Saving Washington City

John Randall Aikman

Copyright © John Randall Aikman, 2024. All rights reserved. Except as provided by the United States of America copyright law, no part of this book may be reproduced in any form, stored in any retrieval system, or transmitted by any means—electronic, mechanical, photocopy, recording, or otherwise—without the prior written permission of the copyright holder.

ISBN: 978-1-7357974-8-9

For: The Truth-tellers

The Main Characters

Fictional

John Gage
Aramis Gage
Jacqueline
Jubal Ford
Victoria Gage Ford
Zeke Alston
Bette Downing
Ransom Pierce
Augustus (Gus) Ward
Jack Spence
The Norton brothers
    Isaac, Henry, and Little Georgie

Historical

Edwin Stanton, Attorney General
Senator Louis Wigfall
Abraham Lincoln
John Hay, presidential secretary
William Seward, Secretary of State
Kate Warne, private detective
General Pierre Gustave Toutant Beauregard
General Ben Butler
Major Robert Anderson
General Winfield Scott
Captain Abner Doubleday, second in command at Fort Sumter
Marshall Kane, head of the Baltimore police
Mayor Brown, mayor of Baltimore

Contents

Part I Remorse　　　　　　　　1
　Chapter 1

Part II Eve of Destruction　　　7
　Chapters 2-5

Part III The Invitation　　　　35
　Chapters 6-18

Part IV A Fight among Friends　109
　Chapters 19-59

Part V City on the Brink　　　323
　Chapters 60-78

Epilogue　　　　　　　　　　411

Afterword

About the Author

List of Maps

* Plan of Charleston Harbor, and its Fortifications
 (Chapter 17/18)   Adaptation of Elliot & Ames map retrieved from the Library of Congress. *Plan of Charleston Harbor, and its Fortifications.* Boston, C. D. Andrews' lith, 1861. Map. https:/www.loc.gov/item/99448817/.

* Map of Railroads in Maryland Reaching Washington City
 (Chapter 60/61)   Adaptation of 1848 map retrieved from the Library of Congress. Doggett, John. Railroads in New Jersey, Pennsylvania, Delaware and Maryland; drawn and engraved for Doggett's Railroad Guide and Gazetteer. [New York, 1848] Map. https://www.loc.gov/item/98688351/.

Cover Designs

Cover Design by Stephen Nagy of Nagy+Associates

Front Cover image is from iStock.

Back Cover: Adaptation of photograph retrieved from the Library of Congress, https://www.loc.gov/item/2007678303/. Sartain, Henry, Artist. *N.E. view of the United States Capitol, Washington, D.C. / Drawn and engraved by Henry Sartain.* Washington D.C. ca. 1858. Philadelphia: Henry Sartain. [Note: the Capitol dome was added by the original artist since in 1858 the dome was in the early stages of construction.]

PART I

Remorse

(April 11, 1861)

Chapter 1

John Gage couldn't sleep, but sleep no longer mattered. He stood up from his cot just as the Confederate sergeant approached his jail cell. Looking through the rusty iron bars, the sergeant asked, "Mr. Gage, would you like me to summon a pastor for you to talk to?"

Gage chuckled.

"That sounds like a *No.*"

"Thank you, Sergeant, but I wasn't laughing at your kind gesture. What made me laugh is something I recalled reading in a book about Voltaire."

"And what was that?"

"It was what Voltaire said on his deathbed. A priest asked him to renounce Satan, and Voltaire replied, 'Now, now, my good man, this is no time to go making enemies.'"

"Very amusing," the sergeant replied softly. He didn't know how to help Gage if, in fact, the man even wanted help.

It was four hours until John Gage's execution.

The sergeant returned to his desk.

Gage lay back down on his cot, his feet dangling over the end, for the cot was not made for someone so tall. He stared at the brick outer wall and began contemplating practical matters. Perhaps I should write a will. This made him delve deeper: What would I say? I have few possessions. But then the next question left him thunderstruck: To whom would I leave them? I have no wife, no children and, with the exception of my brother, I'm basically estranged from my family.

This took him down that treacherous path that all people still with awareness must go through on their deathbeds. What should I have done differently with my life? Obvious things came to him. Too much of my life was spent pursuing war, away from family and friends. He recalled another Voltaire passage:

> Men must have altered the course of nature; for they were not born wolves, yet they have become wolves. God did not give them twenty-four-pounders or bayonets, yet they have made themselves bayonets and guns to destroy each other.

As a former artillery officer, that quote had meaning. But suddenly Gage decided to forgo a retrospective of his life. It might prove too depressing. Besides, it would be complicated and there's not enough time.

Gage began to envision the future of a world without him. Cannons, made by the Gage Ironworks Company, blasting away at the White House and the Northern troops guarding the bridges along the Potomac. Blasting away from positions within Washington City by Confederate troops disguised as Northerners. Southerners seize the capital. Heartened by that success, Border States join the Confederacy giving it fifteen states in all. That robust Confederacy is then recognized by France and England, precluding a Northern blockade of Southern ports. A decimated North sues for peace—the Union is broken.

He now had no way to stop it.

Gage brought himself back to the present. He thought of Bette, hoping Jack was able to save her, hoping that Jack wasn't put in harm's way. I seem to have a developed a talent for placing others in harm's way, he thought. And the most obvious one of all was Gus. Two cells down, Gus sat on a three-legged wooden stool, praying silently. His dark skin glistened in the light of the gas lamp across from his cell.

"I'm sorry, Gus, I should never have brought you into this," Gage whispered in a way that didn't interrupt the praying. "You are one of the best men I've ever known. You don't deserve this."

Gage shook his head and began to reflect on the last few months. In January, I was five hundred miles from here, and I didn't even know these people. In that brief time I learned more about the world, and more about myself, than in my prior thirty-five years. Now that enlightenment will be wasted. Another of many regrets.

But his concentration was broken by voices in the outer hallway. They're coming for me early, he thought. I knew this might happen. They don't want my hanging to be a public spectacle.

Just one hundred days. It all happened so fast.

The end is coming so fast.

PART II

Eve of Destruction

December 31, 1860
(One Hundred Days Earlier)

Chapter 2

"The greatest glory in living lies not in never falling, but in rising every time we fall."

John Gage read that inscription . . . perhaps for the hundredth time. It had been hand-written at the front of a tiny book his father gave him fourteen years earlier when John was leaving for the Mexican War. That was the last time he saw his father.

Those were not his father's words. Still, they spoke to him. Probably a Chinese proverb, John surmised, for the book, no bigger than four inches by six inches and aptly named *The Little Book of Wisdom,* was full of Chinese proverbs.

Gage shoved the book to the far corner of the desk. He went back to laboring over a draft of an article for the *Washington Observer,* writing words he couldn't bear to write.

> So different are we that a Union including the Southern states should never have occurred in the first place. Born out of a common desire to rid ourselves of the British . . . .

He stopped and pounded the desktop before crumpling the paper and tossing it on top of previously discarded drafts, now a mound of frustration.

Gage read the inscription again. How will I ever rise from *my fall* if I must continue feigning Southern sympathies? he wondered.

He picked up a copy of today's *Observer.* The front-page stories focused on Major Robert Anderson, commander of the Federal troops at Charleston

Harbor. Just a few days after South Carolina became the first state to secede from the Union, Anderson relocated those troops from Fort Moultrie on the shore to Fort Sumter in the harbor. It was a stealth maneuver, made in the middle of the night, because Anderson had concluded his troops could not defend Fort Moultrie from the militiamen who were massing in Charleston.

Outraged Southerners charged that the relocation of the troops violated a commitment President Buchanan made earlier to make no changes in the status of the forts while negotiations were ongoing. Charleston was now a tinderbox.

Gage put down that newspaper and picked up that of a competitor, the *Washington Journal.* He glanced at the headlines and long sub headlines of a few front-page articles:

What Follows South Carolina's Secession?

Texas, Mississippi, Alabama, Florida, Louisiana, Georgia, Tennessee, Arkansas, North Carolina, and Virginia sure to soon secede.

The South's Threat to Washington City

Will the city still be a part of the Union when Lincoln is inaugurated?

The Former Secretary of War's Aid to the South

The Virginian moved weapons to the South and troops away from Washington.

All those headlines were accurate, but the next article, an editorial, infuriated Gage. It was about him. It was bad enough that they attacked a fellow journalist, but the last line was unforgivable. In a simple statement, John Gage was called "unpatriotic."

All that I have given for this country, Gage thought, and now I'm deemed *unpatriotic.* He flung the newspaper across the room.

As Gage pushed back his chair from the desk, he detected movement under the door. An envelope appeared, followed by one loud knock. He bolted for the door, but by the time he opened it the deliverer was gone.

The addressee on the envelope was prominent:

John Gage

Chesapeake Hotel

Room 321

The rest of the envelope was blank except for a backwards 7 in the top left-hand corner. That was enough to identify the sender, at least for Gage. He sat back down at his desk and opened the envelope. The message was brief:

> Must talk immediately. Meet as usual, tonight at 8:15 local.
> Our republic teeters on the cliff's edge.

As was his practice, Gage analyzed the consequences of his future actions. This one did not assess well. To attend the meeting could prove perilous. Not attending might be worse.

***

Gage struggled on with the article until the grandfather clock across from his desk struck eight, at which point he put down his pen and quite willingly gave up on the detestable task.

He went to the armoire, pulled open the top drawer, and cast aside an assortment of shirts. He ignored what was on the left—a nearly complete portrait of a young woman he had drawn five years earlier. A portrait too painful to finish, too meaningful to discard.

On the right side he found what he was after: a holstered silver-handled revolver and a Derringer. He chose the latter, much more practical for the clothes he was wearing. He slipped the small weapon into his coat pocket.

Late as usual, Gage raced down three flights of stairs until he reached the lobby where young clerks, all Southerners emboldened by South Carolina's secession, wore blue secessionist cockades on their lapels. They nodded Gage's way, gestures made out of duty, not goodwill.

Gage didn't feel at home in Washington City. Carved out of Maryland and bordered by Virginia, both slave states, it was a staunchly Southern city with Southerners dominating the governmental departments and business establishments.

A lanky, young clerk with arms that extended far beyond his sleeves opened the door for Gage.

"Thank you, Billy," Gage said.

Billy Prescott smiled, a friendly smile that Gage acknowledged with a pat on the shoulder. He was one of the few hotel employees Gage trusted. Billy also wore a blue cockade, but he had the ability to put politics aside.

As Gage began walking up Pennsylvania Avenue, he glanced to his right. Black masons—a mix of freemen and slaves—were completing stone work on a new building next door. In one of many compromises, the slave trade had been outlawed in Washington City, but slavery was still permitted. Like many Northerners, Gage viewed slavery as an abomination, an abomination he had become accustomed to.

A light snow shower came at Gage, scattering small flakes randomly. In his haste he had left his hat behind. He pulled the collar of his overcoat up tight around his neck. Others who passed by him, even a few young soldiers, looked up at Gage for he was a tall man—some said as tall as Mr. Lincoln, even though they had never seen the president-elect. He wasn't scheduled to arrive in the city for another two months, a week before his inauguration on March 4th. That's if Lincoln could make it to the inauguration unharmed . . . if Washington City was still in Northern hands then.

Ahead on the right was Willard's Hotel, the centerpiece of intrigue in the capital, where congressmen and their wealthy constituents haggled over prospective legislation. Gage wished he could stay there—it was an excellent location for a journalist—but he couldn't afford it. Five years ago he could afford it, but not now.

An elderly lamplighter, unsteady on a ladder that was itself unsteady, was attempting to light one of the gas street lamps. Gage stopped and held the ladder until the man finished.

A horse-drawn trolley, its bells ringing softly, rolled along blocking Gage's way. He waited for it to pass, then crossed Pennsylvania Avenue, one of the few paved streets in the city. But the rough cobblestone collected mud and manure, and on the other side Gage stopped to clean his boots. At least that was his pretense. He bent down and looked around to make sure he wasn't being followed.

Gage turned west and dashed across the park at the south end of the

White House, its whitewash paint unlit and gloomy. Even the gas lamps inside the mansion were out. Old Buck must have retired early, Gage thought of the lame-duck president. The man probably wishes he could sleep until Lincoln's inauguration day.

On the other side of the park Gage reached Seventeenth Street, a dirt avenue so dark that it seemed as if he had stepped into a cave. He walked north to the corner at F Street where he observed a few lights at his destination: the Winder Building, the tallest office building in the city. Gage leaned down, and this time quite genuinely cleaned his boots of mud. Again, though, he surveyed his surroundings for followers.

A uniformed soldier stood passively at the building's front entrance. Gage chose to walk on. He headed down an alley to the building's rear where he found a door that had been left unlocked for him. After climbing four flights of stairs, he cracked open a door to a hallway and peered out. Convinced no one was about, he sprinted the corridor to the end of the hallway where he took a staircase up to the roof.

At the far side of the flat roof he spotted the red embers of a lit cigar glowing in the dark. The cigar began to maneuver about, the embers and smoke forming the shape of a 7, a backwards 7 from Gage's vantage point.

***

"Over here, Major," the baritone voice behind the cigar boomed.

It had been years since anyone had referred to Gage in that manner, a chilling reminder of his prior life.

Gage moved closer, and the silhouette of the man calling him came into better focus. As his eyes adjusted to the dim light, Gage was able to recognize Edwin Stanton, the recently appointed attorney general of the United States. Although Stanton had served in the position for just eleven days, this was his second clandestine meeting with Gage.

With a nod of his balding head, Stanton directed his assistant to move to the other side of the rooftop. Hot embers fell from Stanton's cigar, which he swatted away to ensure they didn't catch his unusual beard on fire, for a two-inch-wide swath of that beard drooped down more than a foot from his chin.

"My apologies for meeting this way," Stanton said as he turned to look out over the parapet. "There are traitors among us . . . there are traitors everywhere. They are present in every building, every household."

There was an awkward silence as Stanton looked out to the west. Certain the man was combing the Virginia countryside for traitors coming across the Potomac, Gage finally broke that silence: "Your note suggested urgency."

"Everything is urgent. *We* must prepare . . . prepare for the worst." He then turned toward Gage. "There are reports that Southerners plan to build artillery positions near the white house."

"The White House?"

"Not *the* White House," Stanton snapped. "On the riverbank of the big, white house near Mount Vernon where they could control the Potomac. Imagine that: they'll be waging war against the country from the land of the man who founded it."

"Probably just rumors," Gage said, now sharing the view to the west. "Intrigue and rumors—that's the stuff of Washington now."

"That's my point. We need intelligence, good intelligence."

"I'm gathering what I can. My articles have produced some new friendships. I've been invited to a dinner with Southern senators."

"That's as worthless as horseshit," Stanton growled.

"All your predecessor asked of me was to write articles conciliatory to the South, so I might make some useful Southern connections."

"I have my own ideas."

"You should keep them to yourself," Gage said defiantly. "I've done what was asked, and I'm paying a price."

Suddenly, as if struck with an epiphany, Stanton turned again toward Gage and asked, "Who all will be at this dinner?"

"Senators Toombs and Wigfall. General Scott will be there, too."

At the mention of Scott's name, Stanton went on alert.

"You don't trust our highest ranking army officer?"

"He is a Virginian. Keep an eye on him. Listen carefully to every word he utters."

"I would think you would be more worried about Anderson surrendering Fort Sumter. He's from Kentucky and is married to the daughter of a wealthy Georgia planter."

"You know him?"

"Yes, from West Point and the Mexican War."

"That's another reason," Stanton said casually as if engaged in a conversation with himself.

"Another reason for what?"

"To get you to Charleston."

"What?" an exasperated Gage cried out.

"Among other things, in Charleston you could watch over Anderson."

"I would never question Major Anderson's loyalty. But you seem to have skipped over an important element. Even if I were willing to go—and I'm not—how would I be permitted to travel to Charleston in times like these?"

"You need an invitation to go to Charleston, and to get that Charleston newspapers must laud you."

Gage shook his head, a declination Stanton was unwilling to accept. "Supporting Lincoln's views won't get you that invitation, Gage. You're going to have to take a step out on the ledge. You must say more!"

"Find someone else!"

"There is no one else." The hard approach wasn't working. Stanton softened, suddenly taking on a fatherly tone. "You've done well so far, and I'm not talking just about your John Gage articles. Your Oliver Blanton has turned the tide in the Buchanan cabinet. You have forced Secretary of War Floyd and two other Disunionists to resign. Those three have had the president's ear."

Gage smiled lightly as he looked out across the Potomac. In his reporting of that story for the *Washington Observer*, Gage had used the false name of Oliver Blanton. He was ghostwriting for himself because he couldn't be perceived as attempting to bring down the Buchanan administration while at the same time extolling its passive approach to the South.

"And you think you can now sway Buchanan to take a stronger position on South Carolina?" Gage asked.

"Yes, three of us have made a pact to resign if the president doesn't publicly commit to reinforcing Fort Sumter. He can't withstand any more resignations. He won't give up Sumter."

"He won't fight for it either."

Instead of contesting that statement, Stanton renewed his demand: "No Northerner occupies a position such as yourself—a former military officer who now counsels peace and conciliation. As a reporter, you're a keen observer of people and events. Combined with your military knowledge, I dare say there might not be a better man in the North to take on this assignment."

Gage ignored the flattery. "If I criticize Anderson's move, I'll be called a traitor."

"Perhaps by some people. I'll set the record straight . . . eventually."

Gage moved to the end railing and looked back out over the city. "Sir, you have been attorney general for only eleven days, and you've just advised me you're prepared to quit. In the best case, you'll be out when Lincoln takes office in two months. You'll be gone, and I'll be left adrift."

"Good God, man, our country's future is at stake and you're worried about your image."

There was some hesitation on Gage's part before responding. "Mr. Stanton, five and a half years ago I had some trouble. I've spent the last five years in the West allowing all the noise from that trouble to die down. Three months ago I returned to the East with the intent of repairing my reputation. Being called a *traitor* hardly serves that purpose."

"You will not be left adrift, I assure you," Stanton said as he moved to within inches of Gage's face. Then he spoke with vehemence: "Why the things you could accomplish in Charleston, Major, are of vital importance. In addition to watching over Anderson, you could surveil Southerners' preparations for war, analyze their citizens' willingness to fight, and find out what government officials are really telling the people."

Gage wasn't listening to Stanton's list. He had his own. And foremost on it was one item: find her. *I think she's back in Charleston.* But that just provoked more internal conflict. She could prove to be trouble again. Not that he had ever feared trouble, at least the kind one could face and defeat. But she was of a different sort, something wild and untethered like one of those prairie fires he had seen in the West.

Then Gage reminded himself: *it's in the past, I've vowed to let it go . . . to let her go.* Another reason Charleston is a place to avoid.

"There is a way to ensure that you won't be left adrift," Stanton said. "Senator Seward could protect you. He will certainly be named secretary of state, the lead man in the Lincoln cabinet. You should talk to him for that reassurance. I'll make the arrangements."

"I'll listen to him . . . that's all I'll commit to," Gage said grudgingly. "What's Seward's opinion of the prospects for war?"

"He believes Southerners will try to capture Washington before Lincoln's inauguration. By my count, only fifteen hundred troops now guard the city. If a war were to start soon, and Virginia and Maryland seceded, this city would be overrun."

Gage shook his head. "Hell, Virginia alone could send ten thousand men this way."

"That's another reason getting Floyd out of the War Department was critical. He's not only sent troops away from Washington, but he's also been sending artillery pieces made in the North to Southern coastal forts where they can be seized by Southerners."

"I thought the Pittsburgh people put a stop to those shipments."

"They did, but there are weapons being shipped from other places in the North—lightweight cannons, easily maneuverable. They could be used along any of the corridors to Washington." Stanton paused before playing his trump card: "The maker of those cannons is Gage Ironworks."

"I have nothing to do with that company—"

"I'm aware. But I thought you might be able to investigate the matter. And there's something else to check there. Three days ago there was an explosion at Gage Ironworks. They've kept it quiet."

"What kind of explosion?"

"The kind you might associate with the making of special ordnance." Then he looked Gage in the eyes and said, "I fear your family's company is being used as a Southern front."

Gage grimaced. "Oliver Blanton will look into it."

"Good, but act quickly. You may have little time before you head to Charleston."

"I have not yet agreed to go!" Gage said in an outburst so intense that it took Stanton by surprise.

Stanton retreated, trying to find something to leave Gage with. "Talk to Seward . . . it should give you comfort."

Gage chose silence.

"And, Gage, one last thing"

"What's that?"

"Trust no one."

"Even you?"

A furtive smile came over Stanton, a smile as distant and cold as the night sky above.

When Gage left the rooftop, Stanton called over his assistant and said, "He's wavering. Learn all you can about Mr. Gage. And look into something that happened with him five years ago in Carthage, Pennsylvania—something that caused him to leave for the West. We may need a way to force him to take on this mission."

Chapter 3

Gage walked north from the Winder Building. He needed time to clear his head. The attorney general of the United States had just asked him—or demanded of him—to become a spy. Every word spoken at the meeting, as well as every thought not expressed, churned in his mind.

With time to spare until his next appointment Gage needed a good diversion, but he was fighting his inclination. *I was there just six days ago,* he reminded himself. *Why do I seek refuge there?* Deep down, he knew why. It was the closest thing to a home that he now knew, a place where he was always welcome.

Two blocks further, he saw it: the huge Federal-style house, notorious in some circles as *Lady B's*. Gage succumbed to his inclination. He had always possessed a proclivity for high-end brothels, and Lady B's was among the elite establishments in Washington. It was rarely crowded, partly because it was so pricey, but there was another reason as well. The house sat atop a small man-made hill that in the flat land of Washington most carriage drivers considered too steep to climb. It required a walk up. As one churlish Gage acquaintance put it, "One must decide whether it's worth it to climb the Hill of the Nymphs."

Slightly out of breath from the ascent, Gage opened the front door. A bell rang that could be heard throughout the first floor, and immediately Lady B appeared from a back hallway. Her hair piled high—some not her own—was dyed a flaming red, and as she passed by one of the dim gas lanterns on the wall she looked like a beacon in the night. Yet, despite her age—which Gage had yet to learn—and her rather garish appearance, she was surprisingly attractive, for her features were clean and well-balanced.

"Johnny," Lady B shouted with true delight. "I'm so glad you've come on this special night."

"You look lovely, Beatrice."

"Oh, Johnny, I am an eighteenth century relic..."

Ah, Gage now had some clue. She is at least sixty.

"Not a holy one, mind you," she added with impish amusement.

Gage laughed. "I can't stay long, Beatrice, I need to be somewhere shortly."

"We'll fix you up with a nice little delight real quick." She turned to ring a bell to the upstairs.

He stopped her. "I'm afraid I don't even have time for that. I've just dropped in to pay my respects."

Beatrice liked John Gage. She had witnessed his pensive moods before, and this seemed to be another of those times. And for reasons even she couldn't understand, she often felt compelled to try to rescue him from his melancholy. Besides, she had something on her mind, too. "Well, come in and we'll swap some gossip."

She showed him to a front parlor where a frail, white-haired lady was already sitting whom Lady B introduced as her aunt Olivia.

"My pleasure, ma'am," Gage said, and he sat down in a velvet-covered chair between the two elderly bookends.

"Are you one of our new boarders, sir?" Olivia asked.

"No, ma'am," Gage replied with a puzzled look towards Beatrice.

"Just as well, they all come and go so quickly."

When Lady B offered a glass of brandy, Gage politely declined: "Thank you, Beatrice, but no. As I said, I can only stay for a moment." He was hunched over as if poised to jump up and rush out.

"Come now, John, just one glass to celebrate the coming of the new year. You seem anxious; I think you need a drink."

Gage acquiesced. He took the glass, held it up, and said, "A toast to the final night of what may be the final year of peace."

Managing a wistful smile, Lady B clanged her glass against his. Then she looked across at her aunt and said, "Aunt Liv, Mr. Gage wrote that wonderful article in today's paper suggesting a peaceful resolution for this whole mess."

"This Lincoln fellow needs to give an inauguration speech like your article," Olivia shouted, for she was hard of hearing. "It needs to be a good one, not like Tom Jefferson's. I was at Tom's inauguration and the man spoke so soft I couldn't hear a word."

Lady B attempted to bring her aunt back to the present by adding, "Of course, Mr. Lincoln needs to make it to Washington in order to give that inauguration speech."

"I'm sure he will," Gage replied, "that is make it to Washington *and* give a fine speech."

"I was here when the British burned the city to the ground," Olivia recounted. "Those were awful times. I don't want to live through that again."

"I'm sure that won't happen," Gage said. "Southerners might like to capture Washington but not destroy it. They would want to make it their own."

"Yes, we Southerners do feel this is our city," Lady B said, acknowledging her Southern roots. "Johnny, where are you from . . . I mean originally?"

"A little town north of Philadelphia called Carthage."

"I've heard of it, home to the Gage Ironworks," she said, pausing as she thought it through. "Well, I'll be, it's your family's company?"

Gage nodded.

"But I know the man who runs it—a Southerner from Maryland. His name isn't Gage. He always comes here when he's in Washington."

"You know Jubal Ford?" said Gage, somewhat shocked.

"Oh, my big mouth! I shouldn't be letting on about our customers."

From the uneasy look on Gage's face, she realized something was wrong. "You're not involved in the company . . . is it because of Jubal Ford?"

"You might say that."

"Are you related to him? Is he your uncle?"

"Not quite. He's married to my mother."

"Oh my, I'm so sorry, darlin'."

"Quite all right. It's a good thing to know."

"Now, Johnny, don't be harsh on your stepfather. Many men away from home avail themselves of our hospitality."

"He's not that far from home. Four hours by train to Philadelphia, less than an hour to his home in Maryland."

"I get John Adams and John Quincy Adams mixed up," Olivia yelled, for she was now off on her own doing an historical analysis of the presidents. "Which one came first?"

"The plain John Adams, Aunt Liv. There's a pound cake in the kitchen. Why don't you start in, and I'll join you shortly."

Aunt Liv tottered off in the wrong direction before Beatrice realigned her. Gage concluded Olivia must know what goes on here because she must frequently end up in the wrong room.

Once Olivia was gone, Lady B addressed her issue with Gage: "Johnny honey, I need you to do me a favor."

"And what might that be?"

"Stop encouraging my girls to leave."

"Beatrice, there's only been one—Lizzie Barton."

"My best girl."

Gage began to nod before realizing he was assessing Lizzie's carnal talents in that affirmation.

"I take good care of all my girls, Johnny."

"I wouldn't come here if you didn't."

"I bring them in, teach them how to save money, and make sure they realize they'll need to prepare for another occupation sometime in the future."

"I've done the same with Lizzie."

"The last time you were with her, John, you spent one hour making love and the rest of the night trying to convince her to never do it again."

"I paid for that night."

"I know you did, and I wouldn't mind it so much if you were trying to convince her to give up this life to be with you. But I know you, Johnny, you don't want that. You want no attachments."

Gage didn't respond; he didn't know how to respond. There might be some truth in her analysis.

"Look at you, Johnny. You're the handsomest bachelor in Washington. Oh, you may not wear the finest clothes or keep up with the latest trends—you really should grow a beard—but you could have any young woman of any pedigree in this city."

After nearly an hour, and two brandies, Gage was ready to leave. Lady B walked him arm-in-arm to the door. On the way out she said, "Johnny, you don't come here out of lust. You may want intimacy, but only for a moment, something you can cast off once you walk out of here. No attachments, no complications. Still, though, I think you're searching for something else."

"Perhaps so," he said with a chuckle. "I should think about that."

"Yes, you should. Self-awareness is important."

Gage smiled. "Beatrice, you're too good to me. You always lift my spirits."

She squeezed his arm tightly and replied, "Yes, but just remember, dear boy, I'm not your mother."

Chapter 4

From Lady B's, Gage walked five blocks through a biting wind to Wiley's Tavern. When he stepped into the building, it was as if someone had opened an oven door. Two massive stone fireplaces and the heat generated by wall-to-wall customers made the place feel balmy.

Searching for an open table, Gage waded through a long line of patrons standing at the bar. The blue smoke of cigars hung in the room like a morning fog, and the crack of hammer against ice was the only noise he could hear above the din of the crowd. One lively inebriate jostled him, knocking him into a brass spittoon that he managed to keep from spilling. It wouldn't have mattered. Most of the spent tobacco had missed the target and lay on the floor.

For once it was his brother who was late. Gage sat down at a small table near a window and began reading from a competing newspaper, the *Washington Intelligencer*. The paper reported that Secretary of War Floyd had resigned in protest of Major Anderson's removal of his troops to Fort Sumter. Gage laughed at the notion. Posing as reporter Oliver Blanton, he had exposed the real reason.

Through the smoke and crowd, Gage spotted someone he would rather avoid. He placed the newspaper on the table and cast his eyes downward. Not good enough. The bombastic senator from Texas, Louis Wigfall, was headed his way.

Most in the room recognized Wigfall and, like Gage, most wanted to avoid him. Sauntering toward Gage, he looked all about, not to take notice of anyone but just to be sure he had been noticed. Wigfall did, however, have a certain flair about him. He was as tall as Gage and dressed well for a man known to be broke. He pulled off a black cape that revealed a fine three-piece suit. Everything about him was dark—his eyes, his full beard, and his long black hair. Looking at Gage, he produced a sinister half-smile. It all combined for a roguish appearance. That was fine—he was very much a rogue, and he didn't mind being thought of that way.

Without asking, Wigfall began to sit down in Gage's extra chair, but the chair of a patron at the next table had him blocked. Wigfall wrapped his black cane against the back of the man's chair. That produced little reaction until the man saw who it was and quickly moved the chair.

Wigfall's cane was necessary because of a bullet he had taken in the leg in one of his many duels. It also served as a weapon if needed, and a reminder that its holder was a hotheaded duelist subject to being easily provoked.

"A whiskey for the senator, Wiley," Gage said to the proprietor. Senators, especially this one, didn't expect to pay for their drinks.

"Hot damn, Gage, these are exciting times!" Wigfall thundered with a slap of his right palm on the table.

"They are dangerous times, too, Senator."

"Yes, made dangerous by these blasted newspaper journalists." Then Wigfall remembered his listener. "Oh, I suppose you're a decent sort, Gage, but this Oliver Blanton at your newspaper I would horsewhip him... if I could find him."

Gage smiled, putting on his best Oliver Blanton expression. "You don't like what he did to the Virginian Floyd?"

"Of course not. Terribly unfair. Another instance of Yankees trying to ruin a Southern gentleman."

"Floyd may have brought the ruin upon himself."

"Perhaps," Wigfall acknowledged reluctantly as Wiley brought their drinks. Wigfall grabbed Wiley's hand, downed the whiskey, and said, "Another, my good man."

Gage grimaced. This encounter might prove costly.

"My great state of South Carolina has seceded," Wigfall bellowed with a celebratory fist in the air. "With Anderson's treachery now exposed, others will soon follow."

Instead of challenging that statement, Gage contested Wigfall's usurpation of another state. "You now claim South Carolina, too?"

Wigfall smiled. "A figure of speech, I suppose, but it is the place of my youth."

There was some truth in that. Only forty-five years old, Wigfall had already tried and failed at many things in South Carolina before moving on to Texas. But politics, the robust, bareknuckle kind at least, is what he excelled at, for he enjoyed being at the forefront of any charge. He became a leader of the movement to protect the "Southern Man" and his way of life, so vociferous he even called Mexican War hero Sam Houston a traitor for opposing secession. The Texas legislature sent Wigfall to Washington as their new U.S. senator, although many suggested it was done just to get him out of the state.

"So, you don't believe the Northern Democrats can keep their Southern friends in the Union?" Gage asked.

Wigfall scoffed at the notion, and at the Northern Democrats. "Buchanan, Douglas, it doesn't matter—they're all the same. And they're just like all the Yankees: they believe a woman is a man with petticoat on and a Negro a black white man."

With one big gulp Wigfall downed another whisky, not even showing the hint of a kickback. This alcohol, together with what he may have consumed earlier, was starting to have an effect. He tried to rise, but fell back into his chair. In attempt at some levity, he said, "Well, Gage, you can pay for these drinks with some of that funny money you *made* in Philadelphia five years back. You do have some left, don't you?"

It may have been a joke, but it didn't sit well with Gage. His face turned red, and Wigfall realized he had lit a fire he didn't want to contend with. "Just some New Year's Eve levity," Wigfall added in a weak apology.

The senator stood, this time maintaining his balance, and issued some parting advice: "Gage, I don't want a war. I just want our Southern states to be allowed to go their own way. You're doing a masterful job in promoting a peaceful solution. You keep at it."

Then, like an actor leaving the stage in his final scene, Wigfall swirled his cape around his shoulders and fled.

From across the room, John's brother watched that exit. Aramis Gage, Jr., a four-term congressman from Pennsylvania, shook his head in disgust at seeing his brother associating with a leading secessionist. Just more evidence of John's new Southern sympathies.

Aramis carried with him a small wrapped package and today's *Observer*, opened to an article John had written in his real name. But Aramis didn't start with the package or the article. Instead, he said, "You missed Christmas."

"A Ford family Christmas? I had no such desire."

"It was a Christmas for the Ford *and* Gage families."

"That would have required a lot of pretending on my part, although I might have liked to see the look on old Jubal Ford's face when I showed up."

"John, tell me you didn't spend Christmas at Lady B's."

"They had a nice celebration."

Aramis rolled his eyes. Those eyes were blue and soft matching his laid-back demeanor, unlike John's gray eyes that fired at the least bit of excitement. Aramis was also a couple inches shorter than John and sported a close-cropped beard, but both young men had brown hair, were squared jawed, and handsome in their own way.

"John, it's been five years since your debacle—five years since you went west. You need to go see Mother."

"In due time. She made her choices—she sided with Jubal during my *debacle*." But that's as far as John was willing to take it. He wouldn't reveal the suspicions he had harbored for years about his mother and stepfather. Instead, with hands clasped in front of him, he asked with earnest, "Ari, doesn't it bother you that when Jubal Ford married Mother, the Fords took hold of our family's heritage?"

"The man of the house usually handles business matters."

"But Jubal got hold of the company without paying a penny. The great Gage Ironworks Company is now in the possession of Southerners."

His brother laughed at that statement. "As if you ever had any interest in the ironworks. For me, I've accepted it."

"Accepted what?"

"That ten years ago Jubal Ford saved Gage Ironworks."

"What makes you believe that?"

Ari shrugged. "Mother believes that sincerely. That's all that matters."

"Jubal's always been able to fool her. She denies things about him so as not to have to admit she made a mistake. Did Mother put you up to this conversation?"

Ari avoided the question by asking another. "What makes you think the company was solid before Jubal took over?"

"Because Poppa Joe told me so in August of '46, and he is one person who always told the truth. I had just graduated from West Point, and I stopped at home on my way to Texas for the war. He even brought out the books to show me how well the company was doing."

"Perhaps he was covering, making you feel better . . . you being on your way to the war. I don't know, John, we may never know for sure."

"Do you get money from the ironworks?"

Ari turned sheepish. "I get paid for occasional work and then there are the dividends."

"So he pays you, you're happy, and you don't ask questions."

"You get those dividends, too. At least for the last four years they've been paying them."

"I've never seen any."

"Of course not. They didn't know where to send them. I think in the end they sent them to the First Bank of Carthage to that account you have there. You might ask Freddie Davis at the bank about that."

"I'll do that." John took a quick drink, then asked, "What do you know about the explosion?"

"I know a little. Jubal even talked about it at Christmas."

"They claim they lost fifty cannons in the fire that resulted. What did he say about how it happened?"

"Not much. He wasn't sympathetic. In fact, he was rather mad about it . . . said that the men got themselves killed and destroyed his building."

"That's the kind of man you want running our company?"

Ari looked away, but still spoke. "John, you've come back east, and you still have a chip on your shoulder. You need to move past it."

"It's more than a chip, Ari. Five years ago at the Carthage Fourth of July celebration, a third of the townspeople saw me taken away in handcuffs by Philadelphia police. That's hard to forget, hard to move past."

"I understand how upset you must be," Ari said. "Whoever framed you, took from you . . . they stole your good name." He put on his spectacles and grabbed his newspaper. "But now you come back to restore your reputation, and you write this kind of bull crap."

"I'll restore my reputation when I find the son of a bitch who framed me."

"That won't undo the damage from what you're writing now. Why don't you do good reporting like this Oliver Blanton has done with the secretary of war story?"

John chuckled at his brother invoking John's pseudonym as a person for him to emulate. For a moment he was tempted to tell Ari the truth. Then he recalled Stanton's warning: trust no one. And even though he trusted Ari, he could envision Ari trying to calm his mother with an explanation of the articles and she in turn casually telling Jubal Ford.

Ari finished reading the article, removed his spectacles, and said facetiously, "Yes, such a wonderful piece, Johnny."

"What is it you find so repugnant?"

"All of it, but especially this paragraph:

> The Republican platform aspires to save the Union. How best to do that? Guarantee existing slavery rights. In time the South will adapt, and slavery will die a natural death without a costly war."

"My statement is nothing more than an endorsement of some of the proposals that are coming out of the special committees of Congress. A constitutional amendment that would both protect and limit slavery. A true compromise."

"The John Gage I knew five years ago wouldn't have said such a thing. He would never compromise, never walked away from a fight."

"You're wrong there, Ari. At the insistence of Jubal and Mother, I walked away from a fight five years ago, and I regret it every day. I should have stayed and allowed a trial, even insisted on it, in order to clear my name."

"Yes, and ever since then you've had demons inside you."

John cracked a sardonic smile that caused Ari to clarify: "It's just not like you."

"Perhaps I've changed. Look at yourself, Ari. You're an abolitionist, so how do you justify your friendship with the Fords?"

"They are not secessionists."

"Are you sure of that?"

"I've seen nothing to indicate they are. Do you have proof otherwise?"

"I intend to get it. I'm sure as hell not going to allow Gage Ironworks to make cannons for Southerners."

"Now you sound like you oppose the South."

"I'm for the South to make peace, not war. You, on the other hand, have stayed with the Fords and simply looked the other way."

"I don't believe disassociation is the answer. Both sides need to keep talking with each other."

John slapped the table. "Just what I've said in my articles."

"No, you've said far more than that." Ari looked at his brother solemnly and added, "John, you're already a man without a family. Do you want to become a man without a country as well?"

Despite its possible accuracy, John didn't take that comment well, and he responded with his own charge: "Ari, you take their money and ask no questions. You're happy like a stuffed pig."

Ari shot up out of his chair and said, "Demons, Johnny, demons!" He gathered up his newspaper and package and walked out.

Chapter 5

When he returned to his room at the Chesapeake, Gage went first to the armoire to put the Derringer back in its place. As he did so, he realized its companion was missing. He checked the other side of the drawer. The portrait was gone, too. Looking around the room, he could see that nothing else had been disturbed.

He walked down three flights of stairs to the hotel office where he found the manager, a podgy, balding man named Gardner who was lounging with his feet on a desk while smoking a cigar. When Gage entered, the manager took his feet down but continued to blow smoke rings in the air.

"Gardner, someone broke into my room and stole some important items."

"How long ago, Mr. Gage? I'll alert the police. If the thief is still in the area, they might be able to catch him."

"No need of that. This was obviously done by one of your employees using a key."

"I'm shocked—"

"No, you're not."

"Well, at least I'm surprised. What's missing?"

"A silver-handled revolver."

"That fancy cavalry gun you been showin' off to the clerks."

"That's the one, but I wasn't showing it off. One of the boys caught a glimpse of it and asked about it. I let him look at it."

"Yes, but word does get around. Those clerks talk like a gaggle of ladies at a tea party. Even I heard about it."

A knock on the door interrupted their conversation. It was Billy Prescott, who had a peculiar look on his face when he saw Gage.

"Sorry, I didn't mean to interrupt," Billy said, and he tried to leave.

"Hold on, Billy. What have you heard about things taken from my room?"

Billy winced. "Promise not to tell anyone I told?"

"Of course."

"I heard Reggie Abel talking to someone about it."

Gage sprang to his feet.

"Please, Mr. Gage, leave it to me," Gardner said.

"Do it quick. If my items aren't back to me within half an hour, I'm going after them."

"You said items. What else is missing?"

"A portrait I drew—of a woman. Couldn't be of any value to anyone else."

"But it's of value to you."

Gage shrugged. He left and went to the hotel bar to have a drink in an effort to calm his temper. As he sat down, cheers rang out from the two tables behind him. It was midnight. He hadn't noticed.

After two drinks, and no word from Gardner, Gage looked at his pocket watch. "Time's up," he said to the mystified bartender and he walked out.

Gage climbed the back stairs of the hotel, up two floors where he knew there was a small lounge that the clerks often gathered in. From the stairwell, he heard laughter coming from the lounge.

"I don't know which one's prettier—the lady in the drawing or the silver-handled revolver," Reggie Abel blustered.

Gage burst out of the stairwell and into the lounge. "Give it up!" he demanded.

Abel, a bearded stocky man who in his thirties was one of the older clerks, tried to deny the theft despite being caught red-handed. "Give what up?"

"My things. No one takes from me."

"I don't know what you're talking about," Abel said.

The two clerks began to walk away. Gage grabbed Abel by the shoulder and spun him around. The other clerk lunged at Gage who put him to the floor with one right cross to the jaw.

Abel pulled out the silver-handled revolver and pointed it at Gage. "Is this what you want? Come and get it, Yankee!"

To Abel's amazement, Gage kept walking straight at him. Abel's hand was shaking as he pointed the gun at Gage and pulled back the hammer. When he got to within two feet of Abel, Gage slapped him across the face with the backside of his hand. The slap was so powerful that Abel fell to the floor and dropped the weapon.

"Idiot, there were no bullets in it," Gage said derisively. "Where's the drawing?"

Still sprawled on the floor, Abel began to reach into his coat pocket for the drawing.

"Why in the hell did you take it anyway?" Gage asked.

"When I was taking the gun, I saw her there. She was just so beautiful."

Abel stood up. He pulled out the drawing that he had folded to fit in his pocket.

"You damned fool, you put creases in it!" Gage shouted, and suddenly there was no thought to his actions. He grabbed Abel by the lapels of his coat and threw him against the wall.

Abel then made a horrible mistake: he tried to resist. Gage pummeled him with several punches to the head. A gash opened above Abel's left eye, and a spray of blood littered the carpet. Abel began to slide down the wall just as there was the sound of footsteps in the stairwell. But Gage didn't stop. He yanked Abel up again and was ready to strike another blow when Billy Prescott and Ari Gage raced in.

"Mr. Gage, please stop, you're going to kill him!" Billy shouted.

Those words brought some sense of reason to Gage, and he stopped the onslaught.

Ari saw the portrait lying on the floor. "Jacqueline," he said in a wistful way of remembering the turmoil from five years earlier.

John and Ari left Billy to attend to Abel and his accomplice. They went to John's room where John put the revolver and portrait back in the armoire.

Ari no longer carried the newspaper, but he still had with him the wrapped package and he had added a small bag that was tied with string at the top.

"What are those?" John asked.

"This is a Christmas present for you," Ari said, and he gave John the package. "I forgot to give it to you earlier."

"And what's in the little bag?"

Ari handed it to him and said, "Garlic, to cast out those demons."

They both laughed.

Then Ari put one hand on John's shoulder and said, "I don't necessarily understand your views these days, but we're brothers. I'll always stand by you."

Part III

The INVITATION

(January 14, 1861 – March 1, 1861)

Chapter 6

John Gage halted his horse at the crest of a hill one mile south of Carthage, right at the point where the narrow dirt road picked up the name Division Street. It was the only road connecting Carthage and Philadelphia, running north six miles from the great city before making its entrance in the town. Division Street—such an apt title because it not only divided east from west, but it also acted as a societal partition. The nicer homes of business owners and the Gage Ironworks managers were situated to the west of Division Street. To the east were the small cottages and apartments of company workers and laborers.

The town was in view, but Gage had other things on his mind. Ahead on the left was the giant stone building that housed the Lightwater Institute for Ladies. For the past two decades his mother had been a benefactor of that finishing school for young women, serving on its board of trustees. It was there, six years ago, that Gage met Jacqueline Cordele of Charleston, South Carolina.

But with no reason to visit Lightwater, Gage left the main road and spurred his horse to the west. There was a place he wanted to go, and he knew a battered trail that afforded a shortcut. It had warmed for a mid-January day, and the frozen pathway was yielding mud and exposing open ruts that his horse smartly avoided. They passed by leafless trees, now skeletons of the forest.

A half mile farther, Gage came upon something that caused him to break into a genuine smile for the first time in days: a grove of Norway spruces. I'm home, he thought, although that sensation passed quickly.

He found little need to guide his horse, for there was generous space between the rows of Norways. Three decades ago he, Ari, and his father had planted these trees as saplings to serve as a future windbreak.

At the time, Poppa Joe had said, "We plant them in wide rows to give them room to grow, mature." Then he went on to say such was true of children, too, but he explained it in a way that the boys couldn't understand at the time.

Upon coming out of the trees, Gage arrived at his ultimate destination: the old Gage homestead, a quaint two-story wooden box. It seemed smaller now, but as he looked around everything seemed smaller. The open field that fronted the courtyard was a dwarf to his memory of it. There, he and Ari had chased through the tall grass of summer as butterflies danced about. In the late fall, the tops of those grasses turned a brilliant shade of red, nearly matching the hue of the maples across the way.

The house had been vacant for three years—ever since Gage's stepfather, Jubal Ford, built a mansion a mile to the east. Empty now, it stood as a lonely monument to the Gage family. For ten minutes, John stared at the home as two decades of memories raced at him. I was happy then, he thought, but as he contemplated it further he had a sinking feeling. It wasn't just the comparison of his life then and now. Nor was it the difference in the degree of happiness. What troubled him was that, as he looked back, he liked the person he was back then.

Although it had been years since Gage was last in the house, he still had a key. He entered through the back door, quickly finding himself in the small kitchen that appeared untouched from the days of his youth. A soup ladle lay on the countertop. He wondered how long it had been there. Perhaps the three years.

He stopped briefly at the dining table where the family had played whist. Gage smiled, remembering that he honed his math skills by keeping score in that game, for a running tally was kept over time. He walked into the parlor, and there on a wall was a small, green plaque with a saying on it that his mother had always treasured. It was a quote from Mary, Queen of Scots:

> To be kind to all, to like many and love a few, to be needed and wanted by those we love, is certainly the nearest we can come to happiness.

By the fireplace was his mother's rocker. Why hadn't she taken it to the new house? he wondered. He could understand why she might leave the plaque behind—it was worn and faded, and Jubal didn't share their Scottish heritage—but leaving the rocker was shocking because she enjoyed it so much. He pushed on the rocker. It still had the small squeak from one of its rails.

Around the corner was the stairway to the second floor bedrooms—the place where his grandfather collapsed while coming down the stairs. John caught him and gently lowered him to the floor, but it didn't matter. It was a massive heart attack; he died instantly.

Gage looked up the stairway again, but decided not to go up. Too many ghosts. Instead he went back outside and crossed over to a trail that ran alongside a stream. It was a place where Poppa Joe taught his two sons to fish and where they set up overnight camps. Those were wonderful times.

He looked to the west, but decided not to walk any further in that direction. More bad memories, for three miles into the wilderness was the place where Poppa Joe died in a hunting accident. It had always troubled Gage: his father was such a careful, meticulous man to have died while hunting alone.

Gage picked up a smooth rock and fired it at the stream. It skipped once, hopped straight up in the air, and then buried itself in the water.

"You used to be able to skip a rock five times across that water," a female voice called out from behind.

Gage turned, and shouted out, "Lottie," and the two old friends rushed to each other and embraced.

With her hands on his shoulders, she pushed him back and said, "Let me look at you . . . why you look wonderful."

"As do you."

"Oh, yes, the same tomboy look I've managed so well during my three and a half decades." It was a style she had never changed, for she wore corduroy trousers, a loose-fitting sack coat, and a shawl pulled over her butterscotch colored hair.

"I was just thinking about all the good times at this creek—fishing, camping, swimming . . ."

"I remember one in particular," she said.

Gage laughed. "You caught Ari and me in our birthday suits. But you didn't run away. Instead, you jumped right in."

"We three were inseparable." She hesitated for a moment and then spoke softly, "Such good times. And then it ends."

So well put, Gage thought before asking, "What brings you out here?"

"I have a cabin a half mile from here. I take this trail into town."

"And the town? How is it doing?"

She shook her head. "It's not the same. Jubal Ford is the problem, and of course the explosion has made things worse."

"I can imagine. There has to be fear it will happen again."

"There's fear, Johnny, but it's coming from something else. You ever heard of the Miller Corps?"

"No."

"Not surprising, not many have. It's a private police force."

"They're here?"

"Yes, at least eight of them hired by Jubal. If he's done nothing wrong, why does he need them?"

"Probably to stifle any discontent among the workers."

"Well, they won't stop the feeling that people aren't being told the truth about what happened."

"What do you know about it?"

"They claim it was just an unfortunate accident, but some things don't make sense."

"Such as?"

"The men who died were all common laborers. What were they doing testing explosives?" Then quite emphatically she said, "You should talk to Doc Brown."

"Why?"

"Because he's one of the most talkative people in these parts, but he doesn't want to talk about how those men died. Maybe you can get some answers from him."

"I'll give it a try." They began walking toward town with John's horse trailing behind. "Have you seen my mother lately?"

"Rarely. I'm not a part of her social circles. But the last time I saw her she seemed tired, and she was on her way to see Doc Brown. You might ask him about her, too."

"I will."

As more silence set in, she realized that after all these years she could still divine what he was thinking. "She's still in Charleston, John."

"She still writes you?"

"Surprisingly, yes."

"Why surprisingly?"

"Look at me, Johnny, I'm not exactly in Jacqueline's class. I was cleaning rooms at the Lightwater Institute while she was a student. I've never understood why she befriended me."

He turned to look back out at the stream, trying to decide how to put his request. Finally, he said, "I'd like to read her letters."

"Why do you want to revisit it?"

"I just want answers, some kind of resolution."

"I wish I could give that to you, but her letters from the last few years are gone."

"Gone? Gone where?"

"Stolen from my home, about five days ago. They didn't take anything valuable, just the box with the letters from Jacqueline as if they were hoping I wouldn't notice."

He stopped to look at her, a puzzled expression on his face.

"Johnny, someone wanted those letters for a purpose."

***

Gage found Doc Brown in his office rummaging through cabinets, his back to the office door. "Now where are those darn things?" the doctor said out loud to himself.

Not wanting to startle the elderly physician, Gage knocked on a desk.

Doc Brown turned around immediately and said, "Well, well, Johnny Gage, how's that leg of yours?"

It was their standing joke, dating back thirty years when John fell from a tree and broke his leg, a fracture that Doc Brown set.

"Better than a wood stump," Gage replied in the expected refrain.

"Good to see it didn't stunt your growth any," the doctor added with a chuckle.

The past five years had taken a toll on Doc Brown. His white hair had thinned, his skin had turned pale, and his once wiry frame was now stooped. Gage wondered how much longer he could practice medicine.

They reminisced for a few minutes and then Gage asked, "Doc, what happened in the explosion at the ironworks?"

The smile vanished from Doc Brown's face. "What do you mean? It was an accident."

"An accident, yes, but how did the men die?"

"It was an explosion, John. It was horrible."

Doc Brown returned to searching the shelves, then suddenly stopped. "What was it I was looking for? Must not have been important." He turned back to face Gage.

"You signed the death certificates for those men, but their injuries weren't identified."

Doc Brown's arms began to flail about, the agitation evident in his voice. "It's hard to specify injuries when you don't know which body part belongs to which man."

"It was that bad . . . for all the men?"

"Yes, for all of them." Trying to calm himself, his voice softened. "Maybe you saw things like that in Mexico, John, but I've never seen anything like it."

Gage realized the man was suffering, but he wasn't sure whether it was because of what he had witnessed or what he was concealing. He probed further: "I'm trying to make sense of this, Doc. You're saying there was this single point of an explosion and these five men, all common laborers with no involvement in making explosives, were all huddled around it when the explosion occurred."

"How the hell would I know where they were standing, or what they were doing? All I know is the result. Why don't you just let this awful thing go, Johnny?"

Now Gage was suspicious. In his years of army service, he had learned that when someone had nothing to hide, they cooperated in an investigation. But when they had something to hide, they often attacked the inquiry.

Doc Brown sat down on a chair, his body slumped over like he had just used up his last morsel of energy. He wouldn't look at Gage. Finally, he said, "I lost my Emily last year, John."

"I'm sorry, Doc, I didn't know. You were quite the couple—I remember you two having your noontime picnic each day under the sycamore tree in the park."

Doc nodded. "She sang to me, Johnny . . . for sixty years she sang to me. Then she just stopped singing. What I wouldn't trade now to have back just a small piece of that time."

Either quite genuinely or as part of a fine acting performance, Doc Brown had managed to steer Gage off course. Convinced the man wasn't going to offer anything further about the explosion, Gage asked, "Are you continuing to treat my mother?"

"Yes, I am," Doc said, his eyes still cast downward. "She's one of the few patients I still have from the west side of Division Street. All the rest of them now go to the fancy doctors in Philadelphia. It's hard for small-town doctors to survive these days."

"I can imagine. I'm concerned, though, I've heard she's had some trouble with her nerves."

"Yes, she has."

"Do you think living with Jubal Ford has brought that on?"

"No, Jubal has been a great help to her."

"How do we find the cause then?"

"Perhaps you might start by looking in the mirror. Could be she thinks one of her sons has deserted her."

Gage didn't respond. Doc Brown finally looked up and apologized, "I'm sorry, Johnny, that was harsh. My point is we never know when a loved one might be taken from us, and a family ends up broken. And a man without a family is nothing more than an animal standing alone in the cold."

Chapter 7

As John Gage came to the half-mile lane leading to the Ford/Gage mansion, he slowed his horse to look all about. A thirty-foot-wide swath of walnut trees had been felled to create the pathway. I'm sure Jubal realized a nice profit from that timber, Gage thought.

He picked up the pace, but three hundred yards farther he stopped again as the house came into view. North of Philadelphia, it looked out of place. It was distinctly Southern, a blend of Georgian and Greek Revival styles. Tall Doric columns surrounded the structure and supported the roof. Their white color contrasted nicely against the red brick. Cast-iron railings framed the second floor balconies. A belvedere sat atop the roof.

It is beautiful, Gage had to admit. But he knew it was titled in the Ford family name—that he had checked at the county land office—and probably built with Gage money.

When he reached the house, Gage tied his horse to a tree and walked up the front steps to the portico. He knocked on the massive front door. An elderly black servant, smartly dressed in a three-piece suit, opened the door.

The two men eyed each other. "What may I do for you, sir," the servant asked guardedly.

"Who might you be?" Gage asked.

Annoyed, the man answered, "My name is Cyrus, sir. What is yours?"

Gage didn't answer—he was busy looking around. Finally, he said, "I've never seen you around these parts, Cyrus."

"Nor I you, sir."

"Where are you from?"

Cyrus recognized the purpose of this inquiry and skipped to the ultimate answer: "I am a free man, sir. I am from Maryland."

Their sparring was over, but before Gage could identify himself a sandy-haired boy of fourteen appeared along the balustrade at the top of the stairs.

"Jamie!" Gage shouted to his nephew.

But Gage didn't receive the kind of greeting he was expecting. Jamie seemed aloof. He didn't move and finally he said, "You've been gone a long time, Uncle."

That cut like a knife, and all Gage could respond with was a promise: "I know, Jamie, but I'm back, and this time I'm going to stay."

That produced a slight smile from the youngster, and Gage yelled up, "Now come down here in the way I taught you!"

Jamie hopped on the railing and slid down, stumbling as he hit the floor. Gage picked him up and spun him around.

"Do you remember where you taught me how to do that, Uncle?"

"What? To tumble until you fall on your face?"

"No, to slide down a stair railing."

"Sure do, it was at Independence Hall in Philadelphia about six years ago. Jamie, what are you doing here?" asked Gage, surprised that his brother hadn't mentioned it.

"We live here... at least for now. Father doesn't want us near Washington in these times."

"Probably wise. Have you seen your grandmother today?"

"No, she and Sally have gone to New York City to visit Aunt Matilda."

"Ah, your little sister will be a good companion for your grandmother on that trip."

"Yes, Johnny, your niece has turned into quite the little lady." Those words came from a striking brunette who walked into the entry from the front parlor. It was Charlotte, Ari's wife of seventeen years. She was fun-loving, and a supportive wife and mother. Ari had himself a jewel.

"You would know that if you ever visited... like at Christmas time," she added.

"I've already been scolded for being a scrooge," Gage said as he gave Charlotte a kiss on the cheek. "How is my favorite sister-in-law?"

"Your only sister-in-law is just fine, Johnny."

Gage stepped back and looked at her. "You look like you're dressed to go riding."

"I am. Jamie and I are headed out on the Tillman Trail."

That trail held some special memories for Gage. With its long, open stretches and gentle curves, it had been a favorite place for him and his father to race their horses.

"You should join us, Uncle," Jamie said.

"That must wait for another day, Jamie. I have some things to attend to."

"Another day would be when your mother is here," Charlotte said. "You could ride with her. She enjoys her time on the trail."

"A wonderful idea."

"Of course, that would require you to make another visit," she said with a twinkle in her eye.

"For today, I'll just say hello to Jubal."

Charlotte grabbed John by the forearm. "Be kind to Jubal, Johnny," she urged. "He seems to be trying."

When Jamie and Charlotte left, Gage walked into the massive den. Cyrus followed him.

This room was Jubal Ford's showpiece. It was huge, nearly six hundred square feet—about the size of the entire first floor of the old house—and with its sixteen-foot-high ceilings it seemed even bigger. Along one wall was a door to an adjoining room. Two leather sofas faced each other in front of a massive stone fireplace. Oak planks for flooring helped seal the impression that this was a man's room.

But, more than anything, Gage was drawn to the large bookshelves that surrounded the fireplace on both sides. "I wonder if Mr. Ford has ever read one of these books, Cyrus."

Cyrus knew not to respond. Instead he asked, "May I assume, sir, that you are Mr. John Gage?"

Gage nodded and began surveying the books.

"Are you looking for something, sir?" Cyrus finally asked.

Gage continued staring at the shelves. He grabbed a leather bound book, beautifully embroidered with gold leaf, and began perusing it. "Madame Bovary," he said. "Rather risqué for this household. It's good that it's in French, so no one around here will be able to read it. But if Louis Napoleon ever stops by, I'm sure he'll be impressed."

Gage closed the book just as Jubal Ford walked in.

The long, wavy hair had grayed since the last time Gage saw him, but otherwise Jubal had changed very little. He was taller than most and robust with an aquiline nose. His movements were fluid for a man in his sixties, and there was still some swagger to his step.

"Jubal, you must spend every hour of the day reading these fine books."

Jubal had no penchant for reading. Gage knew that, and Jubal knew Gage knew that. Many of these were Poppa Joe's books, and Poppa Joe used to read them. For Jubal they were mere adornments, substitutes for the art objects he declined to buy.

Jubal motioned for Cyrus to close the double doors and with a casual wave said, "Have a seat, John." Then Jubal walked over and sat down behind the giant oak desk by the window. It was John's father's desk, the one John remembered his father working at, the one John played at during his childhood while pretending to be an adult.

It was while John was away in the army that Poppa Joe died. Jubal Ford, owner of a Maryland ironworks, came over to counsel the company. Six months later he married Victoria Gage. When John returned a year later from his military engagements in the West, he found another man sitting behind his father's desk. His mother's remarriage was understandable, but another man sitting behind his father's desk was almost too much to bear.

Most sensitive men would have managed this delicate situation, but that was not in Jubal Ford's nature. He could have left the desk at the old house, but he chose not to. It served as a declaration: Gage assets were now his domain, and that included Victoria Gage.

John walked over to examine one corner of the desktop where he had carved a U. S. army emblem almost two decades earlier. When his father caught him doing the carving, he began to yell at him. But when he saw what the emblem was he smiled and said, "Keep going, Johnny."

"It's still there, John," Jubal said with a faint bit of disgust.

John moved his hand across the emblem. Yes, it was still there, but barely visible because the desk had recently been stained dark to match the flooring.

It was a rough beginning for this meeting, but Jubal decided to take the high road, one he rarely travelled. "Wonderful articles you've written, John, very sensible. Words like those, and Mr. Seward's, might make a difference."

"It's unlikely."

"Yes, I'm afraid war is coming." Looking down at the desk, he hesitated before adding, "Do you really want to be a journalist watching from the perimeter? You could join up as an officer. Pick your side."

"Pick my side?"

"A joke."

"Which side would you pick?"

Startled, Jubal said nothing.

"A joke," Gage said without conviction.

"I want a peaceful resolution of this whole thing."

"Really? If you're so disposed to peace, why do you have the Gage Ironworks feverously making the tools of war?"

"We'd have to be fools not to. It's good business... no, it's wonderful business. But I suppose that's not your real concern. You want to know if any of the cannons have been sent to the South."

"That's right."

"My contract was with the United States Army. What the army did with them after delivery I wouldn't know."

"You mean what the secretary of war, a Virginian secessionist, did with them?"

Jubal turned to look out the window behind him.

"What about the accident?" Gage asked with conspicuous emphasis on the last word.

"Not much to tell," Ford said to the window. "Five fools got themselves blown up."

"You don't sound very remorseful."

"I am. They destroyed one of my largest buildings."

"*Your* building?"

"Our building."

"I've heard it was one you planned to tear down anyway."

Jubal spun back around. "It sounds like you've been asking a lot of questions—"

"I intend to ask a lot more."

"—about things you shouldn't!"

"What are you afraid I'll find?"

Ford turned furious. "When Cyrus told me you were here, I thought you had come to visit your mother. Instead, I now learn you're just here looking for a story you can fabricate. Make yourself a big hero at your newspaper. As usual, you're out for yourself . . . not caring who you hurt in the process."

"Good old Jubal. Always able to spin a tale. Always able to make himself the victim. I'm sure this is another thing you'll use to try to widen that wedge between Mother and me."

"All that I've done for this family, and you, and you treat me this way. It cost me a lot of money to get you out of that jam five years ago."

"I was framed."

"I know that, and it was all because of your reporting in Philadelphia. You had to attack all the wrong people—the mayor, the police chief . . . all to further your career."

"I did it to bring wrongdoers to justice, and we don't know whether that was why I was framed."

"Well, needless to say, if you come after me or the ironworks, I won't be there to bail you out this time."

As Gage began to walk out, he pointed back at Jubal and said, "Don't you ever dishonor that desk."

"John, we have two congressmen in the family—my son and my stepson. Both young men making good names for themselves. What are you doing?"

Gage didn't respond to that, instead choosing to close with a parting shot: "Lady B sends you New Year's greetings."

He then looked over at the side door and detected something at the bottom on the other side. He bent down and looked closer. It was shoes . . . a man's shoes. "Nice to see you again, Marcus," Gage shouted. "Honestly, a United States congressman hiding behind a door."

Once Gage was gone, Jubal called out, "Marcus." His son opened the side door and appeared. "Did you hear all that?" Jubal asked.

"Every word. Gage is intent on destroying us."

"Money doesn't seem to motivate him."

"And he's a damn good investigator."

"Yes, and we don't want him investigating us . . . again. Have two of the Miller men watching the buildings during the day and double that at night. Start them at that right away. I don't trust my stepson."

Chapter 8

"We think the most likely building the intruder will try to enter is the Center Building," said Dalton Briggs, the commander of the Miller Corps unit. Then he cautioned his men, "But it could be any of the ten buildings."

"Should we arrest him as he's breaking in?" one of the men asked.

"No, we want to catch him already inside, being somewhere he shouldn't be," Briggs replied. "We've made it simple for him to get into the Center Building. A side door has been left unlocked, and that's certainly the easiest building to trap him in."

"What if he shows a weapon?"

"If so, use yours." Then, with a sinister grin, Briggs added, "I haven't been told who this man is, but I have a sense Mr. Jubal Ford wouldn't mind at all if the man is killed while breaking in."

The four men then began a vigil, patrolling along the north side of the ten buildings from a distance far enough away that they couldn't be spotted. They were there at Jubal Ford's direction whose intuition about his stepson was correct. The very night of his encounter with Jubal, Gage set out to scour the ironworks facilities. He came in from the southeast and stayed along the south side of the buildings, trying to recall each one's history. But three buildings were new, and one building—where nails used to be made—was now gone, destroyed in the recent explosion.

It was that scene of destruction Gage went to first, but the site had been swept clean. Not even a memorial sign stood for the men lost. If this was summer, Gage thought, they would have grass growing here already.

There was one place he thought he might learn something. It was the

Center Building, called that because that's where it stood in the complex of structures. It was the largest of all the buildings, and on one side it contained the administrative offices where the most sensitive documents were kept. The other side was a shipping area.

The building was dark, and Gage didn't bother approaching the front door. It was undoubtedly locked. But at the west end he found a side door unlocked. Carrying his lantern, he walked into the shipping area only to find it nearly empty. Have they shipped everything out through the end of the year? he wondered.

Only six wooden crates were present, and they were not yet sealed. But Gage was shocked by the description on those crates: "Thresher Parts." This ironworks had never made threshers. There was no need. All the major thresher sellers had their own manufacturing plants.

He removed the top to one of the square crates, and in it were two fifty-seven inch iron wheels—wheels for cannons, not threshers. He found an elongated wooden box that was so heavy he couldn't move it. He opened the lid and there was the barrel of a cannon. *Thresher parts?*

The barrel looked somewhat different from artillery pieces Gage was accustomed to, but due to its weight there was no way to examine it fully. He didn't bother with the rest of the crates.

Instead he moved to the middle of the building where the administrative offices began. In the first office he came to, he lit two small gas lamps, but when he saw that the files in that office were in a locked cabinet he decided to return to it later. He left the lamps on and the door open, allowing some additional light in the corridor.

Using his lantern at the next office, he spent half an hour searching cabinets for records of recent cannon production. When he finally found a folder labeled 1860 Army Contract, he knew he had what he wanted.

Gage sat down at a desk and what he read in that document was astounding. The contract called for one hundred twenty rifled three-inch cannons made from wrought iron. When did this ironworks acquire that kind of know-how? Gage wondered. Rifling the inside of the barrel produced more velocity and more accuracy. And using wrought iron instead of cast-iron was something new, intended to make the barrel stronger and prolong its life.

One hundred twenty cannons had been made, and thus far seventy had left the premises, but their destinations were in code. On a separate sheet of paper in that file, there was a listing in code of the destinations of the threshers, forty-eight in all. Not quite fifty, Gage thought, but then he remembered the crates he just viewed. There were the other two.

The four Miller Corps men had just assembled outside the front door of the Center Building. Through the front windows, they had seen the faint light of the lamps inside. They entered the building. "He must be in the offices," Briggs said. "You two go around that way and block the corridor from that direction. Wilson and I will go around from the other end. We'll then have him trapped in the back corridor to the offices."

Gage searched the files for instructions in deciphering the code but to no avail. Then it occurred to him: the locked cabinet in the first office. The code they use must be in there. He left his lantern on the desk and went back out into the dark corridor where there was an eerie glow from the two gas lamps in the first office. But as he was about to enter that office a lantern appeared at the far end of the corridor, almost fifty feet away.

"Halt!" the man carrying the lantern screamed as Gage turned and headed back to the office he came from. The man fired a warning shot in the air, causing Dalton Briggs to yell at him: "Dammit, Wilson, you just put a hole in their roof."

Gage locked the door to the office, although he knew that would do little good because they would soon break down the door. Not wanting them to learn what he was looking for, Gage began putting away the files.

Briggs and Wilson were soon joined by the other two men who had heard the shot fired. They converged at the door with Wilson adamant: "This is the office he went into."

Gage put away the last file. He stood up on the desk just as he heard them outside the office door. The area above was open to the ceiling joists. Gage grabbed hold of a joist and pulled himself up, slithering in between two joists until he was able stand on top of them. He walked along one of the joists almost fifteen feet to his left where he stopped and remained motionless.

Wilson seemed to enjoy firing his weapon. Before Briggs could pull a key out of his pocket, Wilson shot the lock off the door.

"Fool," Briggs said, and he confiscated Wilson's gun.

Hidden in the dark shadows above, Gage watched as the door to the office opened and the Miller Corps men entered with their guns drawn. On the desk in that office they found the lantern, but not the person who had been carrying it.

"The man just vanished," said Wilson, bewildered.

"You've got the wrong office!" Briggs said caustically.

"But I saw him go in here."

"Search the rest of the building," Briggs said, "and listen for any outside doors closing."

But Gage wasn't going to use a door. He smiled as he recalled the whimsical way he had often entered the building as a teenager. It was from above. It had been twenty years since he last did that. It was then that Poppa Joe told him to stop coming in the building that way. By that time, John was bigger than any of the employees and when something so large suddenly dropped down from above, it scared people so badly that as his father put it, "You're going to cause someone's heart to explode."

All he needed to do was to go in reverse order from the way he used to enter. Fortunately, his pursuers left his lantern aglow on the desk. That allowed him enough light to navigate the complex of crossed timbers that supported the rafters. He soon found the wooden steps that he climbed until he reached a four-foot-square box that housed pulleys for the water tank on the roof. He pushed the box open and climbed out onto the roof. Then he walked carefully around the water tower until he reached the east side of the building.

By the time the Miller Corps men finished their search on the inside of the building, Gage was already on the outside. The old iron ladder that attached to an exterior wall was still in place. He climbed down the east side of the building and quickly made his way to his horse that was tethered a mile away.

Gage didn't learn all that he wanted, but now he had a count, and he knew what he was looking for.

Chapter 9

He was one of those people whose age you couldn't guess within a ten-year range. Balding and hunched over at a table in his shop, bifocals glued to his work, Ezekiel Alston responded to the door chime without looking up: "Be right with you."

From Gage's vantage point Zeke looked seventy, but when he stood up straight to greet Gage he suddenly appeared fifteen years younger. Nearly as tall as Gage, he was slender but with big hands and muscular arms. He moved slowly, perhaps because of the nature of his work—the etchings, the fine printing—all things that required meticulous, painstaking effort. The handshake was still strong, the product of massive hands that Gage could never understand their ability to produce such fine detail.

"The years have been good to you, Zeke," Gage said with real affection, for Zeke had been somewhat of a mentor to him after Poppa Joe's death.

"I've been fortunate, Johnny."

"It appears so... this is quite the transformation," Gage said as he looked around. What had been just a small studio for engraving and printing five years earlier was now a gallery more than twice the size. No longer did it house only Zeke's work. Now there were works of art from elsewhere that Zeke was reselling. It was high-end, classy, and one of the few places in town that drew people from Philadelphia.

Gage studied a recent handbill, an advertisement in old-fashioned script for a New Year's party. "Your hand is as steady as ever."

"I suppose."

"And your artwork in that handbill is excellent."

Gage smiled as he looked at the bottom of the print. Some people had a favorite number; Zeke had a favorite letter. This unassuming man signed all his artwork with a Z so flamboyant that it was barely recognizable.

"Do you get time to do any artwork that is not commissioned?" Gage asked.

"No, Johnny, the engraving and printing keep me too busy. Besides, I was never the artist you were—or, should I say you could have been."

"I've been busy with other things, too."

"It's a shame. Your drawings of the California gold rush even made it into *Harper's Magazine*."

"For one reason only: they were scenes people in the East had never witnessed."

"Others were even better," Zeke said with a wink. "Did you ever finish it?"

"What?" Gage said in pretense.

Zeke looked at him from over the top of his glasses. "You know . . . the portrait."

Gage shook his head. "I think I would need to see her again to finish it."

Zeke's eyes came up again. "Are you saying you want to see her again? When you went west, I thought you decided to let all of that go."

"Coming here brings back memories."

"Sometimes I don't know what to make of you, John. Artist, soldier, writer . . . I don't know whether you're the true Renaissance Man or you just lack focus."

Gage laughed. "Probably the latter, Zeke."

"What brings you to town?"

"Looking into a few things about the ironworks."

"Ah, yes, the explosion was a real tragedy."

"Leonard Catlin at the *Carthage Daily* is going to take it on."

"That's a risky undertaking. Jubal won't like that."

"Good."

Zeke smiled, and Gage added, "I'm going to take it on, too."

"I see," Zeke said with a look of concern, and he took a quick bite at one of his fingernails. Gage was convinced Zeke must have been a habitual nail biter in his youth but had cut back so that now, in moments of tension, he only took a quick nibble.

"I'm trying to find out if the cannons were destroyed in the explosion."

"Jubal sure claims they were."

Gage's eyes shifted to another handbill, this one promoting a Maryland secession rally. Zeke quickly put it away, saying only, "We must accommodate all customers, Johnny, no matter their political persuasion."

"What will Marylanders do on the question of secession?" Gage asked since Zeke was a native of the state and his two sons still lived there.

Zeke shrugged. "Hard to tell at this point."

"What do your sons say?"

"Oh, they're not very political. Caught up in their work, you know."

Gage walked over to examine a globe-like structure that had a sold sign on it. "You know, Zeke, I constantly replay in my mind the events of five years ago. At the time, everything seemed to be happening so fast. There was no way to figure it out. The plates disappeared, and then Jacqueline and her brother left suddenly."

"They never found the plates?"

Gage was stunned. "Zeke, don't you know where they found them?"

"No."

"In my apartment. Someone obviously planted them there. The police found them before I did. I only got a quick look at them: three sets—five, ten, and twenty dollar notes in the Bank of New York currency. Then they disappeared after the police took them away as evidence."

"It had to have been Jacqueline's brother," Zeke said. "Why else would he and Jacqueline leave for Europe, and so suddenly? It's as if they didn't want to be found. But why would he frame you?"

"I don't know, but someday I intend to find out."

"Thank goodness Jubal was able to help you out of that mess."

John gave him a queer look.

***

Three doors down from Zeke's was the First Bank of Carthage. Gage walked into the bank, passing by the first teller, a woman who had worked at the bank for more than two decades. "Good morning, Mrs. Gentry," Gage said.

She turned away, pretending not to have heard him. Two other employees turned their backs and feigned a serious conversation. Their conversation is probably about me, Gage thought. They all still regard me with suspicion.

But not Gage's old friend Freddie Davis, one of the bank's vice presidents, who greeted Gage genially and teased him with a backhanded compliment: "Well, well, the big-time journalist has returned to his humble beginnings."

"And you appear to have prospered, Freddie," Gage replied, for his old friend had put on enough weight that two of the buttons of his navy blue vest could no longer be joined.

"Seriously, John, you've done well—moving up the ranks at a top paper in Chicago and then getting snapped up by a big one in Washington. You know, I think it was your interview with Mr. Lincoln a year ago that put him on the national scene and got him nominated."

"He was already on the national scene, Freddie. The debates with Senator Douglas did that."

"But that was more than two years ago. Your big interview got him invited to make his speech at Cooper Union in New York City last March, and that helped get him elected. He owes you a debt."

Gage laughed. "All I want from him is to hold the Union together."

"You think he can do that . . . I mean without war?"

"I don't know, Freddie. Things look bleaker each day. I've supported him because I thought he was the only Republican candidate the South might tolerate. Now it seems they won't even accept him."

Recognizing that Gage had come for a purpose, Freddie asked, "What brings you here today, John? Come to check on your account?"

"So it's true, I have an account here?"

"Yes, and it's been growing."

"How's that possible?"

"Your small share of quarterly dividends from Gage Ironworks. While you were away, Jubal Ford has been sending them here. Over five years they've added up."

"I don't remember setting up that account, Freddie."

"It may not be an old one. Perhaps Jubal set it up for you."

"You allow Jubal to set up accounts in other people's names."

Freddie was becoming uneasy. He steered John into his office, closed the door, and answered: "Yes, Jubal controls just about everything in this town."

"Including information about the explosion at the ironworks?"

"I suppose."

"What do you know about it?"

"I know five men died—all family men."

"Come now, Freddie, you know more than that."

Freddie looked out the window, then said softly, "There are rumors that they were testing exploding shells at the ironworks."

"That's what I've heard as well."

"I said testing, but it was more like experimenting. They had no idea what they were doing. And yet Jubal blames the men for destroying his building. Their families are preparing to move out—they've already been given eviction notices for failing to pay the next month's rent."

Gage suddenly brightened. "How much is in my account?"

"About two thousand eight hundred dollars."

"I don't want money from Jubal Ford, Freddie, but I know how to get rid of it. Take that money and pay the rent each month for those families as long as it will last. Don't tell them where the money came from. Just let them know when it will end."

Freddie slapped his leg and laughed. "It's a wonderful notion. Using the money Jubal pays out to keep Jubal from getting what he wants."

Gage smiled momentarily, then turned serious. "In five years, they've never learned where the counterfeit plates ended up after they were taken from my apartment?"

"Counterfeit plates? John, the plates were real."

"What are you talking about?"

"The counterfeit currency put out there were duplicates, printed from real plates."

"Then they must know who made those plates?"

"Sure, it was the person the bank paid to make them."

"Who's that?"

"You really don't know? It was Zeke Alston."

Chapter 10

In the two weeks since his last visit to Carthage, it had been weighing on John Gage. This time he returned to the town for the express purpose of visiting his mother. But upon arriving in Carthage he passed by the office of the *Carthage Daily Journal* where a small sign in the window read "Closed forever."

Standing on Main Street, Gage could hear construction noise to the east. He followed the sounds two blocks over, passing by several of the row houses that Gage's father built to house his employees and their families. Each building was three stories tall with one family living on each floor. His father had built these homes both as a benevolent gesture and to attract workers to the town.

Jubal Ford had used them for a far different purpose. It was his way of controlling the workers. If an employee was fired, it meant no money for his family, and the family could be evicted once the rent was not paid. The threat of firing thus became a powerful tool.

Gage walked another block where it seemed there was construction activity. But it wasn't construction, it was demolition. Two of the row houses were being torn down.

He stopped in the Carthage Café to ask Lottie about what he had just witnessed. She seemed nervous as she waited on a table of five soldiers. Their uniforms were of a style Gage had never seen.

"What happened to the newspaper?" Gage asked.

Lottie turned her back towards the soldiers, as if to block them from hearing what she had to say. Still, she whispered. "Jubal Ford shut it down when they tried to investigate the accident. That awful man controls everything in this town. Those are his goons over there."

"Part of the Miller Corps?"

"Yes, they watch everything and everyone in this town."

Clearly, their intimidation tactics were working.

"Why are two of the row houses being torn down?"

"The five families of the dead workers lived in those two buildings. Rumor has it that the families were suddenly able to pay the rent, so Jubal Ford ordered the buildings demolished as a way of getting them out."

Gage turned silent. A good deed undone.

Lottie stood up straight, a look of determination on her face. "This town has become a horrid place, Johnny. I'm going to leave here as soon as I'm able."

As Gage walked out he made a point of passing by the Miller Corp men. He stopped by their table and said, "You boys haven't found a rose-colored lantern, have you? I seem to have misplaced mine."

They looked at each other in amazement, so shocked that none of them reacted.

Gage smiled and walked on.

***

This time at the Ford house, Cyrus recognized him. "I will seek out the master, Mr. Gage."

"Cyrus, I'm not here to see Jubal. I'm here to see my mother."

"Do you have an appointment, sir?"

"Do I need one?"

Cyrus escorted Gage to the back patio and left without announcing his arrival. It was warm for a late January day. Gage found his mother standing seventy feet away in the garden, looking up at a brilliant red cardinal roaming about in a now barren walnut tree. She had yet to notice her son. He didn't call out.

She was still statuesque, impeccably dressed, and her long hair that was on its way to a shade of gray was still a youthful-looking platinum. Then Gage watched her do something he had witnessed many times before. As she walked slowly while looking up, she stumbled to the side slightly. It was a childlike maneuver, but a reminder for Gage of just how human his mother was.

When she was thirty feet away, she saw him. She smiled lightly, he did the same. They met and hugged in a perfunctory fashion, then sat down in high back chairs facing each other. A fire pit between them provided warmth.

She appeared tired. He expected anger, but she didn't seem to have the energy.

"It's good to see you, Johnny, but for a writer you don't write much."

"When I'm a writer, I normally know what to say."

They conversed about small things before Victoria said, "Fifteen years, John, and you've hardly been back home."

"Mother, nine of those years I was in the army—either engaged in a war, or stuck in the West. There are no railroads west of the Missouri. Just a request for leave takes six weeks to reach Washington."

"Six years ago, when you took the job as a journalist at the Philadelphia newspaper, I hardly saw you during those four months, or at least until you had your trouble and headed for the West. Why?"

"To be honest, it was Jubal."

"Johnny, what is it about Jubal that you don't like?"

"His lack of respect for Poppa Joe. When I came back the first time, Jubal had already taken over." He paused, then looked her in the eyes and said, "Taken over everything—the company, our house, your heart and mind."

"Oh, Johnny, if you would just believe what I believe. When your father died, Ari couldn't figure things out. Our bookkeeper was no help either. Within two months we were sued by three different companies for unpaid bills. It was Jubal who straightened things out and made the company profitable again."

"I've never understood why you turned to Jubal."

"I didn't. I turned to your friend Zeke. He knew Jubal from Maryland and brought him here because he thought Jubal could help us. You trust Zeke."

"I trust Zeke, not Jubal."

"Johnny, in addition to saving the company, look at all the wonderful things Jubal has done. He built us a bigger, better home."

"With whose money?"

"It's family money, John, and he's part of the family now. And he's done well by the workers, too. He's kept up the row houses."

Gage looked at her incredulously. "He's used them as leverage to coerce the workers. Poppa Joe would never have done that. Jubal is tearing down two of the row houses just to force out the families of the five men who died. Do you think Poppa Joe would've done that?"

"Those buildings were set to be torn down before the accident."

"Who told you that?"

"Well, Jubal, but I believe him. Oh, Johnny, I wish you would just try to get along with him. He takes good care of us. He's a devoted husband."

Gage wanted to contest that last statement—with evidence—but he knew the pain it would cause her. Instead, he simply said, "Jubal may not be the savior you think he is."

"You still resent him, resent me, for what happened five years ago. You shouldn't. Jubal helped you out of a tough situation."

Gage stood up, thought about leaving, but then sat back down. "I've had five years to think about our discussion. That night you sided with Jubal; you told me to leave."

"Not for five years."

"Poppa Joe would've told me to stay and fight."

"That's true, but I'm not like your father."

"That's the only time in my life I've ever run from a fight. Because you, prodded by Jubal, encouraged me to. It will never happen again."

"Why do I think this is more about Jaqueline than Jubal?"

"You never liked her."

"I liked her. I just didn't believe she was right for you."

"Why, because I was seven years older?"

"No, it was more the difference between you two in . . . " she paused, searching for the proper word, then settled on a poor one: "sophistication."

"But, Mother, she went to your institute that trains young women to be sophisticated."

She tried to be delicate. "I meant that she was more sophisticated than you, John."

"What?"

"Perhaps I should say that at the time she was more experienced in the ways of the world than you. After all, at that point you had spent your entire adult life in the army."

"Mother, there were several women before her. But, still, I don't understand what you're saying."

"To be blunt, I felt she was after your money and status—all from the Gage family."

"So you sensed that motive in Jacqueline, but not in Jubal?"

"Was I not correct? She left you as soon as she saw you were giving up that station in life—just vanished somewhere in Europe."

"I don't know the reasons she left. That she left without talking to me was suspicious." He didn't elaborate because he had nothing to go on. But he had always suspected that Jubal, perhaps at his mother's direction, had paid for Jacqueline's trip to Europe.

She was about to ask John for an explanation when Jubal came through the garden gate with a command: "John, you've upset her long enough. Victoria, go inside."

With an anxious look back at her son, she dutifully complied. It was not like her, Gage thought. In the past, his mother would not have obeyed such a command from any man, even Poppa Joe. There seemed to be an indifference about her that he had never witnessed before.

Jubal's comment had caught Gage off guard. He wasn't upsetting his mother. In fact, it was the first meaningful discussion they had had in years.

"What is it you want, John?"

"I want to see the company books for the last ten years."

Ford turned red in the face. "That's not possible."

"Why not?"

"They burned in the explosion a few weeks ago."

"You kept the company records in a building that contained explosives?"

"The fire spread," Jubal said indignantly.

"What really got those men killed at the ironworks?"

Jubal didn't answer. Instead, he said, "Five years ago you promised me you would not come back here and interfere with the company. You've now broken that promise. Don't ever violate it again."

"You better hope that I don't," John said as he turned to walk out, "because if I do it may be with a warrant for your arrest. But, then again, you have nothing to worry about. You just make *threshers*, right?"

Jubal was stunned.

As Gage walked down the steps of the front entrance, he looked to his left. There stood his mother next to a carriage. She seemed unsure of herself, unsure of what to do next.

Gage walked over because he had a question for her: "Mother, why did you leave your rocker behind at the old house?"

She hesitated, as if reluctant to trust him with some vast secret. "Because I want to use it."

She noticed his quizzical look, so she tried to explain. "I often ride to the old house and sit in my rocker. Sometimes I rock there for hours, remembering the wonderful times in that house. It gives me great comfort."

Gage was suddenly overcome. That she shared the same longing for those days made him realize just how joined they were. He moved toward her. They hugged, this time with genuine affection.

Chapter 11

John Gage was in the habit of conducting business in some unsavory places, but this one was unlike any others. He and Ari were meeting at a hole-in-the-wall tavern on the edge of Carthage. As Ari took a drink of some foul whiskey, a rat scampered by, pausing by their table as if checking to see if they might pass a tidbit its way.

"Lovely place you've brought me to, John."

"I didn't want us to be seen by any of the ironworks' officers."

Ari rolled his eyes. "That won't happen here. Look, you're concerned about what happened to fifty three-inch cannons—"

"One hundred twenty three-inch cannons."

"A three-inch cannon doesn't sound that frightening."

"It can shoot a ten-pound ball more than a mile and that ball leaves the muzzle at twelve hundred feet per second."

"Oh, my!"

"Or, it can fire an exploding shell. These cannons are lightweight and easily maneuverable. I'm convinced they'll be the most important piece of field artillery if war comes. And a couple other things about these Gage cannons: they're rifled for greater accuracy and made with wrought iron for greater strength. How did our ironworks company acquire that kind of knowledge?"

"I don't know. And you still don't know whether the cannons went to the wrong place."

"Yes, but I now know that Jubal is lying about the cannons being destroyed in the explosion."

"You need proof of that, too."

"I'll get it, and more."

"You think there's more to it?"

"I don't think the men died in that explosion." He recounted Doc Brown's evasiveness, and then asked, "Why was that building site swept so clean... so fast? Why did Jubal want those families gone so quickly—even to the point that he would destroy their homes to force them out?"

"Look, I don't disagree that Jubal does some strange things, but nothing you've said proves anything so nefarious. It makes me wonder: Are you out to find the truth in this, or just out to get Jubal?"

"They may be one and the same."

"Johnny, do you remember about fifteen years ago Poppa Joe gave us each a small book called *The Little Book of Wisdom?*"

John smiled. Ari had no idea how often John looked at that little book.

"There is a Chinese proverb mentioned in there, John, that you should heed:

'Before you embark on a journey of revenge, dig two graves.'"

John seemed confused, or distracted, so Ari started to explain: "It means seeking revenge often results in your own destruction."

Suddenly enthused, almost gleeful, John said, "Yes, Ari, you've hit the nail on the head!"

"At last, a breakthrough."

"It's the graves."

"What?"

"Where we can get the answers—the truth, or the proof."

"Where? What are you talking about?"

"In the graves at the Carthage cemetery."

When Ari reacted with horror, John said, "It'll be fun, like old times when we went there as kids."

"What I think you have in mind we never did as kids."

***

It was midnight when the Gage brothers drove a one-horse buggy into the cemetery. The gate was closed, but it was simple to drive around. They brought with them four lanterns, two shovels, a hammer, and a crowbar. It was dark and it had begun to drizzle.

They headed out on the main path that snaked through the middle of the cemetery. The horse followed the corridor, which was fortunate because the lanterns couldn't light the way. They went to the far end of the cemetery where those of limited means were buried.

A fox ran across their path, and the horse whinnied. Twice the horse halted, spooked by something unseen.

"I can't believe it's come to this," Ari said.

They reached the new burial area, a small section adjacent to the potter's field portion of the cemetery. Using their lanterns, they sifted through several rows of headstones. Because it was a small town, Carthage had infrequent burials. When they found several headstones with the date of the explosion on them John exclaimed, "Pay dirt. Look at this one."

The headstone was small, and its inscription brief and pleasant:

Harold Wilson
Loving father and husband
May 12, 1825 – December 18, 1860

"A respected man," John added. "Let's pay him a visit."

"Jesus," Ari said, partly in anguish but also in actual pursuit of divine intervention.

They set the lanterns on the ground and began shoveling dirt. Everything around them was dark, and the lanterns transformed their faces into ghost-like images.

"The two of us are the only things alight for miles," Ari said. "We would look like two beacons to anyone passing by."

"No, we would look like two hard-working grave robbers."

They had uncovered no more than a foot of dirt when a screeching sound from above startled them.

"Just an egret," John said.

They went back to work. Not three minutes later a terrifying scream caused Ari to drop his shovel.

"Another egret."

"Bullshit."

"Keep digging."

For the next fifteen minutes they shoveled as Ari continued to complain:

"Good Lord! A United States congressman involved in this. Just think how the newspaper article would read."

"Shovel more, talk less. That will get us done sooner."

It began raining harder. Three feet down, John's shovel struck something hard. It was wooden, a pine box—the final resting place of Harold Wilson.

While Ari worked from above, John shoveled dirt off the top of the coffin. When finished, John said, "Give me the crowbar."

Ari hesitated, then handed it over, along with another round of protest: "I don't know why you want to do this. All we're going to do is see pieces of this man."

John bent down at the far end of the pine box and wedged the crowbar under the lid. He gave it a mighty downward thrust and the nails at that end popped. Next he did the middle. As he started to pry open the final segment, he looked up. Ari stood motionless above, holding a lantern in one hand and a shovel in the other.

"This is a bad business," is all Ari could say.

John slid the crowbar under the pine top. This time when he pushed upward, the last of the nails popped and the lid jumped up three inches before settling back in place.

"It was like it was pushed from within," John said jokingly.

Ari was stone-faced. That's exactly what he thought had happened.

"Perhaps it's those demons inside me clashing with the demons inside this casket," John said with a chuckle.

Ari was not amused.

John pulled off the lid.

Ari, expecting something to come flying up at him, instead was met with the putrid smell of a decaying body. He dropped the shovel and put the lantern on the ground, so he could cover his nose with his sleeve. But Ari's movements were quick, too quick on the rain-slickened soil, and his feet slid out from under him. He was falling, and there was only one place to land. He fell into the coffin and atop the dead man's body.

"Ari, we don't need such a close examination."

Horrified, Ari stood up and climbed back onto the dirt beside the coffin. "This is insane," he said as he flailed his arms about in a useless effort to cleanse his clothing.

"No, Ari, it's not. We have our answer: the man is in one piece."

John bent down by the body and pulled open the dead man's shirt.

"Are those bullet holes?"

"Nope, they're too irregular, too scattered," and John pointed at three entry points in the man's torso. "He was hit by canister."

"What's that?"

"Loose objects held in a tin covering fired from a cannon. When the cannon fires, the objects blow through the tin housing and scatter in all directions."

"Must be devastating at close range. It could kill or maim dozens of approaching soldiers."

"Yes, and that's what happened to these men." He looked at his brother and stated emphatically, "They didn't die in a building explosion. They were killed when someone was firing canister ordnance."

"Surely, they didn't shoot them intentionally."

"No, I would imagine they were testing and didn't realize how wide the canister spread would be. The building explosion was then a cover-up."

"Yes, to hide the cause of their deaths. Come to think of it, that building was the oldest one out there. They've wanted to tear it down for years."

"How convenient. They got rid of the building and gave a more justifiable cause of death for the men. But it was even better than that, Ari."

"In what way?"

"They could now claim that the fifty Gage cannons, which they labelled as threshers for transport, were destroyed in the explosion. And then those cannons could go anywhere they desired."

Chapter 12

It was to be a small dinner party held in a special room at the Tremont Hotel in Washington. Except for John Gage, the guests were all Southerners, and Lord Richard Lyons, the ambassador from Great Britain, was the not so impartial host. Despite opposing slavery, the British enjoyed watching the break-up of the former colonies and were looking for every advantage that might be gained from it.

Gage arrived at the hotel at the same time as his old commander, Lieutenant General Winfield Scott. The hero of the War of 1812, the Mexican War, and many other military engagements, Scott was now seventy-four years old but still serving as Commanding General of the United States Army. He was proud of that title, so proud that even at this informal event he wore his full dress uniform, complete with gold epaulettes.

The general, in failing health, was as tall as Gage but weighed nearly three hundred twenty pounds. He staggered when he walked, winced with every breath. Fortunately, it was only five steps up to reach the hotel's entrance. Even so, Scott seized Gage's arm for assistance and was wheezing at the top of the stairs.

It was at that point that Gage was heartened by what Scott, a Virginian, then said: "Let's go greet the damned insurrectionists."

There was good reason the general referred to them that way. These weren't moderate Southerners. They were swaggering types, dismissive of compromise attempts, and their swagger was now quite evident, for they had been emboldened by recent events. Three weeks earlier the merchant steamship *Star of the West,* carrying supplies and two hundred soldiers as reinforcements for Fort Sumter, was fired upon by the South Carolina artillery batteries in Charleston Harbor. The shots, fired as warning salvos, were enough to convince the ship's civilian crew to turn around and head back to New York.

They walked into their reserved dining room where Senator Louis Wigfall of Texas greeted them. "I seem to recall you bought me drinks on the eve of the new year," Wigfall said to Gage as he tossed his black cape at a waiter. "Tonight, at least, the Queen is paying for it." Turning toward General Scott, he said, "And I see you brought the sage of the army along with you. Good to see you can still get up out of bed, General."

"I can still do many things, Wigfall. Age has its advantages."

"Ah, the wisdom that comes with gray hair," Wigfall said, for his hair was black and impeccably combed.

"No, the wisdom that comes with experience. I've been a general for more years than you've been alive."

"Yes, General, you do seem to be one of the army's most immoveable objects."

Although Wigfall was downing his first glass of whisky, it was evident he had been at it for some time elsewhere. Gage asked him a non-combative question: "What are your current plans, Senator?"

"My current plans, Gage, are to eat a monstrous buffalo steak tonight and drink till I'm three sheets to the wind. My plans for the near future are to head to Charleston."

"Charleston is a long way from Texas."

"Going there to see how I might help," Wigfall said, and then he added in what seemed like a challenge to Gage, "As a journalist, and certainly one of the more rational ones, Charleston might be a good place for you to be right now. I could assist you in getting that invite."

"I might consider that," Gage replied with a nod.

Washington dinners, despite the politics, had always been civil gatherings among adversaries, and Lord Lyons skillfully managed to keep this one as such for the first two hours. But it may have been General Scott who set things awry. As he readied to take each drink of wine, and there were plenty of them, he shouted out, "Lord, save the Union."

At last sufficiently annoyed, Wigfall said, "General, I think the Lord may soon tire of your entreaties."

Even more agitated was Senator Robert Toombs of Georgia who rose to offer a toast. Toombs was disheveled—his long gray hair draped about his head haphazardly covering one ear but not the other, his tie askew, and his suitcoat rumpled. He was also significantly overweight which, when combined with the effects of the alcohol, caused him to stumble as he stood.

But his voice was clear and full of purpose: "I offer a toast to the peaceful retreat of the *Star of the West*."

The *Star of the West* resupply plan had been Scott's, and the general took great offense. He could not frown for his face was cast perpetually in that manner as he if he was forever pouting. Instead, he rubbed at one of his perfectly manicured L-shaped sideburns and then slammed a fist on the table while offering a rebuttal: "I will not drink to an attack against a ship flying the United States flag."

"You seem to have struck a nerve with *Old Fuss and Feathers*," Wigfall said out loud to Toombs. It was a nickname given Scott for his insistence on following army protocols, but it also suggested something about the man's personality of late. When his gout was acting up, and it often did, Scott could be a curmudgeon.

Scott overheard that comment but, aware of the nickname, chose to ignore it.

But Toombs wasn't done. He upped the ante: "Yes, General Fuss and Feathers, your flag has been insulted. Redress it if you dare."

It was killing Gage to stay out of this argument, but he couldn't let the Southerners know his true feelings.

"At least we now know where the Virginian stands," Wigfall said.

"You're damn right you know where I stand. I'm going to plant cannons on both ends of Pennsylvania Avenue, and if any of those secessionists raise a finger, or even show their faces, we'll blow them to hell."

"And who's going to man those cannons, General?" Wigfall asked. "The army has only seventeen thousand soldiers, and many of those are Southerners."

"And Floyd scattered those soldiers all over the country," Toombs said.

"I'll do it myself if need be."

Toombs scoffed. "You didn't do so well with the *Star of the West*."

The red-faced general stood up faster than Gage thought possible. Then he wobbled a bit before lunging in Toombs's direction.

Toombs, himself a huge man, stood and the two masses stumbled towards each other like a couple of angry walruses.

Gage rose and got in between them and simply said, "Let's calm ourselves, gentlemen."

In his inebriated state, Wigfall was not kind to either: "If one of you falls to the floor, we'll have to figure out how to get a team of horses in here to hoist you back up."

Later, as he walked General Scott out, Gage said, "Perhaps you can help me, General. I'm searching for some missing cannons."

Scott turned surprisingly alert. "How many missing cannons?"

"Fifty. I'm concerned they've been sent to the South surreptitiously."

Scott nodded and said, "I am at your service, *Major*. Provide me the details and I'll assign someone to look into it."

It was an awkward, uneasy evening, but Gage had his answer about the old general.

***

The next day Gage met again with Attorney General Stanton who was still determined to see Gage go south. It was a brief meeting with Gage first reporting his opinion of General Scott. "I can assure you, Mr. Stanton, the Virginian is a solid Union man. He practically came to blows with one of the Southern senators."

"That's good to hear," Stanton said, although his mind seemed to be elsewhere. "Loyalty is what we need to look for these days."

Once again Stanton had gone dancing with his words. Gage wasn't going to let it pass. "What are you getting at?"

"That you can demonstrate your loyalty by going south."

"We're back to that again?"

"Such proven loyalty would certainly take care of any lingering liabilities you may have."

"Are you talking about the counterfeiting charges? I was framed."

"I know you were, and that's why the charges were dropped. But there remains an open matter."

"And what would that be?"

"Innocent or not, you and some other persons may have committed a crime in the way you avoided charges."

"I don't believe anyone knows how that happened. I sure don't."

"Look, Gage, I like you, but there's a year to go before the statute of limitations expires on that matter. In a month there will be a new attorney general in office."

"And so you're suggesting if I go south, he will never hear about it?"

Stanton nodded.

Gage smirked, dismissive of the threat. He resisted the urge to let Stanton know that he might have friends in high places, too. But still it was unnerving that his *debacle*, as his brother liked to call it, would not go away.

"Let's get this straight, Stanton. Nothing you say or do will get me to go south. If I decide to go, it will be on my own accord."

Stanton decided to accept defeat graciously, for in Gage's calling of his bluff Stanton saw the same fortitude that had convinced him in the first place that Gage was the right person for the job. "Fair enough, Major. Have your meeting with Seward. He should allay your concerns about protecting your reputation."

Chapter 13

The letter lay unopened on John Gage's desk for two days. It contained no return address, no evidence of its sender. Just a post office reference of Charleston, South Carolina. But Gage didn't need any clues. He recognized the handwriting. It was from her.

Five years since she disappeared, and now she writes. Why now? Gage wondered. To read the letter might result in more conflicted emotions, feelings he thought he left behind. Then he picked up the envelope and lifted it to his nose. He smelled the sweet, light fragrance. It was her cologne.

Finally on the morning of the third day, he opened the envelope and read the letter:

> My Dearest John,
>
> I'm sure you're as surprised to receive this letter as I am in sending it. Perhaps it's the recent events, or what I see is coming our way—the dread I feel that will happen to the country. And I know you, Johnny. I know you won't be able to keep yourself out of this hideous mess.
>
> I suppose that's part of it. But I'm really writing to say I'm sorry. I never should have doubted you. I've since learned the truth about what occurred five years ago.
>
> Keep yourself safe, Johnny. You have so much to offer this world. I don't want to see that lost.
>
> With the greatest of affection,
>
> Jacqueline

He reread the letter three times. Then he put it back in its envelope and stuffed it in a drawer as if closeting it away might suppress the memories.

***

That afternoon Gage was late again, this time while coming back from Alexandria. He sprinted across the Long Bridge onto the eastern shore of the Potomac. Ahead of him were stacked blocks of marble—the monument to George Washington, not quite one-third of its intended height, stalled in its construction for six years because the organization building it ran out of funds. It looked like a loaf of white bread standing on end, so squatty that it had yet to take on the obelisk form of its design.

A mile to the east a derrick sat perched atop the Capitol Building where the new nine million pound dome was still years from completion. Headed north, Gage passed by the canal at the south end of the White House property where the water stagnated from silt and debris. Huge gaps between buildings, unpaved streets, few streetlamps—it is an unfinished capital of an unfinished country, Gage said to himself. As he walked along, he realized it was now in doubt who might be the ones to finish this city.

When Gage reached Hutchison Park, he immediately spotted the man he was to meet. Seated on a park bench was a lonely, diminutive figure whose feet dangled in the air because they couldn't reach the ground. His short gray hair still held remnants of the red it used to be. His face was pale and pulpy, perhaps the result of recent illness.

He hardly looks like one of the most powerful men in the country, Gage thought. A former governor of New York, now its U.S. senator, William Seward would soon become the secretary of state in the new Lincoln administration. It was a position considered the second most important in the country, second only to the presidency.

But in the last few weeks Seward, in an effort to avert war, had transitioned from abolitionist to one promoting compromises that could grant constitutional protections to slave owners. Many Republican politicians were appalled at his sudden transformation, including Lincoln who would allow slavery to be protected where it now existed but was opposed to any compromise that might permit its expansion into the western territories.

"Mr. Stanton sends his regards," Gage said by way of introduction.

Seward looked at him dubiously. "Beware the man."

"He sent me to you."

"I don't know his motives as yet. He is a Democrat, you know."

"Yes, but I believe he's a patriot first."

"Time will tell."

Gage reported what he had learned at the Gage Ironworks. "I have no idea where to look for the cannons."

But Seward didn't come here to talk about missing cannons. He turned blunt: "Gage, we need someone like you to go south and be a keen observer who can report back to us."

Gage hesitated. "My friends now look at me askance. It chills me to the core to think of what I might have to say in order to get an invitation from the South."

"Your country needs you to do this."

"Our country needs far more than that."

Then Seward's tone changed. In a voice that was suddenly quivering, he said, "These are perilous times, Mr. Gage. We all must do things we abhor."

Gage could see the anguish Seward was trying to hold within. His arms were shaking, and tears began to form in his eyes. He reached into an inside pocket of his coat and pulled out a letter, his hand trembling as he handed it to Gage.

"I have not allowed my wife to come to Washington City," Seward explained in a voice that was breaking. "It is too dangerous. However, we write each other constantly. Here is her reaction to my most recent speech."

Why would Seward think a letter from his wife might motivate me? Gage wondered. He took the letter, though, and began reading:

> Eloquent as your speech was it fails to meet the entire approval of those who love you best. You are in danger of taking the path which led Daniel Webster to an unhonored grave ten years ago. Compromises based on the idea that the preservation of the union is more important than the liberty of nearly four million human beings cannot be right. The alteration of the Constitution to perpetuate slavery—the enforcement of the law to recapture a poor, suffering fugitive . . . those compromises cannot be approved by God or supported by good men . . .

No one can dread war more than I do. For sixteen years I have prayed earnestly that our son might be spared the misfortune of raising his hand against his fellow man—yet I could not today assent to the purpose of the perpetration or extension of slavery to prevent war. I say this in no spirit of unkindness . . . but I must obey the admonitions of conscience which impel me to warn you of your dangers.

"You worry what your friends will think of you, Mr. Gage. Look at what my best friend has said to me."

Gage had no response.

"In times like these, we all must make sacrifices."

***

That night, despite needing to write only five hundred words, Gage spent four hours agonizing over his next article. He now had a large readership, both pro and con, so large that his editor always put his columns on the front page.

But to take this step, a step that might be necessary, seemed unfathomable to Gage. *I will be deemed a traitor by my very words, and no one will know the secret purpose behind my mission to the South. They will view me as having sided with the insurrectionists. I will sully my name, and my family's name, forever.*

Unable to finish the article, he left his hotel room and went down to the lobby in an attempt to alter his perspective. He sat in a monstrous leather chair in front of the stone fireplace, his notepad on his lap. Thus far his article was only half written and was merely an historical account of the divisions within the country.

He thought of the anguish Senator Seward must have felt when he received the remonstrance from his loving wife. And then there was the letter from Jacqueline but, deep down, he knew it should play no part in any decision to go south. Nor did he give any weight to Stanton's threat, for he considered it a half-hearted bluff.

He was dwelling on the same things he had thought about all day. A distraction was needed, and the only thing he could come up with was to try once again to break the Gage Ironworks code for the destination of the one hundred twenty cannons.

It occurred to him that perhaps he had given Jubal Ford too much credit in creating that code, for over the past week Gage had tested the random mix of letters and numbers with all known modern codes, but he had been unable to establish a key with any of them.

Thus far he had received only hearsay information that some of the cannons had gone to Northern troops at Fort Monroe. That gave him the one word that he could possibly use to break the code. He spent the next half hour staring at the passage that he needed to unlock:

6HJKMJZ8

Gage concluded that anyone using a simple code probably inserted the numbers just as a diversion. He looked only at the letters, and he tried an antiquated code known as the shift cypher. It was simple to employ once the key was known—just shift the letters in the alphabet right or left by a certain number of letters. The key told you which direction to shift and how many letters.

He also figured no one would make a small shift, so he skipped shifting just one letter. He then tried both directions... two, three, four places. Nothing elicited a meaningful word. About to give up, he tried shifting five to the right and up popped the letters he had been looking for: Monroe.

He had the key. Now he went searching for the destination that had eluded him. He began shifting the letters five to the right:

22XCVMEZNOJI6

CHARLE

He didn't need to finish but, just to be certain, he did. The fifty "threshers" went to Charleston.

He now knew the truth: Jubal Ford was a traitor. But then, Gage thought, what good does knowing that do me without hard evidence? It would be me claiming I broke their code from one flimsy sheet of paper that I don't even possess. My adversaries, perhaps even some of my allies, will suggest I invented that piece of paper.

And now that he knew the truth about Jubal Ford, it rekindled one of

Gage's ironclad resolutions: Gage Ironworks cannons are not going to be used by Southerners to uproot this country. I must find them and the evidence that Jubal Ford was a part of all of this.

Suddenly galvanized, Gage said out loud, "This changes everything. To hell with my reputation."

He penned the final paragraph:

> We are a ship sailing in frozen waters. When nighttime comes we will most assuredly find an iceberg, and all will be lost. This is madness. Mr. Buchanan, Mr. Lincoln, negotiate a peaceful separation. Let the South go.

Chapter 14

The animosity that existed between Stanton and Gage ended the day Gage published what had quickly become a famous quote: "Let the South go." It also produced the desired result. When Gage arrived for a meeting with Stanton and General Scott, he brought with him a letter that he handed to Stanton for his perusal. "I received this by special messenger today," Gage said.

"Hallelujah," Stanton cried out. "You're on your way. An invitation from the Citizens of Charleston Defense Committee."

"Not a request from a governmental body, but I suppose it will suffice," Gage replied, omitting that he did have an invitation from a government. It was to visit Montgomery, Alabama, the current seat of the Confederacy, but he didn't mention that. He was going to Charleston.

Instantly Stanton grimaced. "One of the three signers of this letter, Ransom Pierce, is one of the most... I'll call him influential of men in Charleston."

"That's good to hear."

"No, Gage, by influential I mean he's capable of influencing people—he's a notorious liar. He can whip a crowd into a frenzy, especially young men."

Gage nodded.

"You should try to get to know him, but be careful because he's dangerous. His following is so large, so imposing, that Southern politicians are afraid of crossing him."

General Scott, growing impatient at the discussion that didn't involve him, was quickly taking on his *Old Fuss and Feathers* persona. Having brought with him a young lieutenant, Scott interrupted the conversation to bring them to the purpose of their meeting: "The contract between Gage Ironworks and the army called for the production of one hundred twenty three-inch cannons," Scott said. "The lieutenant was asked to make a search for them."

"I found them—seventy of them located at Fort Monroe where they have been undergoing rigorous testing," the lieutenant reported.

Gage already knew this, but it was good to receive confirmation. "What manufacturer's name did you find?" he asked.

"They had the Gage name imprinted on them," the lieutenant said. "And this I'm sure you'll like, Major. They are so distinctive they've already been given a special name: the *Gage Rifled 10 Pounder*."

Gage winced. No, he didn't like that.

"Are you satisfied, Major?" the general asked.

Gage shook his head. "Where did the other fifty cannons go?"

"They were destroyed, of course, in the explosion at Gage Ironworks," the general said.

"Were they? Did anyone verify that?"

They looked at the lieutenant for an explanation. "I was told not to worry about that."

"By whom?"

"The senator. I figured he knew best."

"What senator?"

"Senator Wigfall."

"Lieutenant, Wigfall is from Texas, a state that seceded three weeks ago," Gage replied sternly.

"I assumed he was a Union man. What's he doing still being around here?"

"That's a good question," Gage said.

It was a difficult issue. For those who asserted that the South had no right to secede, how could they claim that those states were no longer represented in Congress? Most Southern senators had resigned and gone back to their home states, but not Wigfall. He continued to hang around, and Gage was suspicious.

Later, Stanton tried to reassure Gage. "No doubt Wigfall has stayed here to gather intelligence which he sends to the South. We take advantage of that.

We have people leaking things to him that he telegraphs straight to Charleston. One day he reports we're evacuating Fort Sumter within the next week, and then the next day he's telling them we're sending reinforcements. They probably don't know what to make of it."

"That doesn't concern me so much. What worries me is I have reports he's been arranging for rifles to be sent to Texas militia units. Those are soldiers who will come to Virginia when Virginia secedes."

"And now you think that aided by others—such as your family—he's sending cannons to the South."

Gage hesitated. He was not yet ready to certify Jubal Ford as a traitor. Perhaps he sent the cannons to Charleston in accordance with orders from the secretary of war. But then, why the secrecy in that shipment? Why label them as threshers?

"I don't know who all has been a part of it," Gage finally replied. "But you can be damn sure I'm going to find out."

Chapter 15

Aramis Gage walked into Doc Brown's office and stood silently, glaring at the man who delivered him into this world. He had come to confront the physician over his lies about how the five men died in the explosion.

Doc Brown avoided his gaze. He knew what this was about. "I suppose they told you the truth."

"No, I learned the truth on my own. Who is *they?*"

"Charlotte and Jamie, of course."

"What?"

"About Jamie's little fracas."

"What little fracas?"

"Oh, you don't know," Doc Brown said. Realizing his mistake and that Ari would press him further, he decided to disclose what he knew. "I treated Jamie for some cuts to his face, and I set his broken arm. He got into a fight with some boys at school."

"A fight? What about?"

"The boys apparently don't like your politics . . . your abolitionist views."

"How many other boys were involved?"

"I'm told five."

"That sounds like he was assaulted."

"You'll have to talk to your son about that. He and Charlotte were trying to keep it from you."

"I'll talk to him. But now that I've got the truth from you about that, I want to hear the truth about how the men died at the ironworks?"

The doctor didn't deny it. He started to explain, but his stammering was interrupted as Ari said, "Why did you lie about it?"

Doc Brown looked away. "It's not easy for a small-town doctor to make ends meet."

"So you were paid to lie."

"You didn't hear that from me."

"What are you afraid of?"

Doc Brown looked at him incredulously. "It's like you don't even know this town . . . like you don't even know your stepfather."

***

When Ari sat down with Charlotte and Jamie at the Ford/Gage mansion, Jamie explained how it all started. "We had a debate in social studies class about the Fugitive Slave Act."

"I assume you argued that it was immoral to prohibit people in non-slave states from helping a fugitive slave?"

"Yes, that and I argued that if slavery was illegal in a state, then the people of that state shouldn't be prohibited from helping a runaway."

"A very commendable position."

"I mean the whole idea of the act was that the laws of a Southern state should be respected. Why shouldn't the laws of a state where slavery is illegal also be respected?"

Ari nodded in agreement. "But you had a fight in the classroom over this?"

"No, after school they were waiting for me outside."

"And that's when they attacked you?"

Charlotte interrupted. "We need to be clear here, Ari. Jamie acknowledges that he threw the first punch."

Impressed by his son's gumption in taking on five boys, Ari stifled a smile. "Son, what caused you to do that?"

Jamie looked down at the floor.

"What was it, Jamie?"

Charlotte intervened again. "Ari, one of the boys called you a Black Republican Nancy."

"Such an odd combination of derogatory terminology. I can see why they're failing in school."

Jamie laughed, but Ari turned serious: "We may need to move you three back to the apartment in Philadelphia where our politics is accepted."

"I don't want to," Jamie said. "I'll fight them every day if need be."

"That's what I'm afraid of," Ari replied.

When Jamie went to his room, Charlotte came over to Ari and put her arm around him. "Don't worry, darling, I'll vouch for you that you're not a Nancy."

Ari chuckled. "I'm sorry it's come to this."

"Yes, politics consumes everything now," she said. "Every innocent statement seems to turn into a political argument. We don't go into town anymore because of it. We are confined to the house."

"Then we definitely need to move you back to Philadelphia."

"Your mother will be heartbroken. At least, though, we won't be far away, and we'll be sure to visit often."

"That's good because she's not going to like hearing what else I have to tell her."

***

It was to be a difficult conversation with Victoria. She was no longer the strong-willed woman with the ability to think things through on her own. While that should make this discussion easier, Ari had recently noticed something troubling. Victoria was easily persuaded by those who were around her most. For the last couple of years that had been Jubal and Doc Brown, and she seemed wedded to their convictions.

But Ari was determined to see her accept the truth this time. He began by saying, "Mother, you need to open your mind to the possibility that some things may not be as they appear to be, or as we are told they are."

"My, that sounds foreboding. So what is this ominous thing you want to tell me?"

"Johnny and I have learned that the five men didn't die in the explosion at the ironworks."

"Oh, Ari, that's silly, of course they did," she said, and she reclined on the sofa like she had just listened to a soothing poem.

"No, Mother, they didn't," Ari said adamantly.

"And how did you come by this knowledge?" she asked with a bit of a smirk.

"I won't go into the details," Ari said, for he had no desire to relive the grave-digging episode. "I'll just say we discovered it, and I've confirmed it with Doc Brown."

This statement drew a reaction. "Doc Brown lied about it?"

"Yes." He could see she was crestfallen, and he needed to soften the blow. "I'm not saying the men didn't die by an accident at the ironworks. In fact, I know that they did."

"But then why would Jubal not tell the truth about how they died?" She paused with a serious look on her face, then added casually, "I'll ask him."

"No, Mother, it's best that you don't right now. There's no reason for you to involve yourself in it. Johnny is looking into it, and he'll let us know if there's more to it."

"Then why did you bring this to me now?"

It was a good question, one that Ari tried to answer as honestly as he could. "We just wanted you to be aware . . . in case you might notice anything unusual."

She was unsettled; it was obvious from the concern showing on her face. It was the first time she had reason to be suspicious of her husband.

"But there's more you want to tell me, isn't there?"

"About that, no."

"I mean I can sense that you want to move your family back to Philadelphia."

"Yes, that's true."

"I will miss them terribly. I love my grandchildren, and Charlotte has become like a daughter to me. It's been wonderful to have them here the last few months. I take strength from their presence."

"I know, but remember they'll only be eight miles away."

"Yes, although it won't be the same not having them in the house. But I understand . . . I truly do. In times like this, it'll be best for them to be back there."

***

A week later Victoria Ford sat in an examination room of a Philadelphia doctor. She unbuttoned her kid gloves and set them on the table next to her. Those were the only articles of clothing she would remove, however, for she had not come here to be examined. Still, she was nervous, and this time she knew the cause. The two people she relied on most in Carthage had deceived her, and she had come here to learn whether they were deceiving her about something else.

The door opened and in walked a tall, angular man who reeked of cleanliness, for his white coat was unblemished and he was freshly scrubbed, freshly shaved—his cheeks seemed to glow in pink. He introduced himself as Dr. Keller and said, "I understand, Mrs. Ford, you're having trouble with your nerves."

"Only at the moment, Doctor."

"Please relax, I'm here to help."

"I may have given you the wrong impression. What troubles me at the moment is the fear of what I might discover here today."

Somewhat perplexed, Keller ran his hand through his hair. "I'm not sure any kind of examination I can perform today can fix those kinds of feelings."

"It's a different kind of examination I'm after, Doctor."

"I don't understand."

She reached into her purse and pulled out a bottle that was enveloped in a plain, brown wrapper. "I would like you to have the contents of this bottle analyzed to see what's in there."

"Do you suspect something foul?"

"It's been prescribed for me by our town doctor, and I fear it was done for an ulterior purpose."

"Why do you think he would do such a thing?"

"Let's just say I've become aware of a lie of significance he has maintained . . . upon the instructions of others."

"So you no longer trust him?"

Victoria nodded.

Keller opened the bottle and sniffed it like he was smelling a glass of freshly poured wine. "We may not need that analysis," he said, and he dabbed a small amount of the liquid in the palm of his hand.

Upon tasting it, the doctor confirmed his suspicion. "No analysis is needed. It's laudanum."

Victoria cringed. She knew enough about the so-called wonder drug to know that it was not the right thing for her.

"How much do you take each day?"

She pulled a small glass from her purse and pointed to a measuring line.

"This much two times a day."

He shook his head, then turned away slightly in an effort to hide his shock.

"Does laudanum work to calm an unsettled stomach?" she asked.

The doctor chuckled. "What you're taking each day would calm just about everything. But, no, there are much better things for a queasy stomach, and certainly this dosage is outlandish."

"Do you think this laudanum could make me feel tired... rather listless?"

"Absolutely. It's opium doused with alcohol, and you're taking twice the dose someone would take for extreme pain or sleeplessness."

He could see the hurt etched across her face, but he watched as it quickly transformed into a look of hardened determination. "Mrs. Ford, I advise you to stop drinking this potion, but wean yourself off of it gradually."

"Thank you, Doctor, I will do just that."

"Do so and I'm sure you will soon be able to take on your old responsibilities."

"Good, because that's what I plan to do, and much more."

Chapter 16

John Gage's very public exhortation to 'Let the South Go' rattled Republicans throughout the North. Thus he was shocked to have received an invitation to this reception in Harrisburg. Seated at a table for six, he surveyed the crowded room at the Jones House, the hotel at which the president-elect was to spend the night. At least one hundred people were in attendance, but he was one of only a few journalists. This was a Republican event, replete with speeches and toasts celebrating Lincoln's election although little was said about its consequences.

During the dinner, Gage kept a watchful eye on Lincoln. The man seemed a little drawn. Not surprising since thus far on the circuitous route to Washington City for his inauguration the president-elect had travelled eighteen hundred miles, making whistle stops in more than seventy towns and cities. Just today he had delivered two speeches in Philadelphia, a speech earlier to a crowd outside the Jones House, and a formal address at the Pennsylvania statehouse.

But there was something going on that Gage couldn't understand. Rumors of assassination plots were everywhere. Why would Lincoln's advisors allow the public so much access to him?

Gage watched the same man approach Lincoln on three occasions during the dinner, as if urging some action on his part. It was upon the third time that Lincoln suddenly stood, grabbed hold of the governor, and the two of them left the room.

When they hadn't returned after ten minutes, Gage considered following them. But before he could do so a waiter approached and said, "Mr. Gage, there is a man in the back hallway who has a message for you."

Gage got up and meandered through several tables and followed the waiter's directions to a door that took him out into the back hallway. Standing there was a rather tall man with an ashen complexion. He had a long neck and narrow face, but a stomach so large that he reminded Gage of a Canadian goose. The Gray Goose, as Gage thought of him, stood expressionless and silent as if waiting for someone else.

Finally, Gage asked, "What is it you want?"

Before the man could respond three other men, younger and stronger, appeared from the other direction. One of them reached into his pocket, a veiled threat that he possessed a gun that he didn't want to show.

"We would like you to come with us, Mr. Gage," the Gray Goose said.

"And what might be our destination?"

"I'm not at liberty to say."

"Who do you work for?"

"I'm not permitted to answer that either."

"Did Jubal Ford send you? Are you Miller Corps men?"

The four men looked at each other, and Gage could tell from their confused expressions that they didn't recognize those names.

"We would like you to come along . . . voluntarily," the Gray Goose said. "Unfortunately, we can't allow you to see the path we take. You'll need to wear this blindfold." He pulled out a large black handkerchief from his pocket that he handed to one of the other men.

Who are they? Gage kept wondering. Violent abolitionists, Southerners with ties to the Gage Ironworks, or someone I've offended with my articles? Maybe a woman's jealous suitor? He regretted that this was the first time he had traveled outside of Washington without a weapon.

When the young man attempted to place the blindfold over Gage's head, Gage knocked his hand away. "I need to send a telegram to my office in Washington. I have a story to report."

"You won't be sending any stories, Mr. Gage."

"And why is that?"

"The telegraph out of Harrisburg is down."

"The wires cut?"

"The telegraph is down."

Perhaps I could fight my way out, Gage thought, but there was something intriguing about all of this. He decided to go along . . . at least for now.

With the blindfold in place, two of the men clutched Gage by his arms. They were guiding him, although not very effectively because they rarely bothered to tell him when to step down from a curb. Gage counted the blocks and noted the turns made, trying to keep a sense of where he might be.

After seven blocks, Gage could hear the low rumble of a steam engine idling, and he knew they must be near a railroad station.

"We're almost there, Mr. Gage," the Gray Goose volunteered.

"Almost where?"

"Your destination, not ours," and one of the men removed the blindfold.

Gage found himself standing in front of a locomotive at a deserted railroad station, so deserted that it appeared to have been cleared intentionally.

"We were told to deliver you here. You're to wait here . . . right here on the platform by the engine."

The four men departed. Gage waited five minutes. He had left his hat and topcoat at the hotel, and now a brisk north wind was chilling him. The train was peculiar looking. Only one car attached to the tender—a long luxury car, longer than any car Gage had ever seen.

Finally, the engineer appeared and Gage asked him, "What is this train?"

"Don't really know," the engineer replied. "All they told me is some woman rented it for herself and her invalid brother." He stepped up into the cabin of the locomotive. Then, looking down, he added, "They also said I should keep my mind on my own business. You might want to do the same."

Never one to abide by another's suggestions, Gage wandered along the platform until he reached the luxury car. Gas lamps lit the interior but not sufficiently for him to make out the faces of those inside. Several people were gathered about as if in a serious discussion. Someone noticed him, and soon people were gesturing his direction. The discussion was about him.

A slender figure departed the group. Moments later, there appeared at the doorway a prim-looking woman in glasses, her hair wrapped tightly about her head and a wrap draped around her upper torso. She struck a pose as if she was going to scold Gage. Then, in a flash, she removed her glasses and pulled a pin that allowed her brunette hair to drop into its normal fashion.

"Kate!" Gage exclaimed. It was Kate Warne, the first female private detective in the country, whom Gage knew well from his time in Chicago.

"You're going to catch your death of cold out there, Johnny."

"Kate, what goes on here? What was that discussion about?"

"The others wanted someone to vouch for you. I sure as hell wouldn't."

"Who did then?"

"The president-elect of the United States."

Gage smiled.

"Get in here, Johnny."

Gage stepped up into the railcar and looked her over. "You've changed. Are you in disguise once again?"

Without replying, she stepped towards him. He anticipated a hug, but instead she ran her hands up and down his suit coat checking for weapons. Then she dropped her hands down his backside sliding across his buttocks and down the back of his thighs. The hands then turned to the front and came up, ending briefly in his crotch.

"No, you haven't changed a bit," Gage said.

She giggled, a devilish little laugh. "Just doing my job."

"You're very thorough."

"Come, I'll introduce you to the others," and she took him by the hand back to the group that still seemed to be in the midst of a discussion

But these men weren't Lincoln's political advisers, they were his protectors. Among them was Ward Lamon, the robust, young lawyer from Illinois who had come along to guard Lincoln. Also present was Samuel Felton, president of the Philadelphia, Wilmington & Baltimore, the railroad responsible for this portion of the president-elect's journey. And just arrived was army Colonel Edwin "Bull Head" Sumner. From his time in Chicago, Gage already knew Alan Pinkerton, the short, bearded Scotsman who was the founder of the famed Pinkerton Detective Agency and Kate's boss.

And Gage already knew the president-elect. Lincoln strode towards him from the back of the car, looking tired but strangely energetic. He was tall and lean with arms and legs so long that he walked with a machinelike gait, as if those appendages were being turned by giant gears. The long strides were quick, though, adding to that sense of energy.

But Lincoln looked vastly different from three months ago, the last time

Gage met with him in Springfield. The president-elect had recently grown a beard that gave a fullness to his face. As they shook hands, Gage said, "You've added something since our last meeting."

Lincoln smiled, scratched at his new beard, and said, "Supposedly it makes me look wiser than the hayseed they make me out to be."

"I wasn't aware of the beard until I saw that drawing in *Vanity Fair* the other day," Gage said, pointing to the magazine on a table next to them.

Lincoln opened the magazine to the wild caricature of himself and said, "Yes, I suppose that does resemble the creature."

Suddenly Lamon interrupted their conversation with his position on Gage's presence: "I'll be blunt, Mr. Gage, I don't favor you being here."

"Nonsense, Lamon," Lincoln said. "Despite our differing views, I promised Gage an interview before the inauguration, and I intend to keep that promise. Besides, what we're up against now is going to be resolved one way or another before Gage could ever put anything in print, so let's include him."

No one could disagree with that logic, and so Lamon succinctly declared, "We believe there is a plot afoot—possibly multiple plots—to assassinate Mr. Lincoln when he passes through Baltimore. We're discussing alternative routes."

"What kind of plots?" Gage asked.

A perfect set up question for Lincoln who was finding some amusement in all of this. "There are so many assorted groups there wanting to do so that I think they're more likely to end up killing each other than me."

Pinkerton took umbrage. "Sir, I'll remind you that these reports came from three different sources who all arrived at the same conclusion. Not only from Kate, who has been on the ground in Baltimore at the request of Mr. Felton, but also from Senator Seward and General Scott who received reports of plots."

Lincoln smiled at Gage and said, "One of them says that a barber is to do the killing. Hopefully, he will tidy my beard first." The president-elect was having difficulty taking the threats seriously. "Americans don't engage in assassinations," he told the others. "It's not in our nature."

Gage viewed that as naive. But the matter seemed already decided, so he said, "I know you had planned a direct route on the Northern Central from

Harrisburg to the B&O station in Baltimore. What is the plan now?"

"Tonight, my railroad will take the president-elect east to Philadelphia and then to Baltimore," Felton explained. "The whole idea is to pass undetected through that city during the nighttime."

"Sneaking through Baltimore in the middle of the night will be called a damned piece of cowardice," Bull Head Sumner thundered. "Let me round up a squad of cavalry, sir, and we'll cut our way to Washington."

Gage crushed the colonel's notion instantly. "You would have an army unit arrayed against Baltimore citizens. If blood is shed protecting a Northern president against border state citizens, it could be viewed as the start of a war against the South."

"Yes, a clandestine approach is better," Pinkerton agreed.

Lincoln and Gage retired to the rear of the car for what the others thought was the interview. However, this wasn't an interview, it was a report.

Lincoln began the discussion. "You've done well, Gage. When I asked you to return to Washington to watch over the Buchanan administration, I knew you would find your way into important circles. You've always had that knack. But you've gone far beyond what I even imagined. You're on the inside with the Buchanan people and yet you've been able to keep an eye on Seward. I laugh because I get Seward's reports about Stanton, and I already have better reports from you."

"Yes, but to maintain my role with the Buchanan officials I've had to write what I consider some despicable pieces. I am paying a price."

"I know you are. But by doing so, I've heard you've garnered an invitation to Charleston."

"Yes, I leave in three days. My last editorial did the trick."

Lincoln laughed. "Yes, that was a nice touch—you calling me a *Prairie Twister.*"

"My apologies, sir."

"Quite all right. Southerners will like that—it will stick in their minds."

"I don't know what you can do about Senator Seward. He now seems to suggest that a compromise might be possible on the question of slavery expansion."

"Yes, he's been swinging the gate both ways," Lincoln said, as his left eye, a lazy one, wandered slightly out of kilter as if it had gone off to think about something else.

It was something Gage had noticed before. That eye drifted off and took the mind with it. Once, during one of their conversations in Illinois when Gage thought Lincoln was distracted, he questioned him about it and received the only cogent explanation he ever got: "Like many lawyers—at least, the good ones I know—I often think in reverse. What's my client's end goal? And from there I work backwards, exploring all the paths to take and what pitfalls may occur along those paths. I suppose I drift off on those pathways at times."

Gage waited. He assumed the president-elect was thinking backwards about what Seward's statements might do politically.

At last both eyes focused on Gage and Lincoln said, "Southern newspapers have been misrepresenting my views. When you talk to Southerners, Gage, explain to them that their slave practice will be as safe with me as it has been under Buchanan. I will not allow slavery to expand into new territories, but it will be safe where it is."

"I will do that, sir."

Lincoln sat back and looked at Gage earnestly. "John, you'll be taking a big risk going south. If war breaks out while you're there, and you're found out, you will be deemed a spy."

"Our purpose justifies the risk. The Union must be preserved."

"We are of the same mind."

"Any special instructions, sir?"

"Learn what you can of their capabilities, assess their true resolve, and be wary of this Ransom Pierce fellow. I understand he's dangerous."

"So I've heard."

"And one final thing."

"What's that, sir?"

"Try to stall them . . . if you can. We need to buy time."

"Time for you to get into office?"

"Time for us to undo the damage that has been done to the military . . . time for us to save the capital."

Chapter 17

Pinkerton's secret plan required Lincoln to travel in disguise. A felt cap replaced his top hat, and to lessen his height he hunched over with a borrowed tartan shawl draped about his shoulders. All done to enhance the appearance of a sick man traveling with the aid of others.

That appearance was necessary because the plan also called for taking a public train the rest of the way. In Philadelphia the group changed to the regular night train to Baltimore. This presented another problem: the berths in the sleeping car couldn't be reserved.

"Work your magic, Kate," Pinkerton said. "Use the same story."

Kate found the conductor sitting at a tall table at the front of one of the forward cars. She tweaked her cheeks for a bit of color and let her hair fall. Then she undid two clasps that were part of a homemade creation. The clasps, once undone, freed a wrap that attached to the upper portion of her dress and when removed it revealed a dress that was itself somewhat revealing.

When Kate reached the table, she placed her arms on the table and bent over.

The conductor's face went flush.

"Sir, I have a problem. My invalid brother needs a private berth for himself and one other for his two helpers. Is it possible you can accommodate us?"

"Yes, ma'am," the conductor said immediately. "I'll make the arrangements."

Although unnecessary, she tipped him with a two and a half dollar gold coin. The president-elect now had a place to sleep with his protectors nearby, and a conductor looking out for them.

The four-hour trip from Philadelphia to Baltimore went smoothly, but by the time the train approached the President Street station of the PW&B Railroad in Baltimore, the tension in the car was palpable. All the lamps in the car were extinguished. Kate bolted the door. Ward Lamon sat on one side of the car, scanning the darkness outside for any movement. He held a Colt 45 revolver in his right hand. Alan Pinkerton watched the other side, nervously tapping his knee as he peered out.

A quarter of a mile from the station, the train suddenly halted. Lincoln came out from his berth. Lamon bolted upright and stood in front of the president-elect with his revolver pointed outward even though he couldn't locate a target. Pinkerton raced to a window on the other side of the train to look out that direction.

But the conductor quickly reassured everyone: "No cause for alarm everyone. Just a slow-moving cow crossing the tracks."

"Relax, Lamon," the president-elect said, "and please don't shoot the cow. He's probably as tired as we are."

When the train rolled to a stop at the station, Felton stepped down from the car and gave instructions to railroad workers without alerting them to the nature of their precious cargo. Now came the most dangerous part of the journey. The station of the Baltimore and Ohio, the railroad that would take the president-elect on the last leg of the trip to Washington City, was a mile to the west. Because steam engines weren't allowed in the heart of the city, the car would have to be pulled by horses on tracks along Pratt Street.

It was only four in the morning, and yet scattered noises came from the station house. It was as if the train's arrival had awakened the city.

Pinkerton approached Gage and Kate with a directive they were half-expecting: "I was told by Mr. Lincoln's advisors that you two can't be seen coming into Washington City with Mr. Lincoln. Mr. Gage, because your publicly professed opinions are contrary to the president-elect's."

"I understand."

"And, Kate, obviously a young woman can't be seen near Mr. Lincoln's sleeping berth when he arrives in Washington."

"I suppose there are some newspaper editors who would enjoy that," Gage said.

"Oh, it's not them everyone is afraid of," Pinkerton replied. "It's the Hellcat. She would go on the warpath if she heard about that."

Gage chuckled. He had heard the nickname some close to the president-elect had secretly given Mrs. Lincoln.

"Alan, can we be of any further assistance?" Gage asked.

Pinkerton nodded. "I hate to ask this of you, John, since this is not your job."

"Think nothing of it. We all want to get Mr. Lincoln to Washington safely. The fate of our nation may depend on it."

"Good. It would be helpful if you two could get out in front and scout along this mile stretch. Mr. Felton and his assistant will do the same on the south side of the railcars and why don't you two handle the north side. Stay a couple blocks away from the tracks so as not to call attention to the train car. All I want you to do is alert us if trouble is coming our way."

Gage and Kate headed north a block before turning west. There were some people milling about but they were scattered, not part of any group. The duo then walked west three blocks down a narrow alley, surrounded on both sides by rows of tenement houses.

At the intersection of Tremont and Pine streets, they came upon two men who were acting suspiciously and walking quickly in the direction of the tracks on Pratt Street.

"What's your purpose out here?" Gage demanded of them.

The much larger of the two seemed insulted. "Our purpose? We live here."

"Why are you out here at this time of day?"

"I might ask the same of you. We're on our way to catch the B&O train to Washington."

"You two don't look like you've got business in Washington."

"Maybe we're going there to visit our sick mother."

The short man walked over to Kate. "Hey, this little one is a woman."

He grabbed once at her hat and she ducked sideways. "Don't touch my hat," she said.

But he didn't heed her warning. He grabbed again, and this time knocked the hat from her head. He began jostling her hair that was pinned tight. As he tried to pull the pins from the back of her hair, she kicked him so hard in the right knee that his leg buckled. He doubled over in pain, and as he did so she crashed her knee underneath his chin. He dropped to the ground, unconscious.

Assuming that would be the end of the matter, Gage began walking toward Kate. But the big man stuck out his foot and tripped him. Before he knew it, Gage was face down on the ground with the big man on top, holding him in a headlock. The man smelled like wet peat and his odor was almost as stifling as his iron grip.

"That bitch of yours hurt my little brother," the big man shouted down at Gage.

With her arms crossed, Kate sauntered over. She bent down to Gage's encumbered head and asked sarcastically, "Do you need help, Johnny?"

That was motivation enough. Gage grabbed the back of the big man's ankles and pulled hard. The big man crashed to the brick pavement, but that didn't stop him. He got up and charged. Gage hit him with a solid shot to the jaw that staggered him but didn't keep him from charging again. The big man threw a wild right hook that Gage ducked. Gage then landed a solid punch to the man's midsection that caused him to double over. Gage gave the big man a gentle push, and he fell backwards over his brother. He was still conscious, but it was clear he had had enough.

Kate applauded lightly.

The two of them hurried westward, looking for any more trouble, but there was none. Then they watched with relief as Lincoln's horse-drawn railcar rolled safely into the B&O train station.

Gage looked around. "It's four in the morning and no place to go."

"Come," she said, and she took him by the hand. "Our company's safe house is only two blocks away."

***

The safe house was small and nothing about it seemed particularly safe except it did have good separation from the houses nearby. Nobody could see the occupants' comings and goings.

When Kate stepped inside, she immediately took off her coat. She pulled a pistol and a knife from the inner lining and laid them on a table.

"You had weapons and chose not to use them to scare them off?" Gage said.

"It was a lot more fun this way."

Gage's scowl caused her to provide a more rational explanation: "John, if I pulled out a pistol and they resisted, we might wind up in a police report. Neither of us would want that. And explaining why I carried a pistol would certainly ruin my cover. Besides, I figured we could finish them off without any weapons."

She removed the pins holding her hair and brown locks fell to her shoulders which she shook into a wild disarray. She took off her boots and threw them across the room. She poured them both a glass of wine as Gage sat down on the sofa.

"You've been living here instead of Chicago?" Gage asked.

"For the last three months I have. I've played the part of the wronged Southern belle, infiltrating the high society of Baltimore while trying to learn of any real plots against Mr. Lincoln." Then switching to the southern accent she had developed while working undercover in Mobile, Alabama, she said, "I attend all the fashionable parties."

"You didn't use your Mobile name again, did you?"

Kate nodded, a mischievous grin on her face. "Yes, I am still Mrs. Cherry."

Gage laughed with delight. Five years earlier, he happened to be in Pinkerton's office when the young widow, destitute and seven hundred miles away from her childhood home, walked into the Pinkerton office in search of a job. Alan Pinkerton assumed she wanted a clerical position. Instead, she wanted to be a private detective. Impressed by her boldness and convinced that she could accomplish things a man couldn't, Pinkerton hired her. Since then she had undertaken covert roles in several high-profile cases. By being unassuming she could find her way into places that men couldn't, and she had a proven talent for becoming a confidant to others.

Gage walked over to the window, pulled back the curtains, and looked outside.

"Don't worry, Johnny, we're safe here," she said as she detached the wrap from the top of her dress and threw it on a table.

"Suddenly, I don't feel so safe," Gage said with a grin while staring at her chest.

She laughed.

"Still no thoughts of settling down?"

"No, Johnny, I haven't changed. I'll never change. I don't want to be a wife, or mother. I love my job."

"I can tell you love the chicanery of it all."

"Chicanery, an interesting word coming from you."

"What do you mean?"

"I helped you figure out how that western freighting company was getting illicit funds from Washington. Then you joined a Washington newspaper and that paper broke the story, but it's written by an unknown reporter who's never been to the West. There's some chicanery hidden in that."

Gage smiled. "Sometimes we parcel out stories among the reporters."

"Malarkey. And the editorials you've written promoting a peaceful separation. That's not the John Gage I know."

"I am a changed man," Gage said as he sat down on the sofa.

She began to walk towards him. "Who are you trying to fool, Johnny, me or yourself? You're not changed. You and I are still two of a kind: we want no attachments."

That assessment confused Gage momentarily, but the confusion vanished as she came to stand right in front of him.

"We want adventure, John," and she climbed on top of him.

Putting both hands to his face and leaning in, she added, "Adventure is a good substitute for attachments."

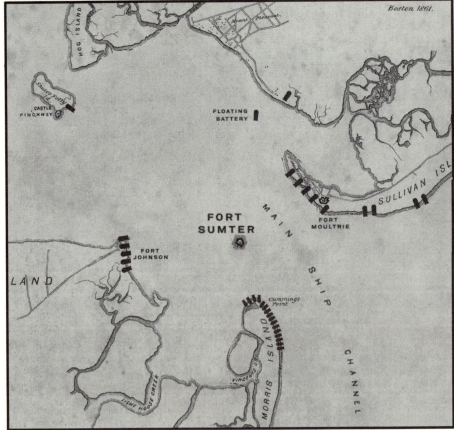

Chapter 18

It was a bright morning with only a few wispy, white clouds decorating an azure sky as John Gage lounged in a deck chair on the port side of the SS *Gadsen*. He was in the final hour of his voyage to Charleston, and when the gulls began squawking overhead he knew land was near.

As the ship approached Charleston Harbor Gage stood up, feeling an unexpected spark of adrenalin. It came about not from the crisis he was about to become a part of, but rather the manner in which he would do so. His adult life had been a paradox, a product of serving in capacities that ran contrary to his unbridled nature. Although always on his own, his conduct had been regimented. In his decade in the army there was always an officer above, always a manual to follow. Even at the newspapers, editors controlled his work. But not now, for there was no manual for the mission he was about to undertake. He was writing his own.

Just outside the harbor, the ship was halted by the U.S. Revenue Cutter *William Aiken*. At first Gage was relieved to see a federal vessel in Charleston waters. A good sign it seemed.

"It's not what you think, Mr. Gage," one of the *Gadsen* crewmen explained. "South Carolina seized the cutter in late December. It's in their service now."

An unusual assortment of men from the *William Aiken*, seven in all, boarded the *Gadsen*. Five were soldiers, each wearing a different military uniform. One was a local pilot, brought in to steer the *Gadsen* through the numerous sandbars and channels of the harbor. One was a civilian who acted like he was in charge. For over an hour the soldiers examined the cargo and questioned the passengers about their purposes in Charleston.

Gage, a keen observer of people, believed you could learn a lot by watching a person's behavior, and the civilian in command of this inspection, a squarish man in his fifties with a smug visage, seemed an interesting study. The man wore a slouch hat, but he never tipped it at a passenger, and he often flashed his prominent white teeth at inappropriate times. Even though he wore no identifying uniform, he still donned the red sash about his waist that leading military men in Charleston displayed. He was an odd individual who demanded respect from others but was unwilling to give it himself. Above all, this man craved attention, seemed to thrive on it.

A young lieutenant bearing a holstered revolver approached Gage. "Please state your name and purpose in Charleston, sir," the lieutenant said.

"John Gage... here at the invitation of the Citizens of Charleston Defense Committee."

A smile came to the lieutenant's lips. "You are an honored guest, Mr. Gage. Welcome to Charleston."

"Thank you, Lieutenant."

"I'm sorry, but I must now demand that you surrender your field glasses."

Gage didn't need the field glasses—at least not at the moment—so he gave them up, albeit grudgingly. Thus far, from outside the harbor, he had been able to observe the construction of artillery batteries along the shore of Sullivan's Island. "Not very hospitable, Lieutenant."

"My apologies, sir. I have my orders."

Just as the lieutenant was about to move on to another passenger, a commotion occurred at the top of the auxiliary mast. The U.S. flag was being replaced by the Palmetto flag of South Carolina.

"A requirement for the ship to enter the harbor," the lieutenant explained.

"Would you require such of a British ship?"

"We are not at odds with the British, Mr. Gage," a shrill voice from the side interrupted. That declaration came from the civilian who had been ordering people about. He then said, "Welcome to our new *nation*, Mr. Gage. My name is Ransom Pierce."

"My pleasure, sir. I'm surprised you busy yourself with this kind of inspection."

"It's my first time actually. I wanted to be here to greet you. You've come at a most opportune time."

"I can see that from the armaments that are being placed along the shore."

"No, no, I mean you've come in time for the annual horse races—the best racing in all the Southern lands. They go on for a week with celebrations each evening."

"It seems a strange time for horse races and celebrations, Mr. Pierce—with a war pending."

"Oh, we're also quite busy preparing for combat. Five militia units arrive each day in Charleston from the interior. Besides, the Yankees won't fight."

"Northerners say barking dogs never bite."

"We aren't just barking dogs, Mr. Gage. You will soon learn that."

"I hope you are just that. Otherwise, you and yours will be leading the South on a course of destruction."

"You don't sound like much of a peacemaker, Mr. Gage."

Charleston residents passed by delivering effusive salutations to Pierce. Gage was quick to sense it. The others were afraid of Pierce, afraid to cross him in any way.

"I noticed that, instead of my newspaper, you chose the *Charleston Tribune* as the outlet for your reports from here," Pierce grumbled.

"Mr. Krause, the editor, has assured me he will share the news articles immediately with the other Charleston newspapers."

"I don't like the *Tribune*."

"I gathered that," Gage said with a chuckle.

"It's run by a German and a Jew. I would've thought you might select an American newspaper."

"Both of those gentlemen are Americans."

"Not genuine."

Finding this informative, Gage decided to treat it as an interview. He asked, "Is it true that a few weeks ago you told an audience of two thousand that Mr. Lincoln plans to eliminate slavery everywhere with one stroke of his pen."

"Yes, I said that."

"You know he has no plans to do so—he may not even have the power to do so."

"I know that."

"So you acknowledge that Lincoln will not interfere with slavery where it now exists."

"Yes, I know that's his position."

"Then why do you tell the public otherwise?"

Pierce let loose a sinister smile with a flash of his prominent teeth. "Those people love me. I must keep them motivated."

"With lies?"

"You are naïve, aren't you, Mr. Gage? The truth rarely rallies the masses."

Their conversation turned to the relocation of Northern troops from Fort Moultrie to Fort Sumter, and Gage asked, "Are Charlestonians really upset because it violated Buchanan's promise to make no changes to the forts?"

"Hell, no. We're upset because it robbed us of an easy victory over the North, a meaningful and loud way to demonstrate our independence."

"So you recognize that taking Sumter would not be as easy as taking Fort Moultrie?"

"Of course not, especially if there's a Northern fleet backing Sumter. That could be devastating for Charleston."

"I appreciate your candor, Mr. Pierce. But despite all your bellicose rants, you don't believe the South can win a war, do you?"

"Perhaps not, but we can win what we need to win."

"And what is that?"

"To fight a war until the North tires of it. When we take Washington City, the Northern government, wherever it may be at that time, will sue for peace."

"Even if true, a lot of young men will die getting to that point, and they will have died because they followed untruths."

Pierce concluded there was no sense in arguing such esoteric matters. Instead he said, "Let's be clear about my *candor*, Mr. Gage. Our conversations are between us. If they end up in a newspaper, you will pay a heavy price."

"Is that a threat, Mr. Pierce?"

Pierce turned and looked out over the harbor before turning back to answer. "Remember, you are a guest in a foreign land. Be careful what you say and do."

Along with the five soldiers, Pierce left on the cutter. Gage now knew the man was more treacherous than he had even imagined. And Ransom Pierce had quickly learned that Gage was not the meek, shallow reporter he was expecting.

The *Gadsen* steamed toward the harbor, slowly maneuvering through the main ship channel. To his left, on Morris Island, Gage could see the batteries used by the Citadel cadets against the *Star of the West* two months earlier. Then they were mere kids firing warning shots at an American merchant ship. They're still kids, Gage thought, but by now they're trained artillerists.

Gage had seen the intelligence reports, and even without the field glasses he was close enough to confirm them. As the ship began to pass by Morris Island, he could see on his left the Confederate batteries being built at Cumming's Point, not more than twelve hundred yards from Fort Sumter. To his right, along Sullivan's Island, Confederates were laboring to finish new batteries there, and looking further ahead on his right, Gage observed the heavy guns of Fort Moultrie.

They steamed within a few hundred yards of the fort, it's five foot thick brick and concrete walls reaching up out of the water more than fifty feet. Several Union soldiers stood atop the parapet watching, waiting. A few hundred feet closer to the city, other Confederate artillery positions came into view. To the left were the cannons of Fort Johnson. Straight ahead, not far from the Charleston shore, was Castle Pinckney, a small stone fortress being readied with additional guns. And further out on the right, Gage perceived something that had not been mentioned in the intelligence reports. It was a floating battery protected by iron, and Gage feared it might be maneuverable on the water.

Sumter was surrounded, a seemingly hopeless position.

"Adventure," Kate had said. You've found it.

PART IV

A Fight among Friends

(March 1, 1861 – April 15, 1861)

Chapter 19

Coming ashore in Charleston, John Gage could remember witnessing a scene like this only once before. It was at the harbor in San Francisco, a decade earlier, when that city was consumed with gold fever. In Charleston there was a fever all right, but it was all about the prospect of war.

"Northern fleet off the coast," a newspaper hawker barked above the clamor. The headline of the newspaper he held high said the same except for a subtle caveat at the end: a question mark. Like Washington City, Charleston was a fountain of rumors.

Gage tried to reach the newspaper hawker, but in the chaos his way was blocked. Passengers scrambling to disembark crossed paths with dockworkers and those there to greet ship passengers, bringing pedestrian traffic to a halt.

Suddenly Gage heard his name shouted from the opposite direction. "Mr. Gage, Mr. Gage," a studious looking man with a light beard and thick-rimmed glasses called out again.

"Are you looking for me?" Gage yelled back.

"Yes, I'm Franklin Talbot."

Talbot managed to weave his way through the crowd, and the two men shook hands. "How did you recognize me?" Gage asked.

"I was told you would be the tallest one coming off the ship."

"Very astute, Congressman."

Talbot smiled. "Thank you, but I'm no longer a congressman."

"Already resigned?" asked Gage, concerned that Talbot might be a hard-line secessionist.

"No, I lost my seat, or perhaps I should say my seat was lost. South Carolina's population has declined so much relative to other states that over the years our number of congressmen has dropped from nine to six. Mine was the most recent district lost."

"I see."

"My friends call me Frank."

"And what should I call you?"

Talbot laughed. "I can tell you're a sly one, Mr. Gage."

"Nevertheless, I'm honored to have you as my escort."

"Don't be, I was assigned the task."

"I figured as much," Gage said with a wry smile.

"I understand you're staying at the Station House. I'll walk you there."

They left the chaos of civilians at the harbor, only to continually cross paths with small units of militiamen. "They're coming in by the dozens from the countryside," Talbot explained. A block further he pointed at some older soldiers maneuvering in an open square. "Firefighters drilling as infantry troops. Everyone is preparing."

But the energy of the people could not mask what Gage was seeing: a worn-out city. Grass was growing in the cobblestone streets. Paint was peeling from the white picket fences of the gated courtyards. There were few new buildings, and the old ones were in need of repair. And like those buildings, the rifles of the new recruits were antiquated, nearly all of a flintlock vintage.

"If I were to describe in simplest terms how I see this city, Mr. Talbot—Frank—I might call it a little tired-looking."

"Yes, despite still being the largest seaport on the southeast coast, we've been stalling economically for years. Some have said Charleston is much like a distressed elderly gentleman . . . a little gone down in the world, yet still remembering its former dignity."

"I like that. May I quote you?"

Talbot stopped abruptly and looked directly at Gage. "You may, if you don't attribute it to me, Mr. Gage. In fact, if you want me to speak candidly, you must agree not to attribute anything directly to me or in a way that I could be identified."

"Agreed," Gage said. His escort was definitely afraid of something.

At the next corner, a huge mural hung from the side of a two-story building. It depicted what appeared to be a judge on the bench shedding his judicial robe.

"Oddly enough, it was painted by one of the wealthiest men in the city, Jerome Cassidy," Talbot said. "It's dedicated to Judge Andrew Magrath who resigned his position as a federal judge just after secession was declared. He did so from the bench as shown in the painting."

"People here seem to enjoy celebrating things like that."

"Yes, we need local heroes."

Gage had studied a map of the city. He realized that at the next corner Talbot deviated from what would've been a direct route to the hotel. Gage knew why: the direct route would've taken them by Ryan's Auction Mart, a slave market established a few years earlier.

But that detour took them down a street where they passed by a small house that had a single red rose prominently attached to a front gate.

"What is that?" Gage asked.

"Someone's daily monument to Denmark Vesey."

Gage recognized the name of the man accused of plotting a massive slave insurrection in Charleston four decades earlier. "Thirty-seven men hung, convicted in secret trials with the accused unable to confront their accusers."

"More than that were acquitted and released."

"Nevertheless, it is a stain on your state's history. Even your governor at the time said so."

Talbot declined to discuss it further, but Gage had picked up on the "daily monument" reference. Someone, or some group, was secretly placing a rose there each day. It was like an open wound that wouldn't heal—a reminder of an evil persecution of the past and the threat of a slave insurrection in the future.

At Transit Street church bells were ringing. "That's the fourth church we've gone by in the last two blocks," Gage noted.

"That's why the city has the nickname the *Holy City*. We have a large number of churches and a variety of denominations."

"It's not from a holy atmosphere?" Gage quipped.

"No, we have more than our fair share of sinners." He pointed to the big brick house up ahead, one of the city's high-end brothels, sitting catty-corner from a Baptist church. "I'm told it's pricey, but well worth it if you're so inclined, Mr. Gage."

Feeling as though Talbot had just accessed his inner thoughts, Gage said nothing.

They walked further with Gage hearing foreign voices at times. "I've heard a fair amount of German spoken."

"We are a cosmopolitan city. Many Germans, some French, Scots, Irish—"

"You omitted Africans."

Talbot turned serious. "Yes, this city is half Negroes, most of them slaves. The percentage is even higher in the countryside."

Just when Gage thought Talbot might comment on the depth of fear of a slave insurrection, the man's face suddenly brightened. Coming their way was a lithe, young woman in her early twenties, wearing a powder blue dress—a uniform of sorts—and a matching hat that made Gage think she was either a nurse or a nun of a special order.

She turned out to be the former. "Mr. Gage, my daughter Jennifer."

"Jenny," she said with a big smile aimed at Gage.

"She is the best nurse at the Charleston Hospital."

"Oh, Father."

"It's true. Everyone says that."

"Only those who survive to tell about it."

Gage laughed. "I'm sure you're quite proficient at your job."

"I only hope you are as well, Mr. Gage. Your mission here is well-known. Perhaps you can bring some reason to all involved."

"I'll do my best."

"It will be difficult. The most intransigent people hold the loftiest of positions in this state. They try to speak for everyone."

After Jenny excused herself to return to the hospital, Gage commented, "You must be a proud father. She's lovely, seems very level-headed."

"In every way but one—the matters of the heart. You see, she has fallen for a Northerner, one of the soldiers at Fort Sumter."

"What a time to do so."

Talbot nodded. "I like the boy, Private Davidson from Ohio. But since Lincoln's election, all they can do is exchange letters."

"He can't come into the city?"

"None of the soldiers can, at least not without escorts. Oh, I don't think the people here would hurt ones like Davidson. But someone like Captain Doubleday, a known abolitionist from Massachusetts, I think they might string him up."

Gage smiled lightly.

"You know Doubleday?"

"Abner and I were together in the Mexican War. Beauregard and Anderson were there, too."

"This whole thing is a tangled affair."

They continued their stroll as Gage realized just how out of place the two of them appeared in their tailored suits. Half of the people they came across were slaves working in the trades. Most of the others were militiamen wearing their backwoods clothing. A throng of twelve such men passed by them to the side, obviously in a hurry to get somewhere.

"They're coming in from the countryside to help defend the city," Talbot said. "At least five thousand so far."

"Why are they so stirred up?"

"Fear. You might enjoy listening to a lecture from someone who plays on that fear—Ransom Pierce."

"I met him on the ship. I'd like to hear what he has to say."

Talbot pointed ahead to an old hotel with a front porch so wide that it extended across the entire width of the building. "That's your hotel. Your baggage should arrive shortly. The lecture is scheduled for three o'clock in the auditorium at Institute Hall. Let's meet there a few minutes before."

Having been in the city for only two hours, things were progressing quickly for Gage. He had already met the city's foremost secessionist—a leader of men, a teller of lies. Gage was eager to hear his lecture, eager to learn the secret of his success.

Chapter 20

With three hours until the Ransom Pierce speech, Gage decided to write his first article. His outlet, the *Charleston Tribune,* was known for its independence. Prior to heading south, Gage had arranged with the *Tribune's* editor to print the articles locally and forward them north by telegraph.

Gage would call his reports *Letters from Charleston.* It was a casual title, as if written by a travel correspondent, downplaying that it was coming from a place that might soon be a theatre of war. In this initial report, Gage planned to provide a cursory assessment of the city and explain his purpose.

The *Tribune* was housed in a small two-story brick building at the corner of Ralston and Third streets. Large windows along the boardwalk allowed generous lighting for the newspaper's office on the main floor. Living quarters were above. When Gage approached the building, five of the so-called militiamen lingered outside on the boardwalk, their rifles rusty but still imposing. A tall, thin woman with one arthritic hand pressed to her face peered out the window at the men. Gage went to the door and tried the handle, but the door was locked.

"Ain't anything worthwhile in there anyway, Mister," one of the militiamen said.

"I'll be the judge," Gage replied, and he knocked on the door. Through the glass panels he could see that the woman was looking his way, but not moving from her position.

Finally, the woman seemed to conclude that Gage wasn't associated with the soldiers. She moved to the door and cracked it open a few inches.

"I'm John Gage, ma'am . . . from Washington."

There was a sigh of relief from the woman along with a faint smile. "Come in, Mr. Gage, we've been expecting you," she said with a hint of a German accent. "I'll fetch my husband. He's upstairs eating his dinner."

She pulled on a cord that rang an upstairs bell, then asked, "Can I get you a cup of coffee, or hot chocolate?"

"No, ma'am, I'm fine, thank you."

"I am Alma Krauss, Mr. Gage." She pointed to a table across the room where a gangly boy of twelve sat across from two blonde-haired girls who were a few years younger. "Those are our children: Martin who is supposed to be typesetting right now and the twins, Marta and Joanna."

The two girls ran toward Gage then halted, mindful of their manners. Martin, wearing a white shirt and checked breaches that were a tawny color similar to his hair, ventured over. He reached out his hand and politely said, "Pleased to meet you, Mr. Gage."

The stairs began to creak and coming down them was a small, balding man dressed in an aged suit decorated with a purple bowtie. When he finished wiping his hands with a towel, he shook Gage's hand and said, "I'm Heinrich Krauss, Mr. Gage. Welcome to Charleston."

A forced cough came from the back of the office. Heinrich gestured in that direction where an older man in a wheelchair was writing furiously. "That, Mr. Gage, is Joseph Greene, the hardest working man in Charleston. Also the most crotchety man in Charleston."

"I work hard because I have nowhere else to go in this contraption," Joseph said. "And I'm crotchety because... well, I'm just crotchety by nature."

"And back in the far corner is the quietest man in Charleston—that's Sam Milton." Heinrich pointed to a large black man wearing a flannel shirt and trousers that were nearly pulled up to his chest by suspenders. He tipped his flat cap at Gage, but said nothing.

The children returned to their table where Martin continued to entertain and frustrate the girls with his version of the shell game. Five times in a row they guessed the wrong location of the pea. Martin then asked Gage to play. Gage sat down across from Martin with the girls huddled next to him. Gage guessed wrong the first time. "That one," he said the second time, fairly certain of his choice.

Martin uncovered the shells. Much to Gage's consternation, he erred again. Martin was a clever one.

"He's very good at that game, Mister Gage," Heinrich said.

"I can see that. It's best I give it up." Gage stood and handed Heinrich a single sheet of paper. "It's the first of what I'm calling *Letters from Charleston*. This one is brief."

Immediately Joseph steered his wheelchair through the openings of the office to come over. He grabbed Gage's report to study it. As he was reading, one of the militiamen on the boardwalk shouted loudly, "It's a damned German newspaper."

"Pay no heed to them, Mr. Gage," Heinrich said. "Just some young hooligans."

"Come now, Heinrich, they've been sent here by Ransom Pierce," Alma said. "They're up to no good."

"Mr. Pierce is unhappy that we're the ones publishing your articles," Heinrich explained.

"All the more reason that we should do so," Joseph said gleefully. "Although Pierce was angry with us well before these articles. He doesn't like having competitors."

"Yes, we must be very careful about what we say and do," Heinrich added.

For Gage, that was disappointing to hear. He had only three possible means for sending secret messages to the North and one of those, the telegraph, was just eliminated. It was obvious Heinrich would not take that risk, and it might be impossible to find another telegrapher who would be willing to do so. And it would be some time before Gage could feel assured that outgoing mail was safe, and even then he would need to send any letter to a private address in Washington. His third method, sending encoded messages within the *Letters from Charleston*, would require hours of work to structure the messages.

Joseph went back to studying the article, which read in part:

Letters from Charleston #1

I arrived here today to a city of grand contradictions. It is a tired-looking city, but strangely full of energy. Amid rumors of a pending Northern invasion, young men are arriving daily from the interior. Someone—the Confederate Army, the South Carolina militia, or Charlestonians—must figure out a way to feed, equip, and organize this new army.

Secession fever grips the city. Unionists are quiet and seem almost stunned to the point of disbelief by what has happened. As one said to me, "South Carolina is too small to be a republic, and too big for an insane asylum."

I have come here as a journalist, a mere reporter of the things I observe. But I will confess to a purpose: I want to see war avoided. I've witnessed the devastation of war, but only on the battlefield. The toll it takes at home is worse. If this war comes, I fear there will be no separation between battlefield and home front. It will spare no one. I don't want to see that happen.

"Snowflakes, Mr. Gage," Joseph chided. "You're sending mere snowflakes to the North, light and fluffy and inconsequential."

Chapter 21

Frank Talbot waived as Gage approached the steps to Institute Hall, a vast Italianate structure where the South Carolina Ordinance of Secession was signed just a few months earlier. Gage enjoyed fine architecture and this building was certainly that. He looked up and marveled at the stone surrounds of the large arched windows.

"You're just in time, Mr. Gage," Talbot said. "More than one thousand people in attendance, most of them young soldiers. You'll get a good sense of the fervor in this city."

They found a place to stand among others at the rear of the auditorium, but they had no problem hearing the oratory. Ransom Pierce's shrill voice carried well. Pierce wore the same clothes he had on when Gage met him a few hours earlier, not bothering to remove his slouch hat.

In just those first few minutes Gage grasped the uniqueness of Pierce's approach. He wasn't particularly articulate, but he had a way of connecting with his crowd. This was labelled a "Lecture," but Pierce didn't lecture. He talked to them like he was talking across a bar room table, often asking, "Do you see that, too?" It was a clever way to keep his audience engaged, but more importantly it invited their constant approval.

"I see collection plates," Gage whispered.

Talbot looked at him quizzically, said nothing.

"The advertisements say the lecture is free, but it seems Pierce expects contributions."

"Purely voluntary, Mr. Gage."

"Where does the money go?"

"Some kind of fund Mr. Pierce has started."

Gage smiled. He had witnessed many carnival shows that employed the same technique.

Pierce removed the slouch hat, displaying a full head of brown hair only slightly tinted with gray. He laid the hat on a nearby table, moving slowly while doing so as if to signify that he was contemplating something of importance. The audience was on edge as he began to speak about the election results:

> Radicals opposed to our peculiar institution have been elected all across the North. Lincoln has called Southerners immoral and unchristian and plans to end slavery. This vice president Northerners elected, Hannibal Hamlin, is a mulatto. Imagine that: we would have to submit to a Negro as vice president.
>
> With these Black Republicans in charge, they will John Brown us to death. Our independence is the only way out.
>
> You see we have some smart men in our state legislature, and they did a clever thing by enacting an ordinance of secession. It makes us our own sovereign entity... our own country. Without that, slaves might think a Northern proclamation to free them meant something.
>
> But, gentlemen, I ask you to consider what secession allows us to do. I envision a grand confederacy of like-minded people. Not just Southern states, but Cuba, Central America, and the West Indies.

Gage looked over at his expressionless escort. Talbot ignored him as Pierce droned on:

> To the merchants of this city, I say think of what Charleston will become: a major free port that will rival New York City.

> To the everyday man, you may not own slaves today but you will. The new confederacy will reopen the international slave trade. That will bring down the price of slaves, and soon you'll be able to buy them for thirty dollars apiece.

Then Pierce lowered his voice, but not in a way that he couldn't be heard. It brought the crowd to even greater attention—as if such was needed—signaling to them to focus on this:

> In our glorious state today, slaves outnumber white folks by more than one hundred thousand. Men, without secession, your children would become the slaves of Negroes!

The audience stood and cheered. Pierce tilted his head back slightly as if taking in a breath of sweet smelling spring air. But it wasn't air he was after. It was the adulation. That was his sustenance.

Gage again looked at Talbot who continued to display no emotion. After a couple minutes, Pierce held up his hand to stop the thunderous ovation. He then launched into an attack on a local newspaper:

> Despite the threat to our God-given way of life, there is one newspaper in this city that proposes reconciliation. It is the *Charleston Tribune*. Do you know who runs that newspaper? Heinrich Krauss. That's right, a German. And he has a Jew who writes his editorials telling us South Carolinians how we should act. Germans and Jews. Are we going to let them run our lives?

The applause was thunderous with shouts of "Hell, no!"

Pierce took his time glowing in the adoration. It didn't matter what he said. He had them and he knew it. He let loose another volley: "That newspaper doesn't belong here. Heinrich Krauss doesn't belong here. They should go north while they still can."

Again there was a huge ovation that Pierce allowed to go on as he nodded his head approvingly. Finally, he said, "Be ready, my young friends. You will be needed in this fight to preserve our way of life . . . to preserve your way of life and your children's way of life."

As they walked out of the auditorium, Gage said to Talbot: "Despite his statements, Pierce has no desire to bring back the international slave trade, does he?"

"Why do you say that?"

"It was hidden in his own numbers. Negroes already outnumber whites in South Carolina, and whites live in constant fear of an uprising. You wouldn't dare bring more Africans here."

"Then why would he propose such a thing?"

"To further rally the common man to the cause. Give them more incentive to fight to preserve the *peculiar institution*."

"Very astute, Mr. Gage."

"What he wants is Charleston as an open port, free of custom taxes."

Talbot nodded with a wry smile. "He is the largest importer in the southeast."

"And you realize he's lying about Lincoln's intentions. Lincoln has been clear that slavery will be permitted to continue just as it was under the Buchanan administration."

"I know that."

"Those young men in there don't seem to know it."

"They believe what they want to believe." Talbot hesitated, a pained look on his face. "In all candor, I fear Pierce is in the devil's employ."

"He seemed to be threatening the men at the *Tribune*."

"These days in South Carolina, one must follow or be run over. They will be run over."

"So, people like you are mere pawns, Frank."

"Perhaps we are both pawns, Mr. Gage."

"Why do you say that?"

"The people of Charleston are very earnest, and you have been invited here to be a witness to that. You are a pawn, too."

They walked back outside, past one of the mercantile stores that Talbot owned. Gage stopped and said, "I might like to go in and buy something."

"What would that be?"

"The most recent *Harpers Weekly*."

"You won't find it. No one in Charleston would dare carry it now."

"But you carry Pierce's newspaper."

"I would be a fool not to."

"For fear of retribution?"

With an anguished look, Talbot said, "Yes, criticize Pierce or cross him in any way and he will retaliate against you. For me, it would mean he would pull his newspapers and then all his followers would boycott my stores."

Gage shook his head. "So much fear. People here believe the lies of someone like Ransom Pierce, but are afraid of the truth found in a non-partisan periodical like *Harpers Weekly*."

"A friendly suggestion, Mr. Gage: you should probably keep thoughts such as those to yourself."

They began their walk back to the Station House on one of the few streets with a little fall to it. Looking down the hill, they observed a crowd gathered at a fountain. When they reached the scene, they found a woman in her thirties cavorting in the pool below the fountain. She wore a floral crown tied into the ringlets of her blonde hair. Her light sundress was soaked and clung to her shapely body.

"It's just Crazy Bette," Talbot said before remembering that meant nothing to an outsider like Gage. "Everyone calls her that. Her real name is Elizabeth Downing."

"She's putting on quite the performance."

"She's always engaging in antics like this, although this is a little extreme even for her," Talbot said, for when she swayed upward and came out of the water her nipples were clearly visible through the thin, wet dress.

Gage smiled.

"She's harmless, lives alone, but she inherited a lot of family money."

Crazy Bette raised her hands skyward. "I am Flora," she cried out in a reference to the Roman goddess of spring. "I invite you all to a festival at the Circus Maximus in celebration of the flowering of springtime."

"She's delusional—can't cause any real trouble. Spends her money helping Negro families. People ignore her misgivings because she is so crazy."

"And because she's so rich?"

"Yes, that too. She's a benefactor for many of the city's most important causes, so she and her contrarian views are tolerated. In small gatherings she can seem quite rational. What she's explained to me privately is that noise can cause her dizziness and confusion."

"Maybe she got into a crowd down here that set her off."

"Perhaps. It'll be interesting to see her demeanor at the Jockey Club Ball."

"What's that?"

"The Carolina Jockey Club holds a fancy ball each year during racing week. It's tomorrow night. It will be your first public soiree—your first chance to meet these insurrectionists, although you may not actually see many of them."

"Why would I not see them?"

"Because this year it's a masked ball."

Gage nodded, but he had only one thought at the moment: Will *she* be there?

Chapter 22

Determined to kill her dependency on laudanum, Victoria Ford followed Dr. Kessler's advice precisely. It had been a struggle, but over the last several weeks she had gradually cut back the dosage to the point that now she no longer used it at all. She did so in secret, however, for she was not yet ready to confront those who had deceived her.

Her energy had returned, and she had begun riding again. One afternoon she went out on the Tillman Trail, but a half mile out she suddenly turned her horse and headed south to the old Gage homestead. It had been months since she sat in her rocker, and she decided that's what she needed now. Just sit and contemplate.

In the past whenever she sat in her rocker, she always thought of the good times in that home. Often those peaceful memories would lull her into a brief nap. But today was different. Today she couldn't take her mind backwards. She was too angry, too unsettled.

She stayed no more than ten minutes, but in that short amount of time she became convinced of things she needed to do. She put her horse to a gallop and rode to Gage Ironworks. Upon arriving, she went to the Center Building and entered through a door to the shipping area. Nestled on sturdy, wooden supports were at least five cannon barrels.

From her right, a man called out, "Mrs. Gage, I mean Mrs. Ford, what a surprise." It was Addison Williams, a two-decade-long employee of the company. His dark beard had taken on a salt and pepper appearance since she last saw him.

"Don't be surprised, Addison. Remember, I am an owner."

"I know, it's just I don't recall seeing you here for the last couple of years."

"Relax, Addison," she said with a smile. "I won't steal anything. And you should get used to seeing me here because I intend to become more involved. But what's going on? I thought we shipped out all the cannons we made for the government contract."

"Yes, ma'am, but we have a new contract ... a very large contract."

"How large?"

"I can't say really."

"Can't say, or won't say?"

"No, I don't know how many."

"Where are the new cannons going to be shipped to?"

Addison was becoming uncomfortable. "That I wouldn't know either, ma'am."

"Come now, Addison, you're a manager. Certainly you must know."

"No, no, Mrs. Ford. The shipping is all handled by another company, so around here we don't know."

"Who knows then?"

"Probably only your husband."

An hour after Victoria left the ironworks, Jubal Ford returned to the Center Building from meetings in town. Addison Williams was quick to find him. "You should be aware, sir, that your wife was here this morning."

"My wife? Was she looking for me?"

"No, she was looking for answers. She was asking all kinds of questions."

With an unsettled look, Jubal said, "In the future, if she asks questions just tell her that she'll have to get the answers from me."

"But, sir, she reminded me that she's an owner."

"Just do as I tell you, Addison!"

***

The next morning Victoria rode in her small carriage to Doc Brown's office. When she walked in, his nurse, Mrs. Blanchard, was showing another patient to examination Room 2. Hardnosed and uncaring, Nurse Blanchard possessed no redeeming qualities for her position. She also was an imposing creature—six feet tall with broad shoulders, and she piled her hair about her head in a manner that made her appear even larger. Upon returning from Room 2, she treated Victoria in customary fashion—she ignored her.

Finally, without looking at Victoria, Nurse Blanchard said, "Doc Brown is with a patient in Room 2."

"Tell him I'll be waiting for him in Room 1," Victoria said, and before the nurse could protest she went into that room and closed the door behind her.

A few minutes later Doc Brown came in and sat down across from Victoria. He looked at her warily and said, "I sense I'm about to be accosted by another Gage family member—that will be the third such occurrence in the past few weeks."

"I'm glad you remember I am a Gage family member."

"What do you mean by that?"

"That I'm not a belonging of Jubal Ford that you can so easily discount." She looked at him earnestly and added, "Arthur, you were there when Joe died and when his father died. You delivered Ari and John, and our two grandchildren. You have treated the Gage family and me for half a century—that's four generations of the Gages. How can a little bit of money convince you to turn on us?"

He couldn't look at her. He spoke towards the floor: "The men at the ironworks died in an accident. It would have been difficult to explain how they died."

"Telling the truth is never difficult, Arthur."

Overcome with shame and tired of lying, his head dropped to his chest.

"But I suppose that's why you didn't tell me the truth about the laudanum you gave me. It would've been difficult to explain."

Victoria got up and walked out. Outside, she stood on the boardwalk trying to decide where to go next. Suddenly, there occurred a loud blast, so loud that it caused her ears to ring momentarily. She recognized it as a gunshot, but she had no idea where it came from. Then there was a scream from inside the office. The patient who had been in Room 2 raced out the front door, a horrid look on her face.

Victoria rushed back into Room 1. There was Doc Brown, seated at his chair with his head hunched over on the desk. His right hand was flat on the desk, still clutching a revolver. From the blood that had pooled on the desk, Victoria knew it was the worst she could have imagined. She screamed once, but she was so overcome she could barely breathe and she was unable to scream again. After several seconds, all she could do was sob.

Nurse Blanchard, on the other hand, hovered over the desk like she had witnessed such a scene a hundred times before. She held up a piece of paper and said, "He left a note that reads, 'I can't go on without my Emily,' but it was dated five days ago like he's been contemplating this for a while. It just took you, Mrs. Ford, to push him over the edge."

***

At dinner that evening, Victoria could not eat. She could barely control her crying. Jubal was no help, put off as he was by her interloping at the ironworks, and he had already come up with a way to handle that: "I need you to pack up some clothing, Victoria. We're going to spend time at my home in Maryland."

"Why?"

He didn't have a prepared response, for this was a decision just made, made after learning of her plans to become active at the company. He hesitated before saying, "I think you need to get away from Carthage for a while. Besides, things will be safer there."

"Safer from what?"

"Safer for the same reasons Ari moved his family away from here."

She dabbed at her handkerchief. "I hardly think you have the same concerns in that regard as Ari. For how long are we going?"

"Why do you need to know that?"

"For one thing, to know how many clothes to pack."

"Plan for a long stay."

As her crying resumed, Jubal said, "You need to take your medicine."

Change was the last thing Victoria needed at the moment. Jubal was taking her away from her grandchildren to a place she didn't know, a place she had never even visited.

The day's events had been too much for her. She stood up from the table and raced upstairs where she fell upon the bed, sobbing. She cried for ten minutes, nearly hysterical at times. Finally, she gathered herself enough to get up and walk to the closet. In there was an open box containing twenty-four bottles of laudanum.

To keep Jubal unaware that she had stopped drinking the laudanum, each day she had been pouring the prescribed amounts into a larger bottle, which she cleverly hid in the upper reaches of a cabinet behind the box of smaller bottles. Whenever Jubal was gone, she emptied that bottle in the woods behind the house.

At the moment the big bottle was half-full. She pulled it out of the cabinet. If ever there was a time she needed the laudanum, she reasoned, this was it. She opened the bottle and raised it to her lips, and drank. Then she carried the box of smaller bottles out into the bedroom to be packed for the trip to Annapolis. She assumed she would need them there.

Chapter 23

Gage wasn't sure how it happened, but it was certainly awkward. He had arrived late for the Jockey Club Ball at St. Andrew's Hall, and just inside the main entrance to the grand ballroom he began a discussion with the mayor of Charleston. Soon he realized he had inadvertently become part of the receiving line. A Northerner was welcoming people to one of the South's most prestigious social events.

Fortunately, most of the guests had already arrived, so Gage's odd situation didn't continue for long. Once the last of the arrivals made their way through the line, he was able to scan the beautiful setting. It was a huge, open room with a twelve-piece orchestra playing at the far end. But it wasn't the room he was studying. He was looking for her, wondering if she might be here, wondering if he would recognize her wearing a mask.

About three hundred people were in attendance with most still mingling, and no one had yet begun to dance. But just as Gage was about to break away to look for Frank Talbot, all conversation stopped, and people in the room seemed to freeze. They were staring at the person making an entrance. A light applause began, quickly erupting into an enormous ovation.

The recipient of that greeting was General Pierre Gustave Toutant Beauregard, recently made a brigadier general by the Confederacy and named the commander in charge of the South Carolina coastal defenses. He wore no costume, for his uniform was costume enough, and it was even more colorful than his name. It may have been standard Confederate gray, but it was adorned with his personal touch: epaulettes of gold braid and a canary yellow sash. Even the brass buttons on his uniform blouse were in segments of three rather than the conventional even spacing.

Nor did he wear a mask, which in itself seemed like his personal declaration of independence: I won't play your silly games, I'm my own man. No one objected. As one of the ladies standing behind Gage whispered, "Why hide such a beautiful face?"

She wasn't exaggerating. Although short of stature, Beauregard was a handsome man and already was the subject of talk among the women of Charleston. Everything about him was dark, the product of his French Creole ancestry. His hair and eyes were black, and he sported a black mustache and goatee. Even his skin had an olive green cast to it.

But there was more to it that had caused the people of Charleston to hold Beauregard in such high esteem. Although quiet, his exotic nature seemed to ignite a romanticism of the city's former glory. He was an outsider, and yet the Charleston elite had accepted him. No, they were in awe.

Gage wondered whether Beauregard would remember him, for they had met before but that was a long time ago. When Beauregard approached, Gage dropped his mask. A half-smile came to the general's face, an uncommon gesture for such an austere man.

"It's good to see you again, *Mister* Gage," Beauregard said, displaying little of his French accent despite not having learned English until his teens.

"And you as well, *General*."

"Our paths rarely crossed in Mexico, but I heard your name often. I still remember you from the academy, though. The youngest West Point cadet ever if I recall."

"I took some punishment from my classmates for that youth," Gage said.

"I believe you served up far more punishment than you received. Even in your first year, you were bigger than anyone at the academy."

"Although you were a couple years ahead of me, I remember you well from back then. First in your class, weren't you?"

"Only second," Beauregard said with a brilliant mix of modesty and boast.

"Your last few months have been a whirlwind."

The general nodded with a faint smile. In January, Beauregard had traveled to New York to assume the position of superintendent at West Point. That appointment was quickly withdrawn when his native Louisiana seceded, making it the sixth state to leave the Union. He immediately returned home and joined the Confederacy.

"We must find a time to talk in depth, Major."

"I look forward to it," Gage said, and the general moved on.

Gage found Frank Talbot standing by a punch bowl. "I see you met the general," Talbot remarked.

"Yes, he appears to have taken Charleston without firing a shot."

"As if he has cast a spell."

Gage didn't hear that last statement. He was busy watching a young brunette gliding across the ballroom floor like a sleek sailing ship on calm waters. Her royal blue gown was long and bell-shaped, the product of a crinoline underneath. It was narrow at the waist, and worn off the shoulders in a way that displayed her ample breasts. Her white lace half-mask hid her identity from others, but not from Gage. He recognized that carriage—it was taught at the Lightwater Institute for Ladies. And he recognized what dangled above those breasts, for attached to a gold necklace was an amber heart pendant that she had purchased from Zeke Alston five years ago.

She was headed for the punch bowl where Gage now stood, although he didn't know whether she had recognized him. Suddenly, the Gage nerves of steel were undone. He wasn't prepared to face her. Questions that had lingered in his mind for five years, he wasn't ready to ask. All he wanted now was to see her, listen to her voice, smell the light fragrance of her perfume.

But as she was nearing the table, a man joined her from the opposite direction. Perhaps a husband, Gage wondered, or a suitor? Gage didn't know what to do.

It was Talbot who interceded: "Mr. and Mrs. Edwin Walker, may I present John Gage from Washington."

Gage decided to follow Jacqueline's lead. He looked at her, she looked away. She didn't want to acknowledge knowing him.

Walker, a stout middle-aged man, shook Gage's hand and said, "My pleasure, sir." The man seemed ill at ease in the crowd. He scratched at his face, for his half-mask scraped against his dark beard.

Jacqueline said nothing, and just when Gage thought she might have to, Crazy Bette passed by the table. Her blonde hair was disheveled and she had a faraway look in her eyes. Turning to Talbot, she said in a drawn out exclamation, "Why, President Davis, if you would just free the slaves, this whole nasty business would be over."

Talbot made his escape by walking over to talk to another group nearby, and when he did so Jacqueline went with him. Crazy Bette moved on. Gage had learned nothing, not even whether Jacqueline now spoke with a Southern accent that she so expertly hid in Carthage.

This left Gage alone with Walker. But what Gage thought would be an awkward conversation was actually enjoyable, for the two men had something in common other than Jacqueline. It was horses.

"It appears I've arrived at a joyous time," Gage said.

"Yes, our annual racing week. We still enjoy the Sport of Kings."

"Is that why the walls in here are decorated with so many paintings of horses?"

"No, these are always on display. Many of them have been painted by the most prominent artist in South Carolina, Jerome Cassidy."

"I've heard the name already," Gage said as he pointed at one painting in particular. "That's a beautiful Arabian in that picture. Is that one of Cassidy's?"

"His painting and his horse."

"Surely he's not racing Arabians."

"No, they're not as fast as the thoroughbreds, but they are beautiful . . . and wonderful to have around. Did you know Arabians have one less vertebrae than other horse breeds?"

"One less rib as well if I recall correctly."

Walker was impressed. "Do you like horse racing, Mr. Gage?"

"I enjoy it thoroughly. I'm afraid, though, what horse races I've seen lately were in the West and usually came about as a result of a bet made in a tavern."

Walker chuckled. "Charleston is the pinnacle of racing in the States," he said and then stopped abruptly, remembering that South Carolina was no longer a part of the States. "Why don't you come along as my guest at the races tomorrow?"

"That would be most enjoyable."

"As a member of the Carolina Jockey Club," Walker said with great pride, although Gage didn't appreciate its significance, "I have reserved seats in a special grandstand."

A few minutes later Gage ran into Ransom Pierce in a sitting area far removed from the noise of the crowd. As Crazy Bette wandered about in the background, Pierce said, "Even with your mask, Mr. Gage, you're quite recognizable. Your height gives you away. It did so yesterday when I could see you standing along the back wall of the auditorium listening to my lecture. Was it all that you expected?"

"It was more than I expected. Tell me something: where did you come up with the notion that Vice President Hamlin is a Negro?"

Pierce smiled lightly. "His brother is named Africa."

"Several of his brothers are named after continents. One is called Asia, and yet you didn't refer to Hamlin as Chinese."

"I'm sure you and your friends at the *Tribune* will attempt to correct me. Although, it won't matter. My people will believe me."

"I'm sure they will."

"Tell me something, Mr. Gage. I've read many of your Washington articles, and yet I've never understood your view on slavery."

"I oppose slavery, sir. I simply don't believe the Union should be destroyed over it, especially if it's by means of a war."

"Ah, like Mr. Lincoln."

"An interesting analysis, given that yesterday you told your audience that Lincoln plans to abolish slavery."

Pierce took a quick bite at one of his fingernails in a way that reminded Gage of Zeke Alston's nervous habit. "So what?"

"You lied to them."

"I told them what they wanted to hear. I merely provide what they demand."

"What a tortured justification."

Behind them, Crazy Bette removed one of the horse pictures from the wall and clutched it to her chest.

Pierce shook his head at her antics, then asked, "If slavery is not to be abolished now, Gage, then what will be its outcome?"

"Like Mr. Lincoln believes, if held in place it will die a natural death in due time."

"That is a sentiment that no one in the South would agree with. All the more reason the North should let us go. It is just and legal that we do so."

Gage looked surprised. "The legality of secession has never been tested."

"What's your point?"

"Secession is either a right or it's treason. Why not ask the Supreme Court and find out? Hell, the chief justice is a Democrat who wrote the Dred Scott decision."

"At this point, Southerners wouldn't want to wait for the decision."

"I think Southerners fear the outcome."

"Southerners fear nothing, Gage," Pierce replied indignantly and he walked away.

As Gage contemplated whether he had just made an enemy out of the most dangerous man in Charleston, Crazy Bette turned to face him. He had a sense she had been eavesdropping on their conversation.

This time when she spoke to Gage, she didn't seem to be hallucinating. "Do you and the Chameleon know each other from a prior life, Mr. Gage?"

She moved on, not bothering to wait for an answer. It was just as well because Gage was somewhat taken aback. First, that she knew him by name, and second by the observation she made. Crazy people, Gage thought, are not normally so astute. And why did she refer to Jacqueline as the Chameleon?

Chapter 24

The next morning Gage rode to the Washington Race Course in Edwin Walker's best four-horse carriage. Jacqueline arrived at about the same time in a small, open carriage. She was dropped off at the rear entrance to the ladies' grandstand where she was escorted to her seat.

It was one of the few sporting activities in Charleston that women were invited to, even encouraged to attend. They were a welcome addition to the pageantry, for the ladies always wore their finest attire. Jacqueline, in a high-collared red dress, stood out from the others because she also wore a modern Tyrolean crown hat in lieu of a staid bonnet.

As their carriage approached the entrance to the members' grandstand, Gage began to understand the importance of the pageantry. People lined the thoroughfare leading to the grandstand, hoping to get a glimpse of the wealthiest patrons and their finest carriages.

But Gage soon detected a sour look on Walker's face, and he knew the reason. When their carriage passed through the throng, there was silence. The crowd ignored Walker's carriage and began scrutinizing the one that followed. The telltale signs of age showed on Walker's carriage—the wood on the maroon side panels was weathered and in need of replacement and rust was present along many of the metallic edges. Even the driver's livery was old and worn.

The Carolina Jockey Club was more than a century old, and over that time a rigid hierarchy had developed among its members. Wealth and social status mattered, but more than anything it was the race results of the members' horses. Winning could take one to the top.

One of the privileges of being at the top of that hierarchy was prime seating in the Jockey Club grandstand. When Walker and Gage arrived, they were forced to make an unpleasant crossing as they scooted by prominent members. One of the club's officers chastised Gage's host: "Arrive here early next time, Walker, so you won't be climbing over everyone."

Walker stopped briefly to speak to Governor Pickens, an awkward encounter because it was clear the governor couldn't recall Walker's name. The governor did, however, recognize John Gage.

When they reached their seats at the far north end of the grandstand, Walker was noticeably embarrassed by their location. But that location put them only twenty feet away from Jacqueline who sat at the south end of the ladies' grandstand. She saw them, and Gage tipped his hat courteously her way. Walker ignored her.

Two rows behind Jacqueline sat Crazy Bette who watched the long distance encounter with amusement.

"Fine seats," Gage said, trying to soothe Walker's ego. Yes, they were fine for viewing the races, but not for that ego. Walker had been cast aside.

Gage's next question further bruised that ego: "Edwin, do you have horses running in any of the races?"

"Not today. I have two running tomorrow."

Gage heard no excitement in that statement, as if Walker had already accepted that his horses had no chance of winning.

In his short time in Charleston, Gage had come to learn the importance of this horseracing. Walker had to suffer the humiliation of not being an integral part of the club of which he was a member. The members raced for honor and prestige. They had purchased thoroughbreds from the finest lineages, bred them carefully, and maintained them by their enslaved trainers. The winners were heroes, exalted by their peers. Prize money and winnings from wagering were secondary.

"What I need is one of the best trainers," Walker explained. "I own a two-year old that could be a champion if properly trained."

Gage nodded, unsure how to deal with Walker's despondency.

"See that tall, rather cocky-looking slave standing out on the track?" Walker said.

"The one in the white trousers, white shirt, and black waistcoat?"

"Yes, his name is Hercules."

"Seems a fitting name—he has a swagger like he owns the place."

"He practically does. He's the best horse trainer in the South, and everyone knows it. His owner is Jerome Cassidy—"

"The artist?"

"Artist, shipowner, planter. Cassidy will rent Hercules out to others to train their horses. It's real pricey, but I'm thinking of hiring him."

Gage doubted Walker could afford Hercules, but chose not to comment. Instead, he asked, "Why is that one grandstand so empty?"

"It's the Visitors' Stands, free of charge to those who visit Charleston, assuming they don't have the connections to sit in these stands."

"So the prospect of war has kept them away?"

Walker nodded. "Normally, we get horse breeders from Kentucky, Virginia, the Northeast, and even England."

Gage looked again at the grandstand to his left. Out of the corner of his eye he caught Jacqueline looking his way. During the next half hour the same thing occurred three times, and Gage wondered whether she was trying to signal him in some way. The final time he studied her closer but was unable to read anything from her gaze. He looked further up in the stands. Crazy Bette was watching, still with that mischievous grin.

When the morning races ended, Gage's host had no desire to stay and watch those in the afternoon. They exited the stands. Walker stopped briefly to talk with someone just as Crazy Bette was coming out of the ladies' stands. Jacqueline came out a few feet behind, conversing gregariously with others.

Crazy Bette came over and stood next to Gage who asked her, "Do you ever bet on these horse races?"

"I only bet on sure things, Mr. Gage."

"Such as?"

"That you and the Chameleon have a common past. I'm now certain of it. I see it in the way you steal glimpses of each other, and the way you evade each other. I saw it in her reaction at the masquerade ball when you removed your mask."

"And I'm now certain that you're not as crazy as everyone says."

"Crazy is in the eye of the beholder."

Gage looked over at Jacqueline. At the moment she was busy flattering the mayor of Charleston. "Why do you call her the Chameleon?"

"That's for you to discover," Crazy Bette said, and she began to walk away. But suddenly she turned back toward him. "I think, in time, you will."

"I sense we both have secrets that need protecting," Gage replied.

***

The following afternoon Gage met Walker at the racecourse, fully expecting to watch his new friend's horses compete. However, it was not to be.

"I pulled both horses," a downcast Walker said.

"Why?" Gage asked.

"Because they had no chance of winning."

The man didn't want to suffer the embarrassment of a poor performance. In fact, he couldn't stand to even watch the races. "My horses are in the stables on the other side of the track. Let's take them out."

"I'd like that."

When Walker pulled his two thoroughbreds out of the stables, he noted, "Both are five years olds." It was his way of admitting that they were past their prime, and he had given up on the chances of either ever winning.

As their horses galloped across an open field to the northwest, Walker looked over and gave a nod. The race was on, along a well-worn trail. The lead went back and forth over the first half mile. Knowing the terrain, Walker positioned his horse to the inside for a curve that was coming in the next section of the woods. He took a lead of five lengths as they came out of the woods and into open ground. But Gage began to close the distance, and as he looked out ahead he could see that a finish line was marked. Both men lashed at their horses, and they came across the line in a dead heat with no one there to declare a winner.

They dismounted and Walker said, "I suppose it's only fitting that North and South should finish in a tie."

"No decision in war would be a horrible proposition."

"Why is that?"

"Because it wouldn't end. The killing would just go on."

"True. That's why I don't favor secession."

Gage was shocked. "I've never gotten that impression from you."

"Don't get me wrong, Gage. Slavery needs to be protected, but your Mr. Lincoln doesn't scare me in that regard. He's said he will leave it alone where it already exists."

"If you oppose secession, then why don't you say so publicly?"

A pained look spread across Walker's face. "It would mean financial ruin for me. I would be ostracized by men of wealth."

"So, instead, you allow men like Ransom Pierce to lead?"

Walker nodded, patted his horse, and took a drink from a flask of whiskey he had pulled from his coat pocket. He held out the flask in an offering, but Gage declined, mainly in an effort to slow his host's drinking. It was clear to Gage that Walker was an ambitious man who was plagued with self-doubt. It must play hell with him internally, Gage thought. Perhaps it explains his heavy drinking.

Over the next hour, as Walker continued to drink from the flask, they discussed a variety of subjects including Walker's concerns about his marriage and his son Ned. "I'm sure you know Jacqueline is not Ned's mother."

"Of course," Gage replied. "There must be less than a ten year age difference between them."

"Yes, and an eighteen year difference between Jacqueline and me."

Gage was puzzled. Walker seemed to be hinting that the age difference was a cause of marital problems. But, instead, Walker again surprised Gage with what he said next: "When I married Jacqueline, I married low."

"What? How can you say that? Your wife is beautiful, charming."

"I mean our marriage provided me no advancement in status."

"You seem to enjoy showing her off."

Walker ducked the comment by pointing across the way at a man standing proudly by one of the stables. "Jerome Cassidy."

"Ah, the artist and businessman."

Cassidy wore the same leather breaches and boots as his jockeys, but instead of a rider's waistcoat he donned a plaid tartan jacket, crimson in color to ensure the world would notice.

Walker shouted across the way: "When might you free up Hercules for me, Mr. Cassidy?"

"When you're able to pay the price, Walker. Remember, I am an artist, and you can compensate me in that regard."

The two men walked on, Walker choosing not to enlighten Gage about Cassidy's cryptic offer. Instead, rather awkwardly, he said, "I like you, Gage.

You seem to understand me."

***

Each night a party was held after the races to celebrate. On the third night, Edwin Walker was so despondent that he and Jacqueline did not attend. But Gage did attend and he had another unusual encounter with Crazy Bette whom he came across smelling, and talking to, a bouquet of roses, her blonde hair so disheveled that when she bent down it entangled in the flowers.

As Gage tried to pass by, she stood upright and said, "I know who you are, Mr. Gage." That comment made him pause momentarily. Then she followed that by asking, "Do you know who you are?"

"Whatever does that mean?"

"That you have things to learn about yourself."

Gage didn't know how to respond. Was she some kind of mystic, a fortuneteller?

"I see you're confused," she said. "Come to my house Friday night at ten o'clock. We'll discuss it. Be discreet—come to the back door."

***

It was after two in the morning when the party ended. Needing some exercise, Gage declined a carriage ride. He decided to walk back to his hotel.

On the way there, Gage came within a block of the *Tribune* office and noticed that the gas lamps were still alight. He walked to within fifty feet of the building. It wasn't just lamps left on mistakenly. It was Heinrich Krause working feverishly, moving from one spot to another, occasionally stopping at the printing press. Gage viewed this scene for ten minutes before moving on. He shook his head in amazement, realizing that Heinrich labors like this seven days a week, barely making enough of a living to support his wife, four children, and Joseph. And he does so while walking a tightrope—struggling to put the truth out there without crossing Ransom Pierce and his followers.

Gage's respect for the man was immense.

Chapter 25

Abraham Lincoln walked briskly down the wide corridor from his second-floor bedroom in the White House to his office at the other end of the building. His long strides showed an enthusiasm not seen for some time. The inauguration the day before had gone well, as had the celebratory parties afterwards, but that's not what had him enthused. He was now the sixteenth president of the United States, a successor in time to greats like Washington and Jefferson.

As the president walked into the office he was greeted by his junior secretary, John Hay, who had come along from Illinois. Handsome but slight of build, the young man appeared even younger than his twenty-two years. Hay smiled hesitantly, a look of concern on his boyish face. He nodded toward the president's desk. One bulky envelope lay on the barren surface. "From Secretary of War Holt, sir."

"Perhaps his resignation," Lincoln joked. Lincoln's choice for secretary of war, Simon Cameron, had yet to be confirmed by the Senate. Holt agreed to stay over from the Buchanan administration until the confirmation.

Lincoln opened the envelope. As was his habit, he stood while reading. The smile left his face. "Mr. Holt says the garrison at Fort Sumter has provisions that will only last the next four weeks."

"We've not heard such a short timeframe before," Hay said.

"And Major Anderson says it would require twenty thousand well-trained soldiers, as well as Navy vessels, to subdue the Charleston island batteries and forts."

"Perhaps a slight exaggeration."

The president sat down. The full weight of his new responsibilities had quickly found him. "John, forward this report to General Scott for his opinion and send for Congressman Gage."

"Aramis Gage?"

"Yes, see if he can come here as soon as possible."

Three hours later, Hay ended prematurely one of the president's conferences with an office seeker and ushered in Aramis Gage. The congressman knew Lincoln but not well, and Lincoln did not know what the congressman knew. He decided to establish that first. "What do you make of your brother's writings about the South and Charleston?"

"I apologize, sir, for my brother's actions. Quite honestly, I don't know what's come over him."

Lincoln swatted away the apology with a wave of his arm. "It's not your brother's doing; it's mine."

"I don't understand."

"I asked your brother—others did as well—to go to Charleston with a few objectives in mind. I wanted him to learn what he could, and if possible slow things down."

"What about these articles he's written?"

"All necessary to get an invitation from Charleston and to be permitted to stay."

"That is a great relief to me, sir."

"Well, not to me. I'm afraid I've put him in danger."

"Johnny can take care of himself," the congressman said assuredly. Then, less assuredly, he said, "This is all good to know, Mr. President, but I suspect that's not why you called me here today."

Lincoln handed him Holt's letter and Anderson's report. "Do you know Anderson?" the president asked.

"No, I don't. My brother does . . . from the Mexican War."

"And I believe you both know Captain Doubleday who is second in command at Sumter."

"Yes, we know him and his wife very well."

"I'm told that Mrs. Doubleday lives here in Washington just a few blocks away."

"Yes, sir," the congressman said, confused about where this was headed.

"Major Anderson seemed very pessimistic in his report."

"Do you question his motives?"

"In times like these it's probably best to question everyone's motives. He is a Southerner—born in Kentucky." Lincoln smiled at the irony since he was as well. "Also, he's married to the daughter of a wealthy slave owner."

"How does this involve Mrs. Doubleday?"

"Perhaps the two of us could pay her a visit in order to review her husband's correspondence. The captain is supposedly an ardent Union man. I might like to see what he has to say privately about Major Anderson."

The president had two horses brought around. They rode east to a residential section of the city with only one guard riding at their side. Lincoln noticed the congressman's look of concern at the lack of security. "They've asked me not to wear my stovepipe hat," the president said in jest. "But we do need to be quick about this."

Three Union soldiers walking along the edge of the street were being ridiculed by a group of teenage boys wearing secessionist cockades. It was a reminder for Ari, and he wasn't going to waste this opportunity. "A good majority of the people of this very Southern city would prefer you dead, Mr. President."

The president chuckled. "I've been told you can be blunt... blunt but fair."

"My point, sir, is that Washington is vulnerable. There is a growing fear that if war comes the capital will be an immediate target of the Confederacy. If Virginia secedes, they could send thousands of soldiers across the Potomac. And if Maryland joins the Confederacy, the city would be surrounded."

"That's a lot of ifs," Lincoln said. He halted his horse and looked directly at Ari. "You see, Congressman, I must play the hand I've been dealt. If I were to call up troops from the Northern states at this point—before hostilities have commenced—it would most certainly cause all the non-aligned states, including Virginia and Maryland, to join the Confederacy."

Ari nodded. They rode on.

Mary Doubleday was about to start her housekeeping chores when she looked out the front window of her home. She couldn't believe her eyes. The president of the United States, only in office for one day, was walking up her sidewalk on his way to her front door.

"Yegads!" she shrieked, and she began scurrying about. She couldn't decide which appearance to try to improve—herself or her home. There wasn't time for both. "What's he doing here?" she said out loud as she began hurling newspapers under a sofa.

When she answered the door, the president smiled lightly before making his unusual request.

Brushing back a ringlet of auburn hair that had fallen across her forehead, she said, "I keep them all in one box, much better organized than my newspapers."

"It's only the letters from the last three months we would like to examine," the congressman explained.

"That should be easy, Ari," she said. "There are only five or six of those." She went to the bedroom to find the box while Ari and the president sat pensively, only now appreciating the awkwardness of their intrusion.

When Mrs. Doubleday returned, she pulled out the pertinent letters and handed them to the president.

He read each one quickly and passed it on to Ari. While reading the third letter, the president's olive-colored face suddenly took on a red hue. He was blushing at what was said in the letter. He gave a bemused look at Mrs. Doubleday and put that one back in the box without handing it to Ari.

When they finished reading the letters, the president said, "Your husband certainly thinks highly of Major Anderson. I can see that even when he disagrees with one of the major's decisions, he nevertheless believes the decision was made in good faith."

She nodded. "I trust in Major Anderson. I trust that he will keep my husband safe and our country in good shape."

***

The rest of the day, and the next, Lincoln heard the same reports about Anderson. He was a man of integrity, bound by duty. While perhaps sympathetic to the South, he would never betray his country.

This presented Lincoln with a dilemma. In his inaugural speech he had pledged to hold and maintain all United States properties. But Anderson's report, even if exaggerated, meant it was impossible to do so. Even General Scott concurred: it would require six to eight months to create such a vast armada of ships and men, he said. The fort had to be abandoned.

Thus began sleepless nights for Lincoln. By surrendering Sumter he would hurt the North's honor and violate his own pledge. But reinforcing it, perhaps just resupplying it, could start a monumental war. Seven states had already seceded and formed the Confederate States of America. The remaining slaveholding states were scrutinizing Lincoln's every move.

It didn't help matters that rumors and misinformation peppered the city like confetti. But one such report had the makings of a scandal, and when John Hay received it in written form, he immediately brought it to the president's attention.

"The *Washington Journal* plans to run this story in the next few days," Hay said. "They're asking if you would like to comment on it."

Lincoln took the page and began reading. When he sat down to study the article in depth, Hay knew the president considered it serious.

"Do you believe these allegations against the Gage brothers, sir?"

"Of course not. I have complete confidence in both Gage men."

"Democrats will probably insist on a congressional hearing."

"Political maneuvering on their part."

"But do you want to comment on the story, Mr. President?"

Lincoln winced. "No, I'm afraid the Gage brothers will have to sort through this on their own."

Chapter 26

On his fourth day in Charleston, John Gage stopped for supper with the Krause family and to deliver his next installment of the *Letters from Charleston*. Gage handed a single sheet of paper to Martin as the girls looked on. "This is just the first paragraph, Martin. Why don't you begin setting the type?"

"But, Mr. Gage, this paragraph is only one sentence long."

"No, it's three sentences," Gage said and he grabbed the paper and moved it near a candle for viewing. Then he handed it back to Martin. "See, three sentences, just as I said."

Flabbergasted, Martin stared at the paper as the twins shrieked. "Those words weren't there a minute ago. You wrote them with the candle."

Gage laughed, as did Martin's parents. "No, the words were already there," Gage explained. "It's a little magic for you called invisible ink. The heat of the candle flame made the words reappear."

He handed the ink and the rest of the letter to Martin, but Alma instead called them all to the table. "I've made your favorite soup, John," she said with a mischievous look. "It's minestrone, the kind you said your mother used to make."

After dinner Alma took the children upstairs to put them to bed. This left the three men plenty of time to engage in a political discussion that Gage had tried to avoid. But Gage quickly came to like Joseph despite the old man's crotchety attitude. Everything he said he believed, and after enough wine had been shared he spoke his feelings with a vigor that belied his age and disability.

Heinrich turned towards Gage and explained, "I oppose slavery, but I do believe the Southern states have the right to secede."

"That's not an uncommon opinion in the North."

"Yes, Heinrich, you oppose slavery, but you do not say so!" Joseph bellowed. "Nor will you allow me to say so."

"We say enough to induce the wrath of Mr. Pierce."

"That wrath is not because of what we say. It's because we're a competitor that he wants to drive out of business."

"That's my point, Joseph. It's why Pierce seizes upon any pro-Union sentiment in our paper. He's using whatever small bits he can to shut us down."

"We are enslaved. Our messages are restrained because we are afraid to speak the truth."

"What good would it do us to speak out vehemently only to lose our newspaper. We would have no outlet for any of our opinions then. We ... you would not have a job. I would be unable to support my family."

"Evil can succeed when good men do nothing," Joseph replied. Looking down at the table, he shook his head until he turned in such a fashion that he fixated on Gage. "You say nothing, Mr. Gage."

"It seems to be your discussion."

"I mean you say nothing here, and you say nothing in your *Letters from Charleston*. They are flowers ... mere flowers that you send to the North."

"Joseph, Mister Gage is our guest!"

"My apologies, sir. Perhaps I've had enough conversation, and spirits, for the night. I shall retire." He turned his wheelchair and headed to his room at the other end of the building. The door slammed shut.

"Forgive him, Mister Gage. He deserves forgiveness."

"He's very passionate about the situation in the South."

"He is passionate about anything having to do with oppression."

"Why is that?"

"He's lived a life of oppression. Have you ever heard of the Rhodes blood libel?"

"No."

"You see a crippled man, lonely and bitter. Two decades ago he stood upright with a beautiful wife."

"What happened?"

"He and his wife lived in a Jewish community in Rhodes then. A young Christian boy went missing. Jews were accused of having murdered him to use his blood in a ritual."

"Who accused them?"

"Greek Orthodox controlled Rhodes at the time, and they were supported in the allegations by European consuls. Joseph was one of several Jews tortured during interrogation. His legs were broken, but that wasn't the worst of it for him. The Jewish community was blockaded for twelve days—completely cut off. His wife, Elena, became very ill during that time and was unable to get the help she needed. She soon died."

Gage shook his head.

"It took six months before it was proven that all the charges were false," Heinrich said. "But the damage had been done."

"Am I to assume that Joseph sees similarities between Rhodes and here?"

"In some respects, yes. Certainly in the oppression of the Negroes. But he also sees it in the way that even good people can be deceived by lies, or fail to do the right thing when they recognize those lies."

"And that's why he's so vehement about Ransom Pierce?"

"Yes."

"My God, Joseph lost everything twenty years ago."

"All but one thing he cherishes: it is a portrait of his wife Elena. Every morning he opens his desk to view her. Before bedtime, he says good night to her. I've heard him speaking to her."

Gage knew Heinrich still had several hours of work to do before going to bed. Heinrich already looked tired, so he said, "I have another *Letter* to publish, but I don't want to give it to you if it means you'll have to stay up all night."

"It's all right, John. That's my lot in life now. Alma is busy taking care of the family. Martin is still too young, and he has school work. Joseph works hard, but he tires during the day."

"You work much too hard."

"I have to. Everything I own is invested in this newspaper."

"For little return it seems."

"We survive . . . barely," he said with a faint smile.

"Ransom Pierce must be a big problem for you."

"Yes, and it's more than his public threats. It's what he does in private that hurts worse. He's run off all major advertisers, and now he starting to scare off our smaller ones."

Gage winced. "Is this all worth it?"

"It is, John. For Joseph and me this is more than a way to make a living. We're trying to make a difference, trying to let people see the light of truth."

"I admire you for that," Gage said.

Heinrich took his next report, and of course it made it into in the morning's paper. It read in part:

Letters from Charleston #4

> There is an intensity of purpose here that is hard to describe. I can assure you, however, that the desire in Charleston for separation is far stronger than the desire of Bostonians for South Carolina to remain in the Union. As far as I can tell, Unionist sentiment is dead here, or at least slumbering.
>
> Despite the preparations for war, life goes on in Charleston. The event of the year, the annual horse races, goes forth at the Washington racecourse. But it is different this year. Horse breeders from elsewhere have stayed home, not wanting to risk becoming trapped in the middle of a war. Much like the Fort Sumter standoff, it is South Carolina's show.

With one exception the people of Charleston viewed that article as fair and impartial. It was Ransom Pierce, contentious as always, who accosted Gage about it when the two ran into each other near the Battery.

"What could you possibly find offensive about that article, Mr. Pierce?"

"I'm not in it."

Gage smirked. "A few days ago you threatened me about what I print about you."

"I threatened you only about things I confide to you." He hesitated, contemplating what he wanted to say. Then he put it bluntly: "Make me famous in the North, Gage."

Looking out across the Battery, Gage let him know that was unnecessary. "I think you'll become *infamous* on your own, Pierce."

Chapter 27

John Gage stood before the hotel room mirror attempting to attach his cufflinks. He was nervous; his fingers fumbled with the tiny gold trinkets. My hands never trembled in battle, he thought. That's the effect she can have on me. But today I will finally get the chance to talk to her. Today I will get an explanation of why she sent the letter, perhaps even learn why she left five years ago.

When Gage rode his horse into the stables at Edwin Walker's Montpelier Plantation for a springtime celebration, he realized he had made a wrong turn. After following the directions precisely to the plantation three miles outside of Charleston, he had turned in one lane too early. An older black man tending the horses asked Gage whether he would like a carriage ride to the main house because it was a half mile away.

"No, I might like to walk," Gage replied. That would be a better way to observe the place.

He began walking and quickly passed by a row of ten wooden cabins. They were slave quarters, but no one was around. The cabins appeared weathered, but otherwise were not in poor condition. They were small, but Gage had no idea how many people might live in each. Most had at least one glass window.

Past the cabins, he could see open fields to both his left and right. He knew Walker grew cotton and a little bit of corn, but it was planting time and there wasn't much to see as yet. He found the celebration being held just outside the main house with about one hundred people in attendance. Those slaves not serving the guests were holding their own celebration in a picnic area along a wooded stream.

As Gage walked up, Edwin and Jacqueline Walker greeted him immediately. This time there was no hesitation on her part and she said graciously, "Welcome to our home, Mr. Gage."

Still, the pretense continued.

"Thank you, ma'am," Gage replied, and he gently kissed her hand.

"Such gentlemanly manners . . . for a Yankee," Walker said.

"Quite an historic name for your plantation—Montpelier, Edwin. I'm surprised Virginians don't object."

"To the contrary, they seem honored. Even Mr. Madison's descendants have expressed that view to me."

"I wonder what the Father of the Constitution might say about your *views*."

"It is a different time and a much different setting," Walker said with a smile.

Jacqueline smiled as well, but that smile disappeared when Edwin Jr. approached. "Excuse me," she said and she walked away.

Dressed in a bright red shirt with cuffs, Edwin Jr. possessed the odor of hard liquor, and he didn't wait for an introduction. The brash twenty-two year old—the son of Edwin Walker and his deceased first wife—reached out his hand and as if to emphasize Southern strength, he grasped Gage's hand tightly to shake. He let go when Gage doubled the pressure.

"I'm Edwin Jr, but everyone calls me Ned." With unnecessary vehemence, he added, "I hope you can quickly come to understand our peculiar way of life, Mr. Gage."

"*Peculiar* is a funny word, Ned. It can have many meanings."

"You need to apply the right meaning if you're going to explain our society."

Edwin Walker intervened. "I believe what Ned means, Mr. Gage, is that you need to witness our way of life in order to report it fairly. I want you . . . I want everyone here to review our children, so you can see how well-maintained they are."

Walker signaled to an elderly house servant standing fifty feet away. "Jeremiah, bring them forward."

Immediately Jeremiah led a procession of twenty young children, ranging in ages from five to twelve, to a location where they stood in a line in front of the assembled guests. The boys all wore white cotton shirts and black trousers, and the girls wore navy blue sack dresses.

Gage knew the scene was staged for his benefit. He looked down the line of children. Their polished black shoes stood out, especially those of one seven-year-old boy whose shoes were about twice the size of his feet.

Edwin Walker spotted those shoes, too, and shouted out, "Little Georgie, whose shoes are those?"

"Mine, Master. I growin' into 'em. I growin' real fast."

Everyone laughed, and then a little white toddler broke through the line of children from behind. He bent down gingerly and tapped on the front of Little Georgie's big shoes, much to the delight of everyone.

That part was too cute, too authentic, to have been staged, Gage thought. "Who does that little fellow belong to?"

"That little guy belongs to Jacqueline and me," Walker said with a touch of pride. "His name is William, and he is almost three years old."

You should have expected this, Gage told himself. In an effort to hide his surprise, he asked, "How many of these children live on this plantation?"

"Some," Walker replied. "Most are from our three smaller estates. You're welcome to visit any of them."

"Unescorted?"

"Unescorted."

"We're not concerned about what you might find, Mr. Gage," Ned said. "We take good care of our slaves. I'm quite certain they live a much better life here than they would from where they came in Africa."

"But they're not in Africa, Ned. They're here."

"I don't understand your point."

"Here they should be entitled to freedom to live and work as they choose."

"Where in the Constitution does it guarantee that for the colored race?"

But their discussion was interrupted when six riders, dressed predominantly in black and riding black horses, approached the group of slaves who were holding their celebration near the stream.

"Patrollers . . . interrupting our celebration," Edwin said in frustration.

The patrollers were volunteers who canvassed the roadways and trails, looking for wayward slaves or those in violation of the curfew laws. Those were the purported purposes of the patrollers. But, more than anything, they were looking for plots of insurrection. For that reason, they were especially suspicious of large gatherings of slaves. They had already asked this group where they were from and when they would be leaving.

"Ned, go take care of that," Walker said to his son.

Ned hurried down to the area of the picnic tables. Gage followed. When Ned got there, he said in a demanding voice, "What are you men doing here?"

"Just doing our jobs, Ned."

"You can do your jobs elsewhere. My daddy doesn't want you here."

"We're not here to cause trouble, Ned. Just wanted to know when this meeting is going to break up and make sure they all are gonna be home by curfew."

"You worry about that off our plantation. We've let it be known that patrollers aren't allowed on this property."

The man then tipped his hat and he and the rest of the patrollers rode off.

"I didn't need your help," Ned said brusquely to Gage.

"I wasn't giving it. Just observing. Tell me, why are you so dead set that the patrollers don't come on your land?"

"About a year ago, one night after curfew, the patrollers killed one of our slaves—one of our best workers."

"That's terrible."

"It was a big financial loss for us."

And suddenly it occurred to Gage. The Walkers weren't protecting their people. They were protecting their property.

***

An hour later Gage wandered about the first floor of the plantation house, admiring all the artwork. He entered a narrow pantry where there were open wine bottles and began to pour himself a glass. Suddenly he sensed a presence to his side. No need to look up—the perfume identified her. The same perfume she wore five years ago, the same perfume on the letter he received two months ago.

"I'm sorry, I've been touring the house without an escort," Gage said.

Jacqueline passed by him, lightly touching his forearm. "It's all right,

Johnny. You've always been inquisitive. I suppose that's what has brought you south now."

He gave her a curious look. "I suppose that and . . . "

He stopped in mid-sentence, partly because he thought she would finish it and partly because of the look she was giving him. He had seen that maddening look a hundred times before.

"And what, John?"

"Your letter."

"My letter?"

"The letter you sent me two months ago."

"Johnny, I sent you no letter."

***

When Gage returned to the celebration outside, he was shocked to see another visitor from the North. Thirty feet away stood a young man of modest build wearing a three-piece suit, appearing markedly out of place on this warm spring day. When the wind blew, he used a hand to brush back his dark, wavy hair. It was Gage's stepbrother, Marcus Ford.

What ensued was an awkward encounter, for each had suspicions of the other's purpose in Charleston. They started slowly, cautiously, talking out of the sides of their mouths while both looked out at the crowd, as if pretending not to know each other even though there was no reason for that.

"Is my mother well?" Gage asked.

"Last I knew, she was. Why do you ask?"

"The last couple of times I've seen her she's seemed tired, rather listless."

"Perhaps the cold weather."

Gage laughed at the absurdity of the response, then asked, "So why does a congressman from a border state show up in Charleston at this time?"

"I'm here for negotiations."

"Negotiations of what? More cannons for the South?"

"Such paranoia, Gage. Being from a neutral state, some in Congress thought I might be a good one to talk to the leaders of this new republic."

"You expect me to believe that?"

"I don't care what you believe. Perhaps I'm here for the same reason you purport to be—finding a peaceful means for separation."

Gage smirked.

"You've argued publicly for an agreement that acknowledges South Carolina's independence, Gage. Your questioning of my motives makes me question yours. What really brought you to Charleston?"

"Perhaps just reporting on the great events of our time."

***

Just outside a temporary tent, there was another awkward encounter when Jacqueline passed by Crazy Bette staring up at the sky.

"I'm not believing your act, Bette, so save your performance for someone who does," Jacqueline said.

Unfazed, Bette replied, "We should pay a visit to Mrs. Lincoln together."

Jacqueline rolled her eyes.

Bette continued looking skyward, but then suddenly brought her eyes back down. "No one is a better actor than you, Jacqueline."

"And what is meant by that?"

"Your ability to hide your feelings for Mr. Gage. Now that's been quite the performance. And now I see you're worried about that Congressman Ford from Maryland."

***

Jacqueline had good reason to worry because it wasn't long before that congressman was able to have a private conversation with Edwin Walker.

"I'm suspicious of my stepbrother's motives in Charleston." Marcus Ford said.

Walker rejected the notion. "Gage is simply trying to prevent a war."

"He's a man of mystery—never settled down, never married," Marcus said with a careful eye on Walker. "I've always been suspicious of a man who doesn't marry."

"That means nothing."

"He was engaged once, but didn't marry the woman."

Walker shrugged. "Why are you telling me this, Ford?"

"Do you not know who that woman was?"

"No."

"Your wife."

Walker was stunned, so stunned he couldn't speak. He simply walked away.

Chapter 28

Edwin Walker was in a quandary. He didn't know what to do about John Gage, a man he liked but no longer trusted. If word leaked of Gage's prior engagement to Jacqueline, he would be the laughingstock of Charleston. And now, in Marcus Ford, there was someone in town who could attest to that relationship.

Walker decided to try to enlist on his side the strongest voice in Charleston. He went to see Ransom Pierce. When Walker sat down in Pierce's office, Pierce seemed harried, disinterested in what Walker had to say. "Who in the name of hell buys the *Charleston Tribune* newspaper?" Pierce screamed to no one in particular. "How can their circulation be so large? I don't know anyone who buys it. Do you, Walker?"

"Of course not," Walker said, uncertain whether he was answering that he didn't buy the paper himself or didn't know others who did, but either way he dared not answer in the affirmative.

Pierce returned to his grousing. Walker needed to grab his attention. He offered Pierce an attractive tease: "I've begun to have suspicions about John Gage."

Pierce looked up from the papers on his desk. "Then we have something in common. I doubt his professed support of the South. What brought you to this realization so suddenly? His opinions, or have you found him visiting places he shouldn't?"

"Oh, perhaps a combination of things."

Pierce walked around to Walker's side of the desk, a serious expression on his face. "You don't sound convincing."

"There's more to my suspicions," Walker said reluctantly.

"What, man? Tell me."

"I learned from Marcus Ford that five years ago Gage was engaged to my wife."

Pierce burst into laughter.

"There's nothing wrong with them having been engaged," Walker insisted.

"No, but why did you have to learn of it from Ford? Did either one of them tell you about that past relationship?"

"No."

"Then, you're a fool, Walker. Have you confronted them about that?"

"No."

"Then you're a coward, too. You should have had Gage horsewhipped by now for not telling you."

"I am going to confront them."

"Hold on a minute," Pierce said, rubbing his chin. "We need to learn all that Gage is about, and you now have a weapon at your disposal to do that."

At first Walker didn't comprehend. Then what Pierce was suggesting came to him. And as he thought it through, Walker realized this was his chance—his chance to enhance his reputation among the Charleston elite. All he had to do was prove Gage was up to something nefarious. Yes, this was his way to step up in society.

***

That night in the Walker mansion Jacqueline sensed something was wrong. Her husband was silent throughout dinner. His drinking—a 120 proof whiskey—had started two hours earlier than normal. When Edwin suddenly shoved his plate to the side and ordered the housemaid to take their young son to his bedroom an hour before normal, she became alarmed.

It was an ugly scene. Edwin grabbed his wife by the upper arm and dragged her into the den.

"What's wrong?" she cried out, for she had never seen her normally passive husband so agitated.

When she broke free from his grasp and asked again, "Edwin, what is it?" he responded without words, only the back of his hand to her face.

The blow knocked her to the floor where she lay with blood seeping from her mouth. She was too startled to ask questions, too afraid to stand.

"Why did you not tell me about you and John Gage?"

She remained sprawled on the floor, looking downward. Now she was silent.

"Answer me, damn you!" he demanded, and he yanked her to her feet and threw her into a chair.

"I didn't think you would understand. I thought you would be suspicious. From your reaction, I can see that I was right."

"No, it's now that I'm suspicious—of him, of the two of you."

"There is nothing between us. What is it you suspect him of?"

"I think he's a Northern spy, and you're going to help me prove it."

She wiped the blood from her mouth. "How am I to do that?" she asked.

"Do whatever is necessary to earn his trust. Find out the real reason he's in Charleston."

She meekly agreed, so afraid at the moment that she didn't bother to ask what was meant by "do whatever."

Chapter 29

The timing of Gage's arrival at the *Tribune* office early Thursday morning was fortunate. It was six o'clock, perhaps still time to get the article in the morning edition. More importantly, though, Heinrich Krause was still asleep.

"Joseph, can you place an article in the morning edition for me?" Gage asked.

"If it's short, and newsworthy. We have a significant lead article this morning: the gold that was seized by South Carolina from the United States Customs House here in Charleston has gone missing."

"That is big news, but I think you'll find this article interesting." Gage handed it over.

Joseph studied the article, then looked at Gage skeptically. "Heinrich might not allow you to publish this, Mr. Gage. Who is this Oliver Blanton?"

"He's the author of the article."

"I realize that," Joseph snapped. "It says that. But where is he from?"

"He's a correspondent with my newspaper in Washington City."

Joseph laid the article down on the desk, and removed his glasses. He looked Gage in the eyes. "Do you have some other source for a telegraph in Charleston because this *article* definitely didn't come in to us?"

"It's irrelevant how it got here. Will you post it as a reprint?"

"Why wouldn't I?" Joseph said with a grin.

"To do so may stir up the locals, especially against you."

"I'm not afraid of them. Besides, what more can they do to me?" He gestured quickly to the wheelchair. "I'll try to soften the message with our own introduction."

"A wise precaution."

Joseph leaned back in his wheelchair. "Yes, I will gladly print it because it says all the right things. But I must confess that I doubt the authenticity of the authorship."

Gage ignored his suspicion. "This is between us, Joseph. I also need you to telegraph the article to the *Washington Observer*."

Joseph tapped a pencil three times on the desk, then looked up. "I believe this confirms it, Mr. Gage."

"Confirms what?"

"You, sir, are a spy."

"Between us, Joseph."

Joseph smiled. "And now that I understand who you are, Mr. Gage, there is something you should know. I have many Union sympathizers in the city who feed me information."

"And just what interesting tidbits have your informants told you?"

"That there are Gage Ironworks cannons in Charleston that are to be parceled out."

"Any idea who is doing the parceling?"

"That they're not sure about."

Joseph's introduction of the article was brief: "As a courtesy to our readers, and endeavoring to present all viewpoints, we reprint this article by Oliver Blanton of the *Washington Observer*."

> I have been away from the newspaper for three weeks while recovering from an ailment. Being bedridden, that time allowed me to catch up on correspondence from friends in South Carolina. There seems to be a common theme: That the madness sweeps through Charleston like the plague. It plays well with the young, the undereducated, and the unprincipled. Too many of those in positions of power are too weak to stop it. It is carrying this society to what will be its certain doom.
>
> This is deception of the worst kind. There are men

here tricking young boys into the savagery of war. Who does such a thing? Old men like Ransom Pierce who stand to profit from an independent South Carolina. He tells the boys lies—lies about Lincoln, lies about Northern invasion plans, lies about the colored race. He will say anything to serve his own purposes.

***

On the night following the *Tribune's* reprint of the Oliver Blanton article, Sam Milton, the *Tribune's* part-time employee, stood on the sidewalk catty-corner to the *Tribune* office. He had just closed up that office and was soon joined by his friend Terrence Woods. Because it was near the curfew hour for black residents of Charleston they were in a hurry to return to their apartment. They dared not run. That could call attention to themselves and the Home Guard patrollers might stop them and accuse them of some crime. They began walking.

But when they were directly across from the *Tribune* office, they stopped and watched three men walking along the boardwalk in front of the building. Suddenly one man threw a brick through the large glass window. The other two men followed closely behind and threw buckets of paint at the printing press that was sitting just inside. The three men stepped off the boardwalk and walked in the direction of Sam and Terrence.

"You better hold your tongues," the brick thrower said to them, and then they were gone.

"I know that man," Sam said. "I seen him befo'."

"Better do as he say," Terrence replied.

"That man works for Ransom Pierce."

"We gotta leave here," Terrence urged.

Sam was torn. He couldn't risk breaking curfew, but Heinrich wasn't downstairs at the moment. This was unusual because he knew Heinrich worked most of the night. At last, however, when Sam saw two gas lamps come on in the Tribune office, he knew he could wait until morning to tell Heinrich who did it. He and Terrence departed.

***

The next morning when Gage arrived at the *Tribune,* he found the Krause family finishing the cleanup.

"It was fortunate we live upstairs," Heinrich explained, "because we heard the glass break. We were able to clean up the paint before it dried. No permanent damage was done to the printing press."

"Any idea who did this?" Gage asked.

"There are witnesses who can identify the men who did this," Joseph said.

Heinrich put aside his broom. "Witnesses who can't testify."

"I don't understand," Gage said.

"It's Sam and a friend of his," Heinrich explained. "Free or not, a Negro can't testify against a white man. It's the law, so there's no sense going to the police."

Joseph was adamant. "Heinrich, something has to be done. These were Ransom Pierce's men."

"You're right, Joseph," Heinrich said, for this time he was incensed. "He attacked us ... tried to put us out of business. We need to respond in the only way we can—by naming the wrongdoers in the paper."

Gage was concerned. "Gentlemen, with so little damage, are you sure you want to do this?"

"This is different, John. We must put the truth out there about what he tried to do."

"I suggest you put the article in my name," Gage volunteered. "That might make it less controversial for the *Tribune*. You just publish it."

And so it was decided to identify Bobby Smith, an employee of Ransom Pierce, as the main culprit.

***

For the most part, the article generated little interest. After all, people said, it was just one window and the printing press must not have been damaged because the *Tribune* was still putting out a newspaper.

Ransom Pierce, however, had a different reaction. He found John Gage the next day at the Coastal Tavern and interrupted his lunch. Pierce demanded to talk with him about the *attack*.

"You mean the attack on the *Tribune*?" Gage asked.

"No, the attack on me."

"What attack on you?"

"The attack on me in the *Tribune,* penned under your name."

"How did the *Tribune* attack you?"

"By reporting that I was behind that foolish prank."

"Hardly a prank."

"Oh, three of my men happened to be passing by the *Tribune* and decided to smash a window."

"And just happened to be carrying full buckets of paint. Come now, Pierce, that was a planned attack to shut down the *Tribune* by destroying the printing press."

"Again, Gage, you're talking about the wrong attack. I won't forget the attack on me." Then, with a look of madness on his face, Pierce said, "The *Tribune* has got to go!"

Chapter 30

The *Tribune*'s accusation created no problems for Ransom Pierce. In fact it provided more opportunity. The day after the story appeared, Pierce was giving another public lecture at Institute Hall. He stood at the podium, holding that morning's *Tribune* in his right hand, while he railed against the newspaper:

> Once again, the Germans and Jews at the *Tribune* have attacked me with their lies. Lies . . . that's all they're good at. They had the nerve to name one of my associates as the perpetrator of a small crime. They claim to have two witnesses—slaves. But do they name their witnesses? No, they only name the alleged perpetrator. It's lies. So here's what really happened: those two Negroes were the ones who threw the brick through the window. They were trying to steal a nice lamp that was just inside, and my men tried to stop them. In fact, one of my men got drenched with a bucket of paint. If that paint had been thrown at the printing press it probably would've destroyed it. So the bigger question is why does the *Tribune* continue to tell lies? Especially over such a trivial matter. They have a broken window, and they want to blame me for it. Why would they bother with such a thing?
>
> The only reason I can think of is that they have some notion that I'm not strong enough to defend myself against such an attack, or that they somehow believe no one stands behind me.
>
> Do you stand behind me?

The crowd roared in support.

"Are you with me?" Pierce shouted again, and this time the ovation was deafening. "Then march down to the *Tribune* office and let them know who stands with me."

Gage had never seen anything like it. Sure, in wartime, he had heard officers give some fiery rallying speeches to their men—he had given several—but this was different. Pierce had these young men whipped into such a frenzy that they might do things they wouldn't have imagined doing just an hour earlier.

Standing at the back of the auditorium, Gage was the first to exit. His horse was tethered out by the street, and he estimated that by riding he could make it to the *Tribune* office ten minutes before Pierce's mob. He put his horse to a dangerous sprint through busy streets. Three blocks along, he barely avoided a collision with a carriage. At the next intersection he circumvented a stopped wagon, narrowly missing a horse on the other side.

Two blocks from the *Tribune*, Gage tied his horse to a post. He ran from there, and when he entered the building he found Heinrich, Alma, Joseph, and Martin all working. "Where are the girls?" Gage shouted.

"Upstairs, taking their naps," Alma said. "Why?"

"Go get them, now!" Gage ordered. "You all need to leave immediately."

"What's happened?" Heinrich asked.

Gage calmed. He placed his right hand on Heinrich's shoulder and said gently, "I'm sorry, Heinrich, but Pierce has unleashed a mob, and they are headed this way."

The full weight of Gage's declaration hit Heinrich so hard that he stumbled backwards slightly. But then, just as quickly, instinct took hold. "Get the girls!" he yelled at Alma. "Martin, pull the wagon around back."

And thus began a burst of effort to collect their most valuable items.

Soon the shouting of the mob could be heard from down the street. They had started a chant: "Close it down! Close it down!"

"Should we barricade the doors?" Heinrich asked.

"Heinrich, no amount of barricades will stop them," Gage said. "There may be five hundred men coming this way."

By the time Alma brought the girls downstairs, the mob had begun to gather outside the building. Their voices, now belting out the chant "Close it down," sounded like they were already on the inside. They began throwing rocks, and the window that had just been repaired was the first victim as it shattered, sending shards of glass across the office.

The family went out the back door to the wagon behind the building, but Joseph was not with them. Gage called out, "Joseph, Joseph," but there was no answer.

The mob was now at the front door, although there was no need to break it down because the front window was gone. Rioters surged through the opening just as Gage found Joseph in the back room of the building. "What are you doing?" Gage asked. "We need to leave."

"Just gathering a few things." The last thing he grabbed was a wooden plaque that read *Tell them the Truth.*

Gage didn't wait for Joseph to wheel himself out. He began pushing the wheelchair. As they came out of the back room they were confronted by four young men. The biggest one seemed intent on justifying his swaggering manner.

"Who are you?" Gage asked, for the reporter in him wanted to learn as much as possible about the rioters.

"They call us the Titans, the Titans of the Winston County militia."

"Playing war, are you?"

"Who the hell are you, and where are you going?"

"Out of our way, Sonny, or you'll get hurt," Gage warned.

"My name ain't Sonny; I'm Captain Stovall of the Titans," he said proudly, and he positioned himself directly in Gage's path.

With one hand Gage pushed him to the side. Stovall looked at his friends. He had something to prove. He charged at Gage. Gage hit him once across the forehead, knocking him backward. Staggered, but only for a moment, Stovall charged again. This time Gage hit him with a solid shot to the gut that caused the young man to double over. Gage then let loose a vicious uppercut to the jaw that seemed to lift Stovall in the air. He crashed to the floor with a jarring thud.

It was all so sudden and so frightening that the other three men backed away as if Gage had just pointed a gun in their direction.

"Some titan," Gage said, and he wheeled Joseph out to the wagon where he and Heinrich hoisted him up into the bed.

Gage turned to Heinrich and apologized. "I'm sorry, Heinrich, if I've had a part in bringing this on you."

"John, it was going to happen eventually anyway."

Suddenly a painful wail of such intensity came from the bed of the wagon that Gage and Heinrich feared someone had been hurt. It was Joseph, and his head was buried in his hands.

"Joseph, what is it?" Heinrich shouted.

"The portrait... the portrait, I left the portrait of Elana behind." His head fell back into his hands.

"In his drawer?" Gage asked Heinrich.

"Yes, but, John, you can't go back."

But Heinrich's pleas were too late. Gage had already jumped down and was headed back into the building. The Titans were gone, having removed their injured friend. In their place were twenty or so men who had come through the front window. They were milling about, uncertain what to do. Some turned over desks and scattered papers. They pounded at the printing press with hammers, but Gage knew where all this was headed. Eventually, they'll remember that their goal is to destroy the newspaper office, and fire is the simplest way to do it.

Gage wasted no time. He ducked into the back room without being seen and grabbed the portrait from the drawer. He was so quick getting back to the wagon that Joseph's head was still buried in his hands.

Gage handed him the portrait. Joseph, with tears in his eyes, said, "God bless you, John Gage."

Chapter 31

Gage didn't go with Joseph and the Krause family. He wasn't even sure where they were going, although he knew they had good friends in a nearby town. Instead, he stayed to observe the mayhem. Once again he was a journalist.

Not wanting to be seen near the building, he walked one block south on the street behind the *Tribune* office. He then came back out on Walton Street at the rear of the horde of men that now numbered more than those in attendance at Pierce's speech. Young men were stepping away from their militia training, joining the mob from the side streets.

As Gage inched closer, he could see that a fire had been started at the *Tribune*. Anything viewed as potentially valuable had been thrown out of the building and lay strewn in the street. Scavengers were sorting through it.

Now the chant had changed, and the entire mob had picked up on it: "Go back to Germany . . . Go back to Germany." It was deafening. As Gage weaved his way through the crowd, he wondered whether he should be shouting that chant so he didn't seem suspicious. But he couldn't bring himself to do so. That would dishonor his friends.

When he was one building away from the *Tribune* office, he began to feel the heat from the fire on his forehead as red sparks flickered above. The police and firemen stood by doing nothing.

Part of the crowd had turned its attention to the mercantile store across the street from the *Tribune*. It was the only store in the city where Gage had found *Harper's Weekly*, and the owners were good friends of the Krause family. Rioters began hurling rocks at the store.

Gage noticed a parked carriage on a side street to that building. He had seen that carriage before, but he couldn't remember where. Then it struck him: it was at the race course when the ladies were leaving. The carriage was Jacqueline's.

Gage began shoving people out of the way, trying to get through the crowd. Suddenly Jacqueline ran out of the front door of the store. Gage was still a good seventy feet away from her, hemmed in by men on all sides. She was pushed, jostled, and fondled as she fought to get through the rioters to her carriage. Gage managed to find a seam in the mob and met her on the boardwalk.

"Oh, Johnny, it's madness!" she cried out, and she grabbed hold of his arm.

He tried to escort her to her carriage, but it was slow going. The crowd's chant of "Go back to Germany" had intensified.

"They're all crazy," she yelled.

"Ransom Pierce has them lit up. They're capable of just about anything right now."

It took nearly five minutes for them to push their way forty feet closer to the carriage. But just as the crowd had thinned at that point, one of the three remaining Titans saw Gage standing out above the rioters. The man yelled to his friends, "Get him."

Gage heard that directive over the din, and with one huge effort he pushed through the perimeter of the mob and out onto the side street. Jacqueline bolted toward her carriage, but Gage yelled at her, "There's no time for that!" He lifted her over his head and dropped her behind a four-foot-tall picket fence. He then pulled himself up and over, and the two of them crouched down behind it.

Minutes later the three men came down the side street. Perplexed, one of them said, "Where did they go?"

"Maybe into that next store," and the three of them went into the building to make a search.

On the other side of the fence, Jacqueline clung to Gage. Flames from the *Tribune* were now shooting sixty feet in the air, and ash was beginning to rain down over the area. Jacqueline put her hand on John's face and said, "Johnny, you shouldn't be here. Why did you come?"

He answered only with a kiss to her forehead. She pulled back and looked him in the eyes for a moment. Then she pressed her lips on his, passionately and forcefully.

Soon they could hear the commands of police and firemen telling the crowd to leave. The desired damage was done. One fireman shouted, "We don't want any worthwhile businesses destroyed."

The crowd was dispersing. Gage and Jacqueline walked out through a back gate of the fence, and he escorted her to her carriage. "Come with me," she said. "You're not safe here."

"I've got my horse a couple blocks away," he said. "I'll be fine," and again he kissed her forehead.

He began walking back up Walton Street.

***

Five hours later, Gage was awakened by a noise at his hotel door. The door handle rattled. Someone had inserted a key in the lock, but was fumbling about trying to open the door.

Gage grabbed his revolver from the nightstand. The door flew open. The silhouette of a person backlit disappeared as the door closed. He lit the small gas lamp beside him, and now the person standing before him came into view. It was Jacqueline.

Gage said nothing.

Surprised by his silence, she said, "Am I in the wrong room?"

"That's for you to decide."

She took a step closer. "It won't take that gun to get me out of these clothes, Johnny."

Jacqueline dropped her coat on the floor. Then clothes fell off her like a waterfall—dress, chemise, petticoats, and corset—until she stood before him naked.

He could tell she was in one of her playful moods. She jumped up on the bed and pulled the covers down. He could smell her perfume now, the same perfume that was on the letter that she didn't send. She straddled him, seizing control for the moment. Then he wrapped one arm around her lower back and turned her half-circle so he was on top.

Their lovemaking went on for an hour after which they fell asleep briefly. When Gage awoke, he wondered if he had been dreaming. But he looked over and saw that beautiful face. *Now I can finish the portrait*, he thought.

But that was the last thought Gage had before the events of the day came back to haunt him. And with it came an anger that was difficult to suppress. He wasn't angry at the Titans or the hundreds of others who engaged in the mayhem. It was Ransom Pierce who did this. He was the one who made the *Tribune* a target, and he was the one who unleashed the mob. Somehow, Gage vowed, I will find a way to make him pay for what he did to Heinrich and his family.

When Jacqueline's eyes opened, it brought Gage back to the moment. She reached out her hand and touched his face, then said, "Why are you really here, John?"

It was such an odd question that Gage recoiled as he tried to decipher it. Was she asking because she wanted to hear him say it was the letter? Or, was she searching for a hidden agenda on his part?

He sidestepped the question by saying, "I suppose in time I'll figure that out."

She rolled over and faced him. Her faint smile faded, though, when he said, "You have a family now. I like Edwin; he seems a decent sort."

"He's a ne'er-do-well, easily influenced by others."

"He does seem troubled."

"He has plenty of ambition, but no will to achieve it. He tries to use others to get what he wants."

"His son, Ned, seems to have ambition."

Immediately tears came to her eyes, but she said nothing.

"From what I've seen, it appears you don't like Ned."

She turned her head the other direction. Tears now flowed, pooling on her chest. She could barely speak, only enough to say, "I detest him."

He grabbed her right shoulder, bringing her back to his direction. "What's wrong?"

Still she hesitated until Gage sat upright, and she realized he wasn't going to let it go. "About three and a half years ago, while Edwin was away, Ned trapped me in the cellar." More tears fell. "He forced himself on me, John. Please tell no one. Ned is a dangerous person."

She had been precise in her timeline for a reason, Gage surmised. He did the quick calculation. Jacqueline's son, William, was nearly three years old. "You . . . ." He didn't have the words.

"I don't know whose son he is, Johnny. I don't know what to do."

"He's your son. Raise him the best you can."

Gage reached to his left and turned out the gas lamp.

Standing on the boardwalk across the street, a man watched that light go out. For the past two hours, he had been watching the shadowy forms through the thin curtains of the room. The spectator was Ned Walker.

Chapter 32

The first letter Gage received from the North was from his brother, and it was full of surprises. Ari started with the tragic death of Doc Brown and details of the elaborate funeral that the town held. "His death was reported as from natural causes," Ari said. "Only a few of us know it was suicide. I suppose it's only fitting given his history of misrepresenting causes of death."

He next reported on an unusual visit from Jubal Ford. "He was in Washington and came to see me," Ari wrote. "He said he and Mother had moved to his home in Annapolis. I pressed him for more, but all he would say is he thought it would be safer there."

Safer? Gage thought, dismissive of the whole idea. There is little abolitionist sentiment in Carthage; it's barely a Union town. Instead, he takes her to Maryland where there is talk of rebellion and violence. It makes no sense.

But Ari wasn't finished with his surprises. He alerted John to a *Washington Journal* article recently published. "The reporter at the Journal confronted me with this allegation a few weeks back," Ari wrote. "The fact that it was published just two days ago convinces me that someone outside the paper has been controlling its publication. Here is the substance of the Journal article:"

> We have it on good authority that the fifty cannons that were said to have been destroyed in a December explosion at the Gage Ironworks factory were not, in fact, destroyed. Instead, at the direction of the brothers Aramis and John Gage those cannons were delivered into the hands of Southerners. With

one of those brothers a known Southern sympathizer and the other a purported Northern abolitionist, this result might seem incongruous. But the shipment of these cannons was not about politics. It was all about money for the Gage brothers, and the cannons went to the highest bidder.

"The innuendo is out there," wrote Ari. "I will try to weather it, but I'm sure some Democrats—perhaps even some Republicans—may seek a congressional investigation. I now have some sense of how you felt in being unjustly accused. I'm hoping, though, that this allegation may help you with your endeavors in Charleston."

Gage found that last notion almost as foolish as Jubal's justification for moving his mother to Annapolis. While Gage was pleased to learn that Ari was now aware of his true mission in Charleston, he knew this article would do him more harm than good. It was obviously planted by someone with a purpose. And if Joseph Greene was correct that the cannons were in Charleston, whoever brought them here knew Gage didn't do it. They may see this as part of some campaign of misinformation intended to confirm my status as a Southern sympathizer, Gage thought. People are going to be watching me closer than ever.

***

That night Ari's letter festered in Gage's mind, but it wasn't because of the allegations regarding the cannons. What had him concerned was his mother's situation. For the past two years, rightly or wrongly, she had depended on Doc Brown and Jubal for guidance and reassurance. Now Doc Brown was gone, and she must be thinking that Jubal has turned against her. He had taken her away from her grandchildren and the town she had lived in her entire life. She knew he had deceived her about the explosion, and perhaps, Gage thought, she has learned about his frequenting of Lady B's.

I need to find a way to give her some comfort, Gage thought, some way to let her know that I'm still with her. That evening he took a casual walk down to the Battery, and along the way he stopped in at one of Frank Talbot's stores. He began browsing and happened to pass by a small room with the door open and saw Frank sitting there.

"Good," Gage said, "this will save me a trip to your office tomorrow."

"What's on your mind, John?"

"The *Charleston Tribune*."

"Yes, tragic."

"Tragic is a word best used for accidents, Frank. This was preventable."

Talbot got up and closed the door. "I'm sorry, I know you and Heinrich Krause became friends."

"Friend or not, that kind of thing shouldn't happen, and there should be consequences for the perpetrators."

"When you say perpetrators, are you talking about the ones who did the damage or someone else?"

"For there to be justice the one who sent them there needs to be held to account, and that's Ransom Pierce."

Talbot ignored that last comment. "I thought you might come see me. You need another newspaper outlet for your *Letters from Charleston*, don't you?"

Gage nodded.

"I can put you in touch with the *Carolina Gazette*, another independent. It's smaller than the *Tribune* and its editor is not as open-minded as Heinrich Krause. But, at least, you'll be able to get your stories out and telegraph them to the North."

"What do you mean he's not open-minded?"

"He's not going to allow you to say anything against Ransom Pierce."

"So Pierce is to come out of this without a scratch, with no one even saying a word against him."

"No one would dare try to call him to account."

"You're wrong there, Frank. Someday, I'll find a way to pay the bastard back for what he did."

As Gage walked down an aisle on his way out, he noticed a small blue plaque for sale. On it was the quote from Mary, Queen of Scots, that hung on the wall of the old Gage house:

> To be kind to all, to like many and love a few, to be needed and wanted by those we love, is certainly the nearest we can come to happiness.

Gage didn't believe in such things, but he had to admit this was like a sign.

His mother needed this now, and she needed to receive it from him. But how would that be possible from Charleston, especially since he didn't even know where in Annapolis she was living? There was only one person living in Maryland that he knew and trusted enough to try to get this done. He drafted a note to Kate Warren to go along with the plaque:

> Kate, I don't know if you ever get to Annapolis, but if you do could you please see that this plaque gets to my mother. Its message is quite meaningful to her, and I believe she could use the solace it will provide. She's living at the Jubal Ford house, and all I know is that it's just outside Annapolis.

He mailed it to a private residence in Chicago, which was the location used to forward confidential material to the Pinkerton office. From there it would be sent to Kate in Baltimore. It was a circuitous route and a lot of things could go wrong in trying to get it through, but he had to try.

Chapter 33

Late Friday night Gage rode to Crazy Bette's not knowing what to expect. As instructed, he went to the back door. A striking blonde-haired woman he didn't recognize answered the door. Her hands were on her hips with elbows extended in an aggressive posture. Her language was just as combative: "State your purpose before I call a constable. Arriving at a lady's house at this hour, why it's shameful."

Gage froze, uncertain how to respond. He studied the woman. Unlike Bette's blonde hair that was long and scattered, this woman's blonde hair wrapped tightly around her head and bunched in the back in a complex pattern of plaits and rolls, terminating in a red bow. That bow matched the woman's sleek red house dress that, in turn, complemented the rouge on her cheeks.

"Speak up, man," she said.

Not wanting to face arrest, Gage chose his words carefully. But as he began to speak, the woman began laughing hysterically. It was Crazy Bette playing a joke on him. She showed him to a front parlor where they sat across from each other.

A middle-aged black servant entered the room with a decanter of wine. As the man left, Gage smiled and said, "And here I thought you were an abolitionist."

"I very much am. Albert is a free man. I pay him good wages. He is free to leave whenever he desires. He chooses to stay."

"Very commendable."

"I've always hoped it would be an example to others around here. I was wrong."

"Perhaps they don't believe they should follow the actions of a crazy woman, although I'm now certain you're not so crazy. I realized that the other night when I saw you eavesdropping on my conversation with Pierce."

She smiled. "No, people around here would prefer to follow someone crazier than me, someone like Ransom Pierce. Newspaper journalists like yourself only aid his kind."

"And just how is it we aid Ransom Pierce?"

"You fail to write the truth. For example, you've been writing articles about slavery, Mr. Gage, and yet you know nothing about it."

"You forget, I've been to a plantation. You were there, too."

She laughed mockingly. "Yes, at the Chameleon's place. There you saw what they wanted you to see, and you reported just as they wanted. Do you ever investigate beyond what you see?"

"I always investigate."

"You didn't even investigate the Chameleon's background before you asked her to marry you."

"Why would I need to do such a thing?"

"Did she not portray herself as being from an elite Charleston family?"

"I suppose she did."

"Perhaps her grandfather was of that kind, but it ended there. Her mother died years before you met her—"

"I knew that."

"Did you know that her father was a drunken derelict who squandered what little was left of the family fortune? There were even rumors he murdered his wife."

"I find little value in rumors. You still haven't told me why you call her the Chameleon."

"Because she is so readily able to change to fit any circumstances."

"And how would you know that?"

"I've watched her maneuver."

"From afar?"

"From close up." She waited for Gage's stunned reaction, before saying, "You see, Mr. Gage, I sponsored her—paid her way—for the Lightwater Institute for Ladies in Carthage."

"If so, why did I not hear of you back then."

"Probably because she didn't want you to know she was poor."

"You two certainly don't seem very friendly now."

"We had a falling out."

"Over?"

"Primarily her marriage to Edwin Walker. I didn't pay to educate her just so she could marry a slave-owning slouch."

"And you grew apart over that?"

"And because I no longer suit her purposes. She's moved on. She is the Chameleon."

"I'm curious. Did you pay for her trip to Europe five years ago?"

"Europe? No, I'm not aware she ever went to Europe."

Gage nodded, momentarily lost in memories before returning. "So you called me here for a reason. What is it you want me to do?"

"You need to dig deeper."

Gage looked down, contemplating an appropriate response. When he looked back up, he said, "You don't seem to think much of me, Miss Downing, and yet you've entrusted me with one of your most important secrets—that you're not crazy. Why?"

"Because from what I've learned about you, Mr. Gage, I think you have potential... potential to do better. Yes, I was listening to what you said to Pierce. You called him out about the truth. Few people are willing to do that."

"Your point?"

"You didn't tell the truth about slavery, nor about your true feelings. When you reported about Montpelier, you were describing a fantasy world, much of it created just for you. Many of the children you saw don't even live on that plantation."

"Nevertheless, Walker seems to care for those children. He protects all his slaves from the patrollers."

"Does he do that for their good or his own?"

Gage hesitated, then acknowledged, "I don't know. Does Walker allow patrollers on his other plantations?"

"Yes, the further inland the plantation the rougher things become. More potential for escapes. The overseers are meaner—more chances for trouble. You should visit a real plantation, spend some time there."

Gage chuckled. "And how would I go about that?"

"I'll take you to what you need to see, if you're brave enough."

"And where might that be?"

"One of Walker's inland plantations. There are many plantations far worse than his, but this should give you some idea."

"I can't be gone too long from Charleston, or others might become suspicious."

"We'll go Sunday."

"All right, but how do you know about this place?"

She smiled. "I've been there many times because I met one of the slaves who lives there. He's a young man sold out of Maryland. He's very talented, and Walker moves him around to wherever he's needed. I met him when he was working on the wharf at Charleston. His name is Gus and I want you to hear his remarkable life story."

"Sounds intriguing."

They talked for an hour. As Gage was leaving, Crazy Bette said to him, "Why in the hell did you come to Charleston to try to save the Union?"

Gage shrugged. "Just seemed like a good place to start."

"You're crazier than me."

Chapter 34

Two days after their late-night meeting, Crazy Bette drove Gage in a buckboard wagon to Edwin Walker's Ashland plantation, twelve miles outside of Charleston. "Ashland is probably not profitable," Crazy Bette explained along the way, "because it's in an area too wet for cotton and too dry for rice farming. They try to grow cotton and corn."

"It's the second Walker plantation I will have visited, and both seem to be marginal."

"They are. A few years ago Walker barely avoided bankruptcy. He tried rice farming in the low country. Rice farming is very specialized. It's gold for those who know what they're doing."

"And Walker didn't know?"

"That's right."

"Why do you want to visit on a Sunday?" Gage asked. "I won't see anything meaningful. They won't be working."

"Because the overseer won't be there. We just need to look out for Ned Walker."

"Why? His father said I could visit any of his plantations unescorted."

"Yes, but he sent Ned here to run things. He's mean, impetuous, and usually drunk. I think Walker really sent Ned here to get him out of the main house because the Chameleon hates him . . . for reasons unknown."

Gage didn't volunteer the reasons. Instead, he said, "You're quite the observer of people, aren't you?"

"I do tend to analyze people."

Gage looked in the bed of the wagon. There was nothing there but a couple of blankets. "I'm surprised," he said, "I thought we might be taking food and supplies to the camp."

She shook her head. "It's too dangerous in daylight. Even at nighttime, I only take things I can justify having in my wagon."

"Why?"

"Too many patrols."

"I thought they would only stop coloreds."

"After the John Brown fiasco, they'll stop anybody who looks to be carrying things they shouldn't. Northerners considered Brown a lunatic, but Southerners fear there are thousands more like him."

"What is it they fear of those thousands?"

"Everything from them aiding escapes to starting uprisings by providing weapons."

"You wouldn't be one of those aiding the escapes, would you?"

She looked at him with a wry smile but said nothing.

They came into the plantation from the north and stopped outside one of the slave cabins. Three brothers, ranging in ages from seven to fifteen, ran to greet them. They were all thin, naturally so, but also the product of a poor diet.

"These are the Norton brothers—Isaac, Henry, and Georgie," Crazy Bette said.

Gage recognized the youngest—it was Little Georgie with the big shoes whom he had seen at Montpelier. But now Georgie was barefoot. When he reached Bette, Georgie flashed a huge smile with bright white teeth perfectly aligned.

Bette reached into her handbag and pulled out several sticks of licorice that she handed to the boys. They were delighted by such a small gift. Other children soon joined them but not because of the candy, but because of Crazy Bette. They adored her. Gage watched with fascination as this childless woman from a society so far removed from theirs bonded effortlessly with each child who approached her.

Gage was astounded by the difference in clothing worn by the children here from what he had witnessed at Montpelier. None seemed to have clothing that fit. Shirts either drooped, or were open because they were too snug to button. Pants were full of patches. Everything was a hand-me-down, perhaps three times over.

Just outside the door to the cabin stood two large bearded slaves, their arms crossed and appearing displeased by the visitors' arrival. The two men resembled each other, but one of them—the one called Buford—was bigger than the other.

"They look angry," Gage whispered to Bette.

"They always look that way," Bette said. "They're cousins, and they're troublemakers for everyone. Always conniving, trying to get Gus into trouble."

Suddenly appearing at the door was Gus, a strapping dark-skinned man in his early thirties. He was nearly six feet tall and muscular, but he looked puny compared to the cousins. He stepped around them because they wouldn't move. Gus bounded toward the others, a broad smile on his face as he looked at Bette.

"Gus, this is the man I wanted you to meet: Mr. John Gage."

"Welcome, sir," Gus said pleasantly. It was clear that Gus had spent much of his life in a more refined environment than this. His diction was good, and Gage surmised he could read and write.

"Thank you, Gus," Gage replied, and he stepped down from the wagon.

Gage looked all about. The cousins looked at him with disdain, but he figured they looked at everyone that way so he ignored them. He turned to the youngest of the three Norton brothers: "Your name is Georgie, isn't it?"

Georgie gave a quick nod.

"You wore big shoes when I saw you at Montpelier."

"Them belong to my brother."

"What happened to *your* shoes, Georgie?"

His head dropped. "Lost 'em in the river." Like many plantations, each slave was given shoes every two years, and the old ones were taken back. There were no replacements.

"What's that around your neck?"

Georgie smiled proudly and held up a large copper two-cent piece with a hole in the middle. A thick string through the hole served as a necklace.

"My, that is something, Georgie."

Buford made a loud snort, and the two cousins wandered off.

"You want to see where I live?" Little Georgie asked.

"Sure," Gage said, and along with Gus and Georgie's brothers, he followed the young boy toward the cabin.

But it took only a few steps in that direction for Gage to realize how poorly constructed this log cabin was compared to those at Montpelier. The logs were old and rotting in places. A soft mud had been used to chink the gaps. Two small openings serving as windows had makeshift wooden shutters rather than glass.

When Gage stepped into the cabin, he found a floor made of dirt. The only piece of furniture was a three-foot-wide table. A poorly constructed fireplace separated two small sleeping areas.

"Me and my brothers sleep here," Georgie said. He stretched his arms out wide, proud to claim a shared domain that was no larger than eight feet by six feet. In that space were the beds of the three boys, each a wooden frame containing straw, rags, and whatever other materials could be found to be used as bedding. Each bed had a single blanket.

"Where are your parents, boys?" Gage asked.

"Mamma live in a cabin across the way," Isaac, the oldest brother, said.

"With your father?"

They seemed surprised by the question. "No, he live on a plantation owned by Master Johnson a ways from here."

"Do you have sisters that live with your mother?"

This time the response was painful. "They sold away a few years back," Isaac said. "Someplace called Alabam'."

Gage looked in the other living area where Gus and the two cousins shared a space not much larger than that of the three boys. He noticed a box at the foot of Gus's bed. Gus opened it, rifled through his meager belongings, and then quickly closed it.

"You checking to see if anything has been taken?" Gage asked.

"No, checkin' to see if anything added."

Gage appeared puzzled.

"I don't trust them cousins. They steal things and at night take them to a man named Harlan Spence who runs the mercantile in Cauldron. He gives them liquor."

"But why would they put things in your box?"

"In the fall, they'll take a hundredweight of cotton to Mr. Spence. Worth about fourteen dollars. He give them a gallon of whiskey worth about a dollar."

"So Spence is stealing from thieves."

Gus nodded. "But in the spring there ain't no cotton, so they steal smaller things—especially from Master Ned. If they get afraid of being caught before they get them to Mr. Spence, they stuff those things in my box so I'll get the whippin'."

"Must make for a difficult living arrangement."

Gus didn't respond, so Gage asked, "Do you like Miss Bette?" He wasn't just making conversation. He was looking for help in understanding the woman.

"Exceptin' my wife, she the only person in the world I trust."

"Where is your wife?"

"Home, in Maryland."

Strange, Gage thought, that the man considers home a place five hundred miles away, especially when he has no prospect of returning. "Any idea why they sold you, Gus?"

"They thought I was gonna run and take my family and others with me. So they sold me south to get some money out of me before I left." Then he added with a bit of pride, "I fetched three thousand dollars at auction."

"How did you come to be in South Carolina?" Gage asked.

"I walked."

"For five hundred miles?" asked Gage, amazed.

Gus nodded. "Chained to ten others."

"How long ago was that?"

"Four years. Me and my wife, Nelly, have a son and a daughter. Little Sarah must be seven years old now—probably startin' to look like her mother. I want to see that so bad."

Gage sensed his pain. "Have you ever tried to escape?"

"It's all I think about. But the first two years after I got here I was too weak to try. Now, if I escape, the only place I want to go is home and I don't know how to get there. Besides, Harlan Spence is pretty good trackin' runaways. That man is only good at two things—catchin' runaways and stealin' from thieves."

"Maybe you need something that forces you to go."

"They try to whip me again and I'll go. I've been whipped twice—first time ten lashes, next time thirty. They say next would be fifty lashes. But that ain't never gonna happen. I'll leave instead."

"It's that painful?"

"Yeah, but that ain't all of it. It's how it make you feel inside."

"Nobody ever resists?"

It was a stupid question. Gus appeared to be formulating an appropriate response, but he stopped when he realized the Norton brothers were getting ready to leave. The two older ones had shoes on. Little Georgie wrapped his feet in thin rags.

It was nearly dusk, but Gage could see the look of concern on Gus's face.

"Master Burl know someone's settin' traps in the woods for them turkeys," Gus said to the boys. A flock of wild turkeys had recently begun to reside in the woods near a swampy area on the north end of the plantation.

"Master Burl too scared of the Pit Man Ghost to go in them woods at night," Henry, the middle brother, replied.

Gus rolled his eyes and muttered, "Ain't no ghost out there."

"Who is Master Burl?" Gage asked.

"The overseer."

"Why do people believe there's a ghost?"

"They only believe it because a white man disappeared in that woods. They say the ghost drop down out of the trees and scoops up people and drags them into the pit."

"Master Burl believe it—that's all that matters," Isaac countered.

"No, it ain't. Mr. Spence ain't scared of that ghost, and Lord knows he don't want you three playin' with his sons."

"That the same Harlan Spence you said runs the mercantile at night?"

"Yes, sir, the meanest man in this area. He hires out to chase runaways with his dogs. He must have twenty of them dogs. Feeds them better than his two boys."

The brothers left, and Gus looked their way with a faint smile. "They good boys, but don't know much. I'm tryin' to learn 'em."

Gage reached into his leather satchel and pulled out a small notebook. "Just going to write down a few things for me to remember."

But when Gus saw that satchel, his demeanor changed dramatically. He became noticeably agitated.

"What part of Maryland did you come from?" Gage asked, but Gus didn't answer. The awkward silence was only interrupted by Crazy Bette's return.

Gus pulled Crazy Bette aside. The two of them had a quick, private conversation.

Now incensed, Crazy Bette hopped back up onto her wagon and said to Gage: "To think I was foolish enough to trust you with my secrets. It's a ten-minute walk to the town of Cauldron. You can get a room there at the boarding house. You need to stay out here a few days and learn."

She drove away.

Gus turned and headed the other direction.

Chapter 35

Gage wasn't sure whom he was more furious with—himself or Bette. As he walked to the small town of Cauldron, he chided himself for being taken in by her. Leaving him stranded without any explanation, now that was the act of a crazy woman. Suddenly, Jacqueline seemed quite rational.

Upon reaching Cauldron he rented a room for the night at the local boarding house and got a meal at the Johnstone Tavern. Having seen how impressed the boys at Ashland were by the licorice, he went across the street to buy some candy at the mercantile.

Gage walked in while the man tending the store for the night was busy at the back door. Gage moved sideways along the counter to get a better view. To Gage's surprise, it was one of the cousins from the Ashland plantation, the bigger one named Buford, at the door.

When their business was concluded, the shopkeeper turned and began to walk toward Gage. The man was balding and heavyset with a significant limp, obviously the result of some injury to his right leg.

"Doing some backdoor sales I see," Gage said.

The man's lips twisted into a scowl. "What business is that of yours?"

"None, just an observation."

"Best you stick to your own affairs around here."

"My name is Gage. I—"

"I know who you is."

"You do?"

"Word gets around this town fast. I'm Harlan Spence. You're welcome to buy here, but there's a stage that comes through Cauldron tomorrow evening and goes back to Charleston. I suggest you take it."

That was already Gage's plan. There wasn't much to see here, and Crazy Bette's friend, Gus, would no longer speak to him, so there was little to be learned. Still, Gage wouldn't let the man have the last word. "I'll stay as long as I want, Mr. Spence."

***

After spending the night at the boarding house, Gage rented a horse and returned to Ashland the next morning. The overseer wasn't around, so he rode in closer. Slaves were preparing the field for cotton planting, still a couple weeks away. He found Henry, Isaac, and Georgie Norton and gave them the candy—licorice and lemon drops—which they greatly appreciated.

There was singing coming from the fields, but Gage was hearing two different songs. Most of the slaves were singing "Nearer, my God, to Thee," a hymn they had learned while sitting in the gallery of the white peoples' church. During breaks in that singing, Gage could hear a different song being sung by a soloist. It was Gus, but Gage couldn't see him anywhere and his voice sounded muffled.

Gage asked one man Gus's location.

"Him in the hole," was the reply and the man pointed about one hundred feet away where there was a pile of dirt.

Gage walked that direction, and he began to hear Gus's song clearly. It was a song about freedom called "Steal Away" in which the slave notes he will not be on the plantation much longer because the Lord is going to help him escape.

> Steal away, steal away,
> steal away to Jesus!
> Steal away, steal away home,
> I ain't got long to stay here.

Gage smiled because Gus changed the tune with the next verse:

> My Lord, He calls me,
> He calls me by the thunder;
> The trumpet sounds within my soul;
> I ain't got long to stay here.

Gage found Gus six feet down. Gus looked up and stopped singing.

"Beautiful song," Gage said. "What are you doing down there, Gus?"

"Diggin'," Gus said, and he threw down his shovel. He was covered in sweat, his white shirt drenched.

There was no water around, and Gage wondered how long Gus could keep up such strenuous work without it. "I know, but what are you digging?"

"A well for water. S'posed to have it twelve feet down by the end of the day."

Gage knew this method. It was an antiquated and inefficient way to go about it. Dig a wide square first, surround that hole with oak boards, and every six feet down narrow the next square. Hopefully, one reaches good water before running out of room.

Gus started to climb a ladder, carrying with him a bucket of dirt.

"Gus, you should use a pulley and have someone up here to bring the bucket up and dump the dirt."

"I know that," Gus said in frustration, "but they won't let me use anyone else."

Gage shook his head. The Walkers were inept plantation operators. When Gus reached the top, Gage asked, "Why don't the others sing with you?"

Gus was aloof, barely responsive. His attitude toward Gage hadn't softened from the night before. He looked quickly at Gage and said, "I told you that already. They don't like me."

"Why don't they like you?"

"Don't know. S'pose it's because I ain't from around here. Maybe because I ain't like them."

"I can see that. I hear it in the different songs you all sing. Their hope for something better lies in an afterlife. Yours lies in this one."

"I s'pose."

"Why is that?"

Gus hunched his shoulders.

No matter how hard Gage probed, Gus wasn't going to tell him anything more. Something had set him off, and Gage couldn't understand what. But at least Gage had learned how Gus was different from the others at Ashland: Gus still had hope.

"Why are Little Georgie and his brothers separated from their mother?"

Gage asked.

"Don't know, been that way since I got here. Someone who been here a long time, like Aunt Abby, might know."

"Who is Aunt Abby?"

"An old woman who takes care of the children during the day, and she also makes medicines for everyone. Some say she a witch."

Gage laughed, Gus didn't.

Gage watched and listened as Gus kept singing louder. An elderly woman in an old gray sack dress strolled by, her right leg dragging a little as she walked. She stopped and yelled, "Gus, you tryin' to get us in trouble with Master Burl?"

"No, I tryin' to get us free."

"He goin' get us all whipped," she said to no one in particular. "All that big talk about the North and freedom."

"Take me to Boston," Gus shouted out, "the land of freedom."

"You ever been there?" she yelled.

Ignoring her legitimate question, Gus again shouted out, "Take me to Boston!"

She saw Gage and said to him: "That man a fool. An even bigger fool than you for comin' here."

Gage smiled. "You must be Aunt Abby."

"They call me that."

"Why do some of the others think you're a witch?"

This time she chuckled. "Maybe it's 'cause I can cure some people. And 'cause I was here the night the stars fell."

"What?"

"Near thirty years back, one night the stars fell like never befo'. Most hid indoors. I stood outside and watched. I told someone I could feel the starlight flowin' in me. They say that give me special powers."

"They say there's a ghost in Pitman Swamp. Do you believe that?"

She laughed. "I believe in conjuring and ghosts, but they made that story up from the name. Ain't no ghost in the pit. The man who owned the woods befo' Master Edwin was named Pitman."

"How old are you, Aunt Abby?"

She shrugged. "Don't rightly know. I was born around the century turn."

"Your parents didn't tell you when you were born?"

"Never knew them."

Gage was stunned. "Did you know any of your family?"

"No, my first recollect is as a child of being at Montpelier. When I got a little older, Master Ned's grandmother took me into the house and I worked as a house-girl for years."

Gage suspected that from the way she talked.

"They was pretty good to me in them days, but not since I was sent out here. Master Ned is a mean man."

"You don't like Gus either, do you?"

"I like him all right. Jus' he a troublemaker."

"Seems to me he has hope, hope for freedom."

"Freedom. What would happen to ones like me? These people here are my family. If they all leave, where would I go?"

***

Later in the afternoon Gage found Gus at the south end of the plantation where there was a pile of oak boards that he was getting ready to haul back to the well site.

"Why didn't they drop these boards closer to the well?" Gage asked.

"Don't know."

More inefficiency, Gage thought. But before he could comment, they began to hear the faint clanking of metal coming from the woods to the south. A dirt road wound through the woods and then came out in the open to form a straight boundary along the Ashland property.

Both men watched as six black men, tied together with ankle chains, came into view. They were flanked by one white man and one black man on horses, both of whom held rifles aloft in case of any attempt at escape.

"They headed to prison?" Gage asked.

"No, they headed to market."

None of the men looked their way, but they appeared a determined bunch.

"So they're going to the auction block?" Gage asked.

"Yep, just like cattle and hogs. Exceptin' they don't put chains on cattles and hogs."

Chapter 36

The next evening, after Gage had left for Charleston on the stagecoach from Cauldron, the three Norton brothers headed out to their turkey traps. When they arrived at the trap site in the woods, their good friends the Spence brothers, Jack and Eli, were there waiting for them. Jack, at age sixteen, was five years older than Eli who looked like a miniature version of his older brother. Both had gnarly blonde hair, but Jack wore a pair of ill-fitting glasses that were too weak for his poor eyesight.

The only concern for this little group was the overseer, Burl Quincy, a tall, grizzled man in his forties whose scratchy gray beard added to his sinister look. That concern was justified, for within minutes they heard Quincy's booming voice call out: "Come out whoever you are. I've found your turkey trap." The crack of his whip added credence to his command.

Quincy was still two hundred feet away. The five boys scampered for cover behind some bushes. It was now dark enough in the woods that he couldn't detect their movement from that distance. He approached the trap. It was one of the large wooden box crates the plantation used for storing items. The box had been turned so the side that opened was to the front, and a rope laid across the bottom served to close the box when tripped.

Quincy turned and shouted toward the woods: "I don't know who set this trap, but this crate belongs to Master Ned, so the turkey inside here belongs to Master Ned!" He took out his knife. He knew Ned Walker would be impressed if he brought home a wild turkey he captured with his bare hands. He started to lift the door. The animal roused.

Suppressing giggles, the boys looked at each other with wild anticipation. Quincy bent down, readying himself to tackle the turkey. He flipped up the door only to be greeted by a snarling, vicious raccoon that came at him so fast that he didn't have time to react. Trapped and unfed for two days, the ornery animal took a bite out of Quincy's kneecap.

Quincy yelped. He then cracked his whip, causing the raccoon to rear up. When the animal looked to its left, Quincy saw his chance for escape. He began running for his horse that was three hundred feet away. But he was a slow runner, and the boys easily outpaced him from behind the bushes. When they got to the point where they were fifty feet ahead of him they stopped for a purpose.

"Now!" Jack exclaimed. "Pull the rope!"

Little Georgie was given the honor. He tugged on the rope and from the trees above a cornfield scarecrow swung down not more than five feet over Quincy's head.

In his haste and confusion Quincy had no idea what it was, only believing that a body had launched at him from the trees above. The boys howled with laughter as Quincy jumped on his horse and sprinted away, convinced he had barely escaped the Pit Man Ghost.

"Master Burl won't be comin' back to these woods," Isaac said.

Quincy had found a trap, but not the real one. The real one was two hundred feet farther out, and when the boys got there they realized they had made a successful capture. They went to work, an unpleasant task but made easier out of necessity. They were hungry.

The boys put their plan into action. When the trap was opened, the two oldest, Jack and Isaac, wrestled the turkey to the ground while Georgie and Eli roped its feet. Then Henry took a hatchet to its neck. It was over in seconds.

They stared at the lifeless animal as blood gushed and the animal jerked a few times.

"Why it movin' when it's head's off?" Little Georgie screamed.

"All just dead things jerk a bit . . . until they've scared the living enough," Jack Spence said.

"It still movin'," Georgie screamed again. But his trepidation at that was suddenly interrupted by something just as troubling: the sound of footsteps crunching dead oak leaves, coming at them from the west. They froze in place. In the dim light, they could make out the pronounced limp of the man.

It was Harlan Spence, and he carried with him a burlap sack.

When Spence reached them, he looked at the three slaves scornfully but said nothing. He then grabbed the forty pound turkey, stuffed it in the burlap sack, and with one mighty heave flung the sack over his shoulder. As he walked away he turned around briefly and said, "Turkey meat is too good for niggers."

His sons looked at the Norton brothers with genuine remorse.

***

A couple days later the five boys were out together chasing rabbits. They had been at it for half an hour. The two youngest boys, Eli Spence and Georgie Norton, were not running well. Their bare feet were cut and bloodied, but they were hungry so still they ran.

Just when it appeared they had two rabbits cornered things changed, for it was as if the rabbits had hatched a plan of escape. The rabbits veered outward, then suddenly darted towards each other. Three of the boys collided, and the other two had to stop abruptly to avoid being caught up in the melee.

Little Georgie picked himself up off the ground. "Them's smart rabbits," he declared.

The chase had taken the boys to within one hundred yards of a decrepit house. In the fading light of dusk, they all looked at the house with apprehension. Even Jack and Eli Spence were afraid of that house, even though it was their home.

Suddenly the back door opened, and a ragged looking woman of about forty years stepped out. It was Liddy Spence, mother of Jack and Eli. She was thin, almost emaciated, looking more like she was sixty. She carried one book and a bag that must have had some weight to it because she struggled moving it about.

She yelled out towards the three Norton brothers: "Little Georgie, you come here."

Georgie and Henry both ran to her. When they got there she gave them the bag. It contained half the turkey meat.

"Thank you, missus," Georgie said, and he bowed quickly in such an awkward manner that it caused this sorrowful woman to break into a gentle smile. She liked Georgie and his brothers, and Gus. She didn't like her husband. No, to be accurate, she loathed her husband.

Then she handed Georgie the book. It was *The House of the Seven Gables*. "Give this to Gus," she said. "It's small enough that he should be able to hide it. I read it many times and don't need it anymore. You three need to get back to Ashland." Then she turned toward her two sons who were walking her way. "Your pa will be home soon. I don't want him to see you all together."

***

That night at Ashland, Gus began reading the Nathaniel Hawthorne gem. He sat at the only table in the cabin with the book spread open under the light of a single candle. Gus often read stories out loud and everyone in the cabin enjoyed them. It was one of the few transgressions the cousins wouldn't report.

In recent months Gus had used whatever written material he could get his hands on to try to teach the Norton brothers how to read and write. But the Hawthorne novel was a difficult teaching tool. Gus began reading and pointing to words. Even Buford watched what he was pointing to.

But it was no use. The book was complex at times, containing language unfamiliar to Gus, and he stumbled over words that he had no idea of their meaning. He tried reading a long sentence:

> The aspect of the venerable mansion has always affected me like a human countenance, bearing the traces not merely of outward storm and sunshine, but expressive, also, of the long lapse of mortal life, and accompanying vicissitudes that have passed within.

Venerable, countenance, expressive, vicissitudes. Gus had no idea what those words meant, and he possessed no dictionary with which to learn their meanings. Frustrated, he slammed the book on the table. How could he teach them to read if he couldn't understand it himself?

Then Buford said, "Jus' read. No teach, jus' read."

Gus skipped through a few pages and found a part that seemed more intelligible:

> Colonel Pyncheon's sudden and mysterious end made a vast deal of noise in its day. There were many rumors, some of

which have vaguely drifted down to the present time, how that appearances indicated violence; that there were the marks of fingers on his throat, and the print of a bloodied hand on his plaited ruff; and that his peaked beard was disheveled, as if it had been fiercely clutched and pulled.

Before Gus could interpret, Isaac shouted out with glee, "Someone killed that man!"

"Who killed that colonel?" Henry said.

Gus read for another hour as the others listened intently with imaginations that had been starved.

Chapter 37

It was as if once Edwin Walker was violent with his wife, he broke through a barrier. Now it came easier. Again it occurred in their den, again after a bout of Edwin's heavy drinking. He grabbed Jacqueline by her hair, threw her into a chair, and then slapped her twice across the face.

He began pacing about the room. When he stopped, he came back at her and shouted, "John Gage is a Northern spy, isn't he?"

"I don't know," she said, leaning back because her husband again had the back of his hand poised in front of her.

"All the time that you've spent with Gage, all that you've done with him, and you still haven't learned anything about him?"

"Whatever do you mean by that?"

"I mean that I know what you've done with him. I never intended for you to go that far."

"You said do whatever it takes."

"And obviously what you've done hasn't been good enough."

She could see he was distraught, and it seemed to go beyond her infidelity. It became clear when he sat down on a sofa with his head in his hands and said, "Ransom Pierce is after me daily for something meaningful."

"Daily? Edwin, he's playing you for a fool. He enjoys putting you through this and hearing reports of what you make me do. He and his friends at the Jockey Club are probably having a good time laughing at what you tell him."

"Hard evidence against Gage will stop their laughter. You must get it."

"Stop playing Pierce's game!"

"Just find the damn proof!" He walked over to the window and looked out before turning back to her. "And there's something else you must do.

You are to go to Jerome Cassidy and pose for him."

"Pose? Pose how?"

"Anyway he says. The man is the best artist in South Carolina. You should be honored."

"Honored to pose naked for him?"

"You've done far more with Gage. I would think this would be easy."

"And what is it you get from this arrangement?"

"That's none of your business."

"Why don't you just put me in a brothel, or put me out on the street with a *For Rent* sign around my neck?"

"If you keep failing me, I might just do that."

***

Jacqueline arranged to meet Jerome Cassidy at his art studio at one o'clock in the afternoon. The studio was a one-room cabin, nestled in a wooded setting approximately a mile from the Cassidy mansion. Jacqueline came alone, driving her small carriage right up to the front of the cabin. Jerome Cassidy, wearing his favorite red tartan jacket, stood outside the front door waiting for her.

Cassidy helped her down from the carriage. Although it was rare for a woman's bare legs to be seen, she wore a floral dress without stockings. They walked inside and Jacqueline removed her coat. She sat on a stool, her dress open at the top. He could tell she was naked under that dress.

"So what's this all about, Mr. Cassidy?" she asked.

"It's about art, my dear Jacqueline, the beauty of the female form."

"No, I mean the arrangement with my husband."

Cassidy turned to his right momentarily while trying to come up with an appropriate response. He decided on honesty. "We each had something the other wanted, so we struck a bargain."

"And what is it my husband wants?"

"Hercules as a trainer of his two-year old colt for three months."

"So, in this barter you each get what you want. What do I get?"

"Pardon me?"

"What do I receive?"

Cassidy was flustered. He didn't expect this. "What is it you want?"

"One thousand dollars in gold coins," she said without hesitation.

Cassidy coughed, and then said, "My, you do place a high value on yourself."

She crossed her legs, and as she did so the dress opened, exposing her right leg all the way to the hip. Cassidy watched with lurid excitement.

She quickly covered up and said, "As do you."

Cassidy tried to explain. "Mind you, I'm not asking for you to do anything other than pose."

"That's why the price is so modest."

"Your husband is this desperate for money?"

"The money is for me."

Cassidy turned away with his hand to the back of his head, contemplating all that he had just heard.

Jacqueline stood up. "You obviously need time to think about this proposition, Mr. Cassidy, so I'll leave you to your thoughts."

She left the cabin and drove off.

Chapter 38

Gage had returned to Charleston, but his mind was still back at the Ashland slave camp. Something there had him both concerned and intrigued. That morning he struggled to finish another segment of the *Letters from Charleston*.

Thinking his recent absence from Charleston may have been noticed, he needed to be seen by local dignitaries. Where better than a visit to the mayor's office. He started out from his hotel, but after walking two blocks he got sidetracked when he heard the faint screams of a woman in distress. As he rounded the next corner the woman's screams intensified, now broken by an occasional mournful whaling. At Chalmers Street the broadside affixed to the side of a building provided the answer:

> Prime Gang of 32 Negroes will be sold at the Mart on Chalmers Street, by Shingler Brothers on March 19, 1861. Terms: One-half cash; balance secured by a Bond and Mortgage on the property and payable with interest in twelve months.

Slave auctions in public forums were no longer permitted in Charleston. They had to be held out of sight as if that somehow extinguished the shame of the enterprise. Gage walked through a door to the mart and found himself in a place that reminded him of a prison, for it was an open air courtyard with twelve-foot-high brick walls surrounding.

He had some sense of slave auctions, but he wasn't prepared for the pitiful scene playing out at this one. An eleven-year-old boy was being sold away from his family. His mother was screaming in agony.

Gage moved closer just as the woman jumped down from the platform. The auctioneer went after her. She reached her child, and they embraced. She looked up at the buyer and pleaded, "Please, Master, buy us all—our whole family."

"I'll be a good master to your boy," the buyer assured her. "Don't you worry."

"But I won't never see him again. My little Toby will be gone forever."

She whirled about, casting her eyes on the arena, as if beseeching those in attendance to intervene. Then she looked straight up to the open sky and began to pray.

Sensing no intervention from anywhere, she turned again to the buyer. "Please, Master, buy us all!" But that was to no avail, so she looked skyward and cried out, "Lord don't let them do this! You have the power, don't let them!" Then she collapsed to the ground.

The auctioneer grabbed her son and placed him in the buyer's wagon. The wagon went out through a gated entrance in the wall across from Gage. The young boy stood and looked back longingly at his mother lying on the ground. He watched as the auctioneer picked his mother up and placed her back on the stage. She collapsed again, knowing that her thirteen-year-old daughter was next.

Standing on the opposite side of the platform was Frank Talbot who spotted Gage among the crowd and came over. Despite the warmth of the sun-filled day, Gage's face was ashen from what he just witnessed.

Talbot noticed. "An unfortunate aspect of slavery, Mr. Gage."

"Unfortunate is a mild word."

"In the long run it's better for them."

Gage looked at him incredulously. "Better than what?"

"In the long run," he repeated. "You seem shocked. Did you not know this occurs?"

"Seeing it first-hand is more powerful than reading about it."

Talbot nodded. "I have an old slave named Moses at my plantation. He's proud, proud of the position he holds. He came to this country when he was ten years old—right before the international slave trade ended in 1808. He tells the others at the plantation of how bad it was in Africa— constant warfare between tribes, a godless religion. He tells them this life is better for them."

"He doesn't have much to compare it to," Gage said.

"We are bringing Christianity to these people, supplanting their godless idols."

"What we just witnessed, Frank, didn't seem very Christian-like."

***

That night Gage awoke from a terrifying dream. Sweat dripped from the back of his neck, soaking his nightshirt. Certainly viewing the slave auction had been the genesis of the dream, but from there it took on a bizarre mix of fantasy and reality, at times confusing Gus's family situation with that of his own.

The next morning Jacqueline came to his hotel room, but things were not the same. He was consumed with the notion that Crazy Bette was right about something: I know very little about the travesties of slavery. And he wondered to what extent she might be right about Jacqueline.

They lay in bed for almost an hour and no matter how hard Jacqueline tried, he did not respond to her touch. He just stared at the ceiling, lost in thought.

Finally, he said, "Yesterday, I watched a family being torn apart."

"Families come apart in many ways, John. Just look at yours, look at mine."

"But this is preventable."

"And yours isn't?"

He answered with a poor analogy: "Yours was by accident—the deaths of your parents. At least, we both have a brother we're still close to."

"Sure," she said softly.

"By the way, where is your brother?"

She hesitated as if the question had stumped her. "He has stayed in Europe. I'm not even sure where right now."

Gage nodded. "Years ago in Philadelphia, you and I never talked about slavery."

"It wouldn't have been the place to do so. Northerners don't understand how different the Southern economy is. Slavery is necessary for our well-being."

Gage shot her a queer look.

She followed that by adding, "For their well-being as well."

He looked at her sternly. "Do you really believe that?"

She avoided the question by asking, "Is this why you came to Charleston, John? To study slavery?"

"It may turn out that way. I'm headed back to Ashland."

"Why?"

As Gage stood to dress, he said, "I'm not really sure."

Chapter 39

It was late in the day when Gage arrived at Ashland, and work had ended. He found the three Norton brothers and the Spence boys in their usual spot—the woods behind the camp, a place where Burl Quincy was now afraid to visit because of the Pit Man Ghost. They were huddled around a four-foot-square piece of tanned leather.

"What are you boys doing?" Gage asked.

"Eli and Little Georgie need shoes," Jack Spence said. "We're going to make them."

"All right, don't let me stop you."

But no one moved. They continued to stare at the leather.

"What's wrong?" Gage asked.

"We don't know how to make shoes," Jack said dejectedly.

Gage picked up the leather. "Nice and soft, probably from deer skin. The easiest thing to make would be moccasins."

"Yeah," Jack said excitedly, but then the dejection returned. "We don't know how to make moccasins."

"I can help with that," Gage said. "Some Indians showed me how."

Little Georgie's eyes opened wide. "You know Indians?"

"I've met a few."

Astonished, Little Georgie looked at the others. "He know Indians."

"Where'd you see them Indians?" Isaac asked.

"In the West."

"Don't know where that is."

"It's far away."

"Did you kill any Indians?" Jack asked as the boys listened intently.

"Not any of the ones that showed me how to make moccasins. They were friendly Indians."

Using his hand as a ruler, Gage measured the length of Little Georgie's foot and that of Eli's. There was little difference. He took out his knife and cut the leather into four equal parts.

"Why did you do that?" Jack asked.

"We need four moccasins," Gage said, and he wrapped one piece around Little Georgie's left foot. He then used his knife to make notches along the center. He removed the leather from Little Georgie's foot and sliced the center between the two notches. With the tip of his knife, he poked several holes on both sides of the cut.

"Do you have any string?" Gage asked.

They knew of only one long, sturdy piece. They all looked at Georgie. He looked down at the necklace that held his two-cent coin. Reluctantly, he gave it up.

"You keep that two-cent piece safe, Georgie, and I'll find you something better than string to carry it on," Gage said.

Georgie tried on the moccasin, and when he laced it up the moccasin fit snugly on his foot. But Georgie wasn't finished. He took the knife and cut a piece off the leftover leather that he then inserted inside the moccasin.

Gage marveled at the ingenuity. "Well done, Georgie, you just made an inner soul for that moccasin."

With one shoe complete, four of the boys then went to work creating the other three moccasins. But not Jack. He was distracted and was reading a single page torn from a book.

"What do you have there, Jack?" Gage asked.

"A page from a book I found. My mom likes me to read. She wants everyone to read."

"You don't like reading?"

"Nah, I like it a lot, but I don't see good enough to read very fast, even with these glasses." He laid down the glasses in frustration.

Gage picked them up and looked through them. They were very weak.

"And I just don't like the way it gets me to thinkin'," Jack said. "She says the world would be a better place if people do more readin' and thinkin'. There'd be less fightin'."

"She sounds like a smart woman."

"Were you in wars, sir?"

"Yes, in the Mexican War."

"Did you kill anyone?"

"When I had to."

"They say we're going to have a war," Jack said in a way that seemed he was eliciting Gage's opinion.

"It might happen."

"I don't know if I can kill anyone, at least someone I don't know."

"It's easier when they're trying to kill you."

"My father says I'll have to sign up if war comes."

"Your father doesn't own slaves, does he?"

"No, just dogs. He says they're cheaper."

"Why does he care about any war?"

"He says the North shouldn't be telling us what to do."

"So he believes the South should have the right to do things that are wrong. Look at your three friends there. Shouldn't they be free like you?"

Jack winced. "I suppose so. None of it makes sense to me."

"Then why would you ever fight for the South, Jack?"

"I guess if that's what they say we have to do, that's what we do."

***

Despite his distrust of Gage, Gus had always been impressed by the way he interacted with the five boys. He sensed Gage's concern for them was genuine. After Gage finished making the moccasins, Gus said to him, "Thank you for helping them boys with the shoes. They sure do like you."

Gus seemed to have softened; Gage viewed this as his chance. "And so why don't you like me, Gus?"

Gus hesitated, but said nothing.

"What is it, Gus?" Gage demanded.

Gus pointed at the Gage Ironworks emblem on Gage's leather satchel and said, "Because of that!"

"What?"

"You make cannons for the slavers!"

"I write stories for newspapers."

"I seen that mark on cannons," Gus said, pointing again to the insignia.

"Where?" Gage said so demonstrably that it alerted Gus to the importance of the inquiry.

"By the ocean?"

"When did you see that?"

"When they sent me there—a few weeks back."

"What? Who sent you there?"

"Master Edwin hired a few of us out to work at a place. There were cannons there with these marks on them. Then, me and a few others helped haul them to another place."

"In Charleston?"

"Yeah."

"Where was that?"

"That way," he said pointing to the east. "By the ocean."

"The ocean's a big place," Gage said, and he pulled out a map of Charleston and spread it before them. "Show me on here where the cannons are."

Gus looked at him incredulously.

"You told me you can read."

"I can read."

"Then what's the problem?"

"Don't know what I'm readin'."

And then it struck Gage. As astute as Gus was, like most slaves who had travelled little, he had no sense of spatial relationships outside of his immediate area. "It must be like being lost on an island," Gage said softly.

That statement perplexed Gus even more, so again he didn't respond.

"Did you hear them say where the cannons will go from Charleston?"

"Yeah, I heard."

"Where?"

"To Maryland."

"Are you sure?"

"Whenever someone say Maryland, I always listen good."

"Take me to the cannons!" Gage implored.

Gus's look of disbelief served as his response. Finally, he said, "What good would that do for me?"

Without hesitation Gage replied, "I'll get you back to Maryland."

Chapter 40

The next evening, with Gus watching over them, the three Norton brothers went to check the traps. They were hungry, but they found that the traps were empty. They sat down, dejected.

"Master Gage brought us some jerky," Isaac said as he handed some to the others.

"He a good man," Henry added.

"And he know Indians," Georgie said, bringing a smile to Gus's face.

They heard footsteps coming from the far side of the woods. Gus picked up a hatchet and stood up. It was the footsteps of one person, and soon that person appeared: it was Eli, the younger of the Spence brothers. This was unusual because the Spence brothers went everywhere together.

"Where Jack?" Isaac asked.

Eli's head slumped and tears began to flow down his face. He couldn't speak, but he handed Isaac a pair of oval glasses.

They were Jack's glasses, ones that had done him little good. Once, however, when Isaac tried them on they had helped his eyesight immensely.

"Where Jack?" Isaac asked again.

"It's my pa," Eli stammered. "He's makin' Jack join the militia."

"What's a milita?" Georgie asked.

"It's the army," Gus said. "They gonna make him fight in the war."

"Po' Jack," Isaac said.

"We got to help Jack," Georgie said.

"No way to help him now," Gus said.

Georgie bolted upright and began sprinting back toward the cabin. Gage saw him and, detecting Georgie's anxiety, came running to meet him.

"Georgie, what's the matter?"

"It's Jack, Master Gage. His pa makin' him be in the war."

"He's not old enough to join. Where is Jack?"

"In the town."

Gage hopped on his horse and rode to Cauldron. Broadsides were posted everywhere for the new Thompkins Militia unit. The biggest one warned:

Marauding Yankees to land on the South Carolina shore. Be there to greet them.

But it was the big print at the bottom that Gage knew was Harlan Spence's motivator:

$20 Dollar Gold Bounty Paid for New Enlistees

By the time Gage arrived, Spence had already signed Jack up and pocketed the money.

"Spence, what are you doing? Your son's not eighteen."

"You think they care about that? They just want fifty young men to help fight the Yankees in Charleston."

"You've sold your son!"

"Yes, *my* son, and this ain't none of your business."

There was some truth in that and Spence continued, "Besides, they'll feed him better and learn him to be a man better than I can. They'll even get him the right glasses."

Gage couldn't disagree with those things either.

As Spence began to walk away, he called out to Jack, "Make us proud, boy. But whether you come home dead or alive don't let it be with a bullet in your back."

Jack began walking slowly, disconsolately, in the direction the recruiter pointed.

Gage caught up to him. He wanted to give the boy some parting gift, but he had nothing with him except for one thing. He reached into his pocket and pulled out the *Little Book of Wisdom*. He stared at it and said, "Jack, I have something for you."

He handed it to the boy and added, "My father gave it to me when I went away to war. It talks a lot about the meaning of life."

Choked with emotion and tears in his eyes, Jack was unable to speak. He simply nodded.

"I wish you the best, Jack."

***

Gage stayed that night in Cauldron and spent the next morning observing the townspeople, but he learned very little. Jack's militia unit had already left for Charleston, and the town was buzzing with war talk even though the residents there had no more information than what they had been supplied by Ransom Pierce's newspaper.

In the early afternoon Gage road to Ashland. When he arrived, several wagons of white neighbors, along with their slaves, had formed a horseshoe in one of the fields.

Gage found Gus and asked, "What's going on here?"

"They're going to whip a sick man."

"Why?"

"For not workin'."

"Who is it?"

"Tandy. He didn't work yesterday or this mornin'. Aunt Abby can't help him, the doctor neither."

"Show me to him," Gage said, and Gus led him to the barn where they found Tandy, a thirty-year-old field hand, curled up in front of a stall. He was sweating profusely even though it was only sixty degrees outside.

"Tandy, what did the doctor say when he visit you?" Gus asked.

"He say I got some kind of 'fection."

"How long have you had it?" Gage asked.

"'bout three days."

But before Gage could ask more, the cousins arrived with orders from Burl Quincy to bring Tandy to the whipping post. They each grabbed an arm. With ease, the cousins lifted Tandy up until his feet were off the ground, for they were much larger than the sick man.

"Buford, this man is sick," Gage said to the biggest cousin.

"I jus' do as told," Buford replied, and they hauled Tandy out to the whipping post.

The cousins had been put to this task many times before, and when Burl

Quincy said, "Arrange him," they knew what to do. Before binding Tandy's feet and hands, they stripped him of his shirt and pulled down his pants because Quincy wanted to tear the skin on his back and buttocks.

"You're not going to be able to sit down after I'm through with you," the overseer yelled. He then ordered all the slaves from Ashland and the two adjoining plantations to gather around. This included Tandy's wife and children.

This was not just a lesson, it was a public shaming as well.

It took only six lashes before flesh was breached and blood drawn. On the seventh lash Tandy finally cried out, a pitiful cry for help from God, for he was struggling with not only the pain inflicted by the whip but the weakness from his illness.

Each lash thereafter produced a smaller cry for help as if Tandy was resigned to his fate.

After fifteen lashes it appeared Tandy could still withstand a few more, but Gage couldn't. He stepped forward, grabbed the overseer's wrist, and yelled, "Enough! Can't you see this man is ill?"

"What I see is a slave that's been loafin' for the last week. Three times I warned him that he was gonna get a whippin'."

"Look, the man has a fever; he's sick. He can't work."

"Who the hell are you to tell me how to do my job? Mister Ned Walker gave me authority to punish when I see fit."

"I wonder what Mister Edwin Walker would say about this."

"I answer only to Ned, and he will be pleased to see that I got him to work."

Gage changed his approach. "Ned answers to Edwin, and what will you say if your brutality makes it so Tandy can never work again? A young slave cut down in his prime because of your foolishness. You'll have hell to pay with the Walkers."

It was a thought that confounded the overseer, and he stood there speechless for a moment before backing down. "Cut him loose," he said softly. Then he turned to the crowd and yelled, "Let this be a lesson to all the rest of you!"

The Norton brothers walked away impressed by what Gage had just done, but Gus had a different take on things. "Why did you do that?" he asked.

"To help Tandy of course."

"You gonna stay here forever to protect him? As soon as you gone and Tandy is healthy, he'll get the whippin' of his life."

"At least he might be healthier then . . . able to take it."

Gus waved his hand in the air and stormed off.

Gage was desperate. He needed Gus's help. He went after him, but as he began speaking Gus would not stop working, wouldn't even look his way. Gage decided he needed to do something dramatic to command his attention. He was not a particularly religious man, but he suddenly dropped to his knees and began praying.

Gus looked over at him and asked, "What are you doin'?"

"Praying for the end of slavery."

"What?" Gus put down his axe. "You think you the only one who ever prayed for that. It ain't worked yet."

"Maybe if enough of us get smarter and start praying it will happen."

"You got smarter by being here?"

Gage nodded.

Now Gus came over and sat by him. "Why you care so much about these cannons?"

"Because there's going to be a war, and if the North wins slavery will end."

"If the South win?"

"Slavery will go on, perhaps for a long time."

This news seemed to have an impact on Gus. "How you gonna get me to Maryland? I don't want to walk five hundred miles with no food and water."

"As soon as you show me where the cannons are, I'll put you on a ship to Baltimore."

"You got a plan on how you gonna do that?"

"Yeah, a real good plan."

"You ain't got a plan."

"I'm working on it."

"You got a ticket for me?"

"A ticket? Oh, you mean like a pass." Gage recalled that all slaves in South Carolina to go anywhere needed passes that set out their name, where they were going, and for how long. "Where do we get one of those?"

Gus looked at him incredulously. "From the overseer, or the master hisself."

"Oh," Gage said. "Perhaps we could make one."

Again Gus looked at him incredulously. But he offered a glimmer of hope when he said, "I got an old one they forgot to take back from me, but the date ain't no good."

"I might be able to fix the date," Gage said.

"No, you can't. But it don't matter anyway because I ain't goin'."

"Gus, I don't understand. All you sing about is escaping, but you seem unwilling to try. Why is that?"

Gus put his head in his hands as he thought for a moment. Then he said, "Somethin' tells me that I'll only get one chance to get away. I can't fail at it."

"I understand that," Gage said, contemplating. Then he launched into a story. "When I was a young boy, I always forgot to wash behind my ears. But many times I would wake up in the morning to find a washcloth hanging beside my bed. I never woke up when someone used that washcloth on me."

"What you sayin'?" a confused Gus asked.

"That a lot can be done while others sleep. We would explore the buildings late at night. Little risk of getting caught. Does that make sense?"

"No, I never had anybody to wash behind my ears."

"That's not my point."

"You talkin' about how we would find the cannons, but you not sayin' anything about how you'd get me to Maryland. All I hear you say is you'll put me on a ship . . . like it some kind of magic trick. You get a real plan, a good plan, and I'll listen."

Chapter 41

Gage was staring at Jacqueline's face—that beautiful face—now lit by a soft morning sun. Even though still asleep, she seemed to sense his presence and rolled onto her side towards him. As she did so, her hair fell back, and he noticed a one-inch laceration along the side of her neck. It was a clean cut that looked to be about a week old but was healing nicely.

"What is that?"

"It's nothing," she said sleepily.

"Tell me."

Tears began to fill her eyes, but she remained silent.

"Tell me!" he again demanded.

"It was Ned," she said haltingly. "He tried to attack me again last week."

"Tried?"

"I think a noise scared him off when someone came in the house. He's deranged. He carries this two-foot-long German sword with a brass handle. He had it up against my neck. I swear, John, he would've used it on me if that person hadn't come in the house."

Gage sat back, stunned. "What are you going to do? Tell Edwin?"

She laughed lightly through the tears. "Ned would probably kill us both."

"What then?"

She looked him directly in the eyes and said, "I need you to take care of it."

"What?"

"I mean kill Ned before he kills me."

"This is a matter for the police."

"Around here things work differently. It's a family matter—handled within the family."

"I'm not family."

"Johnny, I'm scared. I'm scared to death." She clung to him.

I won't kill Ned, Gage thought, but I may beat a confession out of him . . . put the fear of God in him.

Gage was going back to Ashland.

***

Later that morning, as militia units passed by on their way to the island forts, Jacqueline practically ran into Crazy Bette on a busy street near the Battery. Standing together until the troops passed by, there was no avoiding each other now.

"You seem to be quite . . . shall I say, coherent today," Jacqueline began.

"I'm always coherent, darlin'," Bette replied.

"Yes, that's true. Even when you're at your worst, you see and hear everything."

"With people like you about, there is much to see and hear."

"At least when you put on your act, you pretend not to know me," Jacqueline said. "I'm grateful for that."

"You've never been grateful for anything."

"I must say it's been smart the way you've implemented your act gradually over the past few years. People feel sorry for you, so they won't condemn you for the things you do. Your frolic in the fountain may have been a bit much, though."

"My act is not as impressive as yours. Despite being married, you appear to have hooked John Gage. You've been after the Gage Ironworks money for years."

"What are you talking about? There's no money in that company for Johnny."

"How do you know that?"

"He hasn't been in involved in that company for the past decade. His stepfather runs it. Johnny hates the man . . . has nothing to do with the company."

Bette was stunned.

"Perhaps you don't know quite as much as you think you know,"

Jacqueline said as she walked away.

***

Bette now realized the horrible mistake she had made. She headed straight to Gage's hotel and found John packing a small bag to take to Ashland. It was the first time she had seen him since leaving him stranded there.

She began with an apology: "I'm sorry, John. I may know Jacqueline better than you know her, but I don't know you well. I thought your company was building cannons for the Confederacy."

"I'm trying to find those cannons."

"I understand that now. But why are you going to Ashland to find the cannons?"

"Because Gus knows where they are. I'm trying to convince him to take me to them."

"You want him to run?"

Gage nodded. "I've told him I will get him home to Maryland."

"Oh, John, how can you make such a promise?"

"I'll find a way to keep it. I'm also going there to have a talk with Ned Walker."

"Ned? Whatever about?"

"I'll just say his treatment of Jacqueline."

She wasn't surprised by that. "I've noticed there's tension between them, probably because Ned stands between her and Edwin."

"In what way?"

"Think about it. A terrible war may be coming. Edwin has a military background and will surely be given a command in the Confederate army. If he's killed, his eldest son will control the vast majority of his estate. Jacqueline, as a second spouse, at most will inherit a one-third life estate in the homestead. That's not much to live on, especially for the lifestyle she desires."

"Yes, and I suppose she didn't inherit much of anything from her parents' estates, and even that was split with her brother."

"Her brother?" Bette said with a confused look. "Jacqueline is an only child."

Gage didn't question this stunning revelation, choosing instead to put it to the back of his mind for the moment. "I'm also going back to Ashland as an observer, a reporter of things. There are things I didn't know or see before. You were right about that."

She smiled.

"The friendship between the Spence brothers and the Norton brothers is fascinating. They're best of friends. They don't see skin color. Their minds haven't been poisoned."

"A breakthrough," she said, and she walked over and hugged him. "Be careful with Ned Walker. He's dangerous."

Chapter 42

Gage arrived at Ashland late in the afternoon just after Little Georgie cut his arm on a sharp piece of iron. Gage stopped the bleeding with a handkerchief and then escorted him to Aunt Abby.

She washed the cut with a lye soap that stung so bad that Georgie screamed. "That will learn you not to cut yo'self," she said. She then covered the wound with a homemade remedy made from powdered leaves.

While she worked, Gage asked, "Do you expect it to be a bad year, Aunt Abby?" He was contemplating the changes that might occur from a war, but she didn't grasp his point.

"We only had one good year at Ashland since I been here. That was 18 and 57."

"What happened then?"

"Crops was good, but most of all Master Ned was gone."

"Gone? Where to?"

"Somewheres beyond the ocean. A place they call Ger . . . "

"Germany?"

"That's it."

"Are you saying he was gone all of 1857?" Gage said intently, for if true Jacqueline's claim that Ned might be the father of her child was a fabrication.

"As best I recollect. I don't know my birth date so we celebrate it on the first day of the year. He come home the day after that in 18 and 58. A mighty po' present for me."

An hour later, as Gage watched slaves work in the field, Ned Walker rode in. Obviously somewhat inebriated, he waved a short sword wildly about while continually shouting, "Labor omnia vincit." Gage recognized the Latin phrase *Work Conquers All*, but the slaves had no idea what Ned was saying.

Ned dismounted fifty feet away. As he began walking towards Gage, he shouted out, "You've been spending a lot of time out here, Gage."

"Your father approved it."

"My father doesn't run Ashland, I do."

Ned stopped twenty feet away. He held the short sword at his side. It was about two feet long with a brass handle, just like Jacqueline had described. Gage felt the outside of his coat pocket. His Derringer was in there.

Gage moved closer. As he did so, he could discern that the entire edge of the sword was serrated, not something that would make a clean cut like that on Jacqueline's neck.

"Mighty interesting sword you carry, Ned. How did you come by it?"

"I got it when I was in Germany."

"Why were you there?"

"I went to school at the German Military Academy."

"When was that?"

"All of 1857, returned in '58."

Gage was stunned. "You never came home during that time?"

Surprised by the question, Ned replied, "Too damned far to travel for that."

Gage's mind was reeling from these disclosures. He began to walk away only to have Ned leave him with a warning: "Gage, I don't care what you do with my stepmother, but you'll pay a heavy price if you embarrass my daddy."

***

For the next two hours Gage sat in the woods of the Pit Man Ghost, thinking. He was furious with Jacqueline. What is she trying to do? he wondered. Then he tried to dismiss her from his thoughts. I can't allow her to take me off track. I have to find the cannons, and I've got to do it soon.

He kept going over things in his mind. Why would those cannons be sent to Maryland as Gus said? As he thought it through, the conclusion he reached was frightening: Virginia may soon secede, and if that happens Maryland will possess the only viable avenues for Northern troops to reach Washington City. Shut off those avenues and the capital will fall to the Confederacy.

Maryland, with so many rabid secessionists, was the key. Whether the cannons were shipped to Baltimore or Annapolis, they would be no more than fifty miles from Washington. They could already be on their way, Gage thought. I can't sit and wait; the answers aren't going to find me. But I have no sources, and I've produced nothing in days of scouting about Charleston. Ask the wrong person and I could wind up in prison or worse. There's only one person who can help get the answer, and that's Gus. I'm desperate, and desperation demands desperate action.

And now Gage had a plan.

He returned to the camp, arriving there while everyone was still in the field working. Laundry hung from a long clothesline near the main house. Gage rode his horse over to a shed near the clothesline where he found Ned's favorite red shirt hanging on it. He grabbed the shirt and stuffed it in his saddle bag.

Gage headed to the woods to wait, and after an hour he went looking for Gus. He found him working alone at the far end of the plantation, once again digging—this time a drainage ditch.

Gus looked at Gage quizzically, expecting to hear some significant news since Gage had made a long ride out to find him.

Instead, he heard from Gage, "Someone stole Master Ned's favorite shirt."

"That don't matter to me," Gus replied, and he went back to digging.

"Yeah, it does."

"Why's that?"

"Burl Quincy found it in your box."

Gus dropped his shovel in despair. "The cousins must've put it there."

"Could be," Gage said. "They were probably going to sell it to Harlan Spence tonight and were afraid of getting caught with it in the meantime."

"I won't take another whippin' from Burl Quincy. I'll kill him this time."

"Then you need to get away."

"I got no place to go."

"How about going to Maryland?" Gage said with a half-smile. "I'll be waiting for you down around the bend on Crawford Road."

***

Twenty minutes later, when Gus determined no one was in sight, he threw down his shovel and began running for Crawford Road. Gage had a horse waiting for him.

"You got that fake pass you always carry?"

"I got it," Gus said.

"Good, you might need it."

"No, *you* might need it."

"I might?"

"You runnin' off with Ned Walker's property. I'm worth somethin', you ain't. We get caught, and things will be worse for you."

Gage realized Gus was right. Helping a slave escape was a serious crime, and the penalties were severe.

The two men began riding east, but just a few minutes later Gus suddenly halted his horse. Gage was afraid he had changed his mind.

"I need to go back," Gus said simply. "I forgot somethin'."

"Gus, you can't go back."

"I have to."

"You can't. They'll be looking for you."

"I'll go around and sneak in from the woods." Gus took off, promising he would return in no time.

When he reached the woods, Gus tied his horse to a tree and surveyed the area of the cabins. Fortunately, people were still out working. He ran to his cabin, and inside he went straight to his box. Ned's red shirt wasn't in there. Burl Quincy must have taken it out of there already, Gus figured. He grabbed the one thing he was after and stuffed it in his pocket.

Gus sprinted away from the cabin, unaware that Buford was watching him go. When he rejoined a confused Gage, Gage asked, "What could have been so damn important that you took that kind of chance?"

Reticent as always, Gus hesitated. Finally, he pulled something from his pocket and showed it to Gage.

"A lock of hair?" Gage exclaimed.

"Nelly's hair. It was the only thing she could give me to remember her by when I was being taken away."

"Hell, Gus, you won't need that bit of hair. You'll soon have the whole woman . . . if my plan works out."

"Your plan? What's your plan?"

"I'm still workin' on it."

"Figured as much."

"Don't worry. You're halfway to Maryland."

Gus looked at him. Now he was confused.

"What I mean is that you making the decision to go was half the matter."

Gus accepted that, and the two men began riding east. Two miles further, however, Gus stopped again, this time near a creek bed.

"I should clean myself up, get some of this dirt off my shirt. I don't look much like a slave who's goin' some place on his master's business."

"Why didn't you grab another shirt when you were back at the cabin?"

"Don't have one."

"I've got one," Gage said. He reached into his saddle bag and pulled out Ned Walker's fancy red shirt and threw it to Gus.

Gus shook his head. "I shoulda known."

As Gus changed shirts, Gage noticed several small scars across his back, the product of earlier whippings. Once Gus had put on the red shirt, Gage said, "Now you look like a man of means."

As they began riding again, Gus suddenly came to understand what Gage said to him earlier. He had put Master Ned and the Ashland plantation behind him. He was moving on. He was halfway to Maryland.

***

Two hours later, Burl Quincy went looking for Gus and couldn't find him. He sounded the cowbell bringing all the slaves together.

"Augustus Ward has gone missin'," he announced.

This brought a titter from the others. They knew Gus would take off sooner or later. All that freedom talk on his part.

"Anyone knowin' somethin' about where he went, this is your one chance," Quincy added. "If you don't tell me now, you'll get as many lashes as Augustus when we catch him."

It was Buford who stepped forward. He knew there would be a nice reward in this for him, but there was more to it than that. With Gus gone, they would have no one to read to them. "I seen him, Master Burl. He on a horse and rode towards Crawford Road."

"Ain't no reason 'cept one for him doin' that," Quincy said, and he got on his horse and headed for the Spence home.

When Quincy arrived there, Mrs. Spence said, "My husband ain't home, Mr. Quincy."

"All right, Liddy, you tell him I have some work for him trackin' Augustus Ward."

Trying to hide her shock, she drew her hand to her face.

"Same deal as always," Quincy added. "You tell him to take his dogs and head east."

An hour later, Harlan Spence returned home and Liddy told him about the job he had to do.

"I knew Augustus Ward would run sometime—him bein' a Northern nigger and all. Which way did Burl Quincy say he went?"

"North," she said without hesitation.

***

Five miles into their journey, Gage noticed the sullen look on Gus's face. "What's the matter," he asked.

"Everythin' so sudden. I didn't get to say goodbye to Aunt Abby or the brothers."

"True, but you should be happy. You're going home."

Gus didn't get a chance to respond to that. The sound of horses was coming at them from around the next bend in the road. Four riders carrying rifles soon appeared.

"Patrollers," Gus said softly.

"You still got that pass?" Gage asked.

"Yeah, but the date ain't right."

"Damn . . . give it to me, anyway," and Gus handed it over.

The patrollers were very young and carried rifles, pistols, and whips. Gage sized them up as lowlifes, enjoying this rare position of authority.

"State your purpose out here," their apparent leader said forcefully.

"I explain my business to no man," Gage said with equal force.

It was a response the leader had never heard before, and suddenly he was on the defensive.

Gage piled it on. "Why haven't you all joined up?" Gage said with a fractured Southern drawl that caused Gus to wince. "The militia needs all the men it can get."

The young man squirmed in his saddle a bit and looked over at his associates.

"We need to get to Charleston," Gage said. "You all need to let us be on our way."

"He got a pass?" the patroller finally said, pointing at Gus.

Gus pulled lightly on the reins, readying his horse to run.

Gage had assessed the youngster and doubted he could read. Gage decided to test him. "You ever heard of the steamship *Shenandoah*?"

"No, why should I?"

"It's a big ship that came into Charleston two days ago." Gage pulled out a newspaper from his satchel that had a picture of a ship on the front page and handed it to the young man. "There's an article about the *Shenandoah*. All the newspapers wrote about it."

Gage watched the young man's eyes closely. They weren't moving across the paper; they were just staring.

"I don't care about no ship. He got a pass or not?"

Now Gage was certain who they were dealing with, and he pulled out the old pass and handed it to the patroller. "Yeah, he's got a pass to go meet that ship."

The young man stared at the pass. Again his eyes were not moving.

Gage pointed to the pass. "You can see right there that it says this man is the appointed agent of Mr. Ned Walker."

Knowing it didn't say that, Gus looked at Gage in astonishment.

"Yeah, I can see that," the young patroller said hesitantly.

Still, the youngster seemed intent on showing off in front of his friends. "It don't seem right that Mr. Ned Walker would appoint a slave to be his agent." He looked at the others who nodded in some form of concurrence.

"Whether you think that's right or not doesn't really matter. It's not your job to interfere with Mr. Ned Walker's business."

"I'm thinkin' we should go back to the Ashland Plantation and make sure."

"What's your name, young man?"

"Why'd you need my name?"

"Because Mr. Ned will need to know who to take it out on if this man doesn't get to Charleston before dark. He's to make purchases of seed off the

Shenandoah, and that ship leaves for Savannah at ten tonight."

The young man fidgeted in the saddle. He had to back down, but not without trying to save face by getting the last word. "What's your name?" he asked.

"You don't need to know my name if I don't know yours," Gage said, and he and Gus rode off.

Gus was still shaking ten minutes later. Gage looked over and chuckled. "You weren't worried he was going to figure out we were pretending about that pass, were you?"

"No, I was worried about him figurin' things out from yo' Yankee voice." Gus shook his head. "You got the worst Southern accent I ever heard. And *Y'all* ain't two words."

Chapter 43

When Cyrus answered the door at the Ford house in Annapolis, Kate Warne said, "Good day, sir," in such a charming fashion that he was immediately taken in by her.

"Thank you, ma'am, what may I do for you?"

"I am delivering this gift for Mrs. Ford from her son."

"From Congressman Gage?"

"No, from Mr. John Gage."

"Oh my!" Cyrus said. "Please come in."

"I just meant to drop it off. I don't want to be any bother."

"Oh, no, I'm sure the missus will want to talk to you," and Cyrus went off to find Victoria.

Kate wondered what she should do. She was certain John never anticipated her meeting his mother. And should she use her false name? She decided she must. She had too many contacts in Annapolis to risk using her real name.

It took five minutes before Victoria appeared, and when she did she seemed groggy, as if she had just awakened from a midday nap. But she also seemed excited by Kate's arrival.

"Hello, Miss—"

"Actually, Mrs. Ford, it's Missus. I am Mrs. Constance Cherry."

This surprised Victoria. Johnny having a special relationship with a married woman? But she, too, was enchanted by this beautiful brunette with the delightful smile, despite the demure look of her clothing.

"I understand you've brought something from my son," Victoria said.

"Yes, ma'am, I have."

"I don't receive many visitors here in Annapolis," Victoria explained, and then in a pleading manner, she said, "Please come into the parlor and sit."

"All right, but just for a few minutes. I have a horse to return to the livery, and then a train to catch back to Baltimore."

Victoria wasted no time. "So, tell me, how did my son become so acquainted with a married woman in Charleston?"

Kate was getting in deeper. The more questions she had to answer, the more she had to fabricate. But she'd come this far, so she decided to go on. "Actually, Mrs. Ford—"

"Please call me Victoria."

"All right, Victoria, I'm not married. I'm widowed."

"Oh, I'm sorry."

"And I've never been to Charleston."

Cyrus brought in hot tea. He was surprised to hear their guest now speaking with a Southern accent. She didn't have it when she arrived.

Kate watched as Victoria's hands trembled when she tried to maneuver the teacup.

"Then how did you come by this present?" Victoria asked. But without awaiting the answer, she added with a sudden burst of enthusiasm, "And how do you know Johnny?"

Now Kate was fully immersed in spinning a tale, a mix of fantasy and partial truths. "My husband and I were living in Mobile when he died. I then moved to Chicago to live with my sister. That's where I met John. We stayed in touch when I moved to Baltimore—even got together a few times when he moved to Washington."

Victoria didn't know what to make of that last statement, and didn't ask.

Kate went on. "John knows I come to Annapolis often, and so he sent the package to me hoping I could find you."

"Well, I can see why Johnny is so attracted to you. You are a true delight."

Suddenly, Kate felt she was being sized up as a possible daughter-in-law. "John and I are just good friends," she explained.

Victoria pretended not to hear. "Oh, I know he can be a tough one to pin down."

Their discussion went on for a half hour with Victoria becoming more captivated with Kate by the minute. This was the woman for Johnny.

And Kate found Victoria so friendly and accommodating that she couldn't help become concerned as she observed Victoria's actions. Not only was Victoria shaky, but she occasionally became drowsy only to suddenly burst forth with inordinate excitement as if her real personality was trying to emerge.

Kate had spent time in high society, and she had seen the signs before. She was convinced Victoria was taking laudanum, the so-called panacea for everything from sleeplessness to female disorders, and that was the cause of her problems.

They had talked so long that they had almost forgotten the gift. When Victoria unwrapped it and saw what it was, tears came to her eyes immediately. It was a new wooden plaque with her favorite saying from Mary, Queen of Scots:

> To be kind to all, to like many and love a few, to be needed and wanted by those we love, is certainly the nearest we can come to happiness.

It came with a brief note from John that said, "Mother, I saw that you left the plaque with this quote behind at the old house. I know how much it meant to you. It's started having meaning for me as well. You need to keep it with you."

"Constance, I used to stop and read these words ten times a day. But for the last three years I've been without them. Now, thanks to you and Johnny, I can enjoy them again."

Once again she had painted Kate and John as a couple. This time Kate merely smiled, but when Victoria picked up the plaque and had trouble holding it securely, Kate had seen enough. She had to say something... had to do something.

She was blunt. "Victoria, I know we've only just met, but I must say that it appears to me you are using laudanum, and it is causing you more harm than good."

Victoria was taken aback, but she sensed in Kate only good intentions. Victoria didn't deny it, and instead opened up: "Yes, it's true. I know I shouldn't. I stopped for a while, but then things happened, and I had to start taking it again."

"What things happened?"

Victoria then recounted how Jubal and Doc Brown had lied about the explosion at the ironworks, and how they had deceived her about the laudanum. And then, worst of all, Doc Brown's suicide.

Kate was adamant. "What your husband and Doc Brown did was wrong, and using the laudanum only gives in to them."

Victoria nodded at Kate in a way that acknowledged her agreement with that assessment.

"The pain Doc Brown felt was not from your private shaming of him, it was from his guilt for what he had done. His guilt shouldn't become your guilt."

"Yes, that's true."

"The laudanum has weakened you, Victoria. Drinking it limits your ability to resist it. That's why it's so addictive. You need strength to stop taking it. Johnny would want you to end this practice."

Victoria smiled approvingly. "Johnny sending me this gives me strength. Just knowing that he cares and that I can count on him emboldens me. I'm going to quit this awful drug."

***

"This is a strange place for an interview, Keene," Ari Gage said as he approached the man sitting casually on a bench in Hutchison Park.

"Oh, this is not an interview, Congressman," replied newspaperman Ethan Keene, a balding bespectacled man of about forty years who spoke in slow, drawn-out phrases that both enticed and annoyed the person on the receiving end. "In fact I think for the good of both of us we can agree that anything said here today will not be repeated."

"I assumed this was some kind of follow-up to that false article you wrote in the *Washington Journal* about the fifty Gage cannons."

"That article was conjecture on my part," Keene admitted. "I'm starting to believe it was untrue."

"That's good to hear, but the damage has been done."

"I think I can repair that damage."

"Pardon my skepticism."

"So what's out there right now," Keene began in his slow, annoying manner, "is that the fifty cannons were not destroyed and you and your brother sent them south, thereby securing the riches."

"That about sums up your falsehood."

"I could go to the whole other extreme."

Confused, Ari asked, "And what would that be?"

"I could say that I now believe the cannons were destroyed, and even if they weren't you and your brother had nothing to do with sending them south because you are both abolitionists dedicated to preserving the Union."

"That might get him killed in Charleston."

"Perhaps," Keene said nonchalantly.

"What is it you're after, Keene?"

"I could write something in between."

"Such as?"

"I could say that I now believe the cannons were destroyed, but even if they weren't your brother would've had nothing to do with that in view of his true Southern sympathies. However, that would amount to a retraction of my earlier article. It would be damaging to my reputation, and I would need compensation for that."

"How much compensation?"

"From my perspective, it's a matter of how much the damage to my reputation is worth. For you, it's how much your brother's life is worth. All in all, I think five thousand dollars would be very fair."

"Good Lord," Ari said, shaking his head. "And that would be the end of it?"

"For me, yes."

"Someone else wants something? Who? What?"

"You'll be contacted. Do *we* have a deal?"

Ari hesitated. "Assuming your partner's demand is reasonable, we do. I'll wait till I hear it."

Chapter 44

It was eight in the evening when John Gage and Augustus Ward rode into Charleston. It was fortunate timing because Gus's old pass, now with a printed over current date, would not entitle him to be out after nine. Despite having time to spare they were careful, riding through the back alleys and seedy parts of the city. When they arrived at Crazy Bette's house, they stabled their horses in the barn, and even though it was nearly dark they waited another fifteen minutes until it was pitch black. Then they scurried across the courtyard and knocked on the back door.

Bette answered quickly, a bemused look on her face, for she had a feeling Gage would eventually convince Gus to run. "Come in," she said.

Surprised that she answered the door herself, Gage asked, "Where's Albert?"

"I've sent him home for the next few days," she said as the smile vanished, a sign that she no longer trusted anyone fully. She showed them to a kitchen table and served them leftover stew.

"We're headed to Ransom Pierce's factory buildings," Gage explained.

"Not tonight you're not," she said.

"Why not?"

"Gus needs a pass, a special pass."

"If we get caught inside the factory, it's not going to matter what kind of pass we have."

"True, but if you're stopped outside the factory it would matter. He needs a special pass, signed by the mayor, to be allowed along the wharves."

"That's right," Gus said. "I had one of them when I worked there befo'."

"I doubt we can get the mayor to sign a pass for you," Gage said. He looked at Bette and asked, "Any idea where we can get a fake one?"

"Now you're really diving into the deep water, John."

"You didn't answer my question."

"I know someone who's scoundrel enough. He's done it for me before. He'll charge a hefty price, though."

***

The next morning Bette made the arrangements, and when she returned to the house she reported the details: "He says he can make the pass today. It will cost fifty dollars, and he won't give it up until I pay him. I plan to do that at eight o'clock tonight. You two can meet me there, but don't come in. I'll bring the pass out to you."

That night Gage and Gus left the house ten minutes after Bette. When they arrived at the location, they found Bette's carriage parked just outside the building. The sign on the building read "Beckman Carriage Repair."

As each minute passed, the two men became increasingly concerned. There was no sign of Bette. After twenty minutes, Gage said, "I'm going in there."

"Miss Bette told us to wait here. She can take care of herself."

"No doubt, but I'm worried something's gone wrong," Gage said. He dismounted and slowly walked toward the building.

Gus followed him.

The two of them peered through small windows in the door. Bette was talking, perhaps arguing, with a man who stood behind a counter. The man was standing in a way that his back was towards the door. They watched for another five minutes while Bette continued to gesture in a way they had never seen before. Finally, the man behind the counter turned in the direction of the door.

"I know that man!" Gus said in a loud whisper. "He work for Ransom Pierce."

"You sure?"

"Yep, I seen him with Pierce."

"She's walked into a trap, Gus," and Gage put his hand on the doorknob.

"Wait," Gus said, and he grabbed Gage's hand. "She done this with this man befo'."

"So."

"She knows best."

"I know what I see."

"You not thinkin' with your head."

"What?"

Gus pulled him down away from the porch. "I mean you' lettin' your feelings for her make you decide to go in there. She a smart lady."

"She may be smart and still be in trouble."

"Think. What are you gonna do if you go in there? That man gonna know who you are. You gonna kill him? Because if you don't kill him, then you in trouble . . . we all in trouble."

Gage nodded just as the door opened. Bette came out, waving the pass in the air. "What are you two doing up here?" she asked. "I told you to wait out in the drive."

"*We*," said Gage, glancing at Gus who had a dubious look on his face, "were worried something bad had happened."

"And if you charged in there what were you going to do? He's one of Pierce's henchmen and he would know who you are."

Gus had a smile on his face.

A contrite Gage said, "But you were talking so long and gesturing wildly."

"Just conversation. Sometimes you need to build a relationship with people you do business with . . . even if it's unsavory types."

Gage gave Gus a quick nod and said, "Let's go." They set out for the wharves.

Chapter 45

Gus's guidance in scouting the Pierce warehouses was definitely needed. It was a huge complex of one-story wooden buildings, stretching along more than three city blocks. The buildings sat across the street from the Pierce wharf along the Ashley River, far to the north—even past the huge rice mills—as if in an effort to hide them from the rest of Charleston. Pierce's newspaper may serve as his mouthpiece, but here were the businesses that were the foundation of his financial success.

Gage looked all around. "A lot must go on here. Where do we start?"

"Those last buildings," Gus replied. "That's where we took the cannons."

They walked along a back alley in the dark, not daring to light the lanterns they carried. The sign over the third to the last building referred to it as Building G, but the door was locked, and that lock was too sophisticated for Gage to pick.

"Let's try the windows," Gage said. But they found that all the windows on that side of the building were locked.

"There's one way I know I can get in," Gage said, and he handed Gus his lantern.

"Where you goin'?"

"Up," and Gage climbed onto the brick ledge of one of the windows. The gutters above were sturdy. He grabbed hold of them and pulled himself up onto the roof. Ten feet away was a skylight window. As he expected, it had no lock and was easy to pull open. He slithered through the opening, held himself suspended in the air momentarily, and then dropped to the concrete floor. In the darkness, he was able to feel his way to the entryway door only bumping into one chair along the way.

Gage let Gus in, and they each lit their lanterns. "Gus, take yours to the other end of the building and put it down there. Let's not move them around much." All the windows were shuttered and a faint light showing through those shutters to the outside would not be suspicious, but any movement of that light would be.

Gus began walking toward the other end of the building and, as he did so, the full extent of Pierce's work came into view. The building was a single open room, about thirty feet wide by eighty feet long. Scattered everywhere were parts of cannons, as if the weapons had been disassembled for clandestine travel. In one area were ten barrels, in another area twenty wheels, and everywhere were wooden crates with nondescript markings.

"They're definitely getting ready to send these cannons somewhere," Gage said.

"Let's blow them up," Gus said.

"You got any explosives with you?"

"We need that?"

"Yeah, and I'm not even sure that would do any good on all this iron."

"Damn, I like fireworks."

"When did you see fireworks?"

"At Master Edwin's place. He put on a big show. He call it the Fourth of July."

Gage shook his head. Secessionists celebrating the birth of the nation. "Are these some of the cannons you moved before?" he asked.

"Looks like 'em." Then Gus pointed at the imprints.

"Yep, the Gage Ironworks name on them. But there's something different about these cannon barrels, Gus." Gage moved to the muzzle end of one of the barrels and began to feel about. "There are rings added around the ends of these barrels. I've never seen that before—maybe it's to reduce the heat. Let's get onto the next building."

As they were leaving, Gage unlocked one of the windows. "Just in case we want to come back." He also noticed some other peculiar things: containers of zinc, nitric acid, and large buckets of paint.

At Building H they were fortunate because one of the shuttered windows was unlocked. They quickly entered the building, and at this end they found tables with bolts of cloth and sewing materials scattered about.

Gus took his lantern to the far end. Small, wooden boxes were everywhere. Some were full and others looked like they were still being filled. "They makin' clothes now?"

"These aren't just clothes," Gage said in amazement. "They're uniforms—Northern uniforms!" He sorted through the stacks. "Look at these emblems: New York Fifteenth, Massachusetts Twenty-second."

"He makin' uniforms for Northerners?"

Gage shook his head. "More likely he's making uniforms for secessionists posing as Northerners."

After finding few answers, Gage said, "Let's go on to the next building."

"No, you need to go back there." Gus pointed to a small walled-off area in the far corner. "That's where the big man sit."

"You mean Ransom Pierce's office?"

Gus nodded.

Gage took the lantern into the office and sat down at the desk. Suddenly he heard a commotion just outside the paper-thin walls. A militia unit was passing by in the alley. For the first time it occurred to him the extent of the risk of being caught in here: it would mean certain death. The noise subsided; the soldiers had moved on.

The lower right-hand drawer of the desk was filled with letters that Gage quickly sorted through. Most were irrelevant, but then he stumbled upon one that was cryptic. Its authorship was intentionally withheld, and the only clue as to its source was the postmark of Annapolis, Maryland.

It was a letter of instructions and what Gage could decipher was chilling. It read:

> Send the children's clothing now because the children will soon arrive.
>
> Send the authorities rum, painted with olives.
>
> Do all this and that big white house will crumble and the bridges will open.
>
> We will create a Washington City that is as impregnable as Gibraltar—a Southern Man's Gibraltar.

Gage found other letters, presumably from the same sender, that were not so express but in each the same word was used: Gibraltar.

Gus had heard the militia unit as well, and their proximity caused him to want to end this caper now. "There ain't nothing important in the next buildin'," he assured Gage. They left and rode back to Bette's house, Gus clutching the fake pass in his pocket the whole way.

At Bette's house Gage sat back in a chair, thinking about the mysteries of the things they found in Ransom Pierce's buildings. As he contemplated, he watched Bette in the kitchen preparing dinner for the three of them. Even while cooking, this beautiful woman moved about with a gentle grace. Everything was fluid. Poise, that's it, he thought. She is always poised. Even while pretending in her Crazy Bette role, she remains poised.

Gus sensed what Gage was thinking. "She a special lady, ain't she?" he whispered.

Gage nodded, but he didn't take his eyes off Bette.

After dinner the three of them discussed the findings. "Ransom Pierce values money above all else," Bette said, "but he's not making uniforms for Northerners. There's another purpose here."

"Yes, that's true," Gage replied, "and I know what their plan is."

"What is it?" Bette asked.

"They intend to take Washington City from within."

"How would they manage that?"

"Secessionists disguised as Northern soldiers will take the cannons into Washington from Maryland under the ruse of being there to defend the city. Then, probably in the middle of the night, they will reposition them and use them against the White House, the artillery positions defending the bridges of the Potomac, the armory, and who knows what else. Troops from Virginia will stream across the bridges and seize the city."

"Oh, my Lord!"

"But I can't figure out the second sentence of the letter. It's disguised, as if written in some kind of code."

Bette read the sentence out loud: "'Send the authorities rum, painted with olives'. Certainly a message being sent, but what could it mean?"

Gus looked at the others earnestly. "Mrs. Spence always say that when I look for the meaning of somethin' written I should look at it in pieces."

"Interesting notion," Bette said. "John, write it out just as you saw it."

Gage did so, even to the point of leaving the small gaps that he saw between the letters in the word "authorities."

Send the au thor ities rum, paint ed with olives.

Bette reached for the piece of paper, and as she did so Gage saw her gold ring next to the word authorities.

"That's it!" Gage shouted. "Those rings! They've got gold, and they're painting over it—with an olive green color."

"How did you arrive at that?" Bette asked.

"Put the letters together. Aurum—the Latin word for gold. The rims of the cannon barrels, with the olive green-colored paint on them, are hiding gold. He's sending that gold to Maryland along with the cannons and Northern uniforms."

"It could be the missing gold from the customs house," Bette said.

"Yes, you're right. That explains why that one sentence is in code. It's the one sentence that could get Pierce in trouble with Southerners. He's stolen their gold, and it looks like it's been melted down and hidden in those rings."

"What can be done?"

"I want to be sure," he said, looking at Gus. "We've got to go back there tomorrow night."

"To blow it up?" Gus said with glee.

"Have you found any explosives in the last two hours?"

"Let me snoop around tomorrow, and I'll find some."

***

The next night, using the window Gage had unlocked the night before, Gage and Gus reentered Building G. Gage went straight to one of the cannon barrels and scraped away the heavy paint on the ring. He soon had his confirmation: the ring was made of gold, alloyed lightly with some other metal, and painted over with an olive green color to match the barrel.

They continued to search Building G, unaware that Ransom Pierce along with seven soldiers were on their way to the wharf, and were now only a block away. With the window cracked open slightly, Gus heard them. "Militiamen comin' our way," he said to Gage in a hushed voice.

They put out their lanterns. Light from outside lamps came through the windows allowing them to see their way to the door. But Pierce and his men were approaching that door from the other side. The door handle rattled.

Gus looked over at Gage for guidance.

"Gus," Gage whispered, and he pointed to a back door out ahead of them. Gus tripped over a box before recovering.

"You four check out back," Pierce commanded, "and you three come with me."

Gage and Gus went out the back door just as Pierce was coming in the side door. They were barely outside when they heard the four soldiers coming at them from around the far corner of the building. They hid behind trash containers.

Inside, Pierce carried his lantern as he walked through the building, looking for anything out of place. He soon found it. There on the floor, beneath one of the cannon barrels, were the paint shavings Gage had carved from the gold ring. Not wanting the soldiers to see what he had found, Pierce called out, "Collect the rest of the men and head down to the wharf. I'll be with you shortly."

When the soldiers at the back of the building suddenly turned and left, Gage and Gus couldn't believe their luck. They waited a few minutes before leaving, but they did so just as Pierce looked out a back window. He was able to see the face of one of the intruders, brightly lit under an outdoor gas lamp. He recognized John Gage.

Upon arriving back at Bette's house, Gus was still shaking. He had never been through something like that, but in some strange way he found it exhilarating. "That was a load of fun," he said.

"Glad to hear that because we're going to do it all again soon."

"It ain't that much fun."

"I promise a new wrinkle next time." He turned to Bette and asked, "How much kerosene do you keep around here?"

"Plenty, but what are you planning on doing with it?"

"We're going to start a bonfire—a big bonfire that will put Mr. Pierce out of business."

"Ah, fireworks," Gus said.

"Of sorts. Pierce has probably already shipped out most of what he's sending to Maryland. But perhaps we can get rid of a few cannon barrels and those Northern uniforms that are still around."

"John, think about this," Bette said. "If Pierce suspects you at all—"

"He does. I'm certain of it. I saw him peering out the window, looking straight at me while I was under a lamp."

"He could have you arrested."

"He's not about to do that."

"Why not?"

"Because I now know the truth about him, and he can't risk having that told."

"You mean his plan to help rebels in Maryland?"

"No, his theft of the gold that South Carolina claims. There's no gold mined around here, and the only gold that is missing is the gold that was on hand when the Charleston Customs House was taken."

"So, he's not going to tell on you for fear you would tell on him. A nice little standoff. But if you told the Charleston people, you would be a hero to the Confederacy."

"If I tell them, the Confederacy will keep both the gold and the cannons and put it all to their use. Pierce obviously has a way to get all of it to Maryland. I'll let him send it. We'll grab all of it in Maryland."

"If you can get out of here."

"I . . . we have to get to Maryland as soon as possible," Gage said emphatically. "Washington could be attacked any day, and I'll be damned if cannons made by Gage Ironworks are going to be used in that attack."

He didn't identify "we," and Bette didn't want to ask. Instead she said, "You can't just leave abruptly, or the authorities will question that. You need to plan your departure and say your goodbyes."

"That makes sense."

"I believe there is a ship heading north in three days."

"How do we get Gus on that ship?"

"That will take a lot of cash."

"You've done it before?"

She nodded. "I know someone at the harbor who can make the arrangements, assuming he knows the right people on the ship. He may need to parcel out the money to four or five people."

"Can you book passage for three?"

She looked at him sadly. Then with tears in her eyes, she said, "John, this is my home."

Chapter 46

Gage had a sense that his recent absences had cast suspicion his way. When he called on Frank Talbot the next morning, Talbot was not a happy man. But Gage couldn't discern whether he was the cause, or the man was simply preoccupied with the prospect of war.

"Where have you been, Mr. Gage?" Talbot asked in a remote sort of way. Seated at his desk, he barely looked up at Gage.

"Just enjoying the delights of the city."

"Rumor has it that one of those delights has been a beautiful married woman."

"Hardly," Gage said quite honestly, for he no longer considered Jacqueline a delight. "Rumors can be misleading."

"John, your disappearances have made my job difficult since I am the one assigned to keep track of your whereabouts."

"I'm sorry, Frank, but I'm a journalist. I need to observe things."

"Well, your observing has been observed."

"How's that?"

"You were noticed studying the floating iron battery."

Gage chuckled. "You mean the sinking floating battery. It's merely a curiosity. Beauregard would have to be crazy to try to make use of it in battle—it's a death trap."

Talbot waved a hand in the air. "I understand, forgive me. It's Sumter that has me bothered. There's a rumor that a Northern armada is on the way, and its mission goes far beyond resupplying the fort. It's said that they will have two thousand soldiers ready to occupy Charleston."

"Charleston has three or four times that many soldiers to oppose such a force."

"Not if fifty thousand slaves join the Union soldiers."

***

Gage left Talbot and stopped in a nearby jewelry store. He needed to find a nice chain to hold Little Georgie's two cent piece.

As a clerk was showing Gage a metallic chain, Ransom Pierce suddenly appeared from a back room.

"Mr. Pierce, you seem to be everywhere."

"As do you, Gage," Pierce said with disdain.

"Coming from the back room of the store, you must know this place well."

"I should, I own it."

"Yes, I've learned that you dabble in gold *surreptitiously*."

Pierce shot him a menacing look.

"Of course, I just meant operating this establishment under a name other than your own."

"And you've never operated under a name other than your own?"

"What do you mean by that?"

"I receive all the Washington newspapers, including your *Washington Observer*."

"You're well-read, so what?"

"That Oliver Blanton article that ridiculed me appeared two days earlier in your newspaper here than it did in Washington."

"There are often delays in printing at the *Washington Observer*."

"Bullshit, that article originated here. Make your purchase, Gage, and get out!"

Gage smiled, and laid down his money. As he was leaving, he looked back and said, "Of all people, Pierce, you shouldn't be complaining about any harm done by a newspaper."

***

The next stop Gage made also had nothing to do with demonstrating his presence in the city. He went to see Jacqueline, and he found her at the apartment she and her husband kept in Charleston. When she answered his knock on the door, she threw her arms around him and pulled him close in what seemed like true affection.

Gage backed away, determined to resist.

"What's wrong?" she asked.

He pulled back her hair to reveal the tiny scar. "What did you use to cut your neck?"

She didn't deny it. Instead, she said, "This can all be ours, Johnny."

Gage laughed, so she maneuvered in a different direction—something close to the truth. "You should know that people are watching you."

"How would you know that?"

"Because I'm supposed to be one of those people. My husband, at the insistence of Ransom Pierce, is out to prove you're a spy. He thinks that would make him a hero with the right people."

"I suppose it would."

In order to avoid his eyes, she made a small pirouette before delivering a threat: "One wrong word from me could provide him that evidence."

"No doubt you are good at inventing things."

She turned back towards him. "Oh, Johnny, you know I wouldn't do such a thing. I'm just trying to get you to face reality. War is coming. You could stay here, and we could have the plantations. I see some real business opportunities from the war."

"You are quite the schemer."

"A woman has to fight to survive, especially in the world we'll soon have. Just get rid of Ned, Johnny. That's all I'm asking of you now."

"In Philadelphia you didn't leave me because of my bad publicity, or that your fine Southern family couldn't withstand the scandal. There was no fine Southern family. You left me because I was pushed out of Gage Ironworks. You left me because you thought I was no longer wealthy. You latched onto Edwin because you thought he was wealthy. Once you realized that Ned's position threatened your eventual status, you decided you wanted him out of the way."

"We could have it all, John. Just you and me."

Gage turned and walked out.

***

That night Gage and Gus returned to Pierce's buildings only to find that the Northern uniforms and remaining cannons were gone.

"Damn!" Gage said. "They're probably already headed to Maryland."

"We can still have our bonfire?" Gus asked hopefully.

A frustrated Gage nodded. "Let's get to it."

They drenched the floor of Building G with kerosene in the area of the leftover paint. Starting the fire from outside the door would leave a telltale sign that the fire had been set. Instead they ended the trail of kerosene just inside the unlocked window.

They did the same thing in Building H, but they ran out of fuel at the point of Pierce's office. "This will do," Gage said.

The two men then stood at the opposite ends of the breezeway that connected the two buildings. When Gage said "Now" they each lit a handkerchief and threw it inside the window.

They didn't wait around for the result. Quickly they walked east three blocks where they had hitched their horses. They smiled as they looked back at the orange glow coming from the buildings.

Within ten minutes they were back at Bette's house but, once there, Gage said, "We're going to have to find a better place to hide you away, Gus. I have a feeling things are going to get much more treacherous."

Chapter 47

For weeks it had been a strange situation at Fort Sumter. Food supplies from Charleston to the fort had occasionally been shut off by Confederate authorities, but never the mail. Late in March, however, that changed. Gage got wind of it from two sources. First, from a friend who happened to be at the Charleston post office when Fort Sumter's outgoing mail was seized. The second came later in the day from a friend of Major Anderson, a Charleston resident, who said to Gage, "The major has requested that the outgoing mail be returned to Sumter, but the governor denied that request. He wondered if you might intercede." The man also hinted that there was a letter from Major Anderson that could prove damaging, but he didn't elaborate.

This provided Gage with a good excuse for visiting Governor Pickens and General Beauregard. He was anxious to see if their attitude toward him had changed, anxious to learn whether Ransom Pierce had managed to turn them against him.

When he arrived at the governor's office, Gage said to a clerk that he had come to see the governor with a request. He was soon escorted into the office where the governor, General Beauregard, and Judge Andrew McGrath huddled around a desk covered with mail.

"Your constituents appear to be unhappy, Governor," Gage said.

That lighthearted comment drew little laughter. The three men looked stupefied as they focused on the unopened mail, as if looking at a giant jigsaw puzzle with pieces missing. In actuality, they didn't like what they were thinking of doing.

"Opening their mail would not be a gentlemanly thing to do," Gage said.

Judge Magrath, whose recent resignation from the federal bench had caused quite the noise, was thinking of bigger things. "It would also be a federal offense."

Gage chuckled. "Gentlemen, if you attack Fort Sumter, you face far greater charges than mail tampering."

"What is it that brings you here, Mr. Gage?"

"This very thing, Governor. I have a request: if you're not going to allow the Sumter mail to go through at least return it to the fort."

"Is there something in here that concerns you, Gage?" the judge asked.

"How would I know what's in there? I'm just suggesting that it would be the honorable thing to do."

"In peacetime perhaps so, John, but we are now on a war footing," Beauregard replied.

"Go ahead, Governor," Magrath urged. "Open Anderson's letters."

Once a name was put to it, things became even more delicate. Prior to that it was just an assortment of generic mail. Now it was Major Anderson's private correspondence.

The three men continued to stare at the mail. Gage stared at them.

Finally, the governor picked up two of Anderson's letters, both written by the major the day before. He broke the seal of the first one and opened it. Directed to Secretary of War Cameron, it was a brief soldierly response to Cameron's letter a few days earlier in which Cameron had stated that a relief expedition led by Captain Gustavas Fox would soon be on its way to Fort Sumter.

The second letter, however, was written to Colonel Lorenzo Thomas, Adjutant General of the Army, a friend of Anderson's. It was not soldierly. It was Anderson's catharsis, and in it he called Fox's expedition a "scheme" that will be "disastrous to all concerned." He warned that he did not have enough oil left to keep light in one lantern for a single night, so there would be no way to guide the ships to the fort. It would definitely cause the start of the war, Anderson said, a war that he had been so desperate to avoid and that his superiors in Washington had told him to avoid.

The governor glared at Gage as if asking Gage if he knew about this "scheme."

"All I think you've confirmed, gentlemen, is that the major seeks to avoid war," Gage said.

"And that an *armada* is headed our way," the governor replied.

"That's a big word, Governor. I hardly think the North could assemble enough ships at this point to constitute an armada."

"Time will tell but thank you, Mr. Gage, for your input and while I respect your request that the mail be returned, as you can see that request has been denied."

Gage took the governor's statement as his cue to leave. He shook hands with everyone and walked out.

Once the door closed, the governor said, "General, we will soon find out about your friend Mr. Gage. He is being followed as we speak."

"What does it matter?" Beauregard asked. "We learned yesterday, directly from Mr. Lincoln's emissaries, that a relief expedition is on its way."

"Yes, but Gage doesn't know we know that. He thinks we just discovered something with this letter. Let's see what he does with this new information."

"Would you not expect him to report it to the North?" Beauregard said.

"Only if he's acting as a spy," Magrath said. Then the judge mentioned something he had just noticed: "There's something inconsistent with what Lincoln's emissaries said and the relief expedition described in Anderson's letter. Lincoln's message said the ships will only resupply Fort Sumter with food, not soldiers."

"A very clever ploy on Lincoln's part," the governor replied. "If we fire on ships carrying food to starving men, we will look like the aggressors, the ones who started the war."

"That's why we need to release Anderson's letter publicly, Magrath said. "He's critical of the Fox mission—he says bringing more soldiers to Sumter will be what causes the start of the war."

They all concurred. The Anderson letter would be sent to newspapers in both the North and South.

"But we also now know they're sending warships," the governor said. "We need to get our victory before those ships arrive."

"We will soon have it," Beauregard replied, "I've been ordered to demand the fort's surrender."

"And if they refuse?"

"My orders are to reduce it."

Chapter 48

Three men followed John Gage when he left the governor's office. They watched with field glasses as he entered Bette's home. Of course they had no way of knowing what was being said inside. They hoped to get the answer from the next person to leave the house. That occurred thirty minutes later when Bette came out and began walking north.

Two of the detectives followed her while the other stayed behind in case Gage soon left. Bette walked up King Street, her pursuers about fifty feet behind. At one point she sensed she was being followed. She stopped and pretended to look in a store window. But when she glanced back, the two detectives had already ducked into another store.

Bette walked another block to one of the few stores in the city with a telegraph. She knew the operator, Walter Tobin, a young man opposed to secession but, like so many, afraid to voice his opinion. Bette thought that sending a message like this was one way Walter could voice his opinion, a way to help stop the madness that had seized Charleston.

Bette smiled pleasantly at Walter as she entered the store. When he stood to greet her, she towered over him for he was a minion of a man. "Walter, I need you to send a telegram," Bette said, and she handed him a note with a message to Colonel Thomas, the army's adjutant general. It read:

Officials in Charleston know of the Fox expedition.

Beware of shipments landing in Maryland from Charleston.

Fences are down on the flat ground of Tibet. The Aurum is sprinkled from here to eternity.

J. Gage

"Oh, my," Walter said, nervously adjusting his bifocals as he read the message. "Sent from here, Southerners might say this is treasonous."

"No, Walter, Mr. Gage is just trying to prevent a war. He's telling them not to launch the naval expedition."

"I see that in the first sentence, but this second sentence sounds like a spy sending a secret message. And the third sentence is gibberish." Again he toyed with his glasses for a moment. "No, to be correct, it's not gibberish to someone who knows the code used."

She sat down next to him and leaned over. Her fragrant perfume was overwhelming. "We don't want a war, do we, Walter?"

"Of course not."

She smiled at him and placed her left hand atop his right hand. Walter momentarily lost track of their discussion. He recovered and sat in silence thinking for a good thirty seconds. Yes, he concluded, sending this message might help prevent a war. He abruptly stood and walked over to lock the back door just ten feet away.

As Walter sat down at the telegraph and began to formulate the message, the locked door began to rattle. Perhaps just a customer looking for a shortcut, Walter thought. The noise stopped. Then came an incessant knocking that Walter still did not answer. The knocking ended, only to be followed by a blast that showered wooden splinters everywhere as a huge man came through what was left of the door. He held a gun and shouted, "Stay as you are!"

An older, white-haired man with steely eyes then entered the front door, locking it before walking back to the others. "My name is Carson," he said with a heavy Southern drawl. He was obviously in charge because he immediately told the big man, "Put your weapon away, Greer." Then he added in a sinister way, "I don't think these people will cause us trouble ... unless they refuse to cooperate."

Walter stood up and gallantly said, "This is my store. I am ordering you to leave at once."

Greer seized Walter by the left arm and flung the little man against the wall. Bette rushed to his side to help him up. With one hand she grabbed him along the right elbow and her other hand grabbed his right hand. As she did so, she took Gage's note from his right hand and deftly slipped it into the top of her dress.

But Carson was not so easily fooled. "Hand over the note that you so expertly hid away, Miss Downing."

"Whatever do you mean?"

"I will quite gladly retrieve it myself if need be."

"You are a cad, sir." She pulled out the note from her dress and handed it to him.

After reading it, he grabbed Bette by the arm and said, "You're coming with us."

"What about him?" Greer asked of Walter.

"You stay in good health, Mr. Tobin, so you can testify against her. You give that testimony and you will maintain your good health."

Then Carson looked at Greer and said, "I'll take her to the city jail for now. You go pick up John Gage."

***

Gage went willingly when he was arrested. With no place to hide, what else could he do? He spent the night in the small jail at Fort Moultrie, and the following afternoon General Beauregard summoned him. Outside the door to Beauregard's office, Gage encountered former Senator Wigfall, resplendent in a fresh military uniform decorated with a red sash about his waist. A gleaming steel sword hanging from his right side clanged against his black cane.

"Your new home, Senator?" Gage inquired.

"Colonel now, Gage. And my new home is merely my old one."

"You've been quite busy."

A perfect entree to Wigfall's next boast. "Yes, have you seen the soldiers now manning Castle Pinckney? All one hundred from a recruiting station I established in Baltimore."

"I'm sure those young men must constantly cheer your name, confined as they now are to a rock with Sumter's guns aimed their way."

"I've been busy with many other matters as well over the last few months."

"Yes, I'm aware and all while under the pretense of still being a United States senator."

"Well, neither of us is pretending anymore are we, Gage?"

Wigfall chose not to attend the meeting. Perhaps he wasn't invited. But one person who insisted on being allowed in was Ransom Pierce. When he heard Gage was meeting with General Beauregard, he rushed to the general's headquarters and demanded entry.

An apprehensive lieutenant tried to explain that he couldn't let him in: "Mr. Gage has been arrested."

"I know that, but what specifically did he do?"

"I shouldn't be telling you this, Mr. Pierce, but it's believed Mr. Gage was attempting to send messages to Northern officials . . . messages contrary to the interests of the Confederacy."

"All the more reason I should be allowed in," Pierce insisted. "I should be consulted on this matter."

Realizing Pierce wasn't going away, the lieutenant knocked on the door and explained the situation to the general.

"Let him in, but only briefly," the general said.

Now the two men, each holding deadly secrets about the other, stood before a man whom they would not disclose those secrets to.

"Why is this traitor in your custody?" Pierce demanded.

"Why do you ask, Pierce?"

"South Carolina has arrested him. This should be no concern of the Confederacy."

"It is a concern of the Confederacy . . . a legitimate concern."

"He probably still has powder burns on his hands from torching my buildings."

"And what evidence do you have of that?"

"None, as yet, but I feel certain that he and his escaped slave did it."

Gage held out his hands and smiled. "Clean as can be."

Pierce scoffed and said, "May I talk with you in private about this, General?"

The lieutenant took Gage out of the room. Surely, Pierce won't disclose what he knows, Gage thought. If he does, he knows I'll disclose my secrets about him. But then Gage remembered this man has a remarkable ability to spin a set of facts. How might he spin this to explain away his theft?

Inside the room Pierce pressed his case vehemently: "Gage should be executed as a spy, swiftly and publicly, General. So too should the escaped slave he has harbored."

"There is nothing that the slave, Augustus Ward, can be charged with right now, other than being a runaway. As for Gage, I hardly have grounds for treating him as a spy."

"They've tried to commence an insurrection."

Beauregard chuckled. "An insurrection within an insurrection—an interesting notion. Why do you care so much about this, Pierce?"

"You're not from here. You don't understand the—"

"Fear?"

"—apprehension of our people. I know for a fact that the escaped slave has met with several local Negras. And why hasn't Gage returned home? He's obviously a Northern plant."

"Him remaining here hardly proves he's a spy."

"You speak only for the Confederacy, sir," Pierce said with a sneer. "These two have committed crimes against South Carolina, and I'll make sure our new republic punishes them appropriately." Then he stormed out.

"He's a dangerous man," Beauregard said when Gage was brought back in.

"I'm glad you recognize that."

"Don't get me wrong. The Confederacy taking over South Carolina's position in this matter would be controversial. Here we are having just seceded on the basis of the rights of an individual state to make its own laws. How would it look for the Confederacy to overrule one of South Carolina's first determinations? It would be a bad outcome for our new coalition."

"Even worse for Gus and me."

The two men sat down at a small table. Beauregard poured two glasses of a cabernet.

The general seemed to want a distraction from war, but Gage refused to give it to him. "Have you thought of how different this war might be? I mean friend fighting friend."

"I think about that all the time. War is after all murder that is licensed by the carrying of a flag. That may justify it on the outside, but internally we can reconcile it only by not knowing the person you're trying to kill. Obviously, we won't have that here."

"Did you find that to be true in Mexico?" Gage asked.

"Actually, I engaged in very little fighting there. We engineers were busy trying to discover the right routes to outmaneuver the enemy."

"Then you've never really commanded men in battle, have you?"

"Not really. I've never been given the command I've deserved."

"You've got a top command now."

Beauregard nodded, a look of some despair on his face.

"You may order the shot fired that starts the bloodiest war in the history of mankind."

"Yes, we are at the cliff's edge," the general said softly.

Chapter 49

"John William Gage and Augustus Ward, the latter charged in absentia because his whereabouts is unknown, you stand charged with crimes against the republic," bellowed Colonel Alexander Drummond, chairman of the three-member tribunal hearing the case.

Colonels were everywhere these days, usually friends that the governor had appointed. Drummond had been one for only three days. His military experience consisted of twenty years earlier having organized a group of ten men to chase a few lost Cherokee Indians back across the Georgia state line.

Was this hastily convened tribunal legal? No one knew since laws were still being created under the new South Carolina constitution. The governor sanctioned it quietly, then looked the other way.

The Colonel stood up from his chair and adjusted the flaming red sash that drooped about his body. The sashes had been made to fit the majority of the colonels who were usually rotund. Drummond, slight of build—almost sickly-looking—found it difficult to keep the sash from falling to the floor.

Drummond turned the proceeding over to the prosecutor, Thomas Kemp, a bespectacled, redheaded man barely thirty years old. Kemp knew this was his chance to make a name for himself. As he stood to speak for the first time, he didn't face the tribunal members or the defendant. Instead, he spoke to the one thousand people sitting as an audience in Institute Hall.

It was then that Gage realized the severity of his situation. This was theater, and he was to be the prosecutor's foil. With Ransom Pierce the only civilian member of the tribunal, a conviction was virtually assured.

"For the sake of expediency," Prosecutor Kemp began, "I call as my first witness the defendant John Gage. It is my understanding that he has waived his right against self-incrimination, is that not correct?"

"Against my recommendations, yes," said Albert King, legal counsel appointed for the defendants, although he understood Gage's reasoning for doing so. Gage believed his public testimony would bring notoriety of the trial in the North. King was such a highly respected member of the Charleston bar that his opposition to secession was tolerated by Charlestonians. But not the crowd in attendance here. They were from all over the state and would be quite willing to see King sink along with the defendants.

"Please state your full name, Mr. Gage, and where you reside."

"John William Gage, and I currently reside in a small hoosegow on Sullivan's Island."

The audience laughed, the prosecutor glowered. "Very clever. Where did you reside prior to coming to Charleston?"

"Washington City."

"And what was your occupation there?"

"I was a columnist for the *Washington Observer* newspaper."

"And during the last few months in that position you wrote several articles in support of the Southern cause, did you not?"

"That's your interpretation."

"Did you believe those things you wrote?" Kemp thundered with a glance toward the audience.

"I believed then, as I do now, that a peaceful solution should be sought."

"We all believe in that. Did you believe Lincoln should let the South go peacefully?"

"No."

"Aha. So when you wrote the words 'Let the South Go' those were not your true feelings. Were they written with the intention of prompting the people of Charleston to invite you to come here?"

"Yes."

"And you've come here to observe and report your observations back to the North?"

"As a reporter I have naturally engaged in certain fact-finding."

That drew a titter from the audience, and just as the prosecutor was ready to label the purpose of Gage's visit that of spying, he was interrupted by

Ransom Pierce. "May I interject a question or two, Mr. Prosecutor?"

Kemp was miffed, but grudgingly relented. What a break, Gage thought, because Pierce had broken the prosecutor's grandiose moment. But Gage wasn't prepared for what Pierce had coming.

"Mr. Gage, in your work at the Washington newspaper, did you also write columns under any fictitious names?"

Gage coughed lightly. "Yes, I did."

"Oliver Blanton, perhaps?"

"Yes."

Now the prosecutor jumped back in. "So *you* wrote the articles that forced a Southern secretary of war to resign?"

"Yes."

"My, my, Mr. Gage you are a deceptive fellow. So this ruse that you put on as a person sympathetic to the Southern cause was still maintained at the time of your arrest?"

"I suppose you could say that."

"And the information you were passing back to the North, in code I might add, was intended to hurt the Southern cause and aid the North?"

"It was intended to help stop an unlawful rebellion."

"That we'll get into later. For now, let's just focus on the message you sent," Kemp said as he began positioning a five-foot-tall stanchion on one side of the courtroom. He then walked slowly back to his desk where he grabbed a thin, wooden placard. He looked at Gage momentarily, and again took a leisurely stroll back to the stanchion as if hoping his delay would unnerve Gage.

But when the prosecutor placed the placard on the stanchion there was only one person in the room who was unnerved, and it wasn't Gage. Ransom Pierce's face suddenly went ashen.

Displayed on the cardboard was Gage's message in three parts:
- Officials in Charleston know of the Fox expedition.
- Beware of shipments landing in Maryland from Charleston.
- Fences are down on the flat ground of Tibet. The Aurum is sprinkled from here to eternity.

J. Gage

The prosecutor stared at the placard while addressing Gage: "Now, Mr. Gage, the meanings of the first two parts of your message are clear. But you used a code in the final part, didn't you?"

"Perhaps so," Gage said with a wry smile.

Pierce gnawed at his fingernails, then looked over at Gage who, sitting with his hands folded under his chin, stared back for a good five seconds.

Pierce looked away. Surely Gage wouldn't disclose the gold theft, Pierce thought. But there it was: Aurum, the Latin word for gold. Fearing the worst, Pierce needed to come up with something to stop this.

"And is the third part of this message related to the second part?" Kemp asked.

Pierce continually clasped and unclasped his hands, only interrupting that practice occasionally to take a quick bite at one of his fingernails.

"You might say that," Gage responded.

"And in this part you warn—

"Mr. Prosecutor," a desperate Pierce interrupted. "I don't believe it's wise to have the defendant decipher that message because it was stopped. To decipher it publicly would be tantamount to sending it for him."

"A very good point, Mr. Pierce," Colonel Drummond said. "Besides, the defendant has already acknowledged it was sent to aid the North."

"Very well," Kemp said. "And Miss Elizabeth Downing and the defendant Augustus Ward joined in the conspiracy to send this information, didn't they?"

"There was no such conspiracy. Miss Downing merely delivered a message for me. She had no idea whether the message was in support of or against what you call the Southern cause."

"We'll save Miss Downing's actions for another proceeding. And how about the defendant Ward?"

"He had nothing to do with sending messages."

"But he did involve himself in helping you acquire the information that you tried to send to the North?"

"Where is the crime in that?"

"Any act of rebellion against lawful authority is a crime."

Gage smiled. "My point exactly. How can this tribunal be lawful since it was created by people in rebellion against lawful authority?"

"Your true colors are shining brightly, Mr. Gage. And in support of the North you sent messages such as these?"

"Is that a crime?"

"When two sides are in a time of war, yes."

"What war? There is no war."

The enthusiasm of the audience was dashed. The befuddled prosecutor could only say, "You're engaging in semantics now, Mr. Gage." He changed the subject and for the next two hours honed in on Gus's escape from Ashland, aided by Gage, and Gus's subsequent involvement in spying.

At times the questioning turned into what Colonel Drummond called an "esoteric debate" between Gage and prosecutor Kemp.

When Gage stated he and Gus had merely engaged in freedoms guaranteed by the United States Constitution, Kemp naturally argued that there is no longer any United States Constitution in South Carolina. "The new Confederate Constitution clearly permits slavery," Kemp said.

Gage shook his head. "No, I am speaking now of a fundamental moral principle, so elegantly expressed in the Declaration of Independence—of which South Carolina was a principal contributor to—that all men are created equal."

"Then you consider Mr. Ward, a colored man, your equal?"

"No, in all honesty, I believe him to be a superior man to me."

Gage may have been winning over the audience, but none of it mattered. The die was cast before the trial even began. The guilty verdict was expected, but the punishment came as a shock:

> "Death by hanging," Colonel Drummond said with a serious tone in his voice. "That sentence shall be carried out at dawn five days from today at Fort Moultrie."

Chapter 50

"I don't really blame you for what you did, John," Beauregard said. "I would've done the same in your position."

"You mean my jousting with the prosecutor?"

The general laughed as he sat down on a stool in Gage's jail cell at Fort Moultrie. "You did get your licks in."

"A lot of good it did."

"It certainly dampened the enthusiasm of the crowd."

Gage looked up. "Can I assume you recognize the absurdity of that trial?"

"The nature of the proceeding is irrelevant. I'm only concerned with the outcome."

"As am I. That hanging business doesn't sit well with me. But, unlike me, you have to worry about the aftermath of our hanging. You have a predicament."

"How is that?"

"You must now navigate a delicate situation. If I'm hung, it won't matter whether South Carolina or the Confederacy did it. You will all be viewed as barbarians by the North, probably by England and France as well. It might also be deemed the first act of war."

Beauregard was suddenly silent. Gage was right. To hang a private citizen as a spy for actions taken when there was not yet a war could have serious repercussions. And this private citizen, a popular journalist and brother to Congressman Aramis Gage, was famous.

Still, Beauregard continued his posturing: "Perhaps true, but the citizens of Charleston are in an uproar. They now know a Northern fleet is headed to Charleston, but they don't know whether it's to bring supplies, reinforce Sumter, or bombard the city. Given that last possibility, they're inclined to follow the lead of Ransom Pierce."

Gage leaned back, striking a relaxed pose. It was just three days until his scheduled execution, but now he seemed to have the upper hand. "I just realized something. If the South hangs me, I become famous in the North as a patriot—"

"As a spy."

"As a patriot! What better way to have my name unsullied."

"You won't be around to enjoy it. Good God, John, now you sound like you want to die a martyr."

"You will end up putting my name, perhaps even my picture, on every enlistment poster in the North."

Beauregard shook his head in frustration. "Why did you have to make an enemy out of Ransom Pierce?"

"I'm not even sure how that happened."

"Well, he's been out to get you. You saw that at the trial. He bullied his way onto that tribunal."

Gage resisted the temptation to tell Beauregard why Pierce was so ardent. If Beauregard knew the truth, he might be able to safeguard the ship's arrival in Annapolis. Instead, Gage asked, "Is that tribunal even legal?"

"Who knows? Things are in such flux now, no one knows who's in charge. The normal ruling authority has been fractured. Now it's an uneasy triumvirate of elected local officials, Confederate officers, and popular private citizens like Pierce."

"Why don't you show them that you're the one in charge."

"And how would I do that?"

"By letting Gus and me sail out of here."

"That I can't do . . . I'm inclined not to intervene at all."

Gage looked down at the floor momentarily before training his eyes directly on Beauregard. "General, let Bette Downing go."

"I can't, John. That one is clear. She's a South Carolina citizen. They won't let me decide her fate."

"She is just a delusional woman who fell under my spell."

Beauregard laughed again. "No one in Charleston believes her act anymore."

"Will you let me see her?"

"I can't do that either," Beauregard said, shaking his head. "Why did you choose a woman to send that telegram anyway?"

"She has some persuasive powers that I don't possess."

"Sounds like that persuasiveness extends to you as well."

"No doubt."

As Beauregard stood to leave, he said, "I can't get anyone to even consider a different penalty for you and Augustus Ward unless I have him in custody. I need you to tell me where he is."

"I can't do that."

"You must do that."

"Why is he a part of your predicament?"

"His situation is all local. People here are demanding that he be executed as an example to others. Even his owner, Walker, supports that view."

"I can't do that to him."

"Think about it, John. Eventually he's going to be found. If he's not with you, he'll be hung for sure. Unlike your death, no one in the North would hear about his."

Gage's head dropped as he thought it through. Beauregard's argument was sound. It was the only hope for Gus. Without looking up, he said despondently, "He cleans stables at the Hobson Livery—sleeps there at night too."

***

Within three hours Gus was found and taken to the Fort Moultrie jail where he rejoined Gage. Their initial discussion was not an easy one.

"I was livin' like a free man."

"Did you like it?"

"Yep, I had good work at the livery. How did they find me?"

"I told them where to look."

"You had me put in jail?"

Gage nodded.

"Why'd you do that? You just want company on the scaffold?"

"It was the only way I could get you out of Charleston and back to Maryland. That's what I promised to do."

"This ain't Maryland," Gus said, looking around at the tiny jail cell.

"If you're out there on your own, they will eventually find you and hang you. No one will care . . . except me. I'm a pawn that they're afraid to hang. If you're with me, you have a chance."

"Oh, you got a plan?"

"I'm working on it."

"Better work damn fast. I hear they gonna hang us in three days."

Chapter 51

With Charleston friends and neighbors constantly visiting the militia camps, rumors spread like wildfire among the soldiers. When Jack Spence heard the description of two Northern "spies" locked up in the Fort Moultrie jail, he was certain they were his friends. On the evening of the tenth, just after dark, he went looking for them.

What he found was a jail without guards. Gage might be notorious in Charleston, but he seemed a mere curiosity to the soldiers at the fort. They paid little attention to the small jail, and only occasionally went to check on the prisoners.

The only occupied cells were at the far end of the jail where Gage and Gus sat on stools in one cell while an inebriated soldier slept one off in the cell next to them.

When Jack came in, both prisoners jumped up to greet him. The youngster had new glasses, provided by the Confederate army. They were bigger than his prior ones and made him look older and wiser than his sixteen years.

With both hands on the iron bars, Gage asked, "Jack, do you know where Bette is?"

"I've heard that Miss Bette is locked in a room at the Moultrie House."

"No telling what they plan to do with her. I suppose she's in a safe place for now."

"I don't think so, sir. That hotel could be in the line of fire, and I'm afraid war is going to break out any minute."

"What makes you think so?"

"There's a Northern ship right off the coast."

"Probably just another rumor."

"No, sir, that ain't a rumor. I seen it. A warship, not real big—maybe a couple hundred feet long. Someone said it's called the *Harriet Lane*."

"That's a Navy ship," Gage explained, "but not much of one. It's a revenue cutter with only small guns."

"It's anchored two miles offshore to the northeast where the South Carolina cannons can't get to it. It's just sittin' out there like it's lost, or they don't know what to do."

"Probably waiting for more ships." Then with intensity in his voice, Gage added, "We need to get Miss Bette to the *Harriet Lane*, Jack. Do you understand? We need to save her."

Jack didn't hesitate. He went looking for the keys and found them in the only piece of furniture in the place, a small desk with a single drawer. With little thought of the risk to himself, Jack opened the cell door. These were his friends and they mattered most.

As they exited the building, Gage grabbed Jack by the shoulder and looked at him earnestly. "Jack, I know how much you care about Miss Bette, but you can't go with us. You can't risk being caught with us."

Just as Gage finished saying that they heard a commotion from the other side of the building. Two soldiers were headed their way.

"Pull your revolver, Jack!" Gage said.

Jack pulled out the new Colt revolver he had been given and aimed it in the direction of the corner from which the soldiers would soon come.

"Don't aim it at them!" Gage exclaimed. "Aim it at us!"

Jack did so just as the soldiers turned the corner and came into view.

"Well, well, what do we have here?" the lieutenant in charge of the jail asked. He turned to the sergeant who was with him and said, "It appears the young private has captured two escaping prisoners."

Gage put his hands up, and Gus followed his lead.

"Put them in different cells, Private. The others have more secure locks."

"Yes, sir," Jack said, and he marched his friends back to their new cells.

As the door clanged shut, Gage whispered, "It's up to you now, Jack. You've got to get Miss Bette to that ship."

"I understand."

"Once you get her there, whether you get on that ship, too, is entirely up to you."

Jack nodded.

***

It was only ten o'clock, and Jack assumed guests wouldn't be asleep yet at the Moultrie House. The building was more of a boarding house than a hotel. Getting inside was easy because the front door was unlocked, and there was no clerk at the desk.

Jack looked at the guest roster. Bette's name didn't appear, but Room 12 showed as rented by "the military." There were no other possibilities among the list, so Jack charged up the stairs to the third floor where he found Room 12. It had a heavy door with a strong lock that couldn't be opened from the inside. There was no sense in knocking, and Jack had no idea where to look for a key.

Instead he went to the outside of the building and climbed up a wooden fire escape. He felt fairly certain which window belonged to Room 12, and so he tapped lightly on the glass. The curtains flew open. Staring back at him was the scarecrow face of an elderly woman.

Jack jumped back, but she opened the window anyway.

"That's all right, darlin', the woman said. "You tryin' to see your sweetheart one last time before the battle begins?"

That was a better excuse than Jack could come up with, so he said, "Yes, ma'am, that's right."

"Well, she ain't in here, but good luck. I'm sure you'll find her soon."

"Thank you, ma'am."

Jack was now certain it must be the next window to the right. When he looked at that window, however, he found that several boards had been nailed across the sash. He tapped on the glass, and this time when the curtains pulled back there appeared the radiant face of Bette Downing peering out through gaps in the boards. He signaled her that that he would be back in a minute.

He ran down the fire escape, but at the ground level he finally found the missing night clerk. The man was standing with his back Jack's way, relieving himself in a clump of azaleas. Jack ducked behind a maintenance shed door just as the man turned around. The clerk didn't notice Jack's feet below the door. Fortunately, he was too lazy to come over and close the door.

When the clerk went back inside, Jack looked in the shed and found a small metal bar. He charged back up the fire escape and at the window, as Bette watched, he wedged the bar in under the nails. They quickly popped, the boards fell away, and she was able to open the window and climb out.

"I know where there's a rowboat along the shore ... about a mile away," Jack said.

"A rowboat to take us where?"

"To a Navy ship just off the coast. That's where Mr. Gage said I should take you."

"You've seen John?"

"Yes, ma'am."

"We've got to go back for him, Jack."

Jack Spence was not a good liar. His mother had warned him never to lie. The good book said liars will be punished. But there must be good lies, he reasoned, and then he let loose of one: "Mr. Gage said he and Gus will meet us on the ship."

While Gage being at Fort Moultrie may not have been newsworthy to the soldiers, the presence of the beautiful Bette Downing was. Jack knew she would be recognized if seen, and thus they took off on an erratic journey along back trails and dirt paths, sometimes even venturing through wooded areas. At times Jack took her by the hand to guide her through the tight spots. When they reached the rowboat, her white dress was frayed in places and splattered with mud.

Because it was a large rowboat with five sets of oars attached, it would be slow-going. Jack sat down to take the oars at the bow. Bette took hold of a set of oars at the aft end.

"What are you doing?" Jack asked.

"I'm helping. I've rowed before."

Fifty yards from shore, they realized just how slow it was going to be. Despite calm waters, it might take two hours to reach the ship. That's if they could find it. Thick clouds overhung the ocean, blocking any light that might come from a near half-moon. Five hundred yards out, they lost all light from the shore. They were suddenly ensconced in blackness.

"How will we ever find it?" Bette wondered.

"I know directions."

"In the dark?"

Jack shrugged. "I just hope it hasn't moved."

They rowed for the next half hour. Suddenly Jack stopped rowing and stood up to look around. All the times he had traipsed around the Ashland plantation in total darkness he had never felt like this. At Ashland there were markers, things that he remembered that would help guide him on his course. Here, there was nothing—just water, and always the same.

Bette sensed his fear and said, "It's all right, Jack. We'll find a way."

"But I promised Mr. Gage to get you to the ship safely."

She chuckled. "Mr. Gage has made some promises to me that he hasn't kept."

Jack looked her way, even though he could barely see her. She realized he idolized John Gage, and this was no time to besmirch his idol. "John is a good man, Jack. He wouldn't have chosen anyone to take on this assignment that he didn't have confidence in."

Suddenly, there was a slight break in the clouds, and a sliver of light came through, enough for Bette to see that Jack's face was brightening along with the sky. They began rowing again, and fifteen minutes later the low lights of the *Harriet Lane* came into view.

When they were within one hundred feet of the ship, someone called out from the deck above: "Who goes there?"

"Elizabeth Downing, friend of the Union," Bette shouted. "I seek safe passage to the North."

It was not an unusual request. She was the third person to make their way to the ship.

The ship's deck was too high for a ladder, and so the crewmen lowered a tethered sack to the rowboat. Jack helped Bette position her feet on the bottom of the sack as she grabbed the ropes with her hands. As the crewmen began to hoist her upwards, her now shabby dress snagged on one of the ropes, lifting it skyward as well.

Jack stood below, looking up. This was the most he had ever seen of a woman, but at the moment he took no delight. As if frozen in place, he stood in the rowboat as Bette landed on the deck.

The crewmen dropped the sack down into the rowboat again.

Jack just stared at it.

"Jack, aren't you coming?" Bette yelled down to him.

Jack wasn't prepared for this. This decision had been thrust upon him out of nowhere, and he had had no time to think it through. To go meant casting aside forever the people and places he knew . . . perhaps never seeing his mother and Eli again. Perhaps never seeing Isaac, Henry, and Little Georgie ever again. It was ingrained deep within him that he owed some allegiance to those people and places.

He tossed the sack out of the rowboat and began to row away. Fifty feet farther, he stopped rowing briefly and stood to wave to Bette. She blew a kiss his way.

He would be a Confederate soldier, and he wasn't sure why.

***

With only one person rowing, the return trip was long and exhausting. But the clouds had lifted enough so that the moon gave Jack enough light to find his way. It was past five in the morning by the time he approached the shore. Many soldiers were already stirring.

Jack realized he couldn't simply row this boat in because there would be no explanation for him doing so. He had to think fast and could only come up with one thing. He jumped in the water, finding it was only four feet deep. He grabbed onto a rope and walked the boat into the shore.

A sergeant saw him come in and shouted, "You there. What are you doing?"

Jack tied up the rowboat and walked up to him. The sergeant held out his lantern and looked at Jack. "You're soaking wet, Private."

"Yes, sir, I noticed the rowboat had gotten loose and drifted out about a hundred feet. I swam out and got it." Another lie. *I'm surely going to hell,* Jack thought.

"Good work, Private. What's your name, anyway?"

"Jack Spence, sir."

"Well, Private Spence, I really appreciate your efforts because that rowboat is needed this morning down at Fort Moultrie."

Chapter 52

The voices in the outer hallway died down for the moment. Perhaps they haven't come early for us after all, Gage thought. With three hours until their executions, he returned to his self-analysis.

One thing he realized is that he held on to grudges far too long. *I did that with my mother for her failure to see thru Jubal. It wasn't her fault. Funny, she could see thru Jacqueline when I couldn't, and I could see thru Jubal when she couldn't. We were two of the same—blinded by love, blinded by need.*

Gus stood up from his stool. He seemed to be finished with his praying.

This time Gage shouted his apology: "I'm sorry, Gus, I should not have gotten you into this."

But instead of anger, Gus remained positive. "I still have hope. I still think you gonna get me to Maryland, John."

Never before had Gus called Gage by his first name, and it elicited an emotional response from Gage that was rare: "Gus, I want you to know that if we die here today, we will die together as brothers."

Gage returned to his thoughts. One was of the frustration of not having found the answer. *I came here partly because of the letter, and I still don't know who sent the damned thing. I'll die not knowing.*

But this harsh journey was interrupted when the muffled voices in the outer office resumed. The door to the outer hallway opened and three soldiers came in and removed Gus from his cell.

"What are you doing with him?" Gage shouted. "What are you doing?"

Gus looked back in despair as he was escorted out of the cell area.

The door closed and for the next few moments there was silence until

Gage began pounding at his cell door. He yanked on the metal bars so violently that the entire wall of iron rocked back and forth. When he screamed at the jailers, "Bring him back here!" the voices in the outer hallway resumed.

This time one of those voices contained a French accent. It was Beauregard, and he called out to the others, "Remain outside."

The general was barely through the door from the outer hallway when Gage started in on him: "What have you done with Gus Ward?"

Beauregard didn't answer. One of the soldiers opened the door to Gage's cell and let the general in. The soldier then locked the cell door and left.

"If he's been hung, you better not be in this cell when I learn that."

"Calm yourself, John. I came here to talk. I have not yet decided Augustus Ward's fate."

"Then why has he been removed from his cell?"

"So we can speak candidly."

The general sat down on a stool. He was tired, having had little sleep for the past week. And he was different now, for he seemed to carry the weight of the world. "There is a concern that Major Anderson is stalling, stalling until the Northern fleet arrives," he said. "I can't allow that."

It was the wrong topic at the moment for Gage, but he went along because hidden in the general's remark of indecision about Gus's fate was the hint that the general had the authority to decide his fate. "He may be under orders to force you to fire the first shot," Gage said.

Beauregard looked up and said glumly, "President Davis has left it up to me to determine whether Major Anderson will surrender before being resupplied."

"And if he won't?"

"I am to destroy the fort, and everything in it."

"You mean everyone in it."

Beauregard eyed Gage forlornly. "John, I am about to throw bombs at my good friend and mentor. I know his wife, Eliza, and his daughter, Maria. When that first shot is fired, I will see their faces."

"Then why do it?"

"Because I believe in our cause . . . in our right of self-determination. I feel obligated to stand behind that."

"So your sense of duty is your demon?"

"Yes, we're on our own hook now. Making do as we go, as God sees fit."

"What does God have to do with this? Don't try to justify your actions as God's will. It's you who will give the order to fire at people who are your friends. It's you who will permit our hanging, not God."

Beauregard shook his head in frustration. "Discussing it will not do me any good."

Tired of listening to Beauregard's troubles, Gage said, "You seem to have come here to unload your problems. I have my own."

"You are one of my problems."

"Yes, if you hang me, even Democrats in the North will assail you."

Beauregard stood and took a couple of steps before turning back towards Gage. "There might be a solution."

"And what is that?"

"I could send you to Fort Sumter. There you can live or die in a fair fight."

"You said *you*. I assume you are including Augustus Ward in that?"

"No, I was just talking about you."

"I won't go there without Gus!" Gage shouted.

"It's not as if you have a choice. We can take you there in chains if need be."

Gage stood up from his cot, red in the face with anger. "If you hang Augustus Ward, you better pray to God I don't survive Sumter."

"Why is that?"

"Because I will tell the world how you hung an innocent man."

"He was found guilty of insurrection."

"In a phony trial where he was not present and absolutely no evidence of *his* insurrection was presented. Your image will be worse than if you hung us both."

Beauregard stood up from his stool with his hand to his chin and walked about pensively. "All right, the two of you. But I need you to do something."

"What?"

"Advise my adversary to surrender without a fight."

"General, in all candor, I will go there and analyze the situation and give Major Anderson my honest opinion."

"I was afraid that might be your response. You have integrity, stubborn integrity."

"You consider our old friend an *adversary*?"

"I have no desire to bring a war against him. That's why I need you to convince him to leave."

"Is this a condition to our being allowed to go there?"

"No, it's my plea . . . my earnest plea, John. Please realize I'm taking a big risk in sending you to Sumter."

"With the politicians?"

"No, not just that, but because your presence at the fort might change things."

"I'm only one man. I could hardly change things."

"I know you, John, you're a tenacious fighter. Your spirit might embolden Anderson to take a tougher stand. I'm asking you, for the good of everyone, to bring him to reason."

"I will do what's best."

Beauregard, intent on concluding this ugly matter quickly, said, "May we meet again in gentler times."

The two men shook hands.

***

Once Beauregard was gone, Gus was brought back into his cell. He shouted down to Gage: "What did the top dog say?"

"Don't worry, we're getting out of here."

"Where we goin'?"

"To Fort Sumter."

Gus's eyes swelled. "This is worser and worser. You think it's going to be safer there when they start throwin' bombs at us?"

"Maybe not at the start, but I'm betting in the end it will be, Gus. Anyway, you said you wanted to see some fireworks."

"I said I want to light some fireworks."

"Look, neither side wants to be accused of starting this war. I'm betting that any battle ends quickly. Then they'll let us all get out of there."

That made sense to Gus. "You did have a plan. But what do we do at Fort Sumter?"

"Keep our heads down."

Chapter 53

Thanks to Kate Warne's encouragement—or that of Constance Cherry from Victoria's perspective—as well as a sensation of support from her sons, Victoria Ford had once again stopped taking the laudanum. As she had done before, each day she poured the prescribed amount into a larger bottle that she eventually emptied outside just so Jubal wouldn't know. She had been off the laudanum entirely for two weeks, and this time she was certain she had ended her dependency once and for all. Her strength was back and with it came a determination to find answers to questions she had ignored for quite some time.

One chilly afternoon at the Ford house in Annapolis, as Victoria read by a roaring fire in the living room, there was a knock on the front door that none of the servants heard. Victoria answered it instead. A young man from the telegraph office handed her an envelope. "It's for your husband, Mrs. Ford, a telegram from Carthage, Pennsylvania," he said quite pleasantly.

"Thank you," Victoria replied. "I'll see that he gets it."

She was going to place it on Jubal's desk. But as she started towards his office, she noticed the name of the sender: Gage Ironworks Company.

She was suspicious, and with good reason. It wasn't just because her husband had deceived her. Things were swirling about that she couldn't understand. The *Washington Journal* article that alleged her sons had conspired to sell cannons to the Confederacy was an absurdity. So absurd that she was certain someone planted the story. And if it was true that the cannons weren't destroyed in the explosion, then she wanted to know where they went.

I am a part owner of the company, she reasoned. I'm entitled to know what's going on. She opened the envelope. The telegram inside was from Addison Williams and it read:

> Need to know whether to start production of the next one hundred cannons. Your son advises he has a new means for delivering them. If we don't start producing them immediately, our normal production will cause us to have insufficient anthracite to start production of them for at least a month. If I don't hear from you, I will assume we are not to start production of the cannons.

Doubts about her husband had now turned to suspicions, and Victoria was even more suspicious of her stepson. At best, Marcus was leaning to Maryland secession, but his secrecy on the question might just be a ploy to allow him to maintain his seat in Congress. Then she assured herself: Marcus would not involve himself in sending cannons to the North. Once built, these cannons are headed to the South.

She tossed the telegram in the fire.

The next morning Jubal Ford walked into the bedroom as Victoria stood before a mirror brushing her hair. She didn't turn around, but she could see his reflection. "I thought you left already," she said.

"I came back for something." Then he announced, "I'll be staying the night in Baltimore."

That was surprising enough to cause her to turn and face him. As she did so, she noticed that on the dresser behind him was the large bottle that contained the laudanum she was going to discard. She moved closer, trying to distract him. "What business do you have in Baltimore?"

"I have a meeting with Marcus."

"And others?"

"I don't know. He arranged the meeting. I've also found a doctor for you in Baltimore. He's going to give me bottles of the same medicine Doc Brown prescribed for you. I'll bring them back with me."

Her heart sank. She was down to the last couple of prescribed bottles, and she had hoped Jubal had forgotten about it, so she could stop playing this crazy game. But obviously it was important to him, so important that she was afraid of his reaction if he learned what she had been doing with the bottle on the dresser.

He was about to leave and started to turn in the direction of the dresser. She tried to get him to turn the other way, but it didn't work. He saw the bottle. "What's this?" he said as he picked it up.

Cyrus happened to be walking by the open bedroom door, and he poked his head in the doorway as Jubal studied the bottle. Victoria was in a panic—she was about to be found out.

But Cyrus came into the room and immediately said, "I'm sorry, Missus. I meant to take that bottle downstairs and put fresh water in it." He took the bottle from Jubal and left the room.

Later in the morning, after Jubal had left for Baltimore, Victoria met Cyrus at the back door as he came in from the outside with the bottle. "I emptied it in the same way you do, Missus, burying the liquid under a little bit of dirt so no animals will get to it."

"Cyrus, I had no idea you knew."

"I seen you do it on a few occasions, and I know why you do it. I've watched you get stronger as you stopped drinking it. It's a good thing."

"Thank you, Cyrus, for what you did, and for those kind words."

"Don't get me wrong, Missus. I like Master Jubal, and I think he truly believe that the medicine is good for you. He cares about you."

"I don't know, Cyrus. We'll have to see about that."

***

It wasn't surprising that the two stepbrothers rarely interacted in Congress. After all, they were from different political parties. But the animosity between Marcus Ford and Ari Gage had been growing, for their alienation went far beyond politics.

So when Marcus Ford suggested a meeting between the two to "discuss family matters," Ari was truly surprised. They met in a library in the Capitol Building where they sat across from each other at the only table in the room, a room so small that it held only ten stacks of books.

The meeting did not begin well when Ari asked about his mother's status.

"I'm told she's doing fine," Marcus said.

"How can that be? She's been taken away from her grandchildren."

"Send them for a visit."

"Into the troubles that are brewing in Maryland? We're not about to do that."

"Your choice."

"I feel as though she's been kidnapped."

"That's not true, and you know it. But your mother's condition is not why I called for this meeting."

"No, it must have to do with the allegations made in the *Washington Journal* article. That story has your handwriting all over it."

"Why would I leak a story that says that the fifty cannons that we said were destroyed in the explosion were not actually destroyed?"

"Because the rumor of that fact is already out there, and it's starting to make its way into the press. So you decided to blame the disappearance of those cannons on someone else—the Gage Brothers."

"Oh, I can do better than that."

"And how might that be?"

"You're correct that I've got the ear of the *Washington Journal*. I plan to push the story further to the point of an investigation into the Gage brothers. That investigation will expose John Gage in Charleston for what he is not."

Both men were under a misapprehension, unaware that John Gage had already been found out in Charleston, for word of his trial had not yet made it to the North. "That would undermine your whole allegation," Ari said. "You would be saying that my brother is a Northern spy, but he sold cannons to the Confederacy. It makes no sense."

"No, remember your transfer of those cannons to the South was not about politics. It was about the two of you making money."

Ari shook his head. "Keene said there was another conniver in this scheme who would want something. So, what is it you're after, Ford?"

"Sign over to me your ownership interest in the Gage Ironworks Company, and I will kill the allegations."

"I see. You realize, of course, this would cause a rupture between our two families."

"The rupture of the country will cause that anyway."

Ari sat back in his chair, suddenly at ease. "I would prefer to go through a congressional investigation."

"No, you wouldn't. Your fellow Republicans aren't standing behind you on this."

Suddenly there was rummaging in the stacks behind them, the sound of a book opening and closing. Then a book began to appear from the side of one of the stacks. It was open and held high, as if by a tall person. The book came out further, and Marcus Ford could now see that the holder of that book was Abraham Lincoln.

"Excuse me, gentlemen," the president said. "Would you believe it that there are no law books in the White House library? I just came over to brush up on a few things, and one of those is the definition of the crime of extortion. What you just did, Congressman Ford, fits that definition perfectly."

Ford was dumbfounded, and said nothing.

Ari spoke instead. "And I think you can now see, Ford, that I do have the support of Republicans."

Looking back into the stacks, the president said, "Did you write all that down, Mr. Hay?"

The president's young secretary stepped out from behind the books. "Every word of it, sir."

Lincoln smiled approvingly. "While you have an entrée to one newspaper, Congressman, I have entrées to a hundred others. If you like, Mr. Hay and I will sign sworn affidavits of your extortion attempt and give them to those newspapers, as well as to the attorney general. Should we do that?"

"No, sir," Ford said contritely.

"All right. Now here's what's going to happen: you're going to publish a letter in the *Washington Journal*, denying the allegations against the Gage Brothers. We'll let you still claim that the cannons were destroyed in an explosion, but you'll also state that, even if they weren't, the Gage brothers could not have had any decision in sending cannons elsewhere because they're not involved in the management of the company. So do you want to go that route, or the first one I described?"

"Definitely the latter, Mr. President."

Chapter 54

Word of Jack Spence's eventful night, at least most of it, spread throughout the Confederate camps, even reaching the ears of General Beauregard. When told of Jack's capture of the two prisoners and his later saving of the rowboat, the general ordered Jack to come see him.

The meeting was brief, Beauregard thanking him for his efforts during the night. Then he said, "Private, I've got a special mission I want you to undertake this afternoon. I want you to take the *Jacky Boy*—for that was the name the soldiers had already given the rowboat—and row those same two prisoners over to Fort Sumter. I figure you captured them escaping, so now it's your duty to deliver them to their destiny. Now get some sleep until then."

"Yessir, General, sir."

***

Reports that Beauregard had made a final decision concerning the two prisoners spread quickly as well. When Ransom Pierce heard about it, he raced to the general's headquarters where he interrupted a conversation between Beauregard and Colonel Wigfall.

"The Confederacy is taking over the punishment of John Gage and Augustus Ward," Beauregard explained to Pierce.

"And when will they be hung?"

"They won't be."

"What?" Pierce thundered. "They're traitors! A precedent must be set."

"A fair precedent will be set."

"Then what will you do with them?"

"I'm sending them to Fort Sumter."

After contemplating that for a moment, Pierce nodded approvingly. "That's smart. You won't have Gage's blood on your hands. He will simply die in a fair fight. Very clever."

"It's the correct approach," Wigfall said with a bemused smile. "A condemned man, seemingly willing to die a martyr, has had us in shackles."

Now feeling the weight of what was ahead, Beauregard said, "To this point, gentlemen, this has all just been great theatre. But now we have orders to fire on our countrymen."

"Our former countrymen," Ransom Pierce reminded.

Wigfall, feeling that weight as well, said, "But still our friends."

***

Two hours before he was to be transported from the Fort Moultrie jail to Fort Sumter, John Gage received two visitors—Frank Talbot and his daughter Jenny.

"I'm here to ask a favor of you, John, not for myself but for Jenny."

Jenny was in agony. She dabbed at the tears in her eyes with a linen handkerchief that she pulled from her nurse's dress.

"It's about Private Davidson at Fort Sumter, Mr. Gage," she said haltingly. "We were to be married, and then the soldiers were no longer allowed to come to Charleston. And now the mail is shut off, and my last letter didn't reach him. I'm so worried about him. Will you take my letter to him?"

"Of course."

"And will you look out for him at the fort?"

"I'll do my best, Jenny."

Jenny thanked him and left the jail. Frank looked at Gage and said, "Ransom Pierce told me he thinks your removal to Sumter is a death sentence. I hope and pray that it is not."

"As do I," Gage said with a smile.

The two men shook hands and Frank departed. Thirty minutes later, another visitor arrived. It was the last person in the world Gage expected. It was Jacqueline.

They stared at each other for what seemed like a good two minutes. Gage realized that, for once, Jacqueline didn't have the right thing to say. She always had the right thing to say, even if it was some twisted notion of the wrong thing to do.

Finally, she said, "We'll probably never see each other again, John. The last time I thought that I didn't say goodbye. At least this time I have the chance."

"Last time you had the chance as well, but you left with your *brother*. Who was it pretending to be your brother?"

This was a deception she couldn't escape. She went with the truth, at least some version of it. "Thomas Gentry—one of my former suitors from Charleston. He came to Carthage to convince me to marry him instead of you. The first time you saw him was when you caught us in an embrace. I didn't think you would understand, so I panicked and told you he was my brother. Thomas thought it was funny and played along."

"And I assume he planted the currency plates on me to try to get me out of the way."

"Oh, I don't think he could've done that."

"I think he did because as soon as the case against me fell apart—when the evidence disappeared—you two left for Europe."

"We didn't end up going to Europe; we went back to Charleston. But we're talking about the past, Johnny, let's talk about now. All of this war talk has changed me. Others are so enthused, convinced that we will have a new way of life. I see it as the end of our way of life."

"Eventually that's what it will be."

"I know you'll probably never think of me the same as you did in Carthage." She stopped because the things to say were colliding in her mind, a combination of plots and deceptions that even she couldn't keep straight.

"That's true."

"But, perhaps in time, if we were together." She paused, then said suddenly, "Johnny, I can get the key and get you out of here. We can run away together . . . go to the West. We can leave this chaos behind."

Gage smiled. "I'd rather go to Sumter."

She recoiled at that, and tried desperately to evoke something from him. "You never loved me, Johnny. You thought you did. You loved the romance and the intrigue and you loved the thought of being in love. But you never really loved me."

Gage wasn't going to take the bait. He continued to stare at her.

She backed up and then turned to leave. But five feet from the door she stopped and turned back to say one final thing: "I'll get by without you."

Gage nodded. "I'm sure you will."

***

The hands of the two prisoners were bound, but not their feet so both were able to walk to the *Jacky Boy*. As they approached the dock, Gage looked out to his left. Rafts were being built, at least fifty of them by his quick count. They were lightweight—a small tug could pull several of them at the same time—and were definitely being readied for a possible assault on Fort Sumter. Gage estimated each raft could hold at least twenty men, resulting in a landing force of one thousand soldiers against less than one hundred defending the fort.

Five soldiers were assigned to assist Jack Spence in rowing Gage and Gus across to Sumter on the *Jacky Boy*, and even with all of them rowing at a good pace it would take twenty minutes. Halfway there the formidable structure came into clear focus, looking more like a prison than a fort. Its brick and concrete walls rose fifty feet above the water, and there were no windows for air and light. The embrasures, the small openings for the artillery to fire through in the first two tiers of weaponry, were covered over with iron shields. The third tier of artillery sat atop the parapet.

Nearing the fort, Gage turned to Jack Spence and asked, "Private, have you ever rowed a boat on these waters before?"

Jack picked up on what Gage was asking. "Yes, sir, once before. It was at night, and I was able to deliver my passenger without any problems."

Gage smiled with relief.

The fort's wharf was on the far side along what was called the gorge wall, the longest wall of the fort's five sides. It faced a narrow channel that separated the fort from land where only twelve hundred yards away were the Confederate batteries at Cummings Point.

When the *Jacky Boy* was one hundred yards from the wharf, two anxious soldiers atop the parapet aimed rifles at the boat. "Identify yourself," one of the soldiers screamed. These men were on alert for anything, and they were tense.

All the soldiers in the boat were privates and no one knew who was in charge. But young Jack Spence, having captured these two prisoners, held a hero status and so the others looked to him.

"We are delivering two Northerners to you," Jack yelled.

Not quite accurate in Gus's case, but close enough.

The two soldiers looked at each other in amazement. Then one shouted down, "Who are they?"

"Tell Major Anderson that Major John Gage has come for a visit," Gage shouted back.

Five minutes later the officer on watch signaled them to come into the wharf.

The hands of the two prisoners were untied. Gage stood up. He knew he couldn't be too demonstrative with Jack, so he simply reached out to shake his hand and said, "Thank you, Private." Then he handed Jack an envelope. "Will you make sure this note gets delivered to General Beauregard?"

"Yes, sir," and then Jack had something for Gage. It was *The Little Book of Wisdom*, and as he handed it to Gage he said, "Take this book, Major. I've read it and it helped me a lot. I'm sure it will help you, too."

Gage smiled and placed a firm hand on Jack's shoulder as he stepped out of the boat.

Chapter 55

The two newcomers walked from the wharf toward Fort Sumter's main gate, careful to stay on the path for fear of stepping on landmines planted to ward off a Confederate ground assault. The main gate opened. The officer of the guard, Lieutenant Smith, a tall, thin man wearing a uniform smeared with soot, appeared and he seemed genuinely displeased.

"Why have you come here?" the lieutenant barked.

"We're from the post office, delivering a letter to Private Davidson," Gage replied.

"You know Davidson?"

Gage nodded.

"You should go back."

"That's out of the question."

"Who are you?"

"John Gage, retired army officer. This is Augustus Ward . . . a free man."

Gage looked at Gus who had a gratifying look on his face.

"I will inform Major Anderson of your arrival. He will not be happy."

But five minutes later the troubled commander appeared, and when he saw Gage a faint smile came to his lips.

Gage, however, was so taken aback by the major's physical appearance that all he could say was, "Hello, Professor." It was a nickname Anderson had acquired during his teaching days at West Point.

It had been just two years since Gage last saw Anderson. Since then the privation of sleep and decent food, exacerbated by internal conflict, had taken its toll. His hair had thinned and blanched, its only remaining gray near the temples. The only officer at the fort without facial hair, the ashen hue of his face clashed against full eyebrows that were still dark. He had lost considerable weight leaving him with a slight physique and as he approached Gage, who was seven inches taller, he stepped carefully for his balance was poor. But he stood erect and proud, as always maintaining a proper military bearing.

Ever courteous, the major said, "John, it's good to see you, but you've arrived at an inopportune time."

"So I hear."

"No, things are worse. I just received a formal demand from General Beauregard that we surrender the fort."

"And your reply?"

"I rejected it."

"Good."

"I also told his representatives that if he doesn't reduce our fort to rubble we will be out of food within three days anyway."

Gage winced, shocked that such information had been volunteered.

Sensing his dismay, Anderson said, "I did so to buy time . . . to try to prevent the start of a war."

"But I saw your letter to Colonel Thomas. You said an expedition by Captain Fox would fail."

"That's right. The big ships can't make it into the fort, and to try to bring in supplies by small boats . . . well, they would be battered by Beauregard's guns."

"Beauregard is afraid of those ships. He's worried they're carrying two thousand soldiers to invade the islands."

Anderson let loose a slight chuckle. "Where would the army find two thousand soldiers right now? Besides, I doubt Fox's fleet is even coming."

"They're coming. One ship is out there already—the *Harriett Lane*, a revenue cutter."

"That's news to me."

"It's not news to the people of Charleston. They've seen the ship anchored off Sullivan's Island."

"It must be waiting for others."

"Professor, the Confederacy wants a victory over the federal government out of all of this. Those ships pose a threat to that victory. The Confederacy won't give you your three days."

***

Sumter was a depressing place. Confined as it was by the brick and concrete walls that towered above, natural light and air were restricted. Even in the open parade ground, the walls rose more than forty feet above the floor, creating a prisonlike atmosphere.

Only upon the parapet was there a good view of the outside world, and just before sunset Gage went up to look around. He found an old friend standing there, looking out beyond the harbor with field glasses. It was Captain Abner Doubleday, second in command at the fort.

He hasn't changed a bit since our last encounter, Gage thought. Still the dark, curly hair, a dark mustache, and an ever-present troubled look. But at the moment Doubleday seemed especially troubled. He was shaking his head in disgust.

Gage tried some levity: "Spied any fine-looking women yet, Doubleday?"

Doubleday ignored the question and said matter-of-factly, "Aha, Gage, I heard you volunteered for this clambake."

"Better than a noose."

"That's yet to be seen."

"They almost didn't let us in because you're so short of food."

"Hell, two more diners won't make a difference since we're going to run out in a couple days anyway. We're out of almost everything: coal, candles, kerosene—"

"Black powder?"

Doubleday chuckled. "That's one thing we have plenty of, but we don't have enough cartridge bags to put it in."

"Any sign of Captain Fox's fleet?"

Doubleday shook his head. "It looks like we'll have to go it alone." He handed the field glasses to Gage. "Look straight across at Sullivan's Island."

"Nice little battery—four guns. They look to be thirty-two, maybe even forty-two pounders."

"We didn't know that battery was there until two days ago. They built it in the last two months behind a house. Then two days ago they blew up the house. Now, it's aimed squarely our way."

"A sure sign they're getting ready to attack."

"We are surrounded."

Gage nodded. "I've seen what's behind us at Cummings Point and Fort Johnson, and of course there are the big guns at Fort Moultrie."

"Hell, Gage, none of these batteries existed a few months ago except at Moultrie, and we spiked those guns when we left."

"Your point?"

"With ships and a few hundred soldiers we could've taken the harbor and then the city. But Buchanan did nothing, Anderson did nothing." With a look of frustration, Doubleday added, "Anderson never should have been placed in this command."

"You think he's not committed?"

"He's had chances to return fire, especially when shots were fired at the *Star of the West.*"

"Abner, Anderson has been hamstrung by his orders: Defend the fort but don't initiate a battle. We both know the best way to have defended this place would have been taking out all the batteries while they were being built. But his orders didn't allow that."

"I know . . . I know, but I don't think he's had any desire to take out those batteries."

"Come now, he's devastated by all this. One of his best friends, Jeff Davis, has just ordered one of his favorite students to wage war against him."

"And they do so in pursuit of a cause Anderson believes in."

"I'm already aware of your concerns about the major," Gage said sheepishly.

"How is that possible?"

"My brother wrote me about it. He was with Mr. Lincoln when the president reviewed your letters to your wife."

"What? Those were private messages to my wife!" Doubleday said, recalling just how private they were.

"The president merely wanted to hear your honest impressions of Anderson. It wasn't about you. He learned that you believe the major is true to his oath and he follows orders."

"To a fault."

"I think he's loyal to the point of not protesting even if it means taking a shellacking."

Doubleday shook his head. "The man is proslavery, even if he opposes secession. I don't think he wants a war because he knows the North would win and that would end slavery." He hesitated, then asked, "What do you think are the real stakes?"

"The real stakes are the border states. Mr. Lincoln knows that, and he knows we can't alienate border states like Maryland and Kentucky by first attacking Southerners."

"Yes, I suppose we will be sacrificed for that reason."

"It's the hand we've been dealt."

"And now it's going to be a bloody awful one," Doubleday said as he walked away.

Both were artillery men. They knew what was coming.

Chapter 56

(Day 1 of the Battle)

It may have been unusual for an enemy to announce to an opposing force the time at which it would begin its assault, but this was to be an unusual battle. At three thirty in the morning, a note from Beauregard was delivered to Anderson informing him that the shelling would begin in one hour. By then, even though two hours before sunrise, the outline of Fort Sumter against a brightening eastern horizon would come into view.

The message to soldiers at Sumter from their commander was equally surprising: sleep through it. Major Anderson, holding one of the precious few candles, stumbled about in the dark casemates advising his men that the shelling would soon begin. Like a father reassuring his children about an approaching storm, he said calmly, "Stay in the casemates. You'll be safe here. Try to get some sleep. We won't commence our firing until sunrise."

For the most part the men believed his words. Surrounded by five-foot thick walls and ceilings made of brick and concrete, they should be safe in the casemates. But this fort had never been tested. And even those officers who had been in battle in Mexico had never faced weapons such as the ones now aimed their way.

John Gage and Gus Ward couldn't sleep. At four in the morning, they went to the mess for breakfast where they had water and a bit of dried out pork. It was all that was left and soon it would be gone.

"I can't believe these men have been living on this," Gage said.

Gus gave a curious look.

Gage realized his mistake. "Many times you've lived on less, haven't you?"

Gus nodded.

A half hour later they stood in the darkness just outside one of the casemate walls. There was a chill in the air and a light mist was being thrown their way. They walked a few steps out into the one-acre parade ground but stopped there because they couldn't see what was in front of them. The only light anywhere was from two candles flickering in the window panes of the officers' quarters and one small lantern in the casemate behind them.

Suddenly the boom of a cannon came at them from the south, and a red light streaked across the sky before bursting directly overhead in a shower of red sparks.

"Fireworks... beautiful," Gus said, smiling.

"They are punctual," Gage said without elation. "That was a signal shell. Now it begins."

"What begins?"

"A civil war. We just witnessed the first shot."

"What's next?"

"A circle of fire."

But before Gage could explain, a second shell came in. "Get back!" Gage yelled and he pushed Gus back into a casemate. The shell burst in the parade ground where it peppered the area with pieces of sharp metal.

And thus it began. Shots and shells from forty-three guns at nineteen batteries began to rain down on the fort. In accordance with General Beauregard's instructions, the firing occurred in a counterclockwise sequence at two minute intervals.

The men hunkered down in the casemates with all openings closed off. At this point there was little danger to the fort's occupants. Still, it was unnerving. Bombs that lodged in the exterior walls shook the fort, and bombs that struck the parapet were gradually knocking it to pieces.

When a bit of dawn light began to filter into the casemates, Gage saw a lanky, young soldier sitting with his back to an exterior wall, his eyes cast down at the floor. The youngster removed his blue Kepi in order to muss his already tousled blonde hair. He then put the hat back on, only to repeat the process fifteen seconds later. He was distressed. It was obvious he had never been in battle.

Gage asked someone the young man's name and was told, "That's Private

Davidson from Ohio."

Gage walked over and knelt down next to the youngster. Suddenly the wall shook violently. A huge sixty-four pounder had just come in from Fort Johnson.

"Probably best to sit against an interior wall," Gage said.

With a confused look on his face, Davidson said, "I don't understand something, sir. There's no time to prepare yourself. I hear the boom in the distance and the explosion happens at about the same time."

"That's because the sound and the bomb are traveling at about the same speed."

"I see."

"Don't worry, I'm sure the wind will change soon, and we won't be able to hear the boom at all." With a chuckle, Gage added, "Then there'll be no warning at all."

Humor wasn't the cure, so Gage said, "I've got something for you."

Davidson's head came up. "For me?"

"Yes, it's a letter from Jenny."

His eyes came alive. He opened the letter and began to revel in its contents.

Gage patted the young man on the shoulder and walked on.

***

From the view at Beauregard's headquarters along the Battery in Charleston, the bombardment of Sumter appeared devastating. Confederate artillery had been pounding the fort for ninety minutes from six different positions. But, thus far, there had been no return fire.

"Fight back, damn you!" Ransom Pierce blurted out. "What kind of victory would it be if they don't fight?"

"It would be a resounding victory," Wigfall replied.

"We must destroy them," Pierce said pounding his fist on a table for emphasis. "Why don't they fight?"

"They will," Beauregard said, "when there's enough light in the casemates to see what they're doing. It would be dangerous and wasteful for them to fire now."

But there was more to it than that. Fort Sumter was short of nearly everything necessary to carry on a good fight. Designed to accommodate six hundred fifty artillery soldiers, there were only eighty-five present. If fully staffed and fully armed, one hundred thirty cannons could be maintained by crews of five to seven members for each artillery piece.

Anderson determined that, given the limited number of men, he could only fire nine weapons at a time. However, he confounded his officers when he announced the location of those weapons: "I want no one on the parapet. It's too dangerous."

"But, Major, those are our strongest, best positioned, weapons," Doubleday protested. "From there, we could knock the hell out of the Fort Moultrie and Sullivan's Island batteries."

Anderson shot Doubleday a dubious look, a rare thing for the placid major. "Captain, you overstate the chances of success up there. I will not order our men into a death trap."

"We could use spotters for incoming," Doubleday argued.

But Anderson wouldn't hear of it. He ordered the crews to their guns on the lower tiers.

Doubleday stormed off to gather his men. He took his three crews to the lower tier fronting the gorge.

Another reason Anderson limited the number of guns firing was the shortage of cartridges for the cannons. When they left Fort Moultrie in a hurry, they failed to take with them all the empty cartridge bags. Since then, they had been using any material available to create new ones. They also lacked scales to measure the powder put in those bags. A properly made cartridge bag held the right amount of powder for the range and type of shot to be fired. Now they were using old shirts and any other leftover materials to make the bags and were guessing at the amount of powder needed.

Gus Ward felt useless. He wanted to be part of this fight, but he didn't have the training. He wandered aimlessly through the casements, occasionally carrying ordnance when requested by an artillery crew.

Gage soon found Gus looking bored while cannonballs landed all about them. He asked him what he thought would be a stupid question: "Gus, do you know how to sew?"

"Most slaves do. We don't get many new clothes. Aunt Abby teached me."

And so, as war raged all about them, Gus, along with some other laborers who were on site, sat down to fill cartridge bags with black powder and sew them together.

When Gage noticed the look of disappointment on Gus's face, he said, "This is really important." That helped Gus's mood, but only a little.

***

Sumter's guns had been firing for an hour when Gage walked down to the lower tier of the gorge wall and found Doubleday and his crews manning three thirty-two pounders. They were returning the fire that was coming from the batteries at Cummings Point. Just twelve hundred yards away, it was the closest of all the opposing batteries and faced Sumter's weak side from a direction that no one believed a defense would ever be necessary.

Just as Gage entered the casemate, a hardshot came in from across the gorge and struck one of the embrasures. Shards of brick careened throughout the casemate, ricocheting for a good sixty seconds before calm set in. A cannoneer on Doubleday's third crew took the worst of the pelting. Blood dripped from the young man's face and arms, the only cloth available to stop the flow was his own filthy shirt. One of the laborers escorted him out.

This was Gage's chance to break the ice with his old friend. He looked over at Doubleday and shouted, "Doubleday, what in the world is the matter here, and what's all this uproar about?"

Appreciating the levity under the circumstances, Doubleday reciprocated: "There is a trifling difference of opinion between us and our neighbors opposite, and we are trying to settle it."

"Do you need another hand?"

Doubleday nodded. He was hesitant to ask this of a civilian, a retired major no less, but he did so: "We lost a man to injury. Can you fill in?"

"I'd be glad to. Are you making any progress?"

"None at all. We're firing each gun once a minute, but our shots just bounce off their iron canopies." At Cummings Point the Confederates had laid iron rails above their positions at a shallow angle such that the huge cannonballs fired from the lower tier of the fort careened off the iron.

"And are they making any progress with you?"

"I'm afraid so. They've got a new Blakely from England against us. The damned thing is rifled with a muzzle velocity of more than twelve hundred feet per second. It's doing some real damage to our walls, especially when it hits near an embrasure. That's how our man just got injured."

Gage walked over to the weapon he was assigned to. It was dangerous and strenuous work. To avoid injury or death, and function efficiently, the crew had to act as a well-coordinated team. Five of the men had numbers assigned which by army protocol told them where to stand and their duties. The sixth man was called the gunner, responsible for aiming the weapon and the ultimate command to fire.

"Mr. Gage, you are cannoneer number one," Doubleday shouted with a smile. "There is your utensil."

Gage gave a mock salute. He walked over and picked up a ten-foot-long piece of iron with a wooden mallet at one end and a sheepskin sponge at the other. He took his position at the right front corner of the weapon.

The cannon was already loaded and primed, so Gage's only responsibility during this firing was to watch the muzzle and make sure the cannonball was discharged. The gunner cried out, "Ready." Gage and cannoneer Number 2, who was stationed at the left front corner, stepped away from the cannon.

Gage was accustomed to the sound of field artillery firing in the open air, but this was different. When the gunner yelled "Fire," Number 4 pulled on the lanyard and there occurred a blast of such force that the concussion, housed as it was within the casemate, caused the masonry floor and walls to shudder. And that concussion seemed to ripple about, as if bouncing off the walls. For a brief moment Gage lost his balance. The other crew members laughed at the novice.

Smoke and dust filled the chamber, but Gage ignored it. He now had his job to do. He ducked the sponge end of his rammer in a water bucket and quickly inserted it in the muzzle, turning it constantly in order to douse any sparks that might ignite the next cartridge prematurely. As cannoneer Number 3 covered the vent hole to prevent air from getting in, Number 2 was handed a cartridge bag filled with hopefully the right amount of black powder, and he placed it in the muzzle. Gage flipped his rammer one hundred eighty degrees and used the wooden end of the shaft to push the cartridge down to the breach end of the cannon where it came to rest under the vent hole. Number 2 then received the thirty-two pound cannonball from Number 5 and placed it in the muzzle. Gage rammed it into position in front of the cartridge bag. Number 3 uncovered the vent hole and inserted a priming wire through the vent, making a hole in the cartridge bag.

Number 3 then removed the priming wire and Number 4 attached the lanyard to the friction primer which he inserted in the vent hole. He walked the lanyard back until it was taut and gave the signal to the gunner. The gunner again yelled "Fire." Number 4 pulled on the lanyard causing the friction primer to scrape along in the vent tube and that generated a small fire that ignited the cartridge bag. Boom! Again, the explosion rocked the casemate walls.

Thirty seconds later bricks surrounding the next embrasure over exploded, sending pieces of brick and concrete throughout the casemate. The Blakely had struck again, but this time there were no injuries.

After the first hour of firing, the only sound Gage could hear was the ringing in his ears. He watched the lips of the gunner in order to decipher the commands. His eyes now matched those of the other cannoneers, red and burning from the smoke and dust. During brief lulls in their firing, Gage carried cannonballs to a spot near cannoneer Number 2's station. Twice his fingers got squeezed in between the thirty-two pound balls. His hands swelled, intensified by the heat that poured from the barrel as he used the ramrod each time.

As Anderson had predicted, the vertical fire of Confederate mortars and shots from the enfilading batteries were tearing apart the parapet. Large chunks of masonry began to fall throughout the fort. Inside the casemates, however, the men remained relatively safe.

But the men sewing cartridge bags couldn't keep up with the rate of Sumter's firing, so Anderson ordered the number of guns being fired reduced from nine to six: two firing at Cummings Point, two at Fort Moultrie, and two against the batteries on Sullivan's Island.

"It appears we are now outgunned forty-three to six," a dispirited Doubleday said to Gage.

***

After three hours of near nonstop effort, Doubleday's crews were exhausted. Captain Seymour's men came in to take their place. Gage went looking for Gus, and found him sitting on the floor in the magazine area, still filling cartridge bags along with five laborers from Baltimore.

Gage wiped his face and hair with the sleeve of his shirt. There were no towels, shirts, or cloth of any kind remaining at the fort. They had all been used to make cartridge bags.

"Where'd you find a pigpen to fall into?" Gus asked.

"You should've seen me before I cleaned up," Gage said. Wiping with his sleeve did little good because the shirt was full of soot.

Gage looked down at the floor. Black powder was everywhere. "You men need to be more careful," he said. "There are three hundred barrels of black powder sitting behind you. If one spark from one of the shells gets in here and ignites this floor, this whole place will go up."

It was something Gus hadn't contemplated. His eyes lit up.

"You two," Gage said, pointing at two of the laborers standing next to some water barrels, "douse this floor with water. That should reduce the risk of an explosion."

Gus watched as the two men did so immediately, and he realized how differently Gage commanded. Unlike an overseer, Gage achieved obedience out of respect, not fear.

Gage thought Gus might need a little diversion. "You want to have some fun?"

"You got another of your big ideas?"

"Yep," Gage said, and he led the way up two flights of stairs to the parapet.

"The major said ain't nobody s'posed to be up here."

"Yep, too dangerous, so keep your head down."

They were fifty feet above the water, looking through a light drizzle out across the harbor in the direction of Fort Moultrie. Gage took out his field glasses for a better view. He looked at the fort and then continued looking farther east past Sullivan's Island out into the ocean. There, through the hazy mist, he spotted two ships although he couldn't identify them. Part of Fox's fleet? he wondered.

"We need to act fast," Gage said. "I need to tell Major Anderson about those ships."

All the cannons along the parapet were ready to fire with cartridge bags and cannonballs already in place. They found a cannon that appeared to be aligned correctly, and so Gage assumed the powder was in the right amount.

Gage took out his field glasses, ready to follow the cannonball's flight. Then, he said, "Gus, I think I see Ned Walker standing over there."

"How do I make it boom?"

Gage uncovered the vent hole, inserted the priming wire and attached it to the lanyard which he handed to Gus. "Walk out slowly until it's fully extended, but don't pull."

Gus did so, then looked back at Gage who now stood twenty feet from the cannon. "Now what should I do?"

"Pull!"

Gus yanked on the lanyard and all hell broke loose. The huge cannon boomed as it fired its shot and recoiled so violently that it broke from its wooden carriage. The concussion from this blast, out in the open as it was, was not as great as that in the casemates, but still it was enough to cause Gus's feet to wobble.

The two men rushed to the wall and tried to follow the cannonball as it headed for Fort Moultrie. "Just a little long," Gage said as he looked through field glasses. "Probably a little too much powder in that cartridge."

When they turned around, they realized what all the commotion from the recoil was about. When the cannon lifted off its carriage and bolted backwards, it fell down the stairwell behind them. Gage had forgotten to put stops behind the carriage. The barrel alone weighed over ten thousand pounds. It would remain in the stairwell.

"Shouldn't we get out of here?" Gus asked.

"We can stay here for the moment. They probably won't be aiming at us since there's no gun barrel here anymore."

"I was thinkin' of the major's orders."

Gage laughed. "Yep, perhaps we should get back to the casemates."

Actually, the gunners on Sullivan's Island had found a more compelling target. In what was a poor design of the fort the roof structures over the three interior buildings—the barracks and the officers' quarters—reached higher than the parapet. The Confederate cannonballs soon shattered parts of the slate roofs of those buildings, exposing wooden timbers. As Gage and Gus slithered along the parapet, trying to avoid the enemy fire, a shot came in from Fort Moultrie that struck several of the wooden pieces of the officers' quarters. Instantly, fiery shards were cast everywhere.

"What was that?" Gus asked.

"Hotshots," Gage said. "Fort Moultrie has a special furnace where they heat the cannonballs before firing them. They could set fire to all the buildings. Let's get over there."

When they made it to the buildings, Gage began directing a bucket brigade. But the next shots hit the cisterns that held fresh water. That turned out to be for the best because between the water that spilled and the firefighting efforts of the soldiers, the fires were soon put out.

***

Smoke from the fires at Sumter brought out more citizens of Charleston to the highest viewing points. Near the Battery, fifty people stood upon the balcony of the Genesis Hotel watching. From there they could see ships scattered beyond the harbor, although at the moment there were only four.

Standing next to Jenny and Frank Talbot was a neighbor, Francis Haggerty, a stocky woman with plump lips that she often used to assail anyone with an opposing opinion. Mrs. Haggerty looked out at the ocean and scoffed. "Probably just merchant ships. There is no Northern armada headed our way."

"I hope they do come," Jenny replied. "Perhaps it would put an end to this terrible mess."

"What kind of talk is that, young lady?"

"It's the voice of reason, Mrs. Haggerty," Frank Talbot said in defense of his daughter, even though he didn't entirely agree with Jenny.

"No, it's the voice of ignorance. If a few Northern troops come ashore, one hundred thousand slaves will rise up and join them. Is that what you want us to have to deal with?" She turned and walked away.

***

When Gage advised Major Anderson about the ships, the major was already aware of them. In fact, he said, "There are now four ships anchored out there. Some, though, may be merchant ships trying to stay out of the line of fire. But among them is one man-of-war—the *Pawnee*. A true warship, undoubtedly part of Fox's fleet."

For the next three hours the fort continued to receive the shots from the circle of fire which now truly posed a fire threat. Two crews were taken off their weapons to help douse the fires wherever they started.

An hour before nightfall Anderson and Gage commiserated about their situation. "For four months we have done everything possible to make sure we didn't initiate a battle," Anderson lamented. "Now the battle is joined, our ships are at our doorstep, and yet they do nothing to help us."

"It makes no sense," Gage wondered aloud. "Why send them here to do nothing?"

"I suppose it's possible they plan to send troops and supplies during the nighttime by small boats, but I fear such an undertaking would be a disaster. And for what? I can't imagine those ships could be carrying more than two hundred additional soldiers, and they wouldn't be artillerists. I'll order sentries posted for the night, though."

Thinking of the landing rafts he saw being built, Gage said, "May I suggest at all corners, Major. Be on the lookout for friend and foe alike."

***

Near dusk, Gage wandered about in the casemates. In the dim light he made out Private Davidson, again crumpled up along one of the walls. The uplifting effect of the letter from Jenny appeared to have worn off.

"Why aren't you with the others?" Gage asked, for most of the men slept with their own crew where there might be a candle they could share.

"More comfortable here," the young man answered.

Gage detected some evasiveness. "Somebody in your crew treating you badly?"

"No, sir, they treat me fine."

Something had him spooked, but he wouldn't explain it so Gage asked, "How did you handle everything today?"

"I did fine. Well, I was doing fine until . . . "

"Until?"

"Until the fires started."

"You afraid of the fires?"

He nodded.

"How come?"

"My mother and little brother died in a fire . . . in their sleep. A gas lamp tipped over and took them before they ever woke up."

"I'm sorry," Gage said.

It was as if once that disclosure was made, the floodgates opened. For the next half hour Davidson shared his feelings, and Gage counseled the young man about war and his future.

"If I were to leave the army and move to Charleston, I would have to fight for the South," Davidson explained. "I don't believe in slavery. I don't think I could do that. And I don't know whether Jenny would move to the North."

"When we get out of here, you'll be able to send her a letter. Ask her. It doesn't matter whether she's able to get to the North. All that matters is that she's willing to do so."

The more the young man talked, the more his personality surfaced. He possessed a strange combination of confidence and self-doubt, and it manifested itself as he talked about his chances to survive the battle. "I've always been lucky. Even when that fire happened, I was away at my uncle's place, or I would have been taken, too. You know, Mr. Gage, I can flip a coin and call it right nine times out of ten."

Gage smiled. "If you're so lucky, what are you worried about?"

"I'm afraid this battle might be that one out of ten times."

**

One person who had settled in with others was Gus. Gage found him sitting with a group of enlisted men as if he was one of the soldiers. In the common ground of their plight, he was accepted as an equal.

Their conversations focused on predictions for tomorrow. One private predicted the bombardment would intensify, if that was even possible. Another suggested that the Confederates would mount a ground assault against the fort with at least one thousand soldiers, perhaps during the night. That led another to suggest a third possibility: that the Confederate assault would occur when the ships tried to land Union troops. They all agreed that would be the worst of all scenarios because that would mean they would have to leave the relative safety of the fort to join their comrades in hand-to-hand combat.

Their predictions were varied, but underlying it all there was a common sentiment: tomorrow will be worse.

Chapter 57
(Morning of Day 2)

Cannon fire slowed significantly during the night. Sumter did not fire at all since Major Anderson didn't want to waste their few remaining cartridges. Confederate bombs came at Sumter occasionally from the island batteries, but with the fort dark it was a difficult target. It was kept up at fifteen minute intervals as a form of intimidation and a reminder of what was coming in the morning.

With no light in the fort and nothing to do, Gage fell asleep early. However, that sleep was disjointed, occasionally interrupted by a shot from the enemy that struck one of the nearby walls. Three times during the night he got up to wander around in the darkness, clinging to the inner wall of the casemates where he found a sliver of light from the parade ground. Other officers were doing the same. Each was on alert for the possibility of a landing by one side or the other. But a storm had brought in strong winds, and the water was too rough for such to occur.

At four in the morning Gage awoke again. Eighty feet away in his casemate he could see the flickering light of a single candle. He made his way toward the candle, stumbling and feeling his way as he went. From thirty feet away Gage could see that the candle was held by one man sitting in a wooden chair, his head cast downward with his eyes on the floor. A few feet further Gage realized it was Major Anderson, looking as disconsolate as Gage had ever seen him.

The major barely looked up when Gage stood before him. Finally, he said, "I don't know what to do, John." He put both hands to his head and added, "For the first time in my life as a soldier I don't know what to do."

"You mean whether to surrender?"

Anderson nodded. "President Lincoln sent me a message on April 4th. What bothered me most in that message is that he said if in your judgment you determine it's best to capitulate then do so, but he also said I trust you will act as a patriot. He doesn't trust me, John. If we surrender, I will be deemed to have dishonored our flag."

"Nonsense, nearly every newspaper article we've received from the North has said you've shown great honor under trying circumstances. Even the Charleston people recognize that."

"I will be called a coward . . . a traitor. All I've tried to do is my duty and avoid a war."

"You've put up a good fight against impossible odds. People will respect that."

Anderson shook his head. "I've spent the majority of my life as a soldier, detesting the very thing we're taught to do."

It was true. Over his thirty-five years in the army this artillery expert had come to loathe the tools of his craft.

Gage was reassuring. "You once told me you stayed in the army because you believed a strong military could deter aggressors, and thereby ensure the peace. I believe that, too."

"Some of our fellow officers seem to enjoy the carnage of war. I don't understand that. I've never understood that."

"Yes, we saw plenty of that carnage in the Mexican War."

"It's not that I'm thinking of, John. I'm thinking back to the end of the Black Hawk War. We found the bodies of many Indians on the ground—pathetic, emaciated bodies. I don't want this to end that way for my men."

***

The relentless bombardment of Sumter began again just before daybreak. Gage went to the officers' dining area where he ate his half portion of rancid pork. This is what the men had been living on for weeks. They must be impaired, Gage thought. How can they keep up the strenuous work in their depleted conditions?

Citizens of Charleston returned to the rooftops along the Battery for a better view. This morning, however, the scene was less dramatic. A west wind carried sounds out to the ocean, producing noiseless explosions. And those explosions were obscured, for a fog had settled in over the water that made Sumter barely visible.

Jenny Talbot and her father had been on the rooftop of the Genesis Hotel for an hour trying to see through that fog. Mrs. Haggerty, whom Jenny had the encounter with the day before, stood not ten feet away.

Soon the sun began to break through the fog, and it was as if a veil was lifted. What the people of Charleston suddenly saw horrified them. Just outside the harbor there were now twelve ships, and they appeared to be forming a battle line.

"A true armada," Frank Talbot said, for the ships seemed quite capable of bombarding the city or sending troops ashore.

Mrs. Haggerty passed by the Talbots and paused long enough to say, "I hope you're happy, Jennifer. Your wish appears to have come true. I suggest you all hide."

"I don't fear the Northern troops," Jenny replied.

"Then perhaps you should fear our slaves when they rise up to join them."

Mrs. Haggerty left, as did Frank Talbot who went to warn others at his office. But there immediately appeared on the rooftop a young lieutenant from Beauregard's staff who brought news from the general: "I want to assure you all that General Beauregard has the situation well in hand. Many of the ships you see out there are merchant vessels that are stopped because they don't know whether to try to enter the harbor."

"How do you know that?" one man asked.

"The general receives constant reports from Sullivan's Island where they can see out beyond the harbor. We know what ships are out there."

That seemed to satisfy everyone on the rooftop, but the lieutenant couldn't be everywhere. When Frank Talbot purchased a newspaper from a vendor, he had to wait in a line that was thirty people deep. The city was in a frenzy with people rushing in every direction, crashing through that line.

It was headlines like the following in Ransom Pierce's newspaper that triggered this frenzy:

Northern Invasion Force Ready to Strike

Newspaper sales were up, way up, and Ransom Pierce wasn't going to miss this opportunity. That headline would produce a day of record profits.

And yet Pierce knew the truth. He had been in a meeting with Beauregard during which the general told others, "Only two, perhaps three, of the ships are Union vessels." The general was also convinced that Union ships would not dare bombard the city. "This is as much a battle for the hearts and minds of all citizens as it is a battle for Fort Sumter."

It was Ransom Pierce who rejected such a notion. "We battle only for the hearts and minds of Southerners, General. A great victory will win them over."

"Anderson and his men are already heroes in the North," the general responded. "Even here in Charleston people revere them for their dedication to duty against incalculable odds. I don't want to turn them into martyrs."

Pierce became agitated. "South Carolina has called in young men from all over the state, General. You have seven thousand of them at your disposal. You could achieve a great victory by invading that fort."

"No, Pierce, a peaceful surrender occurring through a magnanimous gesture on our part in which we let them slink away will tamp down enthusiasm in the North."

The men at Sumter knew the truth, too, for they had the best vantage point out beyond the harbor. Gage and Doubleday looked through one of the embrasures facing the ocean and could see that the only naval vessels were the *Harriet Lane* and the warship *Pawnee*.

"They're almost all merchant ships," Gage said. "They're just sitting out there, not knowing what to do because after last night's burning they can't get into the harbor." During the night, Confederates burned three old hulks to block the channels into the harbor.

"Maybe that large civilian steamer is carrying troops, but it can't be many," Doubleday replied.

"Even so, they've got nothing to land those troops with."

***

After a day of firing, Confederate artillerists had refined their aim to such an extent that now they didn't just direct their fire at the fort, but at specific targets within the fort. And believing they were making progress, they increased the frequency of their firing. Incoming shots and shells were now arriving at the rate of almost one per minute. It allowed the fort's occupants no time between the aftereffects of a bomb and another bomb's arrival. It was constant chaos.

Gage and Gus made a run for the casemates on the other side of the parade ground. Halfway there a thirty-two pound shell from the iron battery at Cummings Point struck the parapet just above them. The convulsion shook the fort so violently that both men lost their balance and fell to the ground. Pieces of broken brick and mortar rained down on them. As they got to their feet, Doubleday's crew returned fire, shaking the ground again and that was followed immediately by another incoming shell that hit the interior wall and sent masonry fragments spinning in all directions, narrowly missing them.

Upon reaching the casemates on the other side, Gage realized that what had been a trend was now a Confederate strategy. The enemy was lobbing heavy shots at the roof of the officers' quarters. "They know our weakness," Gage said to Gus.

Within minutes additional parts of the slate roof shattered, exposing more wooden beams of the building. Then the ordnance changed, and even Gus recognized it. "More hotshots," he said.

The special furnace at Fort Moultrie was never intended to be used like this. It was intended to heat cannonballs for use against wooden ships—ships from distant shores. Not against a masonry fort, and especially not one manned by Americans. But the Confederates knew this fort well. The roof of the barracks might be made of slate, but beneath that the buildings were entirely wood.

It didn't take long before a blaze began in the upper reaches of the building, this one much larger than the ones the previous day. All the men not engaged in firing the artillery ran to the building to help fight the fire.

Gage grabbed an axe and was on his way upstairs when he found Private Davidson sitting on the landing as if frozen in place. "We need every man, Private," Gage said adamantly. He held out his hand and pulled Davidson to his feet. They raced upstairs to the third floor.

Gage charged up a ladder and began hacking away at burning trim and cornices that might ignite the walls and floor. As he knocked down pieces, men on the floor doused the burning wood with water. Private Davidson found an axe and an extra ladder and went about copying Gage's efforts.

This went on for several minutes until a thunderous explosion occurred right above them as another bomb struck a different portion of the slate roof. Debris rained down. Gage looked over at Davidson and noticed an odd combination of fear and determination on the young man's face, but no panic. Not one minute later another shell struck that rattled the entire building, almost knocking the two men off their ladders. They had just regained their balance when a huge beam let loose and began to swing down their way from the ceiling. It missed Davidson's head by just a few inches.

Bombs continued to pound at the roof as more men joined the firefight from the ladders. But it seemed a losing cause. The roof was being torn away, each time exposing more timbers to the hotshots and fire.

The next explosion shook the building and knocked Private Davidson off his ladder. He sat on the floor for a moment. Gage thought the young man was dazed, or perhaps he had finally panicked. But it wasn't that. Davidson looked up at Gage and yelled, "This floor is warm!"

Smoke began to filter into the room from below, and Gage realized the room under them was on fire. "We need to get out!" Gage yelled to the others. "Let the building go."

The fire was already spreading to the two buildings that housed the enlisted men. The dry wood was like kindling. Gage watched a sixteen-inch thick beam succumb, and when it crashed to the floor flaming shards shot out that the wind whipped about, carrying them out into the parade ground.

Major Anderson was standing stoically across the parade ground, calmly surveying the situation. As Gage started to sprint to him, a shell struck the west tower. Then a series of explosions came at Gage so rapid in nature and so unusual that he knew they weren't fired by the enemy. In the west tower staircase, soldiers had stored nine-inch shells filled with nails for use as grenades in the event of a Confederate ground assault. Gage fell back into the casemates as the grenades exploded, shooting nails throughout the parade ground. The west tower soon caved in.

When Gage reached Anderson, the major said, "John, the magazine is not safe. We have to get rid of the powder." Three hundred barrels of black powder were stored in the magazine, all contained in a masonry vault behind a solid copper door. But it would only take a single spark in the right place to set the whole thing off.

By the time Gage reached the magazine, soldiers were already carrying barrels of powder out to a more secure location where they covered them with wet blankets. But the men were walking through patches of powder and, unlike the day before, they were creating a long trail of powder that led straight to the copper door. One spark would set off that trail, and the fire would make its way under the door into the magazine.

"Flood this entire area with water," Gage yelled to the men and they began bringing in buckets of water to do so.

Gage looked back out into the parade ground. The fire was growing worse. It had now engulfed all the barracks. Now certain of its vulnerability, Confederates intensified their attack on the area.

Hot embers were flying everywhere. They came from the burning barracks as well as the wooden carriages of the cannons on the parapet that had been set on fire by the hotshots. Some of the flaming embers made their way into the casemates, at times finding flammable material such as bedding that the soldiers had brought in from the barracks. Men worked to put out the small fires in the casemates all while dousing the hot embers that attached to their clothing and skin.

Major Anderson concluded that the new location for the barrels of powder was too exposed. He ordered the men in the magazine area to stop their work there and take the barrels already out and roll them down into the water beyond the fort.

Gage was helping to direct their work when a ten-inch ball passed over his head and through a small opening and landed in the magazine area. It pounded the copper door to the magazine, breaking the lock in such a manner that the door could no longer be opened. Gage, along with two other men, tried several times but the door was stuck, permanently shut. Two hundred barrels of powder remained inside the dangerous magazine.

Fire was everywhere but, hunkered down in the casemates, the men could escape that. What they couldn't escape was the smoke, a heavy black variety that the wind was now trapping in the casemates.

So pervasive was the smoke that the Sumter guns ceased firing because the soldiers were unable to maintain enough good air to keep up their work. Everywhere men were coughing, choking. Most lay on the floor with wet cloths across their faces. Gage still had wet sleeves and used them to cover his mouth and nose. Someone pulled the iron shutter away from one of the unused embrasures. Gus stuck his head out of the opening. He and three other men took turns gasping for air from the outside. They were risking being hit by an incoming shot, but there was no alternative.

Gage got up off the floor and stumbled toward the parade ground where shells continued to explode, preventing it from being an area of escape. The Confederates picked up the intensity. Bombs were falling every forty-five seconds. Some of the barrels of black powder that didn't roll all the way to the water were hit by mortars and exploded, sending rocks skyward into the fort where they fell along with the fiery embers.

The barracks were gone, the towers were gone, the parapet and the parade ground were shooting galleries. Now the casemates, the last and only true refuge, were death traps.

For the first time the thought came over Gage that they weren't going to survive this.

People watching from the roof of the Genesis Hotel were appalled. Flames from the burning barracks and carriages were leaping through the thick black smoke.

With tears in her eyes, Mrs. Haggerty looked at a crestfallen Jenny Talbot and said, "My dear, I never wanted this. May God be with those soldiers."

She hugged Jenny.

Chapter 58

(Afternoon of Day 2)

Desperate to help, naval officers on the ships out beyond the harbor watched the conflagration at Sumter in horror. So did Bette Downing. She dabbed her eyes with a handkerchief, not unmindful that it belonged to John Gage.

Both senior and junior officers from the three Navy vessels that had arrived boarded the *Harriet Lane* to debate their options. Their flagship for this operation, the *Powhatan*, which carried the thirty launches that would silently convey soldiers to Sumter, had not appeared. Nor had the tugboats that would tow the launches. Little did they know that the *Powhatan* would not arrive. It was on its way to Pensacola, Florida, in an attempt to relieve the small Union force at that naval base, sent there by a mistake in the orders issued by President Lincoln. Due to the number of Southerners still in the navy, those orders were kept so secret that no one at the navy department discovered the error.

The orders given these officers only complicated matters. The captain of the warship *Pawnee*, Commander Stephen Rowan, had instructions to await the *Powhatan*. None of their orders allowed for a daylight incursion, let alone bombardment of the Confederate island batteries.

The navy ships possessed no means of communicating with Fort Sumter. When the Sumter artillery stopped firing during the height of the battle, the naval officers sent a rowboat carrying two young officers and a white flag to Fort Moultrie to find out what was going on.

It didn't help the mindsets of the senior officers that they were under assault themselves. It came from Bette Downing who assailed them for their vacillation. "What in hell are you doing?" she railed at them. "I'm told the *Pawnee* guns can hurl a one hundred pound shell more than a mile, and yet you do nothing. Instead, you send two sailors in a rowboat to ask the enemy how our side is doing. Why did you even come down here?"

Commander Rowan couldn't stand it anymore. He commandeered a merchant ship headed for the Charleston wharves. He planned to use the schooner to deliver soldiers and supplies to Sumter.

It was a controversial action among the mix of officers. "Seizing that ship was an act of piracy," said one officer.

"I believed it contained contraband—tools of war," Rowan countered.

"And when you found it held ice from Boston why did you not release it?"

"I did release it. I then purchased one night's use of it for five hundred dollars."

The officer looked at Fox. "Do you think his plan will succeed?"

Fox struggled for words. He was distraught watching the fire at the fort, contemplating what must be going on with the men there. His own plan was a failure, not necessarily of his doing, but still it was a failure. And he had come to realize that even if it had succeeded, it would have done nothing more than extend the Union stay at Sumter by no more than a month. The new island batteries were simply too formidable.

"I fear it will not succeed," Fox answered feebly, "but I see no alternative."

"You're talking about helping them tonight," Bette screamed at the officers. "That will be too late. Those men need help now."

"The lady is right," Rowan said adamantly. "We need to act now!"

"What are you suggesting?"

"That we blast our way into the harbor."

"Without a pilot? Without the *Powhatan*? We would likely run aground and sit there as fodder for their guns."

"Then we'll stay outside the harbor on the edges where we can attack their easternmost batteries from an angle they're not prepared for."

"They have forty to fifty guns firing. We don't have enough ammunition to take them all out."

"All we have to do is take out enough of them to get us in closer," Commander Rowan said. "Hell, then we could fire at Charleston."

"What a gruesome act of war that would be."

"The war has already started, Captain."

"I hardly see such an action authorized by the president's orders."

Even Rowan had to agree with that, although grudgingly because he asserted that men in the field had to respond to the exigencies of the moment. Eventually, though, they all concurred that sending the schooner in at night was the only rational option.

Devastated, Bette returned to her small cabin in the *Harriet Lane*.

***

The frightful scene of smoke and fire played out for the next two hours. Then, quite suddenly, the wind direction changed and the men in the casemates could breathe again. Doubleday's crew opened fire against the iron battery at Cummings Point.

When the spectators atop the Genesis Hotel saw that artillery response, they cheered wildly. "There is life at the fort," one man yelled.

Mrs. Haggerty smiled at Jenny, then looked back at Sumter and cried out, "Now, surrender you fools!"

***

Early in the afternoon, General Beauregard convened a meeting of his top aides. Ransom Pierce was also present. A discussion ensued about allowing a negotiated surrender without taking prisoners.

"Let them go?" Pierce screamed at Beauregard. "Are you mad?"

Increasingly irritated by Pierce, Beauregard turned on him and said, "To not take them prisoner will be viewed as an honorable act on our part."

"What kind of war are you waging? You have seven thousand men at your disposal against their one hundred, and yet you don't invade. When their fort burns, you even offered to help them fight the fire. This is idiocy."

"To show compassion for a defeated enemy is not madness, especially in these circumstances."

"What of Gage and the slave?"

"Why are you so fixated on John Gage?"

"You can't let them go . . . assuming they're still alive."

"We believe everyone is still alive."

"What kind of victory is that?"

"A glorious one. We will have accomplished our goal of driving them out without a slaughter."

"This is treasonous on your part, General. The citizens of Charleston will not stand for it."

"I'll ask you once again, Pierce. Why does Gage's status matter to you so much?"

"Because you will have allowed a traitor to go free."

"Two days ago you hailed my decision to send Gage to Sumter as a smart move. I've grown tired of your antics, Pierce." He gestured to a lieutenant standing nearby to remove Pierce from the office.

"You can't dismiss me!" Pierce screamed. "I am the voice of the people."

Beauregard again pointed to the door, and the lieutenant seized Pierce by the arm. But this heated exchange reminded the general that he had a note from Gage that he still had not looked at. As Pierce rambled on, Beauregard opened the envelope and read the short note. A wry smile came to his face.

Pierce finished his rant by yelling, "Why you stupid fucking Creole. You're barely American. I'll have you hung for this."

"Take him to Castle Pinckney and lock him up in the military stockade," Beauregard said to the lieutenant.

"Lock me up? On what charge?"

"Two charges: threatening violence against a Confederate officer and theft of the gold from the Charleston Customs House."

"You're going to lock me up and let Gage go free?" Pierce shouted as he left the room. "This is an outrage . . . " he screamed, his voice trailing off as two soldiers dragged him down the hallway.

***

Artillery fire from Sumter was now mostly for show. The truth was the fort, and its men, were being decimated. But just after one in the afternoon something occurred that changed everything. The Sumter flagstaff finally fell, shot away by the incoming shells. Confederate observers didn't know what to make of it. Was Sumter surrendering?

On Morris Island Confederate officers watched with mixed emotions the conflagration across the water. They had the closest vantage point of the horrific scene unfolding. One of those observing—mainly because he had no real duties—was the recently appointed Confederate colonel Louis Wigfall.

As Wigfall watched, the most ardent fire-eater of all approached him. It was sixty-year-old Edwin Ruffin, his long white hair strewn about that always seemed to confirm an air of madness about him. He was a man so long dedicated to the cause of Southern independence that the soldiers on Morris Island gave him the honor of firing one of the first shots at Fort Sumter.

But Ruffin didn't like what he was seeing. "Wigfall, I've always wanted independence, not a war. I've never wanted to see men die needlessly."

"Nor I."

"Their flag appears to be down," Ruffin added.

"Yes, but did they take it down, or did we shoot it down?"

"Someone needs to find out."

"I agree," Wigfall said.

"What can be done to stop this?"

"That would have to come from Beauregard."

Ruffin scoffed. "Generals, shit. The people should determine independence, and the people should determine when there is war. Not generals."

"I couldn't agree more, Mr. Ruffin," Wigfall said, picking up on the man's enthusiasm. He charged off to one of the generals on the island and, whipping his cane about for emphasis, told him his plan to row across to Sumter. With no way to reach Beauregard, and knowing Wigfall's tendency for manic behavior, the general didn't try to dissuade him.

For Wigfall this was his chance, a chance to prove himself like no other. One man in a rowboat would cause Sumter to surrender, something forty-three guns couldn't compel over the last thirty-four hours. They will cheer me everywhere in the South, he thought, perhaps even in the North. It is well worth the risk. He tossed his cane to the ground.

An old leaky rowboat sat by the shore, and Wigfall walked toward it. Three slaves stood nearby, maintaining a safe distance from any fire that might come from Sumter. "You boys row me across to the fort," Wigfall demanded.

The three young men looked at him incredulously. Sumter might not be firing, but the Confederates certainly hadn't ceased theirs. When Wigfall produced his pistol, the trio reluctantly agreed.

A young private joined the group. As two of the slaves rowed, one bailed water.

But any boat in the harbor, no matter how small, was suspect by both sides. Not one hundred feet from the shore, a ten-inch ball fired from Fort Moultrie as a warning landed just in front of them. The wave created rocked the small boat.

"We need a flag of truce," the private said.

"Yes, of course," Wigfall said. He reached into his pocket and pulled out a white handkerchief that when unfolded was practically the size of a small blanket. He wrapped the handkerchief around his sword and held it high in the air. But not more than a minute later another ten-pound ball came at them, this one flying directly over their heads.

"Damn them, they don't respect this flag." Maybe this wasn't such a good idea, Wigfall wondered. Still, he charged on.

When they arrived at the fort, they found that the small wharf was too damaged to receive their boat, so they stopped out in the shallow water. Wigfall got out and waded through the water up onto land. He had no idea where to go. From his viewpoint, the main gate appeared to be on fire.

He looked at the lower tier embrasures and spotted one that was open and possessed no weapon. That might be a way in, but even the lower tiers were too high to reach. He found a board, propped it up against the wall, and climbed up.

When Wigfall looked through the embrasure opening, there was a face peering back at him. He knew that face. "Gage!" he exclaimed.

"Come to surrender, have you, Wigfall?"

"You're not the man I'm looking for, Gage, but you'll do. Take me to Major Anderson."

Gage was stunned by Wigfall's arrival, but he figured the man must have come for a purpose. He tried pulling him through the opening. Twice Wigfall's sword became stuck on the brick enclosure.

Once Wigfall was inside, Gage led him to Major Anderson. Despite not having seen Beauregard for two days, Wigfall purported to be the general's emissary. "Major Anderson, you have fought nobly in the defense of this fort," Wigfall began. "General Beauregard desires to end this fight."

"As do I, under terms of the Honors of War," Anderson replied.

And now the dance began, for only a few key words could be contentious. Wigfall understood this. "Under what terms would you evacuate the fort?"

Ah, *evacuate*. That was a key word. Not a surrender but an evacuation.

Major Anderson brightened. "I already gave my terms to General Beauregard a few days ago. We will evacuate the fort promptly upon those terms."

Wigfall went through those terms again and agreed that the fight could be ended on that basis. Thirty minutes later he was back on shore at Morris Island where, in a most exalted fashion, he proclaimed to a crowd of soldiers, "The fort is ours!"

They carried him aloft on their shoulders. Two hours later the same thing occurred in the streets of Charleston as celebrating citizens carried Wigfall to General Beauregard's office where he could explain what he had done.

The real negotiating party, one sent by General Beauregard, had already learned what he had done. It flew in the face of Beauregard's terms that Union soldiers would not be allowed to salute the American flag as they left. But what was done was done, and Beauregard eventually agreed.

Chapter 59

Soldiers at the fort were up early the next morning, preparing to depart. Despite their first decent night's sleep and good food in a long time, they were different this day. They were somber, their enthusiasm lost. The adrenalin they had been operating on was gone.

Using undamaged artillery from the parapet, Major Anderson planned a one hundred-gun salute for his departing garrison. But halfway through the tribute one of the cannons fired prematurely. It blew the arm off one of the artillery crewmen, Private Daniel Hough. As the others on his crew scrambled to him, sparks from that misfire set off cartridge bags lying on the ground. They exploded, shooting leftover shards of brick and other debris flying about. Private Hough died instantly. Every other member of the crew was injured, including Private Davidson who suffered substantial wounds to his right leg.

Major Anderson cut the salute short at fifty guns. The injured men were carried on stretchers down to the lower tier to be loaded onto the *Isabel*, the small steamer that would transfer all the men to the larger ship, the *Baltic*, that was waiting just outside the harbor.

Gage stopped the stretchers and knelt down by Private Davidson.

"Mr. Gage, it looks like this was that one time I didn't guess the coin correctly," the private said.

"You're going to be fine, son," Gage assured him.

"All I wanted was to see Jenny one more time before I die."

"You're not going to die, and you're going to see Jenny again."

Gage stood and walked further out. He saw Confederate Colonel James Chestnut who was waiting in one of the small boats offshore. "Colonel, the only man to die in this confrontation was as a result of an accident—our accident. If one of these men dies on the ship going back north, it will be because of delayed treatment and that will be your fault. Take these men to the Charleston Hospital."

"We can do that," Chestnut shouted back.

"You'll take them to the hospital, fix them up, and send them north later?"

"We'll do that."

"And without exchange?"

"Agreed."

Gage returned to Private Davidson and told him the news: "You're going to the hospital in Charleston. I hear they have some wonderful nurses there."

A smile burst across the private's face as he clasped Gage's hand firmly.

Because of the delay it was not until late in the afternoon that the soldiers left the fort for the *Isabel*. As the regimental band played Yankee Doodle they marched out, saluting the tattered American flag that clung to a makeshift flagstaff.

For the first time in two weeks, Southern authorities permitted delivery of mail and newspapers to the soldiers at the fort. Among them was Ransom Pierce's last edition as editor of the *Charleston Star* that featured a menacing headline:

Confederate Flag to Soon Fly over Washington City

That headline arose out of a speech made the prior day in Montgomery by the Confederate secretary of war during which the secretary predicted, "In three months the Confederate flag will fly over Washington."

Later, as he was about to board the *Isabel*, Gage carried that newspaper with him, for that headline served as a reminder of his mission still ahead. To Gage's left, a small boat arrived with Governor Pickens, General Beauregard, and Colonel Chestnut on board. They tipped their hats to Gage, but he had words for them: "This statement by your secretary of war will arouse the North even more than your attack on Sumter."

"Perhaps so," Beauregard replied quickly, "but I've put an end to Pierce and his newspaper."

"But what about Wigfall, Ruffin, and hundreds of others of your

Southern demagogues who have roused the countryside with their lies, lies which you did not speak up and call out as such? Now you can't stop what they've unleashed."

No one responded and Gage added, "You can celebrate your day, gentlemen, but I mourn for you. You have blindly followed people like Pierce to what will be a certain path of destruction."

Because of low water late in the day, the *Isabel* waited until the next morning to take the men out to the *Baltic*. When the *Isabel* drifted by Cummings Point, Confederate soldiers removed their hats and stood silently in a respectful farewell.

Just outside the harbor the *Isabel* rendezvoused with the steamer *Baltic*, and Gage and Gus went aboard. Two hundred yards away was the *Harriet Lane*, and on its deck was Bette Downing waving wildly and jumping for joy. When Gage saw her, he responded with the same enthusiasm.

Gus was waving to Bette as well, but most of all he was watching the expression on Gage's face. Finally, he said to Gage, "I never seen you smile like that befo'."

When a lieutenant came by, Gage asked, "Where is the *Harriet Lane* headed?"

"Straight to New York, sir."

"And our ship?"

"To New York after a stop at Fort Monroe."

Detecting some hesitation on Gage's part, the lieutenant asked, "Do you want us to take you over to the *Harriet Lane* so you can go directly to New York?"

"No, we've got to go to Fort Monroe."

The lieutenant walked away. Gus asked, "Why we goin' to another fort?"

"We should be able to find a Navy ship there that will take us to Annapolis. Remember, I'm going to get you to Maryland."

Gus offered a half-smile.

Then, with a smack to the front of the *Charleston Star* newspaper with the threatening headline, Gage added, "Besides, we've got important work to do in Maryland."

This time Gus broke into a full smile. He liked what he just heard from

Gage... he liked all of it.

***

One hour into their voyage north, John Gage went below deck. He sat down at a table and emptied a bag he had been given containing his last month of mail. Sifting through the letters, he prioritized them, putting the letter from his mother first. It contained no return address, only a postmark of Annapolis, Maryland.

Written four weeks earlier, before she learned of his arrest, she spoke mostly about how different her situation was in Maryland. But she began by thanking him profusely for what he sent:

> I've always cherished that quote from Mary Queen of Scots, and now I have it with me again. But even more than that, I thank you for having Mrs. Constance Cherry deliver it. We talked for over an hour, and she helped me so much. She is a wonder, and you are fortunate to have her in your life. I hope you keep her there.

Gage smiled at that.

His mother's mindset seemed much stronger in the letter. Gage found that comforting until the last few paragraphs in which she said:

> Other than the visit from Constance, my life in Maryland has been unpleasant. I'm basically confined to the house—Jubal doesn't want me to go anywhere. He claims it's for my own good... for my own safety. And yet Jubal keeps making trips to Carthage and Baltimore for reasons he won't explain.
>
> Jubal is so different here—it's as if I don't know this man. He is moody, aloof. Is this the person he really is? I intend to find out. I won't rest until I learn the truth about the man I married and the truth about the explosion at the ironworks.

His mother was once again feisty. He could see it in her language, a sure sign of her renewed vigor. Until her recent health setbacks, she had always been feisty. He laughed as he recalled the time when he was six years old, and he watched her use a broom to chase a black bear out of their garden. But she didn't just chase the bear out of the garden. She chased him for a good quarter of a mile with that broom raised overhead. The bear never returned.

A woman who would take on a bear with a broom wouldn't hesitate to challenge Jubal Ford. And that's what had Gage troubled. "Mother, don't, please don't," he said softly.

***

Up on the deck of the *Baltic,* Gus Ward held tight to the railing on the port side of the steamer. He stood alone, bracing himself against strong wind gusts that rocked the ship. Having been so consumed with the battle and its aftermath, this was the first time in days he had had a chance to reflect on anything else. He watched the paddle wheel tumble in the water. The constant revolutions had him mesmerized. Like the paddle wheel, his life was turning over. Softly he began to sing "Steal Away," the tune he sang so often in the field:

> Steal away, steal away,
> steal away to Jesus!
> Steal away, steal away home,
> I ain't got long to stay here.

"It's come true," he said as he held his hands together and looked skyward. "Thank you, Lord, thank you."

He reached into his pocket and pulled out the little bag that contained the lock of Nelly's hair. He felt the strands inside, careful not to expose them to the strong gusts. Then he said out loud, "I'm coming home, Nelly . . . coming home a free man!"

"I am a free man!" he cried out. Then, overcome by the magnitude of his sudden change in life, he collapsed to the deck sobbing.

***

Four hours into the voyage north, the wind had calmed and John Gage joined Major Anderson on the deck. They stood along the railing, looking out over the water. Neither man spoke.

Gage was contemplating all that they had just been through. Anderson was thinking about what was to come. Finally, he said, "They will condemn me, John."

"Who's they?"

"The press, the public, the army. They will call me a coward, perhaps a traitor, for surrendering Sumter."

"You didn't surrender. The terms you negotiated were an evacuation."

"I'm not sure they'll appreciate the distinction."

"I think the reaction will be quite different. You held out and fought to your last cartridge against overwhelming odds. At least four thousand cannon shots fired into the fort by the enemy, and no one was killed."

A slight smile came to Anderson's ashen face. "God was with us . . . with all of us. No one died on either side in the battle."

"Neither side wanted anyone to die in that battle. That was a fight among friends. Tomorrow will be different."

PART V

City on the Brink

(April 17, 1861 – April 25, 1861)

Chapter 60

The day word of Sumter's capitulation reached Washington President Lincoln issued a proclamation calling for seventy-five thousand troops to be supplied by the states to put down the "insurrection." It was a number arrived at by consensus in the cabinet, but still it stunned the members for it was five times the size of the current standing army.

Within two days of the proclamation, its impact throughout the country was clear. In the North the attack on Fort Sumter rallied people behind the flag, and men quickly volunteered. But nonaligned slave-owning states, such as Kentucky and Missouri, rejected the call for troops. Virginia and Maryland teetered on the verge of secession.

On the afternoon of the seventeenth, Aramis Gage received a message from President Lincoln requesting his presence at a meeting of the cabinet. The president had come to appreciate Ari's ability to placate different factions of the Republican Party, and he deemed it advisable to have someone present who could act as a liaison to Congress.

When Ari arrived at the White House, he bounded up the staircase to the second floor. Between that exertion and the excitement of the moment, he was out of breath when he reached the meeting room. He tapped lightly on the door. Lincoln's secretary, John Hay, opened it and escorted him in.

The cabinet was a fractious group, full of giant egos—four of the seven members had sought the Republican nomination for president—brought together by Lincoln to accommodate a variety of political opinions and geographic locations. As the congressman sat down, all the cabinet members looked at him with suspicion. None offered salutations. Ari took no insult.

They regarded each other in the same way.

It was during this cabinet meeting that the consequences of the proclamation in the critical state of Virginia were first confirmed. Hay interrupted by whispering to the president: "There is a Republican legislator from western Virginia standing outside. He brings news."

"See him in," Lincoln said, and Hay opened the door. In walked a lanky man dressed so strangely in corduroy pants and a flannel shirt that most in the room paid him little attention.

The news he brought from Virginia was not good: "Today the Virginia Convention voted to secede, subject only to an approving vote of the people on May 23rd."

This was surprising, but not startling. It was what the legislator said next that caused the others to sit up and listen. "The secession ordinance is to be kept secret, at least until notice is given of a vote by the populace."

"Strange, but why does that concern you so?" Secretary Cameron asked.

"Because the Virginia secessionists aren't going to wait for a vote of the people. They have established what they call a provisional government with authority to take actions during the interim. I think they have plots they intend to carry out right now."

"It does seem there's a purpose to using a provisional government," the president noted.

"Sir," the legislator said bluntly, "I believe they have designs on Washington City... immediate designs."

The dilemma was clear to everyone: a temporary army of seventy-five thousand troops might soon be raised, but how many of those troops could reach Washington in time?

General Scott tried to lessen the anxiety. "Three regiments of well-equipped and well-trained soldiers from New York and Massachusetts—nearly three thousand men—are already on their way."

"When will they get here, General?"

"They should be here in two days."

"*Should?*"

"They should. Of course, for them to get here, we are dependent on the railroad routes through Baltimore."

The general's subtle caveat was disturbing. There were only two rail routes from the north—one from Harrisburg and one from Philadelphia—and they both came through Baltimore, a hotbed for secessionists.

"At best, we now have only fifteen hundred loyal troops guarding the city," said Secretary of the Interior Caleb Smith, one of the conservative members of the cabinet. Then he turned to Aramis Gage and added, "And where are the troops from Pennsylvania, Congressman? We've heard nothing of those."

"The governor has assured me that two regiments are on their way, and two more will soon follow."

"Hah," Smith said derisively. "Pennsylvania should furnish ten times that amount. After all, it's Northern abolitionists like yourself who have gotten us into this mess."

Ari stood up immediately and pointed his finger at Smith. "I will not apologize, sir, for attempting to right the most morally reprehensible wrong of our nation. You should reflect on that the next time you're in church."

Lincoln winced, then whispered to Seward, "So much for my notion of the congressman being a calming presence." "His mettle is to be admired, however," Seward murmured. Lincoln nodded with an approving smile.

"Don't lecture me, Congressman!" Smith shouted. "I will consider whatever I want to in church, and one of those things is that the Bible recognizes the existence of slavery!"

"So you support slavery?"

Now Smith rose in anger, but before he could speak again the president stepped in. "Gentlemen, let's remain civil."

The noose about the city was tightening, and everyone was on edge.

A discussion began about possibly stationing troops in Maryland to secure the rail route to Washington. Lincoln paced about the room as he so often did when there were tough questions to be decided. Then he said solemnly, "I'm worried, gentlemen, that if we do so we will lose the support of Unionists in Maryland and then lose the state to the secessionists. We cannot play into their hands."

But it was General Scott's reminder that ended the debate: "Based upon the rumors we've heard, the number of secessionists active in Maryland is extensive. It would take several thousand soldiers to subdue Baltimore alone. We don't have those numbers available now."

It wasn't just rumors that fed the anxiety. Some things were visible, like the campfires of Virginia soldiers just across the Potomac. Although their numbers were unknown, it was becoming clear that those soldiers would soon have responsible commanders. Major General David Twiggs, Brigadier General Joseph Johnston, and Samuel Cooper, the former adjutant general of the army, had all just resigned and joined the Confederacy. Lincoln's secret efforts to induce Robert E Lee to lead the Union troops were rebuffed. Lee resigned his commission and joined the Confederacy, telling his fellow Virginian, General Scott, that he had to act in defense of his home state.

As Ari Gage and John Hay were leaving the White House to go out for dinner that evening, they found Senator-elect James Lane of Kansas at the foot of the stairs proudly displaying a shiny steel sword with a curved blade. So desperate was the situation in Washington that Lane had taken it upon himself to organize a ragtag group of fifty volunteers into what he called the Frontier Guards. They were given new muskets and, clad in civilian dress, took up a position in the East Room of the White House where they drilled upon velvet carpet under the gleaming chandeliers.

***

The attack on Fort Sumter and the call for Northern troops exposed not only the divisions within the country, but also divisions within households. One of those households suddenly divided was the Ford home just outside of Annapolis, and what triggered it was a statement issued by Congressman Marcus Ford to the *Baltimore Sun*.

> I call on all good Marylanders to demand that the state legislature convene and vote for secession.

Jubal Ford was about to leave the house for a meeting when Victoria Gage Ford read that quote. This time she didn't hold her tongue: "Your son is now calling for Maryland to secede from the Union. He should resign from Congress immediately."

"Victoria, you said 'your' son. We've always called the three boys 'our' sons."

"Don't change the subject."

"All right, perhaps this is a discussion we need to have. My position has always been that we should remain neutral in all of this, and I thought you agreed with that."

"I will not remain neutral about secession, or any plan to break up the Union. There can be no neutral position about that. A person is either for it or against it."

Jubal was startled by her fervor. "Well, at least my son is forthright about his position."

"What do you mean by that?"

"That he's honest in his stance, unlike John who we now know went to Charleston to spy while pretending to support a peaceful separation."

"I applaud him for doing that—it took courage. He did so for the sole purpose of trying to preserve the Union."

Jubal took a step towards the door, then turned back around and asked, "Have you not been taking your medicine?"

"That's my business."

"It's my business, too."

"Why? Because you want me too weak to express myself?"

"I can tell you're not taking it."

"Laudanum of all things. You made Doc Brown convince me to start taking it—"

"He said it would help you."

"—just like you got him to lie about how those five men died at the ironworks."

Jubal was shocked that she knew that. He didn't try to deny it, instead replying, "That's my business."

"No, you seem to forget: that is very much my business."

For the first time she was challenging what he considered his domain, intruding upon the ironworks just like her son was prone to do. "I have to go to my meeting," he said as he headed for the door. "Take your damn medicine!"

"Or what?"

"I'll force it down you if need be!"

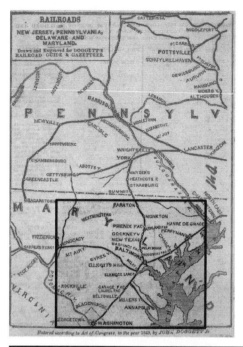

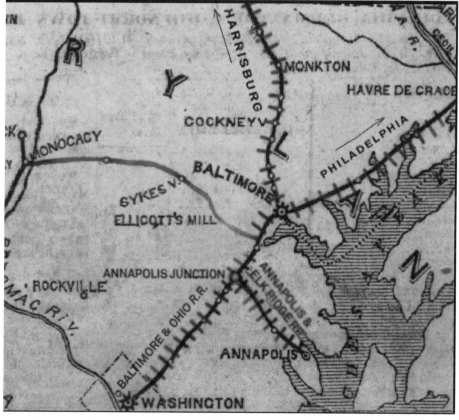

Chapter 61

For three months Kate Warne had cultivated her image in Baltimore of a transplanted Southern belle. She first went there as an agent for the Pinkerton Detective Agency, assigned to look for threats against President-elect Lincoln. Then, at the request of Northern railroads, she stayed on to look for threats against the country that might impact those railroads.

She was the eligible, young widow from Mobile, Alabama, known as Mrs. Constance Cherry. She was a delight to men and, once she had assured their wives that she would never engage in "home wrecking adventures," she was included in their social circles.

Single men constantly vied for Kate's affection, and none more so than Zeb Pierce, a thirty-year-old ardent secessionist from Annapolis. Her nickname for him, the Black Knight, stemmed from his appearance: black hair, black eyes, and dark suits. He could have passed for an undertaker except that he always wore a bright red cravat with his white shirt.

Recently, Pierce had been spending more time in Baltimore, claiming to be there in pursuit of his family's business interests. But Kate had detected two other purposes for his visits. One was his secessionist activities, although Kate had yet to learn how much of that was just talk on Zeb's part. The second was his efforts to fend off Kate's competing suitors.

Kate needed those suitors. The more she had, the more she could move about in Baltimore's "Southern Society." She had no intention of giving in to Zeb's advances, for she considered him an evil young man, capable of abhorrent conduct. On one occasion, after she had shared a glass of punch with another man, Pierce steered her into a cloak closet where he slapped her across the face. The episode ended quickly when Kate slammed her knee into his crotch. She left him doubled over and apologizing. Since then he had not struck her, but Kate remained wary.

On this day Kate happened to be having lunch with Zeb at a restaurant across the street from Camden Station when scores of Baltimore police began to assemble there. Purportedly, the police were there to see to the safe passage of Union troops as they boarded the Baltimore & Ohio Railcars for their short journey to Washington where they would protect the capital.

"Why are the police here at Camden Station?" Kate wondered.

Zeb had no answer, but he knew what she was alluding to. Soldiers coming into Baltimore from Philadelphia on the Philadelphia, Wilmington, and Baltimore Railroad arrived at the President Street Station on the east side of the city. Because of the Baltimore ordinance prohibiting the use of steam engines in the center of the city, the PW&B cars were then pulled for a mile by horses along tracks on Pratt Street to the B&O's Camden Station. Kate figured the police should be positioned along Pratt Street because it was there, on the previous day, that two thousand secessionists turned out and hurled insults and rocks at soldiers in the railcars.

"Today will be different," Zeb said. "There will be more protesters. The passage will not be as easy for the Yankees as it was yesterday. Let's go see."

They had walked no more than one hundred yards when they began hearing the noise of the crowd. It grew so loud that they soon had to shout to each other to be heard. Fifty yards farther, they heard gunshots. Kate looked at Zeb who smiled like that was what he was hoping to hear. In another quarter of a mile they saw Union troops marching their way, hemmed in on both sides by the protesters.

"Why are they on foot?" Kate asked.

Again, Zeb had no answer, but they soon got it from one of his friends who was among the crowd. "We blocked the tracks at South Street," the man said. "Made the troops get out and walk. Once that happened, all hell broke loose."

"There were shots," Kate said. "What were those?"

"Both sides started shooting at each other. We must be ten thousand strong."

Kate and Zeb had to stand back as the police now moved east in an effort to get in between the soldiers and the crowd. Suddenly a Union supporter yanked down a secessionist flag. Five men pummeled him, and he fell to the ground.

Kate started to bend down to help the man up when Zeb began kicking him in the ribs.

"Zeb, stop, you'll kill him."

Zeb stopped, but it was the second time Kate had seen a maniacal look on his face. She was certain he wouldn't have stopped beating the man had she not been there.

Afterwards, Zeb turned to Kate and said, "This was nothing."

"How can you say that? It was horrible."

"I just mean soon we'll have much bigger battles than this."

"How do you know?"

"Because I'm going to make it happen. I've got something important in the works."

"Like what?"

He hesitated, knowing he shouldn't tell her, but he couldn't stop himself. "I've got my own cannons."

She tried to hide her astonishment. "Where did you get cannons?"

"I have a source in the South."

She wondered whether this was just more big talk on his part. He was always trying to impress her. "You need trained artillerymen to fire cannons."

"I will soon have them."

He wouldn't tell her what he planned to do with those cannons. She pressed him further, but he was only willing to divulge one other thing: "I am now Captain Pierce, although don't tell anyone that just yet."

It all seemed unbelievable to Kate, but there was a passion in Zeb Pierce that she dared not underestimate.

Chapter 62

At the same time Kate Warne was witnessing the riot in Baltimore, Aramis Gage was attending another cabinet meeting where the focus was the trouble in the adjacent states. President Lincoln started the meeting by saying, "Shall we begin with the rumor of the day, or perhaps as it's now becoming the rumor of the hour?"

It was General Scott who was often the announcer of rumors, although he was always careful to delineate which he thought probable and those upon which he could not opine as to their accuracy. The one he opened with on this day was a bombshell: "We believe the Virginia military is erecting artillery batteries along narrow passages of the Potomac in an effort to shut off ship transport to the capital. The most prominent of these locations is near Mount Vernon."

"God damn, on President Washington's own land," one of the attendees said.

Those in the room were aghast. Even the pious Salmon P. Chase did not chastise his fellow cabinet member for the use of the Lord's name in vain.

"We are therefore," the general continued, "solely dependent on the forty miles of railroad and telegraph route between here and Baltimore. If we lose that avenue, Washington will be cut off from the world. No mail, no telegraph, no supplies."

"And, no troops," said Caleb Smith. "General, where are your three regiments from New York and Massachusetts you promised would be here by today?"

"I made no such promise, and they are not *my* regiments!" Scott fired back. "They are soldiers of the state from which they come."

"Nevertheless, where are they?"

"We are attempting to locate them. It is difficult under the conditions."

Smith guffawed so loudly that everyone took that as his response.

Once again a discussion ensued about stationing troops in Maryland to secure the train routes. Secretary Seward led the charge in favor. Lincoln remained opposed. The argument went on for thirty minutes while more rumors floated into the room about a bloody confrontation in Baltimore between secessionists and soldiers passing through the city.

A half hour later a telegram came in from Governor Hicks of Maryland reporting the riot. By then other messengers had confirmed the extent of the melee. At least four soldiers of the Sixth Massachusetts Infantry were dead and even more from the crowd that opposed them.

A pall settled over the room. Seward drummed his fingers on the table. Chase prayed silently. Lincoln stared out the window. The first significant regiment trying to reach Washington City, almost eight hundred soldiers, had been opposed.

They returned to General Scott's list of rumors that he rated as probably true: "There are believed to be fifteen hundred Virginia militia just across the river at Alexandria. They could be being assembled for a raid on Washington. It is possible they will be joined by most of the two thousand secessionists who took over the Harpers Ferry armory. We believe that any attack on Washington will be led by former Governor Wise of Virginia, now General Wise."

Having delivered all his bad news, General Scott seemed spent. He relinquished the floor without saying he was finished. Others were perplexed by his "intelligence report," for it was full of qualifiers, qualifiers that only added to the uncertainty and churned the anxiety in the room.

During a short break in the meeting, the president pulled Aramis aside. Now, Ari thought, I will learn the real reason the president sent for me again. They walked into Lincoln's office where the president sat down. Ari considered this unusual, perhaps the weight of everything was finally wearing on him.

But it was something else that was bothering the president. "Do you know where your brother is?" Lincoln asked.

"No, sir, I don't. I haven't heard from him for several weeks."

"There is a rumor at the War Department that he may be headed to Annapolis."

"I heard that rumor as well, sir."

"But you never know about rumors these days. To be honest, my concern is not just for his wellbeing. He could be put on another mission at this point. There are few with his loyalty and multitude of talents. Are there others you might inquire of to see if they've heard from him?"

The congressman thought for a moment. "There are a couple of people I can ask."

Ari left the White House immediately. It was only two blocks to the office of the *Washington Observer*. There, the paper's editor told Ari he had not heard from John since the last of the *Letters from Charleston*.

Since it had been days since he had been back to his room at Willard's Hotel, Ari stopped there to see if he had any recent mail from his brother. Walking through the lobby, Ari had to wind his way through the throng of people and suitcases. People were getting out. Southerners, with their blue cockades pinned to their lapels, whispered amongst themselves, a far cry from their normally boisterous conversations. Northerners not essential to the government were leaving as well.

"This is the last mail received, Congressman," a clerk said. "The only thing that comes through to the city now is by private messenger."

Ari quickly perused his mail. There were letters from a few of his closer constituents who chose not to send mail to his office and a letter from his mother. It was sent from the Annapolis home of Jubal Ford before she learned of John's trial and that he had survived Fort Sumter. Nothing from his brother.

The letter from his mother was only six paragraphs long, most of which bemoaned the effect the war talk was having on Jubal. "He's just not the same person here in Maryland," she said. She ended the letter by saying, "Where is John? I'm worried sick about him."

Hopefully, she will get the letter I sent her yesterday before the mail stops completely, Ari thought. In that letter he told her there was a possibility that John was headed her way.

As Ari was about to leave, the hotel manager, Cedric Mullen, called him over. When Ari reached Mullen at the far end of the lobby, Mullen waved him over to an even quieter corner as if he had some vast secret to tell.

Mullen looked around cautiously. "Congressman, you have a present upstairs."

"In my room?" Ari said, for it seemed a strange time to receive a present.

"Yes, sir, brought by a woman, a fine-looking lady who claims to be your wife."

"My wife? My wife is in Philadelphia."

Mullen smiled. "Then perhaps you have two presents up there."

When Ari opened the door to his room, he couldn't believe his eyes. "Charlotte, what are you doing here?"

She stood next to the bed, seeming crushed by his reaction. "Aren't you happy to see me?"

"Of course I am, but not here . . . not now. A war has started, and this city might be the next battlefront."

"That's why I came."

"You can't stay here; you have to go back home."

"Not until you unwrap your present?"

"And what is this present?"

"Me!" she exclaimed wildly with her arms outstretched.

He couldn't resist, and they tumbled onto the bed.

An hour later they came out from under the covers. Ari returned to his serious tone: "I have an important meeting I need to get to, and you need to get on a train back to Philadelphia. I'll walk you to the station."

Ari carried her one small bag as they walked out through the hotel lobby. Mullen beamed at Ari when he saw them.

At the train station they learned that a train to Philadelphia had just left. Another train was scheduled to leave in an hour, but the ticket seller warned that the schedules had been unreliable lately, and there was no telling what delays might be encountered in Baltimore.

"Go to your meeting," Charlotte insisted. "I'll be fine waiting here for the train."

"Yes, but promise me you'll get on the train."

"I promise."

"Honey, these are strange times, times that have never been encountered in this country before. We have no way of knowing what might happen. Please don't take chances."

"And the same to you, husband. Stay safe."

They kissed and Ari left.

***

Ari didn't tell Charlotte that his next stop was not really a meeting, and that it was at a brothel. It was the only other place he could think of to look for recent correspondence from his brother. His destination was Lady B's, and as he walked the five blocks he mused to himself whether he should introduce himself to Lady B by saying, "I have been sent here by the President of the United States."

But that five-block walk reminded Ari of the city's current peril. He passed by four shops in a row with boards barricading the windows and doors, their owners having left the city. An elderly woman standing outside a grocery complained, "A loaf of bread is twice what it cost a week ago." Not surprising, Ari thought, because the government had taken over the local grain warehouses to make sure the grain didn't leave the city. The threat of famine loomed. At the treasury building just two soldiers stood guard at the door. What could they do if a thousand Virginians suddenly came at them?

When he arrived at Lady B's, he opened the front door slowly, not knowing whether they were open for business at this time of day. He heard no voices and found the furniture in the front parlor covered with tarps. Finally, he heard some commotion off to the left of him from the back of a dining room. There he found a young woman, whom Ari presumed to be a slave, packing boxes.

"What's going on here?" Ari asked.

"We leavin'. Headin' for N'orleans."

"You as well?"

"Free or not, I stay with Lady B."

"Why?"

"Don't know nothin' else. Besides, she good to me."

Before Ari could ask anything more, Lady B entered from the kitchen. "I'm sorry, sir, but we're closed," she said.

"For good?"

"I'm afraid so. My girls have all gone home . . . I suppose I sent many of them home."

"But business should be booming—the city will soon be flooded with young soldiers," Ari said, although he didn't know from which side.

"Soldiers are not our kind of clientele," Lady B replied with a chuckle. "We've always catered to gentlemen. We wouldn't know how to survive in a world of drunken soldiers."

"I see. I'm sorry to see you close down. I mean I've never been here myself—"

"That's all right," she said, sensing his discomfort.

"My brother's been here, and that's what brings me here today."

Her confused expression asked the question.

"My brother is John Gage."

"Oh, Johnny," she said, brightening. "One of our favorites."

"I'm aware. I'm trying to locate him. By chance, have you heard from him lately?"

"Other than his *Letters from Charleston* in the newspapers, just once. It was about four weeks ago."

"No, I meant in the last few days?"

"No, sir."

"Well, I'm sorry to have troubled you. I wish you the best, ma'am."

As Ari reached the door he turned back and asked, "I'm curious. That letter you received from him four weeks ago, did he say anything important?"

"For me, yes. He spoke about what was coming and said, 'Our world is going to be turned upside down.'"

"True enough."

"And so, the question you seek an answer to, Congressman, is: 'Where in this upside down world is John Gage?'"

***

For the last few days on the voyage from Charleston to New York City, Bette Downing had been wondering the same. She expected an answer soon. The *Harriet Lane*, the fastest of the ships returning, arrived in New York City several hours before the others. This gave Bette a chance to go freshen up at the home of the only person she knew in the city.

When she returned to the harbor, she struggled to find a spot to watch the other ships come in. One hundred thousand people had gathered to welcome Major Anderson and his gallant men as heroes. The American flag had been fired upon. Northerners were rallying to its defense.

After being jostled about in the crowd, Bette bought the evening's *New York Chronicle* and sat down to read it on a bench further inland. Four headlines immediately grabbed her attention:

> Major Anderson and his garrison return here today.

> Confederate Secretary of War predicts the Confederate flag will fly over Washington in a few weeks.

> Four soldiers and at least nine civilians dead in Baltimore riot against Northern troops.

> Maryland now the most dangerous place in America.

The harbor was littered with small boats awaiting the arrival of the navy ships. When the boats began vigorously tooting their horns, Bette knew the ships were approaching.

As the *Pawnee* docked, Bette stood twenty people deep in the crowd. But then the police came and opened a corridor for the soldiers to pass through. When that occurred, miraculously she found herself in the front row.

Laborers came off the boat first, then the enlisted men, and finally the officers. But there was no John Gage. She grabbed the shoulder of one of the few officers she knew as he passed by. It was Abner Doubleday. "Captain, where is John Gage?" she yelled and then repeated it so she could be heard over the din.

"Gage got off the ship when we stopped at Fort Monroe," Doubleday shouted. "He's headed to Maryland."

Maryland of all places, she thought, the most dangerous place in America.

Chapter 63

Out in the open air on a vacant lot along one of the busiest streets in Annapolis, John Gage sat at a table covered with papers. Behind him, a large sign promoted the services he offered:

Thomas Millsap Company
Providing Free Travel to Charleston

"Why do you want to join up?" Gage asked the young man.

"I got nothing better to do, sir. I thought it might be fun."

"That's no reason to go to war, son," and Gage ripped up the young man's application.

Gage's young assistant, Jimmy Palin, shook his head and looked at Gage. "Mr. Millsap, we've been at this for more than a day now, and you've rejected half the men that apply. At this rate we'll never put together a Confederate army."

"We want real soldiers, Jimmy. That lad would turn tail the first time a Yankee pointed a rifle his way."

Jimmy wasn't the most reliable assistant, but there were few things for him to mismanage. All he had to do was line people up and handle the paperwork. Jimmy had a ruddy, freckled complexion and red hair that he tried to hide under one of the new Bowlers. The hat, so unique and stylish, was only recently introduced in America, and it was a source of pride for Jimmy. He was only twenty-one years old, but he had one asset Gage considered potentially helpful: he knew many of the young secessionists in Annapolis.

A monstrous young man with a swagger that matched his size stepped up to the table. "My name is Stetson," he said as he handed over his application.

"You understand you're not joining the Confederate army now?" Gage explained to him. "It would be illegal for me to sign you up here. I'm merely providing you free travel to a place where you can sign up."

"I got that. Heard you say it to twenty boys before me."

"What's your reason for wanting to join up, Stetson?"

"I want to kill me some Yankees."

"Why's that?"

"To stop them from taking away our rights."

"What rights are those?"

"To own slaves for one."

"You own any slaves?"

"Not yet, but I might like to someday."

"You'll do just fine, Stetson. Be at the harbor tomorrow morning at nine o'clock. Bring no more than twenty pounds of gear. Don't bring any weapons with you. Those will be provided."

As Stetson walked away, Gage said to Jimmy, "That's the kind of soldier we want."

Late in the afternoon there was a lull, and the two recruiters were able to relax. Jimmy looked out towards the Naval Academy and said, "I've got my men down there drilling with other recruits by the Navy yard... right in their faces."

"Your men? How many?"

Jimmy grimaced. "Only six, but there could be more." Then he got up the nerve to finally ask a question he had wanted to ask Gage since they first met: "Mr. Millsap, did you go to West Point?"

"No, there would've been too much reading for me there."

Jimmy chuckled. "I don't like readin' either."

"That's gonna make it tough to follow in your daddy's footsteps," Gage said. Jimmy's father was a judge in a nearby town.

"No, I ain't gonna do that. I want to do something important in the cause."

"I could send you and your men south."

"No, I want to do something around here. Something big ... something that gets noticed."

Gage watched the young man seem to drift away, a faraway look in his eyes. Upon his return, he asked, "What did you do in the Mexican War?"

"I was with an artillery unit."

"Were you an officer?"

"No, I enlisted as a private—made it up to sergeant, though. They called me a specialist."

"At what?"

"The use of canister shot. It isn't pretty, mowing men down like that, but it works."

That last comment gave Jimmy a sudden spark. "I know someone you should meet. His name is Zeb Pierce, and he's an important man in Annapolis. He's been looking for someone like you, someone who's been around artillery."

"I'd like to meet him, Jimmy." *Perhaps he's the just man I'm looking for too,* Gage thought.

***

Gage was unaware that at that very moment his mother was living less than five miles away in Jubal Ford's home north of Annapolis. Just two days before, she received Ari's letter advising that John might be headed to Annapolis. That letter arrived the same day that Jubal said to her, "I'm going to Baltimore for a few days ... on business."

She asked no questions, for lately he had been acting so strangely, even to the point of making veiled threats towards her. But she couldn't understand why he would go to Baltimore with all the trouble that was occurring there. He had said he would take no sides if war came, but here he was headed to the place where secessionists were most active.

She didn't try to dissuade him. This would give her a respite from him, and she would use that time looking for Johnny.

Chapter 64

Kate Warne trusted her intuition. She had relied on it many times in her covert missions, and this night was to be another one of those times. She was seated at a round table in the bar of the Atlantic Hotel having drinks with Zeb Pierce along with a Baltimore councilman, Alfred Bowman, and his wife Marguerite.

Kate had detected some restlessness on Bowman's part. When he wasn't staring at Kate's cleavage, he was checking his pocket watch or glancing over at Mayor Brown sitting three tables away. Kate sensed something was afoot.

Precisely at seven thirty, Bowman nodded to Mayor Brown. Zeb Pierce and Bowman excused themselves, saying they would return in less than thirty minutes. The mayor followed them out the door.

Just when something important was in the works, Kate was stuck with Marguerite, a large, unpleasant woman with bulging black eyes. She seemed to resent Kate for her beauty and her ability to charm the important men of the city.

Kate was thinking of something provocative to say in hopes of driving Marguerite away when Marguerite, emboldened by the wine she had been gulping, took care of matters for her: "So, I am stuck here with the Queen Bee. You should cover yourself, Mrs. Cherry. Your bosoms seem to be scanning the room."

"You shouldn't be looking at my bosoms," Kate said stiffly.

"I'm not, but all the men in this room seem fascinated by them. You should start charging them—perhaps a penny a peek."

"My, my, Mrs. Bowman, you are a spiteful bitch, aren't you?"

Now justified, Kate excused herself and walked out.

Once outside the hotel, she observed the hulking figure of Marshal Kane, the head of the Baltimore Police Department, entering the front door of a building just down the street. Aware of Kane's Confederate allegiance, she followed him, certain he would be part of any plot.

She knew the building well. It was home to the Baltimore Club, historically an apolitical organization, but in the past year it had come to be dominated by Southern sympathizers. Now, not only was the Baltimore Club a place for parties and celebrations, it was also a place for Confederate intrigue.

On the second floor there was a small meeting room just off a parlor. The room was noted for paying homage to Francis Scott Key, and over time it had taken on the pseudonym of the Flag Room. Kate surmised they must be headed there.

She took off her shoes and carried them as she walked up the creaky wooden stairs to the second floor. She could hear muffled voices, but they were both male and female. Perhaps I jumped to conclusions, Kate thought. They would never include women in such a meeting. But once at the top of the stairs she realized those sounds were coming from a different direction. The ladies were in a room on the opposite side of the parlor from the Flag Room.

Kate crept into the parlor. She pressed her ear against the wall of the Flag Room. The walls seemed paper-thin because she could hear every word being said. My God, she thought, they're plotting treason... in the Flag Room of all places.

She listened intently. The voices were recognizable, and even to her amazement she heard the voice of Governor Hicks. But there was one voice she couldn't make out. She waited for someone to address the man by name, but no one did. The double doors to the Flag Room had a half-inch gap between them, perhaps large enough that she could see him through that gap.

But as she approached the doors, a voice from behind called out, "Have you heard anything interesting?" The inquiry came from Marguerite Bowman. "I will let them know you're here, and that you've been listening."

Kate winced. "I'm sorry, Marguerite, but I can't let you do that."

"You're going to try to stop me from speaking to my husband?"

"I'm not going to try; I am going to stop you."

Marguerite tried to pass by. Kate grabbed her forcefully by the upper arm and pushed her backwards out into the balcony area at the top of the staircase. Marguerite grabbed a three-foot-long fireplace poker and came at Kate with a determined look. The two women circled each other, waiting for the other to strike. Kate's back was against the balcony railing. When she took a quick look down over her shoulder, Marguerite took advantage by thrusting the poker at Kate. Kate did a sidestep and kicked outward, striking Marguerite in the stomach. Marguerite stumbled and lost control of the poker, which fell harmlessly down the steps.

Kate was surprised that Marguerite didn't cry out for help. This was personal, as if she had wanted to have this confrontation with Kate for some time.

Marguerite grabbed a tall vase that was sitting on the floor. The vase was bulky, and she struggled momentarily to raise it overhead. But once she had it in that position she took on a look of madness and ran straight at Kate. As Marguerite tried to pull the vase down toward Kate's head, Kate made another quick move to the side. Marguerite's momentum, combined with the weight of the vase, vaulted her over the railing. As she was going over, Marguerite managed to grasp one of the balusters, but now upside down it only slowed her momentum and caused her head to bang against the wall underneath. The impact knocked her unconscious so she couldn't hold on.

Acting on instinct, Kate lunged to grab the only body part she might reach, Marguerite's left foot. But all Kate could take hold of was Marguerite's shoe. It came off in her hand as Marguerite tumbled headfirst towards the marble floor below. The vase crashed first, quickly followed by a loud crack when Marguerite landed.

Kate stared at the shoe she held. And in that instant a strange thought occurred to her: What would I have done if I had been able to hold onto her foot with a chance to save her? Saving her would have meant me being caught and unable to expose the insurrectionists. All might be lost in Maryland. This result was for the best, she assured herself.

Kate tossed the shoe aside and it landed along an open alcove. She then scurried down the steps, and at the bottom of the staircase she looked over. Blood was pouring from the back of Marguerite's head. When Kate heard a door open on the second floor, she bolted out of a side entrance of the building.

Within minutes she was back in her seat at the Atlantic Hotel. Although somewhat breathless, it didn't stop her from quickly downing a much-needed tumbler of whiskey.

After half an hour she was concerned because Zeb hadn't returned. She went to take a look out the front window of the hotel. As she was peering out, a hand suddenly clutched her arm from behind. It was Zeb, and he had a grim look on his face.

Kate's first thought was: he knows. But she asked, "What's wrong?"

"Marguerite is dead."

"Dead? What happened?"

"She was apparently moving a large vase to an alcove at the Baltimore Club and fell over the balcony."

"Oh, my goodness. She did have a lot to drink here. She shouldn't have been doing that in such a condition."

"I suppose not."

"Was she able to speak to her husband before she passed?"

"Not a word."

"Such a shame."

Chapter 65

The twentieth of April was to be another day of stunning developments for the president and his cabinet. The first lightning bolt struck in a telegram from Senator David Wilmot who had been trying to make his way north by railroad through Baltimore:

> Railroad bridges out of Baltimore to the north have been burned to the ground. I've seen it on the Philadelphia route and rumor has it that the same is true on the Harrisburg route.

No one in the room was more horrified by this than Ari Gage. Charlotte had left on the train for Philadelphia just hours before. He ran through all the possibilities: Was the train on time? If so, she should have made it through Baltimore before the bridges were burned. But what if the train wasn't on time, or the transfer between railroads at Baltimore had been delayed? The trains might be stopped at one of the burned-out bridges. He visualized a newspaper headline:

> Wife of Northern Abolitionist Congressman Abducted by Secessionists.

Someone asked him a question that he did not hear. "Congressman . . . Congressman," and upon the second call he seemed to come out of his stupor.

Within an hour there was confirmation of the burning of the bridges, but it came with a startling revelation provided by Kate Warne who had just arrived from Baltimore. "Yes," she told the cabinet, "I was there listening when it was so ordered."

"Who ordered it?"

"Mayor Brown, Marshall Kane who is head of the Baltimore police force, and a few other Baltimore leaders. Governor Hicks may claim that he was not a part of that decision, but he was there and went along with it."

"Treason!" General Scott roared. "Outright treason."

"They will claim that it is not," Kate explained. "They will claim that it was done to prevent more violence between soldiers and their citizens."

"I suppose there could be a morsel of truth in that," the president allowed.

"I can assure you, sir, that Mayor Brown and Marshall Kane are rabid secessionists. Their purpose is to stop troops from reaching Washington."

"Arrest them all!" Secretary of the Navy Gideon Welles shouted.

"All ten thousand of them?" Treasury Secretary Chase said with a touch of sarcasm.

"At the moment we don't possess the means to subdue Maryland," General Scott reminded.

The president held up a hand. He had allowed everyone to have their say, and although he often took a vote of his cabinet on matters this was not one of those times.

"Right now," the president said, "this is also a war for the minds and hearts of our citizens. Let's remember that when we meet with the delegation from Maryland this afternoon."

An hour later a second telegram came in from Senator Wilmot. It read:

> We have bypassed the destroyed bridges by coach and made it onto railcars to Philadelphia. Inform Aramis Gage his wife safely aboard with us.

Only one other person in the room recognized the great relief that telegram brought to Ari Gage. As Kate Warne passed by him on her way out of the meeting room, she patted Ari on the shoulder and said, "Relax, Congressman, now you have only one family member missing."

***

Kate Warne needed to make a quick exit from the White House because most of the members of the delegation from Maryland would have recognized her. That delegation included Mayor Brown, some Baltimore councilmen, and Zeb Pierce.

The president had forbidden the cabinet members from accusing any of the attendees of having ordered the torching of the railroad bridges. "It would serve no purpose at this point," the president said. But he did allow it to be known that he and the cabinet were aware of the burnings.

After expressing his firm desire that no more blood be spilled, Lincoln asked the critical question of the visitors: "What is it you seek, gentlemen?"

Mayor Brown began, "We seek—"

"A commitment that no Union troops will ever again set foot on Maryland soil," Zeb Pierce interjected.

"You speak for all of Maryland, young man?" Seward asked in a most patronizing manner.

"Most all Marylanders."

The cabinet members laughed in such an insulting fashion that it was clear they didn't believe him.

Lincoln declared that the troops must pass through Maryland on their way to Washington: "Our men are not moles and can't dig under the earth; they are not birds and can't fly over it. There is no way but to march across, and that they must do."

A meaningful discussion then took place and over the next hour it was agreed that only two routes were available for the troops to reach the B&O Railroad just west of Baltimore without going through that city. The first involved deboarding the train from Harrisburg before reaching Baltimore and marching southwest to pick up the B&O Railroad. The second was to come north on the Elk Ridge Railroad from Annapolis to Annapolis Junction and catch the B&O Railroad there.

General Scott stated that he knew of no troops near Baltimore at the moment. Mayor Brown pledged that he would use all lawful means to try to keep citizens from leaving Baltimore to attack any troops going around the city.

The meeting adjourned on that rather high note. The cabinet members stayed on, but their discussions were soon interrupted when John Hay entered the room and announced, "They've come back!"

The same committee from Baltimore had returned and this time they brought with them an astounding telegram they just received from the president of the Baltimore and Ohio Railroad. It read:

> Three thousand Northern troops are reported to be at Cockeysville; intense excitement prevails; churches have been dismissed and the people are arming en masse.

The troops were said to be within thirty miles of Baltimore and progressing.

Stunned by this development, this time the Maryland committee allowed Zeb Pierce to speak first. "You called Mayor Brown and this committee here so we wouldn't be in Baltimore when you marched troops into the city. This was all a ruse."

Now they had to be polite to the young fire-eater. It did have that appearance. General Scott assured them that no one in this room knew of any regiments that close to Baltimore.

The cabinet retired to a separate room for a brief discussion because time was of the essence. Seward began the discussion: "Let the New York Seventh Regiment cut their way through Baltimore."

Secretary Welles was even more belligerent. "It's time we end this policy of appeasement toward the rebels. These troops heading to Baltimore may have been sent there in error, but I suggest we take advantage of that error. Let's use them to begin an occupation of the city."

"No, Mr. Welles," the president said, "we need to use those men to fight Confederate soldiers, not citizens of a neighboring state. I believe we can win over that Maryland majority by not being perceived as the aggressor. General, order the troops recalled to the Pennsylvania state line."

Seward was surprised, although not disheartened. Thus far Lincoln had made a habit of polling his cabinet secretaries on crucial matters and the majority usually won out. But this time it was different, and Seward liked that. It was decisiveness, even if he didn't agree with the decision.

Lincoln and the cabinet returned and announced that the troops would be sent back. "This will allow us to keep our commitment that the troops will either be marched around Baltimore or brought up from Annapolis," the president said.

This seemed to satisfy Mayor Brown and most of the committee members. However, it was not satisfactory to Zeb Pierce. He cried out, "That may be good enough for some of us, but not all. I don't want any Northern troops touching Maryland soil."

Tired of Zeb Pierce and the unrelenting demands from Maryland, Lincoln replied, "Gentlemen, go home and tell your people that if they will not attack us, we will not attack them." Then he stopped abruptly and looked at the Baltimore committeemen sternly. "But if our troops are attacked, I will lay Baltimore in ashes."

Everyone in the room was aghast by Lincoln's threat. No one had ever heard him use such aggressive language.

All were moved to silence except Zeb Pierce who stood up and replied, "Seventy-five thousand Marylanders may resist those troops, Mr. Lincoln."

"Then I presume, Mr. Pierce, there is room enough on Maryland soil to bury seventy-five thousand men."

It was an awkward way to end a meeting that most considered successful.

When the Maryland committee left the White House, Zeb Pierce, despite having been ridiculed by the president, was smiling. "There is no good road around Baltimore from the Harrisburg route," he said to the others. "The Harrisburg and Philadelphia routes are dead to them."

Sensing the others needed further explanation for his elation, Zeb added, "Annapolis is now the only path in. They're coming my way."

Chapter 66

Brigadier General Benjamin Butler eyed the ship captain with suspicion. He knew the man and his crew had Confederate sympathies. What was unknown was whether they would act on those sympathies. Thus far in the six-hour voyage they had not.

As they approached the harbor in Annapolis the captain made a sudden turn of the wheel, and the ship veered to starboard. The portly general jumped up from his chair and pulled his pistol. "You run us aground, and I will blow your brains out."

"No, General, I wouldn't do such a thing," said the captain. "I made that turn to keep from running aground. There are a lot of small bars to navigate."

Two weeks earlier, Butler was a lawyer in Boston. In his twenty years of casual service with the Massachusetts Sixth Regiment he had never been part of a military engagement. Through political connections, he managed to be named general of a Massachusetts brigade.

Butler sat back down. A sergeant positioned a lantern that brought to light the prominent features of the general's face—a balding forehead, dark mustache, and dark bags under his eyes.

But ten minutes later Butler was up again, staring in amazement at the town of five thousand.

"It looks like they knew we were coming," said one of the general's aides.

"How could they?" Butler said, looking at the sea of light that stretched from the Naval Academy all the way across the town. "No one knew we were coming by water."

Having learned of the attack on the Massachusetts Sixth in Baltimore and the burning of the railroad bridges, Butler had commandeered this ship, the *Maryland*, to take them to Annapolis. He planned to reach Washington City by the back way, bypassing Baltimore to the west. This meant taking the Annapolis and Elk Ridge Railroad north to Annapolis Junction where his troops would pick up the B&O railroad to Washington.

They stared at the town. At one in the morning nearly all houses were alight. "It's the lamps, the damn lamps," Butler said. "Why are so many of them moving?"

Whether the lamps were being carried by wagons, carriages, or men on horseback the town was in a state of commotion. A peaceful nighttime landing was out of the question. "We'll wait until daylight," Butler said, and he ordered the captain to lay anchor.

Not an hour later a rowboat approached. Like David shouting at Goliath, the man in the rowboat looked up and demanded to know, "What steamer is this?"

There was no response, so the man repeated his call. This time General Butler answered, "Come aboard, or we will blow you out of the water."

The rower, a lieutenant from the Naval Academy, was brought up. He was relieved to see he was on a ship of volunteers from the North. "We were worried your ship was carrying hundreds of plug uglies from Baltimore. We're in a terrible situation here."

"By *we*, do you mean the Naval Academy?" the general asked.

"I mean Northerners. The area is filled with secessionists, and some have come down from Baltimore. The younger ones drill each day right in plain sight of the academy. There is a man openly recruiting for Confederate soldiers."

"I'll soon put an end to that. What's the name of this traitor?"

"Thomas Millsap, although some people just call him the tall man."

"I'll take care of him. Is the Naval Academy threatened?"

"Absolutely, and we're especially worried that secessionists will seize the *Constitution*."

The *Constitution*, or as most people knew it *Old Ironsides*, would be both a tactical and symbolic victory if secessionists captured it. For now it was an albatross, stuck on a bar in the harbor where it was used for training midshipmen.

Suddenly a small rocket shot across the night sky from one end of the town to the other. "We think they use those to signal each other," the lieutenant said. "Our commandant advises that you should not try to land here."

"Why wouldn't he welcome the reinforcement?"

"He's afraid it will arouse the secessionists who might not otherwise take up arms. The governor feels the same."

The general was suspicious, his anxiety heightened by what seemed the lieutenant's desire to keep them from coming ashore. Butler pulled out his pistol and aimed it at the lieutenant. "I'm told that two hundred naval officers have now left for the Confederacy, and at Gosport they took over the navy yard. Do you plan to join them?"

"No, sir, I wouldn't think of it. I'm from Michigan."

Butler lowered his weapon. "How about the other officers? Have you noticed anything adverse at the academy?"

"No, sir."

"We'll wait 'til morning. But let your captain know that if we see any untoward action from the *Constitution*, or from the Naval Academy, we will not hesitate to open fire your way."

"Yes, sir," said the shocked lieutenant.

***

The next day at the recruiting station, Jimmy Palin spotted what he thought was real activity in the harbor. He stood up from the table and looked out that way before realizing the movement he had detected was actually on the shore. "That ship with them Yankee soldiers has been sittin' out in the harbor all morning. They say there's a general on board who's really a lawyer from Boston."

"Yep, his name's Butler," Gage replied.

"A lawyer ... from Boston," Jimmy said, shaking his head. "If he comes ashore, he'll probably try to talk us to death."

Gage chuckled, then cautioned, "We shouldn't underestimate them. That's the Massachusetts Eighth Regiment out there. Upwards of a thousand soldiers—well-trained and well-equipped."

"Well, I wish they would come ashore. We'd teach 'em a thing or two."

"Patience, Jimmy, patience. There's a proper time and place for making war."

"Hell, they can't even get ashore. They wasted the whole damn day trying to get that old frigate—"

"The *Constitution.*"

"—out into deeper water, and now it looks like they got their own ship stuck."

"They're soldiers, not sailors, Jimmy."

Around noon, the crowd dwindled. Only six men remained in the recruiting line, but Gage was watching closely the actions of three men who stood opposite the line. They wore civilian clothes and seemed interested in the recruiting proceedings.

"Is one of those men the person you wanted me to meet—that Zeb Pierce fellow?" Gage asked Jimmy.

"No, I've never seen those men before."

Ten minutes later the men approached the table.

"Who's in charge here?" the shortest of the three men asked.

"I am," Gage replied.

"What's your name?"

"Thomas Millsap."

"Come with us, Millsap. General Butler wants to talk to you."

Jimmy reached for the leather bag he carried.

Gage knew he had a pistol in there. The short man reached inside his coat. Gage pushed Jimmy's hand away from the bag and said, "It's all right, Jimmy. They just want to talk. They can't arrest me for running an honest business."

***

Gage was taken in a rowboat out into the harbor to the steamer *Maryland* where more than eight hundred Union troops were currently housed. He was quickly escorted into the cabin of General Butler.

Before Butler could begin an interrogation, Gage started his: "How did you get here?"

"By the Susquehanna."

"You couldn't get through by rail?"

"Why are you asking *me* questions?" Butler said. "*You're* the one being arrested?"

"Arrested? On what charge?"

"Treason against the United States."

Gage chuckled.

"You find this amusing?" the general roared. "You've been recruiting soldiers to aid in a rebellion!"

"Who told you that?"

"The commandant at the Naval Academy."

"I do not recruit for the enemy. I provide travel arrangements for possible recruits."

"A fine distinction."

"As a lawyer, you should appreciate fine distinctions. Here's one of the papers they sign—an affidavit that says they intend to join the Confederate army. They've acknowledged *their* treason. The paper says I don't enlist them; I merely provide them travel."

Butler grasped the back of his head as if to shake off one more headache he didn't need. To arrest just one of thousands of Southern sympathizers as his first act in Maryland might cause more confrontations. "Where do you take them?"

"To Fort Monroe."

"Fort Monroe has fallen to the Confederates?" the shocked general asked.

"No, General."

"Then why are you sending them there?"

"To get them the hell out of Maryland where they'll cause trouble. Tomorrow night, while they sleep unarmed, their ship will cruise into Fort Monroe where they will be made prisoners."

This time Butler roared with laughter. "How many have you sent there?"

"About six hundred thus far. I reject more than we send. I just want the militant ones, the real troublemakers. And we don't want to risk the ship's crew being overwhelmed."

"Who the hell are you really?"

"John Gage."

Butler recalled the name. "You're the newspaper man, the one who wrote the articles supporting the South. I don't understand."

"Those articles were a ploy... to get me noticed and invited to Charleston."

"And that in turn got you an invitation to Sumter?"

Gage nodded. "More of a command."

"And you came back here to do this?"

"No, it just fell into my lap. On the way back from Sumter, I got off at Fort Monroe where I met Charles Timmons."

"I've heard of him. He owns a fleet of steamers that run the Chesapeake."

"Yes, and he's a true patriot. When he told me about the trouble being caused in Maryland, the two of us came up with this scheme. He provides his steamers for free. He also gave me with a little capital."

"How long can you keep this up?"

"Only a couple more days. Fort Monroe can't handle any more prisoners. Besides, I need to get to other matters. You see, there is an ulterior purpose to my very public display as a Confederate recruiter."

"And what is that?"

"To be noticed by the right people."

"And who might that be?"

"The insurrectionists who managed to steal fifty lightweight cannons made by Gage Ironworks."

"You think the cannons are here in Maryland?"

"I'm certain of it, and I fear they might be used in a plot here or against Washington, maybe even both. I need help finding them."

"No, Gage, I can't help you look for them, at least not as yet. My orders direct me to avoid interactions with the populace. I can't turn my men loose scouring the countryside for your cannons. Bring me precise evidence of where they are, and then I can help."

"Then what are your plans, General?"

"Hopefully, to get to Washington soon, but I'm awaiting orders from General Scott."

"You need to get there as soon as possible. Are you aware that Virginia has seceded?"

"I just learned that. I've also heard that railroad bridges to Baltimore have been destroyed and perhaps track of the railroad we're to use from here to Annapolis Junction."

"I've heard the same."

"We were supposed to come in from Harrisburg, so I don't know anything about the railroad to Annapolis Junction. All I've got is this one stinkin' little map."

Gage had a thought. "There's someone you should talk to about that—a former slave who came with me from Charleston. He was freed there. He's trying to get back to the plantation where his family is, only about ten miles north but right along the railroad. He probably knows that route better than anyone."

"Where can I find him?"

"He's working at the docks to earn a little money, pretending to be my slave."

Gage gave him Gus's location and within two hours the same three men who had seized Gage had Gus on board.

Gage took Gus aside and apologized.

"That's the second time I've been off enjoyin' life on my own and you've had me arrested," Gus said.

"You're not arrested," Gage assured him, and then added, "I'll pick up your pay at the wharf first thing in the morning." The owner of the dock wasn't about to give that pay to a slave. That money belonged to the slave owner.

Gus was fine with that, although he hadn't been fine with the arrangement when it started. It occurred when Gage explained to Gus that he couldn't have him helping at the recruiting station. "It wouldn't make sense for a colored man to be recruiting soldiers for the Southern cause."

Gage had tried to convince Gus to leave and go to his family, but Gus's loyalty had held him back. "I'll go soon," Gus had said, "but not till I'm sure you ain't gonna get yourself into trouble again."

So Gage found Gus work at the wharf for a few days. And as Gus thought about it, he realized it would be a good thing to have some money in his pocket when he returned home. Perhaps he might even take a few small presents to his wife and children.

But Gage was now concerned. He moved closer to Gus and whispered, "I don't fully trust the general. He is a Democrat."

Gus shrugged. He had no idea what that meant.

"He's been supportive of the South in the past," Gage explained. "I fear he might still try to enforce the fugitive slave law. Don't give him any clue that you're a runaway."

"This railroad line to Annapolis Junction," the general began, "what do you know about it?"

It was an imprecise question that confused Gus. He looked at Gage who said, "The general is worried that secessionists will do something that destroys the rail line. Can you think of any places they might attack that would be hard to fix?"

"They could tear up the rails anyplace," Gus said.

Frustrated, the general asked, "How about bridges?"

"They all small—could be fixed pretty easy—'cept for one. The Calumet Bridge right up next to where my family is."

Gage pulled over Butler's small map and pointed to the bridge's location. "That bridge cuts through this valley," Gus said. "It has a lot of wood to it. I don't know much about makin' bridges, but if they torched that one it would take a long time to fix it."

Chapter 67

Zeb Pierce made it back to Baltimore from his meeting with the cabinet in time for dinner with Kate Warne. He was euphoric, almost manic, for he felt he was now a part of something big.

"I told off that old gorilla real good," Zeb said proudly, not mentioning that the president had blistered him in a way that others had never witnessed.

Kate sensed she now had an easy mark. "Zeb, you seem excited. Is something important about to happen?"

"You should believe it so." He scanned the room as if to ensure no one was watching. Then he pulled a piece of paper from his pocket and said, "Here is a copy of the telegram that Marshal Kane sent to his friend, Mr. Bradley Johnson, in Frederick, Maryland."

> Streets red with Maryland blood; send expresses over the mountains of Maryland and Virginia for the riflemen to come here without delay. Fresh hordes will be down on us tomorrow. We will fight them and whip them, or die.

"So Marshal Kane, the Baltimore police chief, is a secessionist?" Kate said in pretense. "The other day I got the impression he was trying to stop the riot."

"Only because the Northern troops had more weapons. That won't be true in the future."

"How do you know that?"

"This Mr. Johnson is an important man. He's going to be a general in the Confederate Army."

Kate threw her hands in the air in mock frustration. "What does that have to do with Baltimore?"

"He's sending troops here from Frederick, just fifty miles away," Zeb said.

"All that message said was for him to call on others to send troops here." Kate zeroed in on Zeb's weakness. She leaned over close to him and wrapped her arm around his before saying, "Zeb, are you going to be a part of this?"

Zeb smiled and nodded. "He's sending eight hundred troops here and half of them are to be mine."

"How are they *yours*?"

"I'm forming my own little army unit with the soldiers from Frederick. They'll get here in a couple days. They're to be my troops, part of my plan."

"Zeb, this is so exciting! What is your plan?"

"All the routes through Baltimore, whether from Harrisburg or Philadelphia, have been shut off. I plan to stop the Union troops from making their way to Washington by the only way still open—Annapolis up to Annapolis Junction where they could hop on the B&O railcars."

"You think you can stop them just with soldiers?"

Again, he smiled with that hauntingly proud look. "I've got cannons. We'll make the route up to Annapolis Junction impassable. I even have some Northern uniforms that my uncle made in Charleston. I can't wait to tell my father about all this, and especially about where I'm going to take those cannons next. He'll be impressed."

"Where is your father?"

"In Annapolis. I need to head back there because I'm in need of a good artillery man. A friend of mine has told me about a former soldier—people call him the Tall Man—who's running a Confederate recruiting service in Annapolis. My friend says he was in the artillery and that he knows all about using canister shot."

"Why is that important?"

"It's the best way to mow down a line of marching soldiers. We'll have our cannons hidden, waiting for them. The Union troops won't make it to Washington."

Kate was stunned by the potential consequences of Zeb's plan. She had to find a way to stop the troops coming from Frederick.

It was a race against time.

***

An hour after their dinner in Baltimore, Zeb Pierce was on the road to Annapolis, and Kate Warne was on her way to try to foil his scheme. She had to delay the troops from Frederick anyway she could. Just a few days could make all the difference.

Kate went to the telegraph office where the telegram from Marshal Kane was sent to Bradley Johnson in Frederick. She knew the young telegrapher, Lenny Tolliver, who worked the office at night. When Kate walked in, she greeted Lenny with an embracing smile and said, "Good evening, Lenny."

Wearing horned-rimmed glasses and a pink bowtie, Lenny looked the part of a telegraph operator, but when he stood up and removed his glasses, he was actually a very handsome young man. "Good evening, Mrs. Cherry," he said politely.

"I have a short telegram to send to Chicago. Can you get it through?"

"To Chicago, probably. So many lines are down—all of them to Washington—but to Chicago sometimes it works."

"I've written it out. Here it is:"

>Thank you for the birthday present. All is well. Constance."

The telegram was to go to a nondescript recipient. What Lenny did not know, and could not know, is that the telegram would ultimately be delivered to the Pinkerton Detective Agency in Chicago. It was Kate's way of checking in and letting the company know that her cover was still secure.

But what Lenny also didn't know is that the telegram was a set-up for a ploy about him.

"When exactly is your birthday, Mrs. Cherry?"

"Lenny, please call me Constance. Actually, today is my birthday but, alas, I have no one to celebrate it with."

"I would be glad to celebrate it with you . . . if I could get away."

"That would be wonderful," she gushed.

"But I can't get away."

"Not even for fifteen minutes?" she said with a sad face.

Lenny looked around. Things had quieted down. No one had come in to send a telegram in the past hour. And this particular telegraph recorded incoming messages on paper, which he could read afterwards. "All right, but just for fifteen minutes," he said.

"Wonderful. Meet me down the street at the Blake Tavern at eight o'clock."

A few minutes before eight o'clock Lenny hung a sign in the window that read: "Returning at 8:15."

From across the street, hidden around a corner of a building, Kate watched as Lenny locked the door and headed for the tavern. Once he was out of sight, Kate raced across to the telegraph office and used one of her many skeleton keys to open the door. She was skilled at the use of the telegraph and in Morse code. She located the listing for the Frederick, Maryland, telegraph and tapped out a short message, purportedly from Marshal Kane, to Bradley Johnson:

> Union troops stopping all B&O railcars going east to Baltimore. Send our friends in from Harrisburg.

It took her no more than three minutes. But in her haste to leave, as she swiveled about in the chair and stood up, a scarf sticking out of her pocket snagged on the desk and fell to the floor. She didn't notice it.

Within minutes she was at the Blake Tavern where she had a drink and a pleasant five-minute conversation with Lenny.

Chapter 68

While her husband was away in Baltimore, Victoria Ford spent many of the daytime hours riding. It was a hobby she truly enjoyed, but now she was riding for a purpose. In the final mail delivery that came through from Washington there was a letter from Ari in which he said John might be on his way to Annapolis. Each day Victoria rode the five miles to town in hopes that she might find him. The town was small, less than five thousand inhabitants, but still she knew her chances of success were slim.

Nighttime was different, and then she roamed about the Ford home. Only Cyrus and a few other servants were present at the house, and they kept to themselves.

The second night Jubal was gone her curiosity got the better of her. She went exploring the house, not even sure what she was looking for. Perhaps evidence . . . evidence that her husband wasn't the man she thought he was. In the basement there was a locked room that Jubal had never opened for her. She wanted to know what was in that room.

The room was built of concrete and stone with a lightweight steel door, much like a fireproof vault, but oddly enough the door could be opened with a key. She possessed two keys for the home and she took them to the cold and damp basement. Not a sound could be heard coming from anywhere, and no servants were around. Still, she had an eerie feeling of a presence as she approached the door. She tried the first key, but it didn't work.

As she was inserting the second key, she sensed movement behind her. She turned around and there was Cyrus, Jubal's most trusted servant.

"I've always wondered what's in there, too," he said.

She exhaled in relief.

When he saw that her second key didn't work either, he said, "I know where there are other keys." He went to a cabinet on the far side of the basement and in a false panel of that cabinet he found a key ring with ten keys on it. He began trying the keys, but each one failed until finally the ninth key unlocked the door. Cyrus pushed the door inward.

The two of them stood there staring, struggling with the notion that they were violating Jubal's sacred space.

Strewn about the room was an odd mixture of things—some artwork, some clothing, a few old books. Nothing that really intrigued Victoria. But there was a desk in the room, and she sat down and began opening drawers. In the third drawer she came across a letter that was in draft form although in beautiful penmanship. It was from Jacqueline to John with a date of January of this year, and in places there were handwritten edits in Jubal's handwriting. It made no sense to her that Jubal would possess such a letter.

That may have been confusing, but the next thing she found truly frightened her: the metal currency plates from five years ago that were used to frame John. She had seen enough. She grabbed the letter and walked out, leaving Cyrus to lock the door.

***

Although it was nighttime, Gage knew where to find Gus. He bunked with three other rented-out slaves in a ten by ten apartment near the waterfront. When Gage entered the room, the other men were not surprised. Their owners often came looking for them. But the conversation that ensued between Gage and Gus they found startling.

"I need a lookout," Gage said to Gus.

"A what?"

"Someone to watch out for me."

"No doubt you need that," Gus said, and he lay back down on his cot.

The other three men were both impressed and frightened by Gus's recalcitrant attitude toward his master.

"Get up," Gage ordered.

"I worked all day. I'm tired, I'm going to sleep."

"You'll come with me now or suffer thirty lashes."

The others reacted with horror at that declaration, and even more when

Gus fired his pillow at Gage.

Struck by Gage's tone, Gus sat up and looked at Gage with a shrug. Then he put on his boots.

"Where we goin'?" Gus asked.

"The Maryland statehouse."

"Why?"

"Well, it's not to see the governor."

It was only a six-block walk to the statehouse, a magnificent Georgian design with a towering dome. They circled the building twice in reconnaissance, keeping their distance because there was a guard standing in front of the main entrance.

"He must be posted there because that's the only unlocked door," Gage said.

"He ain't gonna let us in?"

"No, but I got a plan," Gage said with a wink.

Gus rolled his eyes.

As Gage went to the far side of the front entrance and hid behind bushes, Gus began a rambling gait across the lawn on the other side. When the guard saw him getting close, he came out on the lawn and stopped Gus with a demand: "State your business."

"I just goin' home," Gus said in a drunken voice.

"Where is that?"

"By the Belden Wharf. I just can't find which way."

As the guard walked Gus back to the street and pointed him in the right direction, Gage climbed the front steps and passed through the door. Gus ambled away, disappearing after a half block. He then took a back street around to the rear entrance of the building where Gage unlocked the door and let him in.

They walked down the expansive hallway. The gas lamps on the wall were turned down but allowed enough light to see into the Senate chamber on the one side. On the other side was the House of Delegates.

"This building served as the nation's capital for a short time almost eighty years ago," Gage explained. "Great statesmen like Adams, Jefferson, and Franklin roamed these halls. After the Revolutionary War, General Washington resigned his commission as commander-in-chief of the

Continental Army in this building."

Gus was not impressed. Those men were as removed from his world as the moon, and of lesser importance.

They came to the rotunda that was open to an inner dome more than one hundred feet above with windows surrounding it.

"Impressive, isn't it?" Gage said, looking up.

"Who has to clean all that?" Gus asked.

Soon they found a hallway that turned to the right and led them to the office Gage was in search of: the Maryland Secretary of State. But again they found the door locked. The massive oak door, ten feet in height, had a movable transom window above it.

Gage went to a nearby janitor's closet and found a ladder that he positioned in front of the door. Six steps up he was able to reach the transom and push the glass open. Iron pipes crossed the ceiling. He pulled on the closest one—it was attached solidly to the ceiling joists.

He came back down the ladder and said to Gus, "I don't think I can make it through there, but I'd bet on whether you can."

"Who you gonna bet?"

"No one. Just go up there and grab the nearest iron pipe, then pull yourself through and swing out and drop."

"You bet I can do this?"

"Hell, no. I don't think you can."

Gus accepted the challenge. He went up and pulled himself through, swung out on the iron pipe, and stretched his arms out. Fully extended, his feet were now only two feet off the floor and he let go for an easy landing. He unlocked the door and let Gage in.

The room was dark, but with the door open enough light came in to allow them to see a candle on the large mahogany desk that was the centerpiece of the room. Gage lit the candle and went to work rummaging through the desk drawers.

"What are you lookin' for?" Gus asked.

But before Gage could answer, he found it in the lower left drawer. "This!" he said emphatically, and he removed the velvet surrounding the object and held it up for Gus to view.

Gus was confounded.

Chapter 69

When Gage returned to the recruiting station the next morning, Jimmy was relieved to see him. "I was worried they had arrested you and shipped you off to Fort Monroe."

Gage chuckled at the irony hidden in Jimmy's comment.

There was an extra spring in Jimmy's step because today he would a make a major contribution to Zeb Pierce's plan by introducing Zeb to his boss.

Gus was without work at the wharf today, so he came to see Gage at the recruiting station. He stayed about fifteen feet away from the recruiting table, but his presence no longer concerned Gage. He realized that having what appeared to be a slave by his side gave more credence to him being a Southerner.

The recruiting area was busy at the moment, and as Gus backed up further to make room for the recruits he accidentally bumped into someone. It was Zeb Pierce, and he was livid.

"Get back, boy, or I'll have you horsewhipped," Pierce shouted.

Gage rushed to Gus's defense. Looking down on the much smaller Pierce, he said, "I'll take care of mine; you take care of yours."

Startled, Zeb said, "Of course, sir. I would never interfere with another man's property. I apologize."

This was not the way Jimmy wanted the two men to meet. He raced over and intervened: "Mr. Millsap, this is Zeb Pierce. I want you to hear his wonderful plan for stopping Northern troops from reaching Washington."

Although their agendas were quite different, the two men needed each other. They began a friendly conversation.

"I understand you just spent time in Charleston," Pierce said. "What brings you here?"

"I came here to restart the recruiting service that Wigfall started."

"Senator Wigfall?"

"Yes, but in Charleston we now know him as Colonel Wigfall."

Zeb chuckled. "Yes, the man who singlehandedly captured Fort Sumter."

"Certainly, he would tell you so."

"My father doesn't think it such a good idea for you to recruit men and move them to Charleston."

"Why's that?"

"He thinks we need them here to march on Washington. Last night we seized the telegraph office in Baltimore. The mail is stopped, too. Washington has no means to communicate."

"Well, all I can tell you is that Ransom Pierce of Charleston sent me here to recruit good soldiers for the cause. You related to him?"

"My uncle," Zeb said with a smile.

Gage appeared to be the man Zeb needed, but there was a test he wanted to put Gage to: "And just what all did Ransom Pierce tell you about our intentions?"

Gage thought back to the letters he read at Ransom Pierce's office before burning it to the ground. He recalled the odd language he found in a few and then said, "That we could create a Washington City that is as impregnable as Gibraltar—a Southern Man's Gibraltar."

That was it. The proper password: Gibraltar. Pierce smiled and said, "I am at your service, sir."

"We want eight hundred—perhaps a thousand—good men to take to Charleston immediately," Gage said.

"But why Charleston at this point?"

"Two reasons. We're afraid Lincoln will try to retake Charleston Harbor. If we can solidify South Carolina's position, it will be a clear demonstration of the new Confederacy's viability. These men will help that cause, and in the meantime be properly trained for our mission to secure Maryland and overtake Washington City. They should be back here in six weeks."

Pierce nodded. "I suppose if Unc Pierce says it's all right, then it is. What was it you did in Charleston? Any work with the military?"

"General Beauregard had me training artillery crews."

Pierce brightened. "Jimmy said you were with an artillery unit in the Mexican War. Your role must have been important in Charleston."

"I suppose. There were a lot of raw recruits there. Training is critical. That's why we can't have a bunch of loose misfits trying to take on the Union Army in Maryland. We need a real army."

"And, that, sir, is why I need your help, and very soon."

***

As Zeb and Gage conversed, Victoria Ford was stabling her horse on the south end of town. With Jubal due back anytime, she was desperate to find her son. Today she decided to go to the Naval Academy to ask the commandant whether he knew of John's whereabouts.

She began walking to the academy. A quarter of a mile from there she was forced to walk around a long line of men waiting to sign up at a Confederate recruiting station. When she passed by, she happened to look to her left where two men stood talking. She looked closer at the taller man of the two and stopped dead in her tracks.

"Johnny!" she shouted out.

Zeb Pierce's back was to her, but Gage saw her. A horrid look came over his face because his true identity was about to be revealed.

Overcome to see her son and to know that he was safe, Victoria started rushing towards him. It was Gus who stepped in front of her, using his body to block her approach. He would have grabbed her arm and hurried her away, but it was not something a black man would dare do, especially a slave.

"You must not call him that name," Gus implored her.

"But that's my son. I haven't seen him since—"

"Please, ma'am, say no more," Gus said, and the look on his face was so earnest, so sincere, that she immediately quieted. He explained things to her.

"I understand," she said calmly, "but I need to talk to John. I need to tell him about the strange things I've found."

She began to walk away and Gus relaxed. Then suddenly she turned back and walked again towards Gage. From twenty feet away she cried out, "Mr. Millsap, may I have a word with you about my son Johnny's enlistment?"

Zeb Pierce turned to Gage and said, "You should probably deal with her. I will see you tomorrow evening at the farm." The two men shook hands, and Zeb walked away.

Gage walked towards his mother. They resisted the urge to embrace.

"It's so good to see you, Johnny, and to know you're all right," she said.

"And for me as well, Mother, but this is not a good time or place."

"I know, but I've found things you should know about. Jubal had the currency plates all along."

Gage nodded. "I'm not surprised. Jacqueline denies that her brother, or should I say the person pretending to be her brother, planted those plates in my apartment."

"You know about that man . . . that Thomas Gentry?"

"Yes, she confessed about it. But you knew about him?"

"Yes, I learned of their relationship two months before you were to be married."

"And so Jubal offered them money to leave and go to Europe?"

"No, Johnny, to be honest, I did. But I did it as a test to see if she would choose you or the money. I know I was interfering in your life, and I'm sorry for that, but at the time you were so preoccupied with the prospect of being unjustly arrested. For whatever reason, she chose the money."

Gage chuckled. "You got cheated; they didn't go to Europe."

"I'm not surprised. And there's something else I found that may help shed some light." She handed him the draft letter from Jacqueline.

John looked at the letter—especially the edits. "Yes, this explains a few things," he said, "but not everything."

"So you've seen it before?"

"Yes, I received it. But, Mother, I can't talk now. Is there a place we can meet tomorrow?"

"At Nelson's Café on the north side of town. Meet me there at two o'clock tomorrow."

"I know the place. We'll be able to talk then."

***

When Gage returned to the recruiting table, he was surprised that Jimmy didn't ask about his conversation with Zeb. Instead, he asked, "What did that general say to you yesterday?"

Gage laughed. "The general didn't know quite what to do with me, Jimmy."

"I suppose not. All we do is provide travel."

"That's right. And I told him that if you arrest me, secessionist leaders around here like Jimmy Palin will rise up against you just like what has happened in Baltimore."

"So a general is worried about me?" Jimmy said with pride as a sudden gust of wind caused him to grab hold of his Bowler hat.

"He sure is. It might explain why they haven't come ashore yet."

Of course it wasn't true, but Gage was determined to learn the real reason the troops were still on the ship. He drummed his fingers on the table for a few minutes while looking out to the harbor pensively.

"Jimmy, will you man the station for a while?"

"Sure," Jimmy said with delight.

An hour later, Gage reached the *Maryland* by rowboat just after the general had received another message from the Maryland governor.

The general was in a testy mood, and Gage's abrasiveness didn't help. They stood at a railing along the ship's deck in an area where others could not hear them.

"How many days are you going to sit on this ship, General?"

Butler winced. "Gage, I still have no orders from General Scott."

"And you're not going to get those orders since secessionists have seized the telegraph."

Butler continued to stare out at the water. "If we go forward, we will do so blindly."

"Good God, man, you need to move! Washington may be under attack while you sit here and dawdle."

"The governor says the rails to Annapolis Junction have been sabotaged."

"So, do your men not have legs? March the twenty miles to Annapolis Junction!"

"It's not that simple. We need wagons to transport our equipment."

"Then rent them, or impress them into service if need be."

"We also have no idea of the numbers that will oppose us."

"Sitting here won't give you any better understanding."

"Also, Governor Hicks has sent me a letter requesting I not land my troops here. I replied that we must."

"Yes, I understand you and he have engaged in quite the exchange of letters. But, General, that reply of yours is not the letter that concerns me."

"What letter then?"

Butler was trying to avoid the obvious, and Gage knew it. "The one everyone in Annapolis is talking about. The one you sent to the governor that is on the front page of today's newspaper." He pointed to the pertinent language:

> I have come to understand within the last hour that some apprehension is entertained of an insurrection of the Negro population. I am ready to cooperate with your Excellency in suppressing most promptly and efficiently any insurrection against the laws of the state of Maryland.

"Why would you offer such a thing?" Gage exclaimed.

"I'm attempting to tamp down their opposition to us being here ... give the governor something he can use to quell the hatred of the populace."

"Well, remember, those slaves are part of the populace."

"If Southern sympathizers believe we would help them in such an instance then they may welcome us."

"Would you help them?"

Butler hesitated, choosing not to answer. Instead, he said, "You don't trust me, do you, Gage?"

"I have until now, despite your history."

"My history? Because I attended the Southern Democrats' convention in Charleston?"

Gage nodded.

"I voted for Jefferson Davis for president in that convention. But that was to be president of the United States. I'm as vehemently opposed to secession as you."

"I sincerely hope that's true, General. But from what you said in that letter, it's had me worried you might try to enforce the Fugitive Slave Act."

"I've thought of that."

"What?"

"After all, it is the law of the land. I don't mean to enforce it generally, but just do it once to prove to secessionists that we won't interfere with slavery. It would be quite a statement to them. Just one arrest that is heavily publicized would get the word out."

"Are you mad?"

"No, in fact I've had one easy target in mind—your friend Gus Ward. I can see right through his situation. He's an escaped slave, isn't he?"

Gage shot a look at Butler that caused the general to momentarily fear for his life. Gage's next statement didn't lessen that fear: "After what we've been through to get to this point, I'll kill any man who tries to arrest Gus Ward, or any man who orders him arrested."

Butler realized he was facing a warrior. He took a step back, both in his physical positioning and his approach: "Of course, I wasn't serious, Gage. But I have threatened Maryland that I will use force to put down the lawlessness of white men against our troops. Why should I not agree to do the same for the lawlessness of Negroes?"

"You mean if they rebel against enslavement laws?"

"Yes, like it or not, those are the laws of Maryland."

"They won't be when all this is finished."

"Perhaps, but that's not what this war is about."

"It will be, General . . . it will be."

"We don't differ in our loyalty, Gage, just our politics."

"No, General, it's not politics. It's basic morality. No man should own another."

That seemed to bring an end to their discussion. They both looked out to the water, for there appeared on the horizon an incoming vessel that was loaded with men and casting off shards of reflected sunlight. When Butler looked through his field glasses, he could discern that the light was bouncing off rifles and bayonets.

"Who is it?" Gage asked.

"Could be the secessionists that the commandant feared were headed this way to seize the *Constitution*."

But soon the men on board that ship began haling the *Constitution* with cheers.

Butler looked again through the glasses, and suddenly he yelled out, "My Lord, it's the New York Seventh Regiment—nearly one thousand strong and with light artillery. Gage, this changes everything. We are now a formidable force."

Chapter 70

Jubal Ford was already home from Baltimore when Victoria returned from her chance encounter with John. As she turned her horse over to one of the servants, she noticed two horses she didn't recognize tied to a hitching post.

She walked up the front steps into the entry. Cyrus stood there holding the door, but he wouldn't look at her. He pointed to the den and said, "The mister wants to see you, ma'am."

Victoria sensed there were visitors in the house, but when she walked into the den there was only Jubal. Cyrus closed the doors behind her.

"Welcome home, Jubal," she said. He was standing with his back to her, facing the fireplace. When he turned around, he was red in the face. She had seen this look on only a few occasions before. She knew his anger was about to burst forth.

"Have I not provided well for you over the years?" he said with a slight tremble in his voice.

"Of course you have."

"Then why do you do things that make me not trust you?"

"Jubal, whatever are you talking about?"

"You've taken things from me. And you destroyed an important telegram from the ironworks."

There was no use denying it but, strangely enough, Victoria had no desire to do so. There was something about seeing John earlier, and knowing he was close by, that had given her additional strength. Now she was willing to challenge Jubal.

"Where are those new cannons going?" she demanded.

"That's none of your concern, woman!"

"It's very much my concern!"

"You broke into my personal vault."

"Are things missing?"

"You know there is something missing. You took it."

"Such as?"

"The letter."

"What is that letter?"

"Again, that's my business, not yours," and he slapped her so hard across her face that blood spurted from her lip immediately.

But she wasn't going to back down. "Why do you have those plates?" she yelled back at him.

He turned his head momentarily as if to buy time while searching for an answer. "I bought them . . . I bought the evidence against John."

"That makes no sense. You planted the plates in John's possession, and once he was in trouble you took them back."

"That's not true!"

"You planted them just to drive Johnny away!" she screamed, and this time she slapped him across the face.

"All that I've done for you, Victoria, and this is how you repay me?"

"All that you've done? You drove a wedge between me and my son. But no more. Johnny is here in town, and he knows what you did."

Jubal was so shocked that he had no words. In a rage he hit her with a closed fist that knocked her to the floor unconscious.

"Get in here," Jubal called out, and two of the Miller Corps men entered the den from an adjoining room.

"Take her up to the attic room and lock her in there," Jubal said.

"And after that?" one of the men asked.

"Find her son . . . find John Gage!"

Chapter 71

Aramis Gage was up early, so early that he had time to spare before attending another cabinet meeting. He went to the top of the Winder Building to watch dawn break over the city. Lanterns were being maneuvered about among the Virginia troops on the other side of the Potomac. Awfully early in the morning for that, he thought. Unless the troops are preparing to move.

He waited another fifteen minutes as sunlight began to illuminate the wharves along the Virginia shore where large steamers sat anchored. But were they there because they recently made deliveries, or because they were preparing to ferry Southern troops across the river?

I'll report what I've seen to the cabinet, he thought. Then he decided against that. General Scott must have people watching the same thing. There's no reason to add to the apprehension of the cabinet members.

He wondered what those in the North must be thinking now ... with Washington isolated. In New York they've received no word from the seat of the national government. Every minute they must speculate whether the government has been seized, or the president taken hostage.

When Aramis walked into the president's meeting room at the White House, John Hay immediately pulled him aside. "I'm afraid the president is truly despondent today," Hay said.

"What is it?"

"More defections of military officers. Too many to name them all, but the one that's cut the president the deepest is that of Benjamin Helm."

"My God, his own brother-in-law," Ari said, shaking his head. Helm, from Kentucky, was the husband of Mary Todd Lincoln's half-sister Emile, and over the last few years had become like a younger brother to Lincoln. The president offered him a commission as major with the illustrious role of Paymaster of the Army. Helm graciously rejected it and joined the Confederate army.

"And now Captain McGruder, commander of the most important artillery battery defending this city, has resigned."

Lincoln overheard Hay speak that name and intervened in their conversation. "Only three days before, McGruder gave me his personal pledge that he would remain loyal," the president said as he walked over and in one of those rare occasions sat in a chair. Staring out the window, he added, "If men of the character and rank like McGruder, Lee, Johnston, and Cooper should give way where might we not fear treachery?"

Others joined in. "Over the weekend there were mass resignations in all the departments of the government," Secretary Seward reported.

"Good riddance to them all," Chase said. "It's for the better to have them all out of Washington."

The president noted that General Scott had sent a written statement for his daily report.

"Hopefully, he hasn't gone back to Virginia," another cabinet member said only partly in jest.

No one laughed.

"Congressman, will you read the general's report to everyone?" the president said.

"Of course," Ari replied. "I will begin with General Scott's statement of things he believes to be true."

> First, there are three or four steamers off Annapolis with Union volunteers headed for Washington; second, their landing will be opposed by citizens of Annapolis, reinforced by those from Baltimore; third, it is believed the landing may be nevertheless made through good management; and fourth, many of the rails on the twenty miles of track between Annapolis and Annapolis Junction have been taken up by the rebels. Once ashore, the regiment should be able to march to Washington provided they can secure wagons.

Ari stopped momentarily and looked at the angst on the faces of the cabinet members. Then he added from the report:

> Efforts to communicate with the regiments at Annapolis have failed because the telegraph has been taken over by rebels in Baltimore. We have sent four messengers and we believe at least one should get through.

Again thinking there might be comments or questions, Ari paused, but there was silence. Then the president mused, "Let's hope the general is as good at assembling troops as he is at assembling rumors."

A bit of laughter permeated the room, but it quickly died away as the peril of the situation sank in.

"Yes," Chase said, "five days ago the general promised New York troops would be here in two to three days."

"Where are they?" the president lamented. "Why don't they come?"

***

In Annapolis, there was some movement of those troops as the New York Seventh and the Massachusetts Eighth finally came ashore to the Naval Academy. The men of the Seventh quite willingly shared their provisions with the soldiers of a sister state, but the cooperation ended there. Butler was ready to advance along the railroad line; Colonel Lefferts, commander of the New York Seventh, was not. And without orders from General Scott, and not being in the same chain of command, there was no one to rule upon the disagreement.

John Gage was elated by Butler's transformation. But when the general learned of Lefferts' hesitancy, he asked for Gage's help in trying to persuade him.

"We've had messengers come in who have reported a company of Maryland militia drilling right near the academy," Colonel Lefferts argued.

"That's at most one hundred men, and they're probably drilling because they're untrained," Butler said. "They'll scatter when they see us coming."

"We believe there are hundreds more in hiding, country marksmen just waiting to strike from behind trees."

Butler was beside himself, so agitated that he deemed it best to hold his tongue. Gage spoke instead, and he was not gentle: "It's a fucking war,

Colonel. Did you think men wouldn't be shot at?"

"We just had two newspapermen arrive who said that other than that one small unit they witnessed nothing unusual out there," Butler added. "They even said the townspeople are quite willing to sell us provisions."

"You want to take your intelligence from reporters?"

"Better than taking it from rumors."

"Colonel, I've been able to move several hundred of the militants out of this town," Gage said, "and I can assure you that those still here are basically untrained."

As if in a gesture of finality, Butler smacked his hand down on a table. "With you, or without you, we're going out!"

"Without orders?" Lefferts questioned.

"They didn't send us here to sit and wait in Maryland, Colonel. We were told to come to Washington. I plan to get there."

The Massachusetts Eighth soon occupied the railroad station where they found an old engine that had been sabotaged. Coincidentally, one of the men in the regiment was a mechanic who helped build the machine originally. He went to work that night to repair it as two companies of men started out to restore the first few miles of track.

After cajoling by junior officers, Colonel Lefferts relented, and the New York Seventh soon joined them.

Two thousand Union soldiers were on their way to Washington City. If they could get there.

Chapter 72

John Gage had not prepared himself for something else that was to occur on this day. It was time for Gus to move on . . . time for him to return to his past.

Gus had worked for four days on the docks. In addition to his room and board, there was pay of one dollar a day. As his pretend owner, Gage collected that money for him, but waited until they were in a location where they couldn't be seen before handing Gus the money.

"Thank you, Master John," Gus said with a smile. But suddenly Gus's expression changed.

"What's wrong?" Gage asked.

"What do I do with it?"

"Didn't you tell me you wanted to buy presents for your family?"

"They sell to ones like me around here?"

"Sure," Gage said, and they headed for the nearest mercantile.

Actually, Gage wasn't sure. When the storeowner saw Gus browsing, Gage pulled open his coat and displayed a Colt revolver.

That was all the convincing the storeowner needed. "Money is money," he said. "His is good here."

Gage followed Gus down the aisles as he browsed. While Gus understood money, he had little concept of what all it could buy. He was therefore a meticulous shopper, studying the price tags on each item.

When Gage pointed to a packet of pencils and a pad of paper, Gus looked at him like he must be crazy. "They don't allow that at the Walton plantation."

But Gus soon found something he liked. It was a secondhand silk scarf, pink in color but still in good condition. The price was forty-three cents. "Nelly like this," Gus said, but still he hesitated.

"What's wrong?" Gage asked.

"How much is left?"

"$3.57, Gage answered quickly, and as he did so he realized something shocking. This highly intelligent man, who could do simple addition, did not know how to do subtraction with three digits. Oh, what he has been deprived of, Gage thought.

After finishing with Gus's shopping, they walked one block to a street intersection. This was where Gus would start his journey home. It came as a sudden conclusion for the two men who had been through so much together. Neither had prepared his thoughts for their parting.

Gus looked Gage in the eyes and said, "You kept your word. You got me to Maryland."

"Yes, after I almost got you killed," Gage said with a chuckle. Then he turned serious and added, "I've learned a lot from you, Gus."

Gus nodded, keeping his eyes locked on the eyes of a white man as he had never done before. There was trust, and mutual respect.

"Tell me something, Gus. Why did you go back for the lock of Nelly's hair?"

Gus hesitated, then was forthcoming: "If I get back there and she's died, or been sold away where I can't find her, it's the only thing I would have to remember her by."

Gage understood. Then he grabbed his leather satchel and handed it to Gus. "I want you to have this."

Gus was stunned. He had never owned anything so nice. He ran his hand across the Gage Ironworks insignia, remembering how that symbol had ignited his initial distrust of Gage.

"There are a couple of things in it for you, too."

Folded neatly inside was Ned Walker's red shirt.

"You stole that shirt again?"

"I had it washed. You'll need to look good when you walk in there."

The other item was a pair of field glasses. "I figure you'll be heading north along the railroad tracks—"

"Only for ten miles."

"Yeah, but that's halfway to Annapolis Junction. If you see anything peculiar along the railroad, try to get word back to the Union troops. They should be only a short ways behind you repairing the tracks."

Gus hesitated. "I feel like I'm desertin' you. There's more to be done."

"This was our deal, Gus. I would get you to Maryland if you took me to the cannons. In truth, you've done far more than that. It's time, past time, for you to go to your family."

Gus stuffed a couple of items in the bag. Then he looked up. Gage reached out and the two men shook hands. Gus slung the satchel over his shoulder and began to walk away.

Twenty feet along, he turned around briefly, smiled, and said, "I'm almost home. Thank you . . . John."

***

Precisely at two in the afternoon, Gage walked into Nelson's Café. His mother was not there. He took a seat at a corner table to wait for her. He ordered a cup of coffee, and then after fifteen minutes he ordered another. This was not like his mother; she was always on time.

Gage continued to glance at the large clock on the wall across from him. As each minute passed, he became more concerned. *Why did she give me the Jacqueline letter? Why did I keep it? If she had just taken it and put it back, Jubal wouldn't know she had seen it.* But he tried to reassure himself. *Perhaps Jubal just came home, and she couldn't get away. Even so, eventually he would notice the letter missing.*

After an hour of waiting, a thought occurred to Gage that was both uplifting and disturbing. His mother was back to her old self. He saw it in the letter she sent to Charleston, and he saw it yesterday in town. The mere fact that she came looking for him was a sign of her renewed vitality.

Once again he recalled the time she chased the black bear out of the garden. No, she wouldn't hesitate to challenge the Fords. And that had him worried.

After an hour and a half, Gage declined a fifth cup of coffee. He needed to find the Ford home, but there was no time for that now. He had a meeting to attend, a meeting that might decide the fate of Maryland, perhaps even the fate of Washington and the Union.

Chapter 73

It was only a three-hour walk for Gus to the Walton Plantation. Unsure of what or whom he might find along the way, he stayed to the west of the railroad tracks, even avoiding the easier path of a wagon road that paralleled the tracks on the opposite side. At periodic intervals, he saw rails that had been pulled up and cast aside, but nothing the Union troops wouldn't find themselves when they came north. The wagon road was deserted, and during his entire journey he didn't encounter another soul.

When the Calumet Bridge came into view, Gus turned to the west because the Walton Plantation was only a short distance from there. Not wanting to cause a disturbance, he decided to wait until dusk before walking in. The overseer should be gone by then.

He climbed a hillside to his favorite spot in the area, a place everyone called the Crow's Nest for its commanding view. It was a place he often stole away to for moments of reflection, so important to him that he had arranged boulders that allowed for comfortable sitting and little prospect of being seen.

One of the reasons Gus liked coming to this spot was to watch the railroad at Calumet Bridge. But it wasn't because he enjoyed the trains. What he enjoyed was imagining. Where were the people going? What must it be like to ride anywhere in the country you wanted to go? To go somewhere and see things you've never seen before?

He was relieved to see all the boulders were in the same position. The Crow's Nest had not changed. Gus sat down and took out the field glasses, wondering if Gage had this in mind when he gave them to him.

He knew the Walton Plantation well, even though he had never lived there. He had lived on a different farm a few miles away while his wife and two children lived at Walton. As a husband and father he was allowed to visit there for a few hours each Sunday, and he occasionally managed to sneak over at night during the week.

With the field glasses focused on the Walton Plantation, he quickly realized some things had changed. The cabin his wife and children had resided in was partially destroyed. It appeared to have been torn apart by high winds in a storm. Gus scanned the property repeatedly. Then he remembered: I might not recognize my children.

He would, however, certainly recognize his wife and other adults. But who of them were still here? He spent the next two hours searching but to no avail. At dusk he knew he would now be able to go about the camp in some anonymity.

Gus changed into Ned's red shirt. It was unwrinkled and smelled fresh. With that shirt and the leather satchel over his shoulder, he would cast a fine appearance upon arriving.

He walked into the camp and past several cabins without being noticed. But at the next cabin a man shouted at him, "Augustus!" It was George Gill, one of his best friends, who ran at him and embraced him.

"Augustus, what you doin' here?"

Gus didn't answer. Instead, he simply asked, "Where's Nelly?"

George reacted strangely. He was suddenly hesitant, and Gus sensed something was wrong. George simply pointed at the next cabin.

When Gus was within twenty feet of that cabin, Nelly came around from the far corner carrying a basket of clothes she had just taken off a clothesline. She looked up at Gus. The basket fell to the ground.

"Augustus," she cried out, and then she collapsed next to the basket.

Gus raced to her as did another man who came from a cabin off to the right. They each took one of her arms and helped her sit up. She was moaning and crying hysterically.

Finally, she screamed out, "Augustus, I didn't think you was ever comin' back."

Gus looked over at the other man who said simply, "We married."

There was enough of a stir that it caused the top slave to come by. He was the only slave allowed a rifle, although he was limited to two bullets, and he answered directly to the overseer. He told George to take Gus to his cabin to quell the commotion.

But Gus waited until Nelly was conscious and able to talk rationally. She then said to Gus, "He been good to me. He a good man."

"You have children with him?"

She hesitated, then said, "Two."

"Where are my two?"

"Playin' down by the river."

The night didn't get any better for Gus. When he met his son and daughter, who were now nine and seven years old respectively, he realized instantly that they did not know him. They had been raised by another man whom they knew to be their father.

He stayed that night in George's cabin where he was visited by several old friends who tried to comfort him. What little alcohol they could find he drank, and about three in the morning he finally fell asleep.

Gus did not awaken until the early afternoon. All the slaves were back in the field, but George had left him a few things to eat. After eating, he went back to the Crow's Nest to sit in his favorite spot and think.

I can't hold it against Nelly or her new man, he reasoned. It's not their fault. My children don't know me, and there's no way for them to get to know me. He lay back on the ground. He was unaccustomed to alcohol and, still feeling its effects, he again fell asleep.

Chapter 74

It had been five straight days of disasters and bad news. A sensation was sweeping the capital that John Hay expressed to Ari Gage: "It's as if there is an irresistible current of fate that the capital is being lost. Perhaps even that the South might be victorious. I fear the rebels are sensing the same."

The microcosm in which the cabinet now worked had finally taken its toll. The city was cut off from the outside world. At the end of the cabinet meeting, the president said, "I have come to think at times that there is no North. That the New York Seventh Regiment is a myth, as is the Massachusetts Eighth."

The president's anguish extended far beyond personal concerns. He was the reigning symbol of the country, and that symbol had been reduced to this kind of isolation and threat. But he did now fear for the safety of his family. At one point he took Ari and John Hay aside and asked, "Congressman, is your family living in Washington?"

"No, sir," Ari replied. "They're in Philadelphia."

The president turned to his junior secretary and said, "Mr. Hay, just in case, why don't we have a plan ready to get my family to safety in a big city in the North."

"Perhaps New York City?"

The president smiled. "No, Mrs. Lincoln would spend me underground there. Maybe Harrisburg would be good."

Following the cabinet meeting, Ari happened to be passing by the president's office when he saw the president looking out a window. Suddenly the president cried out in anguish, "Why don't they come? Why don't they come?"

***

Just north of Annapolis those troops were making some progress along the Annapolis and Elk Ridge Railroad. But it was painstaking work. Wherever rails had been pulled up, the track bed had been damaged as well. Finding the rails and hauling them back to the track was always the first thing to do. But when the ties were missing they were often gone for good, and the soldiers had to create replacements from the woods along the way.

Gage rode from Nelson's Café to meet with General Butler along the railroad tracks a mile north of Annapolis.

"We've met no resistance," a relieved Butler said.

"Not yet, but be ready for anything further north," Gage cautioned.

"Like what?"

"I don't know, but I'll find out this evening. I'm being recruited for a mission that involves artillery. I'll get word to you as soon as I know more."

"Unfortunately, I'll still be here."

"What?"

"I've received orders by messenger from General Scott that my regiments are to remain in Annapolis and secure the location."

Gage detected Butler's disappointment, but tried to be encouraging: "That's an important role."

"It's not where I want to be. Instead of my men, the New York Seventh will reap the glory."

"It could be that with the Maryland legislature meeting here in three days to discuss secession, he believes you're the best man to be around. Between that and making sure the harbor is secure so more troops can land, those are critical tasks."

"He gave me no orders about the legislature. The question I'm trying to answer is whether I should arrest the legislators if they vote for secession."

Gage thought for a moment. "Our world seems to operate on rumors right now. You need to start some."

"What do you mean?"

"Unionists need a voice in this state even if that voice is cast about through rumors. Just put it out there that you plan to arrest any legislator who votes for secession. That should do it."

"Yes, I could do that. Still, I worry the legislature will act so soon that those rumors will not have made their way around in time."

"You shouldn't be too concerned about the legislature," Gage said. "They can't make any laws that will be enforceable now."

"Why is that?"

"To be enforceable every new law enacted must have the official seal of the state of Maryland imprinted on it. There is only one such seal."

"So?"

"They may not be able to find that seal."

"Why?"

"Because you now have it," and Gage handed over the official seal of Maryland he had taken from the secretary of state's office.

The general smiled.

Chapter 75

Late in the day Gage and Jimmy Palin rode north on Jackson Road, the only good trail in the area. About two miles north of Annapolis, Jimmy pointed to a path headed east and said, "This way to the Pierce farm."

Gage halted and asked, "Jimmy, have you ever heard of Jubal Ford? Does he have a place around here?"

"Sure, it's somewhere around here farther to the north. I think near a big windmill, but I can't remember exactly where."

Gage didn't move.

"Mr. Millsap, we need to go. They're waiting for us."

Lost in thought, Gage didn't answer. He was still trying to rationalize his mother's failure to show for their meeting at Nelson's Café.

Gage was torn, but he was acting on guesswork. He had no idea whether his mother was in trouble. Nor did he know whether Zeb's plan presented a real threat. What he was certain of is that if Northern troops were shut off from reaching Annapolis Junction, Washington City might be lost . . . the Union might be lost.

"Jimmy, how long do you think it will take at the Pierce farm?"

"I don't know, why?"

"Jubal Ford is an old friend. I might like to pay him a visit tonight before it gets too late."

"I imagine there'll be time for that."

That's what I'll do, Gage decided. I'll meet with Zeb Pierce and learn the plan, then go to the Ford house afterwards.

They rode down a trail that soon split. "That one goes to the house,"

Jimmy said. "We'll take the path to the big barn."

Jimmy's characterization of the barn as "big" was a vast understatement. It was the largest barn Gage had ever seen, and it even had stone pillars flanking the corners. There was some significant wealth here.

Zeb was waiting for them. He immediately took Gage to a back corner of the barn in an area partitioned off by five-foot-high walls. Sitting there were twelve three-inch cannons, nicely arranged in two rows.

"Do you recognize these cannons?" Zeb asked.

Thinking he had been found out, the question jolted Gage momentarily. Of course he recognized them. They had the Gage Ironworks insignia on them. "Very nice," Gage said. "They look to be ten pounders, very mobile. How did you come by them?"

"They were presents from my uncle in Charleston. I've got thirty-eight more at the other end of the barn."

Gage continued to examine the cannons and even though he already knew the answer, he asked the question: "Why are these cannons different? There are rings around the muzzles of the cannons in the back row, but not on these six?"

"The rings are being taken off . . . not sure why really. My father is doing that. He works with all kinds of metals. He says the rings are unnecessary, may even cause a problem."

"And so what are your plans for these cannons?"

"Two things. First, we'll use three of them to destroy the Calumet Bridge."

"Why not torch it?"

"It's recently rebuilt—all fresh wood, and it's been soaked by recent rains. We'd probably have to come back three or four times to burn it sufficiently, and the Yankees aren't going to let us do that. Besides, it's supported by stone columns. If we blow those to bits, the whole bridge will fall. It'll take months to rebuild."

"Sounds smart. What's the second part of your plan?"

"We'll take all twelve of the cannons north to Annapolis Junction, fill them with canister shot, and blast away at Northern troops trying to make their way onto the Baltimore & Ohio trains to Washington."

"Brilliant," Gage said, and he wasn't lying. These cannons were easy to move, and easy to hide for a quick ambush.

"That's another reason you're a perfect fit for our group. You've got experience with canister shot."

Gage nodded. "What's your plan for the other thirty-eight cannons?"

"I'll explain that along the way."

"Along the way?"

"Yes, we need to leave now with the three cannons to get to Calumet Bridge before the Yankees. I've learned they're making faster progress than expected in rebuilding the tracks."

What irony, Gage thought. He had cajoled Butler and Lefferts into getting their troops moving. Now their very movement was making Zeb Pierce act sooner, so Gage was unable to warn those troops of his plan. He would have to go along and try to eliminate the threat himself.

Gage tried to stall. "How many horses do you have available?"

"Twelve."

"That's not enough. You need six horses to trail each cannon. The barrels alone weigh eight hundred pounds each."

"We'll do four horses for each cannon," Zeb said. "It's flat ground. They'll be fine."

As Gage and Zeb left the barn, Zeb's younger brother, Zane, passed by them on his way in. No introductions were made. Zane looked back once at Gage. He then walked over to Zeb and said, "That tall man looks familiar. I think I've seen him before."

"Probably down at the recruiting station in Annapolis. He's made quite a stir there."

Scratching his head in thought, Zane said, "No, I think it was somewhere else."

Chapter 76

When the courier from Frederick, Maryland, arrived by horseback, Marshal Kane didn't know what to make of him. "Why did you ride here instead of taking the B&O train?" Kane asked.

"Because of your warning."

"My warning? What are you talking about? Where are the soldiers Johnson promised?"

"They're headed north . . . to come into Baltimore from Harrisburg."

"Harrisburg? They can't make it in that way."

"But you told them to go that way."

"I did nothing of the sort."

The young man pulled from his pocket a transcription of the telegram. "Here's what you sent."

"I never sent that!" Kane roared.

He looked over at Mayor Brown and said, "*I'll* find out who the hell did."

There was a veiled message for the mayor in that statement. Kane didn't want the mayor to be a witness to what he might do.

Ten minutes later Kane and two of his most trusted officers, all in plain clothes, were at the telegraph office where a frightened Lenny Tolliver stammered about in answering their questions.

"Who sent this goddamned telegram?" Kane demanded.

"It . . . it wasn't me, sir," Lenny replied meekly.

"It was sent two nights ago. You're the night clerk. Who else would've sent it?"

"I don't know."

Kane reached across the counter, grabbed the young man by the lapels, and pulled until Lenny lay atop the counter. Then Kane slapped Lenny in the face, knocking his glasses across the room.

Lenny realized this could get much worse, and when Kane demanded he tell them everything about that night, Lenny did so. He admitted to going to meet Mrs. Cherry for a quick drink, and he ended his disclosure by pulling out the scarf he found afterwards.

"I've seen that scarf before," Kane said. "Constance Cherry had it with her a few nights ago. Brown knows where she stays." The three men charged off to find Mayor Brown.

Lenny was shaken. He did what he had to do to survive. But he was a solid Union man, and he had a sense that the fake telegram was sent to aid the Union. There was one thing Lenny learned from Kate that he hadn't volunteered: he knew where she stayed. He hung a closed sign on the telegraph office door and headed for the Atlantic Hotel.

When Lenny identified himself while standing outside Kate's door, she had an uneasy feeling. I led him on. How do I let him down gently? She put on a robe and opened the door. "Lenny, it's nice of you to come see me, but I have plans for tonight."

"It's not that, Mrs. Cherry. You need to get out of here right now. They know what you did the other night."

"What? Who knows?"

"Marshal Kane. He knows you sent the telegram, and he's on his way here."

Kate didn't panic, but she recognized the extent of her danger. Because the safe house had been given up a month ago, she had nowhere to hide in the city. "Go, Lenny. Get out of here before they see you."

Lenny reacted like a lovesick puppy. "But I want to help."

"You just did, now go," and she kissed him on the cheek and sent him away.

She turned back to her room. She needed to make a quick escape and yet she knew she would never return. What to take? She pulled out a small leather bag. Into it she stuffed her Pinkerton codebook and all her weapons. She looked at her closet forlornly. All those wonderful dresses would have to be left behind.

She put on her most comfortable dress for riding and left the room. But when she was ten feet from the door of the east stairwell she heard voices, men's voices, in that stairwell. She ran the other direction. As she opened the door to the west stairwell, she looked back and saw the enraged face of Marshal Kane staring at her. "Get her!" he yelled, and the two plainclothes officers sprinted in her direction.

Kate hurried down two flights of stairs, but rather than going down to the first floor she stopped at the second floor and peeked through a door. It opened to a banquet room where an elaborate celebration was underway.

She had her weapons—two guns to choose from. She could ambush the two policemen chasing her. They would never expect that coming from a woman. But morally, can I justify it? she wondered. Only if they're secessionists, and I have no way of knowing that. Besides, she thought, to kill a policeman in this environment would create a public outrage against me. Right now I'm only facing a charge of sending a fake telegram. But that would only be the public charge. What Kane might do to me in private would be far worse.

She peeked out again at the banquet hall. Twenty feet away a large group of men stood about a bar. The two policemen were on the steps just one floor above, and sounded like they were coming down two steps at a time. She looked down at her dress and ripped it along the right shoulder. Then she thought, I really need to make this believable. She pulled down the top of her corset, exposing her right breast. When the two policemen were five steps above her, she burst out into the ballroom.

"Those men...those men," she screamed breathlessly to the men around the bar. "They accosted me in the stairwell!"

It made for an easy getaway. By the time her two pursuers convinced the people in the ballroom that they were policemen, she was down another flight of stairs and out the front door of the hotel. She quickly made her way to the livery where she kept her horse.

Chapter 77

Zeb Pierce was not only organized, he was efficient. Within an hour after Gage's arrival, they were headed north on Jackson Road with six men riding on some of the horses that were trailing the three cannons. Only Gage rode without a cannon behind him.

One half mile to the north they cut over to a trail that angled northwest. "This is the quickest route to the Calumet Bridge," Zeb explained. "This will put us out in front of the Yankee troops. They're going to be stuck due west of here for some time."

"Why is that?" Gage asked.

"Because that's where we didn't just damage the rails, we took them out and buried them in a pond. They'll be hours finding a way to reach the next set of rails."

Gage realized he had underestimated the young man. Zeb was clever. He also must have a network of people watching the progress of the Union troops along the rail line.

But there appeared to be another reason Zeb was taking this route to the bridge. They were passing through lands where the people knew Zeb and aligned with his views. The few who witnessed the small convoy came out to hail Zeb like he was a conquering hero even though they had no idea what he was up to. Zeb exalted in the adulation, waving his hat in the air to all who cheered him.

By the time they reached the pathway along the Annapolis and Elk Ridge Railroad tracks, which was halfway to the Calumet Bridge, Gage was perplexed. He had yet to come up with a way to stop this mission.

Zeb soon motioned Gage to ride alongside him. "I mentioned what we'll do with the twelve cannons. It pales in comparison to what we'll do with the other thirty-eight."

"Sounds intriguing."

"I've got four hundred soldiers coming to me, some of them artillery men."

"That's a good start."

"It's all I need."

"For what?"

"To take the thirty-eight cannons right into Washington . . . like we're there to defend it."

"How will you get by the few Union Army troops that are already in Washington?"

"We'll dress in the uniforms of regiments from the Northern states. They will welcome us."

"Aren't you concerned the Union Army will realize they're bogus Northern units?"

"How would the army know that? They know little about the military units the states are sending, and they especially don't know which ones will be arriving. The telegraph is down, so there'll be no way for them to verify anything."

"And how will you use the cannons?"

"The cannons will be strategically repositioned during the night. At first light we will then blast away at everyone and everything guarding the bridges. We'll shell the White House, the armory, the army barracks, and several other strategic locations. Thousands of Virginia soldiers will then storm across the Potomac."

Gage was now certain: Zeb Pierce was a genius at this type of thing.

***

Gus Ward was asleep in the Crow's Nest when noises to the east awakened him. He took out his field glasses and scanned the wooded area where the sound was coming from. Under a clear sky and with a full moon, he was able to get a good look. It was horses hauling cannons, three of them to be exact, and seven men riding along, all only a half mile from the Calumet Bridge.

But these weren't soldiers. They had no distinctive uniforms, and they didn't exhibit any type of military bearing. There was one man who stood out from the others because of his height on the horse. Could that be John Gage? Gus wondered. Then he spotted one other rider wearing a Bowler hat, a new type of hat he had seen worn by only one person. He was certain of it: that's Jimmy Palin—Jimmy Palin, the secessionist. Suddenly Gus remembered his warning to General Butler that this was the one bridge that couldn't be repaired quickly if destroyed. And with that a terrible thought struck Gus: John Gage has been captured by this group, and they plan to destroy the Calumet Bridge.

***

As the cannons rolled across the Calumet Bridge, Zeb Pierce began directing them down an incline where they could be aligned with a perfect angle to the bridge substructure.

"This will be good practice for us," Zeb said to Gage. "Once the cannons get in position, I'll want you to review how the men go about firing."

Gage nodded, then rather than continuing on he allowed his horse to drift back until he was behind the last cannon. They were now at a standstill as the first cannon started slowly down the pathway.

Gage dismounted. A box was attached to the last trailer and he was fairly certain of its contents. While all eyes were on the cannon struggling to negotiate the downhill curve, Gage opened the box. There were the cartridge bags filled with powder. He grabbed the bags and tossed them off the bridge into the water below.

When Zeb Pierce realized the difficulty of traversing the curving, downhill terrain to the riverbank, he decided two cannons would be sufficient to destroy the bridge. He ordered one of the men to bring forward the cartridge bags. When that man opened the box, to his astonishment he found it was empty.

Zeb Pierce was beside himself. "Jake, did you not put them in there when we started out?" he screamed.

"They were in there," Jake protested. "I'm certain of it."

Zeb didn't know whether to believe him, but then one of the other men pointed to the creek bed below. There, stuck on a rock, was a white bag glistening in the moonlight.

"That's one of them," Jimmy Palin said.

"There is a traitor among us!" Zeb exclaimed.

It didn't take much thought to figure it out. Gage was the newest member of the group, the one who had never had to prove his loyalty. Then Jake added, "I seen him back by the box a few minutes ago. I wondered what he was doing back there."

Gage thought of jumping from the bridge into the water, but there wasn't enough current to sweep him away before the others would get to him with gunfire. He began to stealthily move up the railroad tracks, but Zeb saw him and pulled out his revolver.

"You've tricked Jimmy, and you've tried to trick us," Zeb shouted. "You are a spy, and spies are put to death!"

He aimed his revolver at Gage.

"Zeb, you need to give up now before you get into real trouble," Gage said. "Two thousand Union troops are coming this way."

"None of them will make it through here."

"They will all make it through here, and within the next eight hours."

Upon that sudden realization that his plan had been ruined, Zeb screamed, "You're a traitor!" and he pulled back the hammer.

The sound of a gunshot ricocheted throughout the valley.

Zeb Pierce fell to the ground. His companions looked at each other in astonishment. They had no idea where the shot came from.

Now leaderless and confused, they were not ready for the onslaught that came at them. Fifteen black men wielding clubs and shovels, led by a man in a bright red shirt, came charging down the hillside screaming and yelling. It was over in minutes. Zeb Pierce lay dead, and four of his companions were captured. The only one remaining was Jimmy Palin who was standing by a tree fifty feet away as if frozen in place.

Gage moved toward Jimmy and yelled at him, "Is this what you want in life? Is this it? It's only fifteen miles north to Millersburg. Go back there to your family as fast as you can, and stay there!"

Jimmy began to run. The top slave picked up his rifle. He had one bullet left. But Gage held up his hand and said, "Let him go."

Jimmy ran from the tracks across a small grass island to a dirt road that headed north. As he reached the road, the others could detect in the moonlight a lone rider coming slowly in their direction. The rider was slight of build and seemed to have no fear of the men standing about.

Upon reaching the body of Zeb Pierce, the rider dismounted and bent down.

Gage walked over and asked, "You know him?"

The hood shielding the rider's face came off. Kate Warne looked up and said, "Yes, Johnny. Such an inglorious death for a man who wanted nothing but glory."

Chapter 78

The top slave wanted the others to return to the plantation as soon as possible, so they weren't discovered as missing. He gave orders for the quick burial of Zeb Pierce, and he promised to turn over the four captured secessionists to Union troops when they came through.

"Mr. Pierce will be buried with colored folk . . . in a slave cemetery," Gus said to Gage.

"Everyone will be equal there," Gage said with a half-smile.

But Gus wasn't smiling, and Gage thought he knew why. "Did things not go well with Nelly?"

Gus's head dropped. "She with another man. My boy and girl don't know me."

"I'm sorry, Gus," Gage said with genuine sorrow. He had worried this might be the outcome. And then he realized the consequences of that outcome: Gus had no place to go.

And so they started south, as strange a trio as ever had ridden this trail: an exceptionally tall, white man on a mission, flanked by an escaped slave wearing a flamboyant red shirt, and a canny, young woman in a torn dress.

"We need to get word to General Butler that there are four hundred Confederate soldiers arriving here today or tomorrow who will be looking for the fifty cannons," Gage said.

"No, they won't," Kate said. "They're going to be delayed several days, if they can make it here at all."

"How do you know that?"

"Because I sent them north through Harrisburg."

Gage laughed. "The poor fellows. They don't even have their Northern uniforms yet."

After riding four miles to the south, they came upon skirmishers of the New York Seventh. The three of them, appearing more a curiosity than a threat, were allowed to proceed.

Another mile south they encountered four companies of the New York Seventh and the Massachusetts Eighth repairing the railroad tracks. But here the tracks couldn't be repaired because it was here that Zeb Pierce's men had thrown the rails into a nearby pond.

Instead, as if engaged in a game of tug-of-war, soldiers were using ropes to drag the platform cars along the ground almost two hundred feet to the next section of rails still in place. It was exhausting work. Each of the platform cars carried small howitzers that had been mounted for quick use. They moved the cars only inches at a time. As the trio arrived, fresh soldiers were replacing the men on the ropes. Those who just finished went off to the side and collapsed on the ground.

A young lieutenant approached Gage and asked his identity.

"I'm Major John Gage."

"Sir, you're out of uniform."

"Many of us are at this stage, Lieutenant."

"What are you doing out here?"

"We had business to attend to. We've left you some presents up ahead."

"Presents?"

"Three brand-new ten pounders."

"Are they operational?"

"Yes, but you'll need cartridge bags," Gage said. "Some fool lost them in the river."

The lieutenant was confused, but asked nothing further.

"I've also got forty-seven more cannons for you a few miles east of here," Gage said.

"I'm sorry, sir, but I can't deviate from my orders, and I can't spare any men to go elsewhere right now."

"That's all right. Anytime in the next two days should be sufficient. Read this note and then make sure it gets to General Butler. It explains everything."

Again they were allowed to pass, and once they were out of the commotion of the troops, Gus asked, "Where we goin'?"

"Hopefully, to find my mother, Gus. She didn't show at that restaurant."

"We goin' into trouble?"

"Maybe."

"Good, we need a little adventure."

"I only hope we can find the adventure," Gage said. "All I know is it's somewhere near a giant windmill."

Kate looked at him, somewhat confused. "You forget, Johnny. I've been there. Just get us to the windmill and I'll find the place."

Coming from a different direction on a different trail, Gage worried that even with the moonlight they might not be able to see the windmill. He began searching the eastern horizon, but without success. Trails periodically broke to the east from the railroad tracks, but they had no idea which ones connected with Jackson Road. When they reached a trail that looked heavily used, Gage said, "Let's take this one."

A mile to the east they arrived at Jackson Road, and just one hundred feet down the road was the giant windmill. Kate led them south to a lane that took them to the Ford house. They rode into the courtyard three abreast.

"It's not as big as the Carthage house," Gage said as they halted. "Of course this one was built without Gage money."

"What do we do from here?" Kate asked.

"Let's each try to find a way in. I'll take the front door."

While Gus and Kate went around the sides, Gage went to the front of the house. He peered in the windows but saw no one. He went to the front door and found it unlocked. He walked in, but there was complete silence, not even a door chime announced his entry.

Gus managed to climb in through a window on the back of the house where he found himself in the kitchen. An eight-inch long carving knife sat on a counter. He had no weapon, so he picked it up. As he came around a long serving table, a door to the kitchen began to open slowly. A Colt revolver was the first thing to appear in the opening.

Gus held out his knife. The door sprang open. It was Cyrus holding the revolver in two shaky hands.

"There ain't nothin' here for you to steal," Cyrus said. "And that knife ain't gonna do you any good against this gun."

"Your hands shakin' so bad you can't squeeze the trigger. And I ain't no thief!"

"Then why you here?"

"I'm here with Mr. John Gage."

"Then you his slave?"

"Don't get big with me. Me and him's friends."

Unaccustomed as they were to such a harrowing confrontation, the two men stood paralyzed. But then Kate came into the room.

"Mrs. Cherry, what are you doin' here?" Cyrus exclaimed with surprise.

"It's all right, Cyrus, you can put the gun down," Kate said just as Gage entered.

"Cyrus, where is my mother?" Gage asked.

"She ain't here, sir."

"I know that. Where is she?"

"They took her—"

"Who's they?"

"They took her to the Pierce plantation."

That was enough. His mother was one mile south.

As they began to leave, Cyrus handed his gun to Gage along with a warning: "You might need this, sir."

***

Upon arriving at the Pierce house, they were amazed at its size. It was a mansion, dwarfing the Ford home they just came from.

"It so big, how we gonna find anybody in there?" Gus asked.

"*We* aren't," Gage said. "Gus, you almost got into trouble at the last house. You two are staying here. This isn't your fight."

That didn't sit well with the other two, and Kate spoke for both of them: "If we hear trouble, like gunshots, we're coming in."

Gage nodded and headed for the front door. He found the door slightly ajar, and he walked in with his revolver drawn. On one of the walls was another beautiful New Year's poster made by Zeke Alston. At least, the Pierces have good taste, Gage thought.

Ten feet away, a door opened suddenly and young Zane Pierce appeared. He was unarmed, but with a peculiar smile on his face. "Well, if it isn't John Gage," Zane said.

"You know me?"

"Let's just say I've seen you before. Put your gun away, Mr. Gage."

"Why would I do that?"

"Because we have your mother. Follow me, and I'll take you to her."

They walked through that door into a large living room. "Mother," Gage yelled when he saw her. But he was immediately told to stay in place by two of the Miller Corps men. They had weapons pointed at Jubal Ford, pointed at everyone except Zane Pierce.

"What goes on here?" Gage asked because he couldn't understand why the Miller Corps men had turned on Jubal.

Gage would soon have his answer as a door at the far end of the room opened. In walked Zeke Alston.

And now it came clear to Gage—all the signs he had missed. Out loud, he said, "Zeke Alston Pierce, brother of Ransom Pierce."

"Yes, John, that's my name in Maryland."

Gage looked down at a small table. On it was a photograph of him and Zeke taken five years earlier.

"It's the only photograph we have in this house," Zane said. "I happened to run across it a few days ago. When I looked at it again tonight, there was Thomas Millsap."

Gage turned back to Zeke. "And you've committed treason against your country."

"Oh, now you're talking politics. I don't engage in such."

"No, you're just all about the money."

"One of those times he was just about the money, John, was five years ago when he used the plates he made to duplicate bank notes," Jubal explained. "When the duplicates were discovered, he needed a scapegoat. You were getting too close to his friends in Philadelphia with your investigation, and so he planted the plates on you. He was solving two problems with one stroke."

"Jubal handled it by buying the evidence," Victoria added. "He really did help you get out of it, Johnny."

"And I suppose you wrote the letter from Jacqueline that got me to go to Charleston?"

"Some of my best penmanship," Zeke crowed.

"You wanted me gone because you thought I had come back to investigate things again."

"John, he's had his tentacles around me, around the Gage Ironworks, for the last decade," Jubal said. "I've had to do what he wanted."

"And the gold that you and your brother stole from the Charleston Customs House, Zeke, has it been worth it to you? That gold will soon be seized by Union troops along with the fifty cannons. You've gained nothing and lost plenty. Your brother is in prison, and one of your sons is dead."

"Dead?"

Gage nodded. "Zeb was killed tonight at the Calumet Bridge."

And now a fury came over Zeke that Gage did not think possible. With one hand he picked up a chair that was in his way and threw it across the room.

Just as enraged, Zane asked, "What shall we do with them, Father?"

"John and his mother must be disposed of. Jubal will never tell anyone since he'll be a part of it."

"No, Zeke," Jubal protested. "You've made me do some horrible things over the years, but this is a line in the sand I won't cross. You've run my life for too long."

"I've given you life! Whatever you've needed for the past decade came from me. We both wanted John gone five years ago, and I found a way. When your ironworks was about to go under, I bailed you out. Now it's time you repay me."

"You're asking for too big of a repayment. I can't . . . I won't."

Zeke aimed his weapon at Victoria. Jubal jumped in front of her as Zeke pulled back the hammer and fired. Jubal fell to the floor.

Gage pulled out his weapon, but Zeke was already back out the door he came in. When Gage got to the door he found it locked from the other side.

The Miller Corps men didn't know what to do. They just witnessed a cold-blooded murder; it wasn't what they signed on for. When Gage shot the lock off the door, they didn't try to stop him.

Gage was now in full pursuit of Zeke, but never having been here he was at a disadvantage. He reached the end of a dining room and happened to catch a glimpse of Zeke outside, scurrying to an outbuilding behind the main house. Gage opened a window, climbed out, and went after him.

There was a door on the left side of the outbuilding. When Gage was fifty feet from it, the door opened and Zeke fired at him. The bullet missed, and Gage dropped to the ground. Zeke had him pinned down. Gage fired twice toward the doorway, but Zeke had pulled back. As Gage stood up, Zeke reappeared and began firing. There then ensued a cascade of bullets from the two of them until they both had emptied their weapons.

Having heard all the gunshots, Gus and Kate made their way into the house. Just as Zane went out a back window, Kate charged into the living room with her gun drawn. The two Miller Corps men, confused by the situation and having no fear of Victoria, had put their weapons away. Kate ordered them to lie on the floor. Victoria, bent down over Jubal, shouted to Gus, "The shots came from out back. They may be in the building behind the house."

Gage ran for the door of the outbuilding as Zeke disappeared back inside. The building was a large shop, almost a thousand square feet, and it was dark. In the blackness, Gage had no idea where to look for Zeke. He waited a minute, listening for any telltale sound while his eyes adjusted to the low light. Suddenly, a gas lamp on one of the sidewalls came on. Gage wasn't going to fall for the deception. Instead he waited until Zeke made a move towards the back of the building. Gage raced after him. But when he was within five feet of Zeke and reaching out for him, Gage suddenly felt a crushing blow to the back of his neck. The impact knocked him to the floor. He turned to see Zane with an oak board in his hand ready to strike down again. Gage wrapped his foot around the back of Zane's foot and pulled, and the young man's feet came out from under him. From his knees, Gage grabbed the board and swung it outward. It hit Zane solidly in the side of the head, knocking him out cold.

But when Gage tried to get up, he realized the damage done by Zane's blow. He stumbled as he got to his feet and struggled to gain his balance. He turned just in time to see Zeke come at him with a ten-inch hunting knife. He held off Zeke's initial thrust of the blade, but fell backwards into a stack of old furniture. Gage was in a weakened state, and Zeke knew it. He tried a second time and again Gage was able to grab hold of Zeke's hands and hold the knife at bay.

Zeke screamed at Gage, "It looks like I will have to kill both father and son." He could see the confused look on Gage's face and then added, "No, your father didn't die in a hunting accident."

That admission caused a flood of adrenalin to rush through Gage, and even though positioned below Zeke he began to turn the knife the other direction. Zeke pushed back as hard as he could.

The door handle to the building jiggled, but Zane had locked the door when he came in. It was Gus, and this time he rammed his shoulder into the door. Although he didn't break the door open, the commotion startled Zeke so much that Gage was able to fully turn the knife in Zeke's direction.

"You murdered my father!" Gage screamed. He was recovering his strength, and he began to stand up. The fear came to Zeke's eyes as he realized what was happening. He suddenly seemed resigned to his fate. He let go of his grip on the knife and it plunged into his throat. Blood sprayed across the back of an old chair.

"Yes, Zeke, one of us killed both father and son, but it wasn't you," Gage said in the last words Zeke ever heard.

Gus broke through the door on his second attempt, but there was nothing for him to do except take charge of a wobbly Zane. They tied up Zane and marched him back into the main house where they bound up the Miller Corps men.

John came over and hugged his mother. She was sobbing, suffering from a combination of loss and regret. "I'm sorry, Johnny, Jubal was a part of all this from the beginning."

"But he was a hero in the end, Mother. We should give him that."

Then Gage wrapped his arms around Kate. "What do we do next?" she asked.

"Let's dig a couple graves, temporary as they may be. Then we'll go back on the route we took to get here and turn our prisoners over to the army."

***

Late the next morning John Hay sat in his small office at the White House listening to a young lieutenant sent by General Scott. The lieutenant was explaining the plan the general had implemented for safeguarding the president and the cabinet.

"With few troops having arrived, the general thought it best to have a strategy. He believes the treasury building can be the most easily protected.

Sandbags have been placed in front of all doorways except one."

"Why has one been left unprotected?"

"To be able to get in and out, of course," the lieutenant said. "But it's not unprotected. There's a howitzer in the hallway behind the door."

"Be careful entering."

"Food is being stored there. Nothing fancy, mind you, but things like pork and beans and army rations."

Hay shook his head. "This is what the reigning symbol of our democracy will be reduced to: cowering in a hidden location, and eating out of tin cans."

Hay was about to ask whether family members could be accommodated when a messenger arrived and handed him a note. Hay read it and leapt to his feet. "They've come! They've come!" He ran from the room and out in the second floor hallway he began shouting, "They've come! The New York Seventh is at the B&O station house in Washington."

By that time the Seventh had already deboarded and formed up its ranks. Its regimental band led the way with more than one thousand soldiers, well trained and well-armed, marching along Pennsylvania Avenue in parade formation.

The city came alive as people turned out to cheer the Seventh's arrival. President Lincoln and his family came out onto the grounds of the White House and joined in the wild celebration. Lincoln clasped his hands together and vaulted them high in the air in a salute to the soldiers.

The B&O train had also included four weary civilians as passengers. Their exploits were now well known to the officers of the Seventh, and they had been welcomed aboard. But the four were too tired to march with the Seventh.

"We need to get cleaned up and rest," Victoria said.

"We may need some new clothes, too," Gage said with a chuckle.

"Yes, Mrs. Cherry needs a new dress," Victoria said as she hugged Kate. The only thing Victoria could laugh about in this tragic affair was the surprise she felt when a gun-carrying Constance Cherry entered the room.

Kate's dress was torn, and Victoria and John's clothes had bloodstains on them. Only Gus's bright red shirt looked presentable as they entered Willard's Hotel.

Gage walked in the middle with his arms around Kate and his mother.

Gus followed closely behind, looking up and marveling at the grandeur of the lobby.

It had been five years since Victoria had stayed at Willard's and she was amazed by the recent improvements: "My, things have changed since I was last here."

It was an innocuous statement, but it ricocheted in Gage's mind. Things have changed dramatically since I was in Washington just two months ago, he thought. The South is gone. Republicans now control Congress. What an opportunity. The president's plan to freeze slavery in its place in hopes it will eventually die a natural death is no longer valid. Gage thought back to that one line in the letter Frances Seward sent to her husband:

> Compromises based on the idea that the preservation of the Union is more important than the liberty of nearly four million human beings cannot be right.

There can be no compromise solutions now that would allow Southern states to return with slavery protected, Gage thought. The peculiar institution they call it. It's a hideous institution, and it's time for it to end. I'm ready for the fight.

Gage ordered four rooms for them. "Today we rest," he said.

"And what do we do tomorrow?" Gus asked

"We're going to the White House."

"Why?"

"Because I got a plan," Gage said with a wink.

Gus rolled his eyes. "You ain't got a plan," he said hesitantly. "Do you?"

"I do, Gus. I got a real plan. I want you to be a voice for four million souls."

"Me? How do I do that?"

"I want you to tell your story—your whole life story—to Mr. Lincoln."

"What good would that do?"

"It might help change his view of things."

"Don't know why it would."

"It changed mine, Gus."

EPILOGUE
(April 14, 1865)

John Gage stepped forward and presented his invitation to the military guard.

"General John Gage and Mrs. Gage—a group of four in all," the lieutenant read out loud from a list of special invitees. "Yes, sir, your seats are in the second row on the south end."

"Thank you, Lieutenant," Gage said, and he took his wife by the hand, and they started to climb the hastily built wooden stairs on the northeast corner of Fort Sumter. Up to the level of the shattered parapet where they could see dozens of boats that had assembled in the harbor to share in the celebration.

They walked out on a small platform, preparing to take steps down to the open parade ground. Gage hesitated, and with a smile on his face he pointed over to a shattered stairwell and said, "Gus, look over there."

Gus Ward broke out laughing as he recalled that time four years ago when Gage forgot to place stops behind the carriage wheels. They had fired the huge cannon, and it and the carriage went backwards down the stairwell. The broken carriage was still there. The gun barrel was gone.

They came down the steps into the parade ground. Much of the loose debris had been cleared away, but the massive damage to the parapet and the interior walls served as a reminder of what went on here. Cannonballs were still embedded in the masonry walls.

Row after row of wooden benches filled the parade ground. Three thousand people would soon fill those seats. The majority of attendees were sailors and soldiers, many of them black such as the Massachusetts Fifty-fourth Colored Regiment. A raised speaker's platform, enclosed with boughs of myrtle, stood in front of the benches.

It was four years to the day that Sumter had been surrendered.

They were a half hour early, Gage's tardiness a thing of the past—one of his many attributes his wife had improved. But as they sat on their bench waiting, Gage thought he spotted something out in the far right corner of the parade ground, something that was not there before. It was a raised area about ten feet by fifteen feet, bordered by large boulders. He said to the others, "Excuse me for a moment."

A middle-aged sergeant stood guard over the area. It turned out to be a temporary burial ground for the unclaimed bodies of Confederate soldiers killed in recent years while defending Charleston Harbor from Union assaults. Gage said to the sergeant, "We've been searching for the body of a friend of ours. We were told that the bodies here had already been moved out and reburied."

"Not these that have gone unclaimed," the sergeant replied. "They're to be moved to a potters' field in Charleston next week."

"Do you have the names of the three buried here, Sergeant?"

"Sure, they're written on the back of the wooden crosses."

Gage went around to the back side of the crosses, and he became so excited by what he saw that he immediately shouted to the others, "Bette, Georgie, Gus, come quick!"

The others raced to him, and the four of them stood there before the graves. There it was on the back of the middle cross:

Private Jack Spence
1843 - 1863

"Oh, Jack," Bette cried out, "we found you," and she fell to the ground sobbing.

Gage bent down on one side and put his arm around his wife. Little Georgie, now eleven years old, put his arm around her from the other direction.

"Amazing," Gage said, "they never learned Jack's true age. He was only eighteen, not twenty, when he died."

"How many die like Jack?" Georgie asked.

"I'm afraid, Georgie, the number is too big for you to understand."

Gus, now employed by Gage Ironworks where Aramis Gage was its president, had come to appreciate the importance of numbers. He repeated the question: "How many?"

"Six hundred thousand . . . in a country of only thirty million. We wiped out a generation of young men."

"Jack don't belong here," Georgie said vehemently.

"No, he doesn't," Gage said. "Sergeant, can we still make arrangements to give him a proper burial?"

"Of course, sir."

"Georgie, we'll find Jack the best resting place ever. You'll be able to visit him whenever you want."

Now Bette was smiling.

"We'll make the arrangements later, Sergeant," Gage said, for they were being told to take their seats for the ceremony.

After introductions and prayers, Major Anderson was called upon to do the honors. He spoke briefly, then with tears streaming down his face he pulled on the halyards and up went the same tattered American flag that was taken down exactly four years ago. When the flag reached its zenith, it was saluted by blasts from the surrounding artillery guns at Fort Moultrie, Sullivan's Island, and Morris Island.

The audience stood and cheered mightily. It was a jubilant crowd. Within the last two weeks, news had come of the fall of Richmond, Virginia, the Confederate capital, and the surrender of Robert E. Lee's army. The war was effectively over.

The one given the task of bringing clarity to the last four years of madness was the abolitionist preacher Henry Ward Beecher. It took him two hours to do so. In his observations, he stated:

> Hail to the flag of our fathers; glory to the banner that has gone through four years, black with tempests of war, to pilot the nation back to peace without dismemberment; and glory be to God who, above all hosts and banners, hath ordained victory and shall ordain peace.

414 / April 1861

President Lincoln had wanted to attend this ceremony, but the rapid developments of the war had prevented him from doing so. In his closing remarks Reverend Beecher said this about the president:

> From this pulpit of broken stone, we speak forth our earnest greeting to all our land; we offer to the president of the United States our solemn congratulations that God has sustained his life and health under the unparalleled burdens and sufferings of four bloody years, and permitted him to behold this auspicious consummation of that national unity for which he has waited with so much patience and fortitude, and for which he has labored with such disinterested wisdom.

Six hours later, at Ford's Theatre in Washington, President Lincoln was shot dead.

And then the curtain fell.

Afterword

What else in the book is real? The clandestine Lincoln journey to Washington, the Baltimore riot, and the Fort Sumter battle scenes did occur much as presented, and the slave mart on Chalmers Street did exist. President Lincoln did make the awkward visit to Mrs. Doubleday to review her husband's letters. Frances Seward did send that scathing letter to her beloved husband. Senator/Colonel Wigfall did row to Fort Sumter and, without authorization, negotiate what would eventually become the agreement for evacuation.

The Calumet Bridge was not real, but the dramatic campaign of the New York 7th and the Massachusetts 8th to reach the Baltimore & Ohio Railroad at Annapolis Junction did occur.

Also fictitious was Lady B's, the town of Carthage, and the Ashland and Montpelier plantations, although all were based on real places.

A few minor liberties have been taken with dates to accommodate the fictional stories, the most significant being the racing week in Charleston. It was an enormous annual event, but it took place in February rather than March. Also, the seizing of the Fort Sumter outgoing mail occurred a couple weeks later than set out in the book.

In addition to those mentioned in the list of Main Characters, several other historical figures are prominent. All the cabinet members are authentic as are Senator Robert Toombs, detective Alan Pinkerton, and the naval officers Commander Rowan and Captain Fox.

I have attempted to keep real characters true to their words, and where it was necessary to expand their actions I've tried to do so in a manner consistent with their beliefs. Where possible, the actual words of historical figures have been used, especially in the case of President Lincoln. He really did make that out of character threat that if need be he would "lay Baltimore in ashes."

During the day one battle, Captain Doubleday did deliver the humorous remark about the "trifling difference of opinion with the neighbors," but in reality the set-up line came from Captain Truman Seymour. Edwin Ruffin's concern for the Union soldiers ended quickly after Fort Sumter. His hatred of the North soon consumed him, and when the Confederacy collapsed he committed suicide rather than live under "Yankee rule."

Unmasking the cryptic private lives of historical figures is difficult. Certainly in this novel Kate Warne's background is the most challenging because as a private detective she served in covert roles, the details of which have never been revealed. However, the fact that she wanted to work in dangerous undercover situations says a lot about her tolerance for risk and desire for adventure. Those traits have served to create the portrayal in the book.

Finally, a note about language. I did not try to utilize what some might think of as a slave vernacular because the dialect of the slaves was quite diverse based upon their individual circumstances. Instead, language has been used that is readable, generally realistic, and yet still illustrates the education they were denied.

J. R. Aikman
May 2024

About the Author

A dedicated student of history, John Randall Aikman is a former attorney, business executive, and adjunct professor. He lives in Westfield, Indiana, with his wife, Judith. This is his second novel, the first being the sweeping nineteenth-century saga of the fictional Markim and Reynolds families entitled *All Things Touch: a Saga of the American West.*

Made in the USA
Middletown, DE
30 July 2024